CATHI UNSWORTH

WITHOUT THE MOON

This edition published in 2016
First published in 2015 by Serpent's Tail,
an imprint of Profile Books Ltd
3 Holford Yard
Bevin Way
London
WCIX 9HD
www.serpentstail.com

ISBN 978 1 84668 987 1
eISBN 978 1 78283 066 5

CONTENTS

For Caroline Montgomery, John Williams and Pete Ayrton –
The Crucial Three

Soon,
We'll be without the moon,
Humming a different tune,
And then . . .

Irving Berlin, "Let's Face the Music and Dance"

PROLOGUE

Monday, 27 April 1942

Greenaway stood on Waterloo Bridge, breathing in the London night. Above his head, searchlights criss-crossed the sky in broad, geometric sweeps, cutting through the clouds and illuminating the dome of St Paul's Cathedral like some vast modernist artwork, created by the forces of war. Below his feet, heedless of all conflict, the ancient Thames roiled on.

Greenaway's gaze rested beyond the horizon of the blacked-out city and back through time. For two unrelenting weeks this past February, he had chased a pair of killers through the unlit streets of the capital, from bedsit rooms in Paddington and Soho, through Brick Lane barbershops to the place where he now stood – a bridge being constructed even as bombs fell all around it. The carnage he had witnessed flowed through his mind in crimson waves: he had not seen the like of it since he had served his country in the last war. The bitter irony being that both the men he pursued were trained killers – Allied servicemen who used their skills not against the enemy but on the easiest of prey – the women who worked London's streets.

As a Detective Chief Inspector, it had been Greenaway's

task not just to catch these men but also to make sure that justice was done. Today he had failed in that duty. Only one of them was now due his rightful date with the hangman. The other was free, out there somewhere in the dark, with plenty more victims to choose from. Never before had Greenaway arrested a villain who had not been duly sentenced, but today had made a mockery of him. Which was why he had returned here. His ingrained knowledge of the criminal mind and its habitual quirks that so often overruled common sense told him that the killer might just do the same. So he watched and he waited.

Greenaway did not allow himself to think beyond what could happen next. Like everything else today, he faced territory previously unknown. He could only trust that when the moment came, the right instincts would prevail.

He looked down at his hands, began to rub them together. As he did, he caught something out of the corner of his eye. The thin beam of light from a torch, bouncing a trail along the side of the bridge. A figure behind it, coming his way.

Greenaway took a deep breath. His nemesis strolled towards him.

PART ONE

HUSH, HUSH, HUSH,
HERE COMES THE BOGEYMAN

1

MOOD INDIGO

Friday, 19 December 1941

"What's it say, Duch?"

The Duchess could smell her before she even heard the soft footfall, felt the weight of hands on the back of her chair. The scent of soap and violets.

Lil's peroxide curls brushed against her companion's cheek as she leant down beside her. The table was set for afternoon tea, in all the Duchess's finery – a silver pot engraved with an Oriental dragon, matching sugar bowl and tongs, hand-painted Japanese cups of exquisite delicacy – all throwbacks to an era long departed, a way of life neither of these two women would ever know.

Beside them, today's copy of the *Daily Herald* screamed headlines of German retreat from Moscow and Leningrad. But these had been folded beneath an advertisement, ringed around in pencil, reminding readers that the paper's most celebrated journalist, Mr Hannen Swaffer, would be lecturing tonight at the Christian Spiritualist Greater World Association, Notting Hill Gate. A gas lamp of similar vintage to the crockery, shaded in engraved pink glass, emitted a rose glow across the blacked-out parlour. Al Bowlly, by now a ghost himself, crooned on from beyond through the radiogram.

Outside the windows, the traffic of Praed Street rumbled along as the dim remains of the afternoon shaded into evening. The heels of commuters scuffled and clacked their way towards Paddington, guided by the thin beams of torches and the shouts of newspaper vendors at the station gates. Just around the corner, in their rooms at the top of the mews, Duch and Lil were cocooned from all that; the rest of the world passed by as if it might have been a dream.

Duch's lashes flickered as she inhaled Lil's scent, the calling card of a profession that linked them to the time when their tableware was new. It was the first thing Duch had ever noticed about Lil, before she even turned to see her face – that beautiful, aquiline profile and those dark brown eyes that made her think of an Egyptian queen, and the shining silvery sea of curls that foamed around her shoulders – what had attracted her in an instant. Duch considered it her fate to protect this girl, young enough to be her daughter, as well as serve her. Even if the tea leaves kept telling her otherwise.

"Will he be all right?" As usual, Lil was not thinking of herself.

Duch's eyes rested on the speckled whorls while her gaze reached beyond, summoning instead the features of the man she knew resided in Lil's mind's eye.

He was handsome, all right. So handsome he could have been in the pictures, one of those dark-haired, chisel-jawed men who wore his trilby at an angle and his mac folded over his arm, shrouded in the smoke of cigarettes and his own intensity as he chased the likes of Jimmy Cagney across the big screen. This one wasn't quite a private eye though. He was a journalist, on the *Evening Sentinel* – or a *crime reporter*, as he liked to put it. His byline read Frank Power, but he wanted you to call him Tom. A man who liked to live two lives, Duch thought, and this was what unnerved her.

They'd first met him in a club in Archer Street, the sort of place where all the Little Caesars of London, the bogeys from the Yard who pursued them, and the inky-fingered hacks who took it all down, rubbed up together of an evening. He'd lit Lil's cigarette for her, stared into her eyes, breathed in the scent of violets and completed the trajectory of his doubles in the cinema – fallen hard for the wrong sort of dame.

Duch couldn't really blame Lil – there'd been times she'd been no better herself for keeping the wrong sort of company. But there was this strange sort of innocence about the girl, despite the number of men who, on any other day, would have been steaming through this parlour and into the boudoir beyond, faster than the punters at Paddington rushing for their trains. Or maybe it was because of it. Lil went at her work like it was a vocation – Duch had never met a girl before who was so popular, so good at making most every kind of man feel happy – except for him, of course.

"Vocation" was a word Tom Power might have used himself, being as he was a Roman, but he couldn't understand that part of Lil. He kept on wanting to save her, and Duch had been worried, for as long as the affair had been going on, that he might just end up succeeding.

Then he'd got his call-up papers. He was being shipped out tomorrow, his regiment posted all the way to Africa. For all Lil knew, this night could be their last, and her anxiousness transmitted itself as she rested her hand on Duch's elbow, as palpable as an electric current running between them.

Duch exhaled slowly, trying not to take the tension into herself. She knew what she said next must be spun with the utmost care. Lil put a lot of store in what the tea leaves, the tarot and Mr Hannen Swaffer said – and the skill with which her red-haired maid with the green gypsy eyes relayed it to her. All Duch had to do was soothe her friend, repeat how the lines entwined in tiny flecks on the china represented two lives that could not be parted, that this was only a separation and not an ending. Make it sound convincing, keep Lil happy for as long as she pined for her Fleet Street player, while at the same time hoping that for all their sakes this wouldn't really come true, that Lil would soon get bored with waiting and Tom Power would not be back this way again.

Even if the tea leaves kept telling her otherwise.

– • –

Under the clouds that blotted out the moon, across the rooftops where the fire-watchers waited, around Piccadilly Circus and into a narrow thoroughfare just behind, was the club where Lil had met Tom.

Entre Nous, read a small brass plaque by the side of the front door.

Leaning against the bar, Detective Chief Inspector Edward Greenaway wore a frown. In the bevelled mirror behind the optics he could see an assortment of familiar faces milling in the opposite corner of the room: men in handmade suits and women swathed in mink, all dressed as if for Ascot on a Friday night in Soho. By his side, Scotland Yard Chief Commander Peter Beverley studied the form of this little parade with a benign smile, matching memo-rised descriptions of stolen property to the coats, stoles and jewellery currently on display, and planning forthcoming pinches like chess moves. It was a ritual that the two of them would have followed up on together until recently, Greenaway being Beverley's former second-in-command. But the pained expression worn by the newly promoted DCI was not caused by the conspicuous consumption of the Archer Street clientele. It was the racket emanating from the piano, where a tall, gaunt man with a shock of white hair was loudly revisiting his youth.

"*Live for tonight!*" bellowed Hannen Swaffer, long fingers attacking the ivories. "*And scorn the morning's care/Are not the wine-flasks full, the women fair?*"

Greenaway caught the barman's eye, asked for a large Scotch.

"*Evening's for drinking and for making love,*" Fleet Street's finest continued, his mind back in the Roaring Twenties and the music halls where he had once performed. "*And not for asking How and wond'ring Where.*"

"Cheers," Greenaway handed his change across the bar, picked up the glass and said to Beverley: "Think this might shut him up?"

Beverley chuckled. "You can try," he said.

Greenaway crossed the small dance floor, plonked the whisky down on top of the piano as Swaffer trilled out a triumphant arpeggio.

"Dear boy!" the journalist greeted him.

"Swaff," nodded Greenaway, offering his cigarette case in a further attempt to distract attention. The flare of a Ronson lit up cadaverous features, the face of a Victorian undertaker. By contrast, Greenaway's own countenance was that of a sleepy boxer, his heavy lidded brown eyes camouflaging the restless intelligence that sparked behind them. The two men studied each other briefly. Swaffer spoke first.

"How goes life on the Murder Squad?" he asked. "Got used to it yet? Or are you still longing for the great outdoors?" His grey eyes sparked like flints in the candlelit gloom of their basement surrounds.

Greenaway flicked a glance to the swells in the corner, the remnants of one of the racetrack gangs that had recently been interned for their Italian heritage. Throughout the Thirties, Greenaway had pursued the London triumvirate of Elephant Boys, Sabinis and Yiddishers across the nation's turf, a sporting life that had suited him just fine. But the war had changed all that. The Elephant Boys and the Sabinis had dispersed, their leaders respectively fleeing to America or locked up on the Isle of Man. The Yiddishers, with whom Greenaway went back furthest, had found the privations of war limited their gaming endeavours, so had turned their skills to bank robbery. But the spectacular backfiring of a daylight heist had brought their leader Sammy Lehmann to book and since then, with so many younger officers volunteering, Greenaway's superiors had decided his talents would be better spent investigating murders. He missed the Flying Squad.

"I don't need your help with the Ouija board yet," he said.

"Ah," Swaffer touched the side of his nose conspiratorially. "But you're still not comfortable with it, are you, confined to barracks on Tottenham Court Road?" His fingers danced across the keyboard, nicotine-stained dabs plucking out the first few notes of "The Camptown Races". The occupants of the club began to dance, the women twirling their stoles, the men mimicking the actions of jockeys on their horses, all smiling and gesticulating in Greenaway's direction.

"You got me," said Greenaway, wanting to put an end to that number before it went any further. But Swaffer stopped of his own accord.

"Tell me," he said, modifying the volume of his plummy tones, "one of your former colleagues from those halcyon days, a certain Ross Spooner – I gather he's been seconded to the Ministry?"

Greenaway shrugged. "I know they had him up the Scrubs, going through files of enemy infiltrators, at one point." He raised his pint to his lips. "Things could be worse than the Murder Squad, I s'pose."

"A little bird told me," said Swaffer, "he's got a comfortable berth for himself, under the wing of the Chief. Bright boy, is he?"

Greenaway summoned Spooner's face to mind, a pale oval, dominated by wire-rimmed spectacles, fringed with unruly red hair. Unlike himself, Spooner was not a man of action. He was the type that went through files and phonebooks with a magnifying glass, joining the dots to make a case watertight. The type that was just right for MI5. He wondered where this was going and who Swaff's informant might be. The old devil always hinted at powerful sources within the establishment, from Churchill himself to his former employer, the deceased Lord Northcliffe, with whom he still claimed to be in constant communication.

"Apparently there's some funny business going on down in Portsmouth," Swaffer went on. "The Chief's on his way down there now. Have you heard anything about it? I wondered if he'd taken young Spooner with him?"

Greenaway frowned, shook his head. "How d'you reckon I'd know a thing like that, Swaff?" he said. "Spooner ain't really a close pal of mine, you know."

"Ah but—" said Swaffer, plonking out another few notes, "Honeysuckle Rose" this time, "you do go back a way with his guv'nor, if memory serves. Two years back, to be precise – those premises on Dover Street?" Swaffer's eyebrows rose and fell.

Greenaway laughed, shook his head. "What, you mean *The Vault of Vice*, as your firm so poetically put it? If you remember rightly, them premises was empty when I raided them. Apart from the lovely Carmen, of course."

"Carmen Rose! Six-foot tall in her thigh-high boots," said Swaffer, recalling his copy with relish, "and wearing nothing else."

"Nothing else," echoed Greenaway. "But no, Swaff, you're barking up the wrong tree here. If Spooner's boss was one of Carmen's clients, then it's news to me. You better tap up some of your higher-class snouts. I'm just a Murder Squad plod these days, ain't I?"

Swaffer smiled like he knew otherwise, put the lid down over the ivories and stood up. He placed his empty glass on top of the piano and lifted up a frock coat and a battered old stovepipe hat that looked as if it was going rusty round the edges.

"Well," he said, "should any information from Portsmouth happen to come your way, I'd be much obliged to hear it. And now, you must excuse me. I'm due at Miss Moyes's circle in Notting Hill Gate." He tipped the hat at Greenaway before clamping it over his long, snowy locks, and gave a theatrical bow. "Adieu, dear fellow, adieu."

Greenaway made his way back to Beverley at the bar, sank the dregs of his stout and ordered them both another.

"How'd you make our friend Swaff?" he asked his old boss. "How much of it's real, how much is a put-on?"

"Good question," replied Beverley, staring into the foam at the top of his glass. "But I'll tell you this for nothing. If he ever invites you over to his gaff, don't take him up on it. He'll have you up all night talking to his Red Indian spirit guide."

"Right," said Greenaway. "It's funny though. Every time I talk to him, he reminds me of something I'd forgot. He was going on about the knocking shop on Dover Street, remember that? Old Carmen Rose and her leather boots . . ."

"Really?" said Beverley. "The dirty old sod. Mind, I don't see how you could have forgotten that one, Ted."

"You got me," Greenaway admitted. But it wasn't the Jamaican madam he was thinking of, impressive though she had been. It was her green-eyed, red-haired maid.

"Funny business down in Portsmouth," he said, batting her image away. "You heard anything about that?"

2

BLUES IN THE NIGHT

Sunday, 8 February 1942

Miss Evelyn Bourne stood in the hallway of Mrs Payne's boarding house, inhaling the aroma of the first and last meal she had managed to avoid eating there. A medley of liver, onions and mashed swede by the smell of it, and by the fact that there had been scarcely any variation to the menu in the three long months since she had taken up lodgings.

The grandmother clock chimed a sonorous six times as her eyes took final stock of the gloomy interior. Mrs Payne kept one oil lamp lit on the hall table, which emitted enough of a glow to illuminate the brass gong she used to summon her inmates for feeding, a green baize letter rack criss-crossed with black tape, and a typed and framed list of rules about blackouts, meal times and the dire consequences of guests being found in lodgers' rooms.

Miss Bourne tried to leave her gaze there, picking out the various misspellings she had detected in this treatise during her stay, which had given her a kind of bitter comfort against the pretensions of her hostess. But, as if some agent of mischief was controlling them, her eyes rolled across to the other side of the hall, to a thing that had always made her wince – a cartoon that hung next to the lounge door, of a little girl sitting on her father's shoulders with a speech bubble coming out of her mouth uttering the words: "I'se bigger than 'oo!"

It was just the sort of thing her mother would have found amusing. Miss Bourne forced her head away just as Mrs Payne, in her customary matching pinafore and headscarf, finally emerged from the boxroom she called her office, smelling strongly of L'heure Bleue and holding a piece of headed paper.

"I trust this puts everything in order, Miss Bourne," she said, as if challenging her to find otherwise. Mrs Payne was a thickset woman in her late forties, who faced the encroachment of time with a full armoury of face powder, corsetry, setting lotion and an accent adapted from the BBC. Before the war, her premises had been a tearoom, which she had enterprisingly adapted to circumstance. With beady attention to economics, including the strict adherence to her frugal menu and a coal ration that matched the temperature of the household to that of a mausoleum, she turned enough of a profit to allow such little luxuries as black-market French perfume.

"Thank you, Mrs Payne," said Miss Bourne, giving the settlement of her account the briefest of scans before folding it up and consigning it to the depths of her handbag.

Mrs Payne gave what she thought was a magnanimous smile. Miss Bourne had always been a mystery to her. Her appearance she found somewhat severe, those tight buns and old-fashioned cloche hats, the shapeless clothes that hung off her twig of a figure. Her unwillingness to spend each evening in the lounge chatting with the other guests had been read as a sign that she considered herself above the rest of them. But there was little else to fault: Miss Bourne had been tidy to the point that, apart from her bed linen, her room never needed cleaning, was always punctual with her payments and her mealtimes and had never once come home in company.

On paper, Mrs Payne realised, Miss Bourne had been an ideal lodger. Perhaps it was a shame that she was moving on.

"Well, good luck, dear," the landlady said. "Where was it you said you was going to?"

"Grimsby." Miss Bourne scowled as she said it. Perhaps, as the forbidding name would seem to imply, that place was beneath her, too.

"Nice there, is it?" said Mrs Payne. Her smile revealed a dash of coral pink lipstick stuck to her front teeth.

"It's a job," was all Miss Bourne could find to say about it. "Much like any other one, I expect. Well," she extended her hand, "I must be going now if I'm to catch the train to London tonight. I'll have someone come for my luggage directly as I've booked the ticket."

"Yes, all right, dear." On paper be damned, Mrs Payne decided, she had been right all along. There was something queer about Miss Bourne. She opened the front door, watched the woman pick up her one small travelling case and prepared to dismiss her from her mind.

Outside on the pavement, Miss Bourne hurried up the residential avenue towards the High Street and the train station. Hornchurch – she couldn't wait to see the back of it.

– . –

The clock on the station wall read twenty minutes past seven as Miss Bourne at last arrived there. If Mrs Payne had found her ex-lodger self-possessed and aloof, the booking clerk with whom she made her arrangements formulated an altogether different picture of her.

Having spent a career observing people on the move, the clerk had frequently seen women like this: leaving in a hurry, puffy around their red-rimmed eyes and working their hands together in a state of agitation. More of them than ever since the Blitz began. He felt a stab of pity for the woman in the camel-coloured coat, hiding her face under a round, knitted green hat. She stood so upright, as if she was wearing a metal corset, yet anxiety oozed out through her strained vocal cords.

"I'm sorry, madam. Could you repeat that for me?" he asked her. "Did you say that was Miss or Mrs?"

He knew it would be the former even as she choked the word out. There was something vaguely familiar about her.

"Are you quite all right, Miss?" he asked. He remembered now where he had seen her before, working behind the counter at the chemist's on the High Street, the one that had closed for business this past Friday. He wondered if the loss of her job was the cause of her distress, or whether it had resulted from a parting of a more difficult kind, if there was someone she was leaving behind here, too.

The kindness in his voice was almost more than Miss Bourne could bear.

"I'm just fed up, that's all," she said. "Fed up with all this moving about. All I want to do is spend the rest of my days in peace."

The clerk nodded sympathetically. "That's all we can hope for, isn't it?" he said, turning the form around for her to sign. "To get through all of this in one piece."

"Yes." Miss Bourne pulled herself together with a monumental act of will. It was no use having a nervous breakdown in front of this poor man. That could wait until she was on the train to London, chugging through the dark and the cold alone, with nothing else to do except reflect upon her failures. This one, and the rest.

– • –

By the time she had reached Paddington, some two and a half hours of blizzards and frozen points later, Miss Bourne had managed to rally herself. Perhaps, she thought, despite the abrupt ending of the telephone call that had sent her into the snug bar of the Railway Tavern for an hour longer than she had anticipated earlier this evening, if she just turned up at Gloucester Place, they would have to let her in. Where else was she supposed to go so late of an evening in a city she barely knew? Surely they would show some pity, tonight of all nights?

Catching sight of a porter, she walked briskly towards him. "Excuse me," she said, "could you help me to find a taxi, please?"

The porter raised his eyes gloomily up to the station clock. "I'll try, Madam," he said, "but you'll be lucky, this time of night."

However, when they came out of the station, there was a cab just pulling up. It lifted Miss Bourne's spirits: this had to be a sign that she had taken the right course of action after all. She gratefully slipped a shilling into the porter's hand as he stowed her bag in the boot and informed the driver of her destination.

But the cabbie drove so slowly through the unlit streets that her agitation began to stir again. She couldn't shut the image of Mrs Payne's stupid framed cartoon out of her mind. That and the memories that came with it, of her mother's drab little Tyneside parlour, of confinement in a world she didn't want or understand – and which wanted and understood her still less. The brief moments of respite between then and now – other worlds opening suddenly in bright shafts of brilliance: intellectual discourse and political fire, the possibilities of minds meeting, of love being a hair's breadth away – only to cast her back to grey reality again each time. Each time making it harder to swallow, knowing that it could have been so different, but for her own timidity, her own stupidity. The manacles she had forged all by herself.

"This is it, love," the driver's voice broke through her tormented reverie.

Miss Bourne blinked, looked out on the terraced crescent. It had started to snow. "Could you just wait here a moment, please?" she asked. Like the booking clerk at Hornchurch station, the cabbie caught the tremor in her voice.

He watched her pick her way down the street by the thin flicker of her torch beam, go up the steps to the front door and ring the bell. A maid opened it with a disdainful look on her face. She didn't usher his passenger in, but instead just stood there, shaking her head solemnly. As his fare began to wave her arms in argument, the maid simply shut the door in the woman's face.

She stood there for a moment, shouting at the door as flurries of snow swirled around her. Then her shoulders slumped in defeat and she slowly turned and came back to him, her brow puckered and her eyes darting from side to side.

She got back in the taxi. "They must put me up somewhere," she said, more to herself than to him, the cabbie thought. "I've got the money to pay."

"Where you headed, love?" he asked. "Can we find you a room nearer to where you want to get to, d'you think?"

She shook her head. "I've got to be in King's Cross in the morning to catch a train to Grimsby. But I don't want to stay anywhere around there." She looked back towards the house that had just ejected her, desperation in her eyes.

Then, just when he thought she was going to start crying, her head snapped back round. "I know," she said, her expression suddenly quite calm. "The Three Arts Club, just a bit further down the street here. I've stayed there before. Could you take me there instead, please?"

He turned the cab around towards Regent's Park and this time her doorstep enquiry was a success. He carried Miss Bourne's small case to the door for her and got a shilling's tip for it on top of his fare. But he was relieved to see the back of her. The cabbie had seen his share of strangeness during these days of fire and chaos, but there was something proper disconcerting about this one. He thought she was going mad.

– • –

Mrs Carolyn Jones, manageress of the Three Arts Club, showed Miss Bourne up to her room as the clock chimed the half hour past ten. Miss Bourne managed to keep the smile glued to her face until she was alone, and by holding her breath until she heard footsteps receding back down the stairs, she kept the sob from her throat.

Ten minutes later she was splashing cold water onto her face. She stopped when she caught sight of herself in the little square of mirror above the sink.

"Stop it now, stop it," she whispered to herself. Her eyes darted away from her reflection to that of the room behind her. It was small and beige and it seemed to Miss Bourne just then that it was starting to shrink still further. For a brief,

mad second, she wondered if, like Alice, she had taken something that was making her grow. She laughed, and the sound
snapped her out of this thought, brought her gaze back to her
mirror image.

"You haven't eaten again, have you?" she asked herself, in
the tone of voice her mother would have used. "Now you're
so hungry you're starting to see things. You need to eat, my
girl . . . Eat something now."

She lifted her coat from where she had flung it across the
bed, put it back on. Smoothed her hair back into shape and
carefully arranged her hat over the top of it. For a few seconds
more, she scrutinised herself in the mirror, until she was
certain that she looked quite calm.

Then she went back downstairs and asked Mrs Jones where
she might find somewhere open to eat at this time of night.
The manageress suggested the Lyons Corner House at Marble
Arch. It was a bit of a walk, but Miss Bourne said she was sure
she could manage it. She gave a brief, grateful smile as she
closed the front door behind her.

Then she stepped out into the snow.

3

YOU RASCAL YOU

Monday, 9 February 1942

She lay on her back in the gutter that ran across the middle of a surface air-raid shelter in Montagu Place, Marylebone. It was so cold a final resting place that Greenaway could see his breath hanging on the air in front of him as he stooped into the doorway, squinting at the scene in the pallid glow of electric lantern light.

The photographer and the Divisional Surgeon had already done their work, had left the throng of police that currently surrounded the building to develop pictures and write reports. In the few moments between their departure and the arrival of the next officer called to the scene, Greenaway hoped he might be allowed enough peace to think.

A green woollen cap lay across the threshold of the shelter. Slush fell from his shoes as he carefully stepped over it to approach the tangled form beyond. It had been bitterly cold the night before, snow swirling over the city, but for once the Luftwaffe had not come calling. There was no reason for this woman to have come here.

Her feet pointed towards him, her right leg slightly raised, her skirt pulled up to her thighs. A fawn camelhair coat lay rumpled beneath her, her arms still inside the sleeves, though the garment was open, revealing a green jumper that matched the discarded cap. She probably knitted them herself, Greenaway thought, as he knelt down beside her. Now her careful work lay in savage disarray, the jumper pushed up to expose her right breast, the white vest she wore beneath roughly torn away.

Greenaway opened up his murder bag. He extracted a pair of rubber gloves and pulled them on, breathing in the iron scent of blood. The woman's head was propped upwards against the wooden bench that served as a seat, her final scream muffled by her own silk scarf, now wound tightly around her nose and mouth. Her eyes had turned glassy, unseeing, but the horror of her end still registered from the dark dilated pupils, from the swollen tongue protruding between her teeth and the gag, from the livid bruising on her neck.

Her tormented features could not show him for sure, but Greenaway did not take her modest garb and undyed, dark brown hair for that of the kind of woman who would have come in here to entertain a serviceman.

The only jewellery she was wearing was a plain wristwatch on a brown leather strap. No necklace broken in the struggle, no rings on her fingers, no brooch pinned to her coat. Just a matchbox, a powder compact and a packet of Ovaltine tablets lying by her side. Her torch had rolled a couple of yards away from her.

This woman doesn't belong here, Greenaway thought, someone had to drag her here. Someone who thought himself clever, a bit of a card – someone who had gone to the trouble, after his frenzy was through, of picking up her gloves and placing them on her chest, palms outwards in an inverted prayer, the fingers pointing towards her face.

Greenaway felt a throbbing at his temples.

"Any sign of a handbag?" he asked the D Division copper who had made the call-out just before nine that morning, when an electrician on his way to a job had found her here. The thin young man stood just outside the doorway, arms crossed and blinking against the wind.

"No, sir," the PC answered, turning his head. "Not in here. But there's a squad of men out there looking."

"Good," said Greenaway, his eyes travelling around the entrance of the shelter. Loose mortar lay all over the place, fragments of which could easily find their way into the tread of a boot or shoe. He picked out some sample bags from his kit; he'd need to bag some of that up for evidence. And this . . .

Her watch had stopped at one o'clock. But when Greenaway lifted her wrist, it began to tick again.

"Ted." Another shadow across the doorway, and the voice of Detective Chief Superintendent Fred Cherrill, Head of the Yard's Fingerprint Division, a hangdog face under a bowler hat, regarding him with solemn brown eyes. Greenaway was glad to see those familiar, morose features. His comrade's mind was an encyclopaedia of villainy rendered in lines and whorls, prints more vivid than any mugshot to him. Despite his senior rank, he insisted on always working murder scenes himself and nothing escaped Cherrill's gaze. If this killer was somebody they already knew, he would be indexed in Fred's mental rogues' gallery. If he wasn't, the DCS would find a sure-fire way of putting a noose around his neck.

"Fred." Greenaway got to his feet, short stabs of pain in his knees as he rose from the concrete floor. They shook hands and Greenaway stepped back outside, exhaling the bitter aroma of death from his nostrils as Cherrill set up his powerful crime-scene lamp and went immediately to work.

Greenaway's eyes roamed up and down the street, and on to the bare branches of the trees in Regent's Park behind them, stark against the sleeting sky, and the barrage balloons that hovered over them all, like great grey elephants somehow floating in the air. Around him, workers hurried along with their heads down, wrapped and muffled up against the cold. Greenaway wondered if this Johnny could possibly be amongst them, if he was the type who liked to come back and hover around his masterwork, as the boastful arrangement of the woman's gloves suggested he might. Without thinking about it, he lit a cigarette.

Inside, Cherrill crouched down beside the body, raised his magnifying glass.

Greenaway turned a slow circle, taking in a 360-degree mental snapshot of the terrain and everyone within it. Then he fished his notebook out of his pocket, jotted down his first impressions and all the questions that sprang to mind. Finally, dropping the butt of his cigarette into the gutter, he turned his gaze back into the shelter.

"Anything?" he asked.

Cherrill, seemingly lost in his inspection, said nothing for a while. Then he looked up, eyebrows raised. "Seems to have been a left-handed job," he said, nodding.

"Chief Inspector, sir." Another constable approached Greenaway, an older man in the uniform of a reservist, a pair of bottle-thick glasses resting on a nose threaded with red veins.

"Stokesby, sir, Marylebone Lane – the gaffer said I should report to you."

"Oh, yes, constable?" Greenaway took in greasy grey hair, spots of egg on the lapels of a jacket shiny with wear.

"I was on Number 13 beat last night, that is to say, Marylebone Road, Baker Street, York Street, Seymour Place and here." Stokesby waved a notebook earnestly.

"Right," Greenaway opened his own again, licked the end of his pencil, "and what did you see here, constable?"

"Nothing," the reservist replied. "Well, nothing suspicious, any rate. I passed by here first at 11.30 and I always take a look inside. I did last night. I shined my light up and down, but didn't see anyone in the shelters at all. Well, there weren't any call for it, was there? I think if anyone *had* been lying on the floor round about then, I would have noticed them."

Greenaway watched the darting little eyes behind the magnifying lenses. The reservists were usually retired policemen, but he wondered how much worse things could get for a force strained by the departure of so many younger men to the war, if myopic volunteers were all that were left to do this kind of legwork. "Did you hear anything, then, any sounds of a quarrel, a fight?"

"Nothing unusual, sir," Stokesby scratched his head. "It was a very quiet night, last night, not many people about. No moon neither. It was very dark out here. But . . . what people there was about were soldiers. Four or five times I got asked where the Church Army Hostel was, so I directed them to Seymour Place." He flapped his arm for emphasis. "Got called over to Baker Street just before midnight, reports of some shady types coming in and out of a doorway. Well, they must have pushed off before I got there, no sign of any breaking and entering on the premises. Took me lunch from 1.15 to 2.15, and I must have passed by here two or three more times during the night." Stokesby shrugged. "Still didn't see anything out of the ordinary."

"No vehicles parked up here?" Greenaway suggested. "Or any driving away?"

"None that I recall. I didn't see a sentry on duty either," Stokesby looked as if he had surprised himself with this last remark. "Well, like I say, sir, it was very dark."

Greenaway closed his notebook. "Thank you, constable," he said. "That was very helpful. Give my regards to your gaffer, won't you?"

The throbbing in Greenaway's head was more insistent now. He rubbed his temples, hoping for it to clear. Watching Stokesby shambling away in the direction of his station, he felt acutely aware of his own years. Greenaway was a veteran of the last war, who'd taken his skills as a radiographer from the Navy to the Met and risen swiftly up the ranks, thanks to his luck on the racecourses. Swaffer had been right about his ambiguous feelings towards this new role on the Murder Squad.

The men that worked the rackets he could understand. He had grown up with them, after all, knew exactly how their calculating, chancy minds worked and therefore how to deal with them. Takes one to know one, maybe. But this pointless death, this brutal, ugly end of a woman who had managed to survive Christ knows how many air raids before she ended up dead in a shelter on a night when there were no bombs, how could he get into the mind of a man who did things like that?

"Excuse me, Chief Inspector," the younger PC broke into his thoughts. "We've located the lady's handbag, sir. It was just round the corner, on Wyndham Street."

Greenaway looked down at the constable's gloved hands

which held the remains of a black handbag treated much the same way as its owner – left wet, torn and empty.

"Fred," he called to Cherrill. "Something else for you here."

Cherrill, only a few years Greenaway's junior himself, stooped his way out of the shelter. He appraised the sorry artefact with a frown.

"Doesn't look like I'll be able to get much out of that," he said. "But we'll see what comes up when it's dried and dusted. I've done all I can here, better get her over to Spilsbury, now, see what he makes of it. Poor old boy," Cherrill added to himself. "I don't suppose he'll like it much. What'll you do now, Ted?"

Greenaway snapped his notebook shut. "Go house to house," he said. "Try and find out who she was first, what she might have been doing here. And who she might have been knocking about with."

Cherrill nodded. "Well," he said, "we're looking for a left-handed man, I'm sure Spilsbury will confirm it. Good luck, Ted."

"And to you," said Greenaway. "Hope you find him before I do."

For his own sake, he added, mentally.

4

THE MOOCHE

Monday, 9 February 1942

The dull afternoon light did not penetrate the windows of the first-floor rooms of 153 Wardour Street. The windows themselves, hanging in their frames like the bleary eyes of a heavy drinker amid a sagging façade of shell-shocked masonry, were covered with the accumulated dirt of so many bomb blasts that the sun would have had a difficult enough job even on the brightest of days. But this was not the reason for the dim aura of the room occupied by Mrs Evelyn Bettencourt, or, as she preferred her friends to call her, Nina Oakley, this Monday afternoon. Nina had drawn the blackout curtains early in order to best facilitate the atmosphere necessary for the services of her friend and confidante, Madame Arcana.

Madame – or Flo, as she was known by her fellow expatriates in the community that dwelt around Berlemont's pub in Dean Street – was a petite woman in her thirties, who dressed in black astrakhan and a flamboyant red hat with a feather in it. Thus she announced her profession as an occultist: palms and tarots read, fortunes told, spiritual assistance given for 1/6 an hour – a little above the average rate, but, as Madame would impress upon you the first time you met her, holding your hand tightly with red-manicured fingers and gazing with a solemn intensity through a pair of huge, black eyes, that was because she had studied under Madame Blavatsky herself, as a young girl in Paris.

Very few of her clients, including the peroxide blonde sitting next to her, had insight enough to realise that, were this to be true, Madame Arcana would have had to have been at least sixty years older than she appeared to be. Perhaps, even if they had, they might have put it down to awe-inspiring magical powers, for very few of Madame's regulars were ever disappointed by her.

Nina had been seeing her on and off for some months now, since she had first made her acquaintance in the aforementioned hostelry one slow October evening. At first it had been the crystal ball Madame had consulted through, but today, because she was anticipating a change in her luck, Nina had asked her to read her cards.

Nina drew from the Marseilles Tarot by flickering candle-light, while a lump of Indian incense, bought especially from the Atlantis Bookshop, smouldered in the ashtray. Even the most amateur of readers would have found the three cards she chose a challenge, but Madame was skilled enough in psychology not to let her dismay at the chaos she saw revealed transmit itself to her client.

"Tell me," she said, lifting her head, "how was your husband when you last saw him?"

Nina, who had fled to London six years previously, to escape the life of a Lancashire poultry farmer's wife, gave a resigned sigh before she answered. Her trouble, as she had often confided to Madame before, was that her husband still paid her regular visits, always hoping – yet never bold enough to actually ask – that they might be reconciled.

"My Harry?" she said. "He was all right, I s'pose. Same as he always is. Oh, he's a good man right enough, he's kind, considerate, goes to church on Sunday; he's just—" she shrugged, pursing lips around which the first little fissures of middle-age were beginning to show, "boring. You've no idea what it's like trying to make a living out of chickens, love. They smell bloody rotten, they make a right flamin' row and they fix you with their evil little eyes all the time. I'd sooner face Hitler . . ."

Madame shook her head curtly. "I assure you, you would not," she said.

Nina blushed, remembering too late from whence Madame had fled. "Eee, I'm sorry, chuck, I let me mouth run away with us sometimes. No, course I wouldn't. But what are you talking about Harry for? You know I've not changed me mind about him. I thought you were gonna tell us some more about my Canadian . . ." Nina's expression took on a simpering air and she wriggled in her seat, the patched and faded eiderdown she had placed on top of her single bed.

Madame looked back down at the third, most damning card in the sequence. What she wanted to say and what Nina wanted to hear were two separate things that her mind strained to reconcile.

"Your soldier friend," she began to recall their previous conversations. "This is why I ask. You said you were going to introduce him to your husband, no?"

This was not a course of action Madame would have advised, but advice was not really what Nina sought from her. She paid her shilling and sixpence mainly just to air her bewildering plans aloud to someone who was obliged to listen.

"Oh, aye." Nina shrugged. "Well, they got on all right, I s'pose. Nowt Harry could do if he didn't like it, is there? But leave off about him now, will you, love? Tell me about my Joe. Is he gonna sweep me away to Canada once all this is over?"

Fortunately, Madame was saved from pronouncing on the likelihood of this by the loud arrival of Nina's neighbour, whose room was separated from the one they were in only by a pair of wooden doors acting as a shutter. There was a banging, followed by a mewling, as one of the doors came ajar and a huge tabby cat came barrelling through it and pounced upon Nina's knees.

"Hello, Bertie!" Nina greeted the animal effusively, stroking it as it padded around in circles on her lap. "Is that you, Ivy?" she called. "Come through and meet a friend of mine."

Madame's gaze turned to the door. The woman who stood there resembled some kind of ageing variety turn, wearing a fur coat that appeared to have been fashioned from a succession of Bertie's predecessors and a felt Stetson hat. A cigarette protruded from the corner of her mouth and she spoke without removing it.

"Hello, ducks," she said, the fag beginning to droop as her eyes travelled from Nina to the extraordinary creature sat beside her on the bed, with her scarlet hat and piercing, coal-black eyes. To Ivy, Madame looked just like a witch and it was all she could do not to cross herself.

"Ivy, this is Madame Arcana," said Nina, waving her hand and then returning her attentions to the tabby on her lap, who had made himself comfortable and was now sizing Madame up with a hostile green-eyed glare to rival that of his mistress.

Madame gave Ivy a curt nod before turning back to her paying client. "Nina," she reminded her, "our time is almost up for today."

"Oh, course, silly me." Nina gathered the cat into her arms and stood up. "Sorry, love," she said to Ivy. "Can you take him? I'll not be more than five minutes, then I'll make us both a brew."

Ivy nodded, took the furry bundle from Nina's arms and left, closing the door behind her as firmly as the landlord's woodwork skills allowed. Madame thrust the cards back into the pack as quickly as was dignified, snapping her handbag shut over the top of them.

"What were you saying, now, love?" Nina sat back down on the bed. "He's gonna take me away to Canada, was it?"

"Nina," Madame looked into the hopeful, smiling face of this woman who had come to London to make her fortune on the stage and had spent the past six years sliding further away from the variety theatres to hostess clubs and bottle parties and finally the streets around her. A silly woman, many would judge, who stubbornly refused to give up her dreams of stardust and handsome leading men, but who nonetheless had survived all the knocks her aspirations had taken along the way and still managed, in the candlelight, to retain her handsome features and her sense of hope. A face which seemed to Madame as wholesome as a freshly baked loaf of bread. A wave of sympathy rushed over the fortune-teller and with it came the loosening of her tongue.

"If you would just listen to me, for once, please take some advice." Madame took hold of Nina's hand as a puzzled expression crossed the blonde woman's features. "I don't want you to go out with any more servicemen," she said. "In fact, it would be better for you if you went back with your husband now, at least until the war is over. You know I don't like to give advice that is contrary to your hopes, but believe me, it is for the best." She gave the hand a squeeze. "There are worse things than chickens out there, *ma cherie*."

Nina's mouth fell open. "Well," she began, shaking her head, "I don't know what to say . . ." Then a change came across her features and she pulled her hand away. "Has he put you up to this?" she said, scowl lines appearing on her forehead.

"*Quoi*?" Madame was thrown. "What do you mean?"

"Harry," said Nina. "Has he told you to come here and say this? Did he pay you?"

"No, of course not, where ever did you get that idea from?" Madame sprang to her feet. She had never seen an enraged Nina before. Luckily, her client had crossed Madame's palm with silver before the session began and, equally fortuitously, Madame had chosen to sit on the side of the bed that was nearest the door.

"'Cos that's all you've bloody talked about," Nina glowered over her. She was at least a foot taller than the little Frenchwoman. "Him and his flamin' chickens! Even if it's not, what right have you to tell me what to do and who to see?"

Madame stuffed her handbag firmly under her left arm. Her eyes flashed, defying the other woman to come any closer.

"Nina, you asked me to read your cards for you and that is what I have done. If you don't want to take my advice, you don't have to. But I can assure you," she stepped backwards, feeling behind her with her right hand for the doorknob. "I have never so much as met your husband. I cannot be paid to do anything so despicable as you suggest and I will not stand being treated like this."

"Is that right?" Nina jutted her chin. But the anger was

cooling in her almost as quickly as it had ignited, replaced by a feeling of despair. She had been so sure Madame would tell her that a new future awaited her in Canada. Even though it was better than the farm, the life she had here was taking its toll on her.

"I'm sorry, chuck," Nina said, sinking back onto the bed. "Don't mind me, I just . . ." She twisted her hands, as if wringing out an imaginary rag. "I've just got too much on me mind, that's all. You go, I'll be all right."

"If you are sure?" Madame was caught between the remnants of her sympathy and the urge to flee.

"Be seeing you," Nina said, turning her head away.

– • –

Next door, sitting at her kitchen table, Ivy tried to keep her eyes on Swaffer's column in the *Herald*. But she couldn't help overhearing the conversation taking place between Nina and her strange little friend. She reached in her drawer for her rosary beads and didn't put them down again until she heard the fortune-teller leave.

5

PAPER DOLL

Tuesday, 10 February 1942

"Bleedin' nice, ain't it?" Lil flopped back in the hairdresser's chair, rolled her unmade-up eyes at the ceiling. "My local bogey stops me on the way into work last night, tells me to be up bright and early for Bow Street in the morning; my turn on the rota, he reckons. Then he goes and invites himself in for a cuppa Rosie, scares off all my regulars clomping up the stairs in his size ten boots and makes himself at home in the kitchen with Duch – all before I've even had time to make a couple of quid. Talk about being a lady of easy virtue," she huffed on. "I ain't seen nuffink easy about it yet."

"Oh dear," Gladys, the Cardiff-born chief lady of the rollers at the basement salon in Shaftesbury Avenue, sympathised. "We'd best get you a nice cuppa on before we get started, eh?"

"Thanks, Glad." Lil wrinkled up her nose as she smiled, like a mischievous child. She kicked off her high-heeled shoes and stretched out on the chair, settling into the lazy, steamy warmth of the place, the sound of Peggy Lee slinking out of the wireless.

Getting pinched by the local, friendly bogey on the beat was an occupational hazard that cut both ways: he got a few extra shillings in his pay packet for bringing her up to court, she pleaded guilty and got off with a two-quid fine. Justice was seen to be done, at least for the next month or so, and the Crown got its form of tax on Lil's earnings. Plus, it made sure she never got mentioned to any of PC Plod's superiors.

On such occasions, Lil always came down to Glad's for a trim, set and manicure after they let her go. It was an in-between time, too late to go back home, too early to get back to work. This made a treat out of an inconvenience for her.

"Wonder where she's got to?" Lil mused, meaning the Duchess, whom she had arranged to meet here. She glanced around the small, cluttered room and her gaze stopped on the woman sitting to her left. There was something familiar about her, but it took Lil a few moments to work it out.

"Lorn?" she said, watching one of Gladys's apprentices, a girl called Dot, who had arms like a docker and a fag hanging out of the corner of her mouth, applying a tube of brunette hair dye to the woman's previously platinum locks. "Is that you, girl?"

The woman, with whom earlier in her career Lil had once shared a West End corner, swivelled red-rimmed eyes at her and grunted an affirmative.

"What you doing to your hair, love?" Lil looked aghast.

"Here you go, my lovey," Gladys plonked a cup and ill-matched saucer in Lil's hand. Lil's expression didn't change as she looked down into dark brown depths. Strong, Glad always made her brews strong. Not refined and perfumed like the Duchess poured them.

Gladys patted her on the shoulder, bent down and whispered: "Don't bother Lorna right now, lovey. She had a bit of a bloody shock last night, is all. Don't think she really wants to talk about it . . ."

"It's all right, Glad," Lorna's voice was croaky. "I don't mind telling Lil. Probably should spread the word, case we ain't seen the last of him." Her eyes travelled back in Lil's direction. "I got a right bastard last night," she said. "RAF, he said he was." A shudder travelled up her body. "Oh, you tell her, Mol. It hurts to speak."

Lorna's companion, a short, stout brunette with a round face, her hair already set in rollers, had been sitting quietly on a chair in the corner, reading a magazine while Glad's daughter, Angie, painted her toenails. She looked up, fixed Lil with a steady gaze. "All of it?" she asked. She had a strange, high-pitched voice, like a little girl's, that was at odds with her matronly appearance.

Lorna nodded. Molly put her magazine down on her lap.

"All right," she said. "We was outside The Monico, you know, on Piccadilly Circus, 'bout half-past ten last night. Business was slack and we was starting to get royally pissed off with these Canadian soldiers hanging about being all mouth and no trousers. Lorn was just saying to me, if they can't afford the merchandise then move along, this ain't Madame Tussauds."

"I should cocoa," said Lil, unable to nod now that Gladys was brushing back her hair.

"Then these other geezers came along, like Lorn said, RAF blokes in uniform. Aha, we thought, that's more like it. Surely our boys'll know the score? We start shining our torches and one of 'em, this strapping great tall fella – looks a bit like Douglas Fairbanks Jr, I thought – comes up to Lorn. He had this funny little white slip sticking out of his cap. She asks him what it is, and he says it means he's training to be an officer. Right plummy voice he had to go with it, and one of them little moustaches. So, we thought *ooh*, we are going up in the world.

"He said his name was Gordon and his mate, the one I got talking to, was Felix. Felix had a slip in his hat an' all, only not such a posh voice, reckon he was more local. And he weren't like them Canadians, this one got straight down to business. Well," Molly looked down at her toes as Angie moved onto the next foot, "my room's closer than Lorn's, so I said I'd show him the way back after to wait for his friend.

"But he never showed up. Felix weren't bothered, he went off to get pissed, and I s'pose it ain't all that unusual, but I suddenly come over all queer, thought I'd better just go over to Lorn's, see how she was getting on. Good job I did an' all. She was in a right state." Molly looked over at Lorna to make sure it was all right to go on. Lorna gave the flicker of a nod.

"What happened was, this Gordon couldn't get it up. Lorn said he was half-cut anyway, stank of booze, so she starts to get worried about what's gonna happen next, you know, is he gonna take it out on her? First of all, it seems like he's all right, he laughs it off and gives it another try. This don't work neither, and now she's starting to get annoyed with him, wasting her time.

"She tells him to get off and he does, still sort of bashful like, apologetic. So Lorn takes pity on the geezer, tells him to come and sit with her by the fire. He likes this idea, starts stroking away at her hair, telling her how much he likes it, and she can see he's coming round again, so she sticks another French letter on him quick as you like, don't want him making a mess all over her carpet.

"Soon as she does it, he starts getting rough. Winds all her hair up into his fist and starts pulling her head back, going on and on about how much he loves her hair and how he could tell she was a dirty bitch when he saw her, how he can always tell. He puts his hand around her throat and starts squeezing, really hard."

Little Angie, sitting at Molly's feet, stopped painting and sat up, staring at the storyteller with her huge brown eyes. "My godfathers," she whispered.

"What happened then?" straining against Glad's rollering hands, Lil was on the edge of her seat.

"Well," said Molly, flicking her glance around all the women in the room, "thank God, at that moment he manages to get himself off. He drops her like a stone, puts his head in his hands and starts rocking back and forth like a baby. Stays there for a while, moaning to himself, like he's not even in the same world as she is. Then he snaps out of it, tells her he's sorry for keeping her and hopes she makes lots of money tonight. Drops a *five quid* note on her and leaves. Now, what the bleedin' hell do you make of that?"

"Sounds like he was going to kill her," Lil's voice came out a whisper.

"Don't it just," said Molly. At her feet, Angie crossed herself.

"So that's why she's changing what she looks like? In case he comes back after her?" Lil asked.

"No," croaked Lorna, "'cos he said he liked blondes. All that stuff . . ." she broke off and started coughing, loud, wretched hacks.

"All that stuff about her hair," Molly finished the story for her, "was 'cos she was blonde." She raised her crescent moon-shaped eyebrows. "You better watch out, Lil. Don't go with no fella in an RAF uniform, if you know what's good for you."

– • –

"Yes. That's her." Carolyn Jones stood in another basement room, a quarter of a mile east of Gladys's salon, in Gower Street. A room that was large, white and antiseptic. The goosebumps that pricked her skin as Sir Bernard Spilsbury pulled back the white sheet were caused not just by the mortuary conditions, but by the recognition of the woman who had checked into her boarding house only two nights previously. "That's Miss Evelyn Bourne," she said.

"Thank you," said the pathologist, replacing the shroud.

Carolyn Jones put a hand up to her mouth.

"Let me drive you home," said Greenaway.

A detective from Marylebone doing house-to-house enquiries had called on Mrs Jones's establishment that morning and ascertained that Miss Bourne had rented a room there at 10.30pm on the Sunday night previous. Miss Bourne had come back downstairs twenty minutes after she'd been shown to her room and asked if there was anywhere nearby where she could get a meal. Mrs Jones directed her to the Lyons Corner House at Marble Arch – and that was the last she had ever seen of her.

They drove back to Gloucester Place in silence, Mrs Jones staring out of the window in a daze. Greenaway didn't trouble her with any more questions, let her try and get over her shock. He thanked her as he dropped her off and headed straight to the restaurant.

Outside Lyons was a world of bomb craters, sandbags, barbed wire and windows bound up in tape to stop them from shattering in the event of a blast. More barrage balloons swayed above Hyde Park, restless in the wind.

Inside, however, the atmosphere resembled that of the ocean-going liner the building had been designed to resemble. A curved, mahogany tea-bar ran the entire length of the ground floor, fringed with ornate stools. Behind it, gigantic copper cauldrons stretched from floor to ceiling, a network of pipes gurgling and steaming between them, brewing a constant supply for the thirsty masses. From one of the three floors above came the sound of a live jazz band, doing their best impression of Benny Goodman's repertoire.

A Nippy with a loaded tray swung out from behind the bar as Greenaway approached. He flashed his warrant card at her by way of introduction.

"You weren't by any chance working here on Sunday night, were you?" he asked.

"Yes, sir," she said without missing a beat. "I was."

"Good. Would you mind having a chat after you've got rid of that little load?"

Ten minutes later, he was back in his car. The waitress had remembered Evelyn Bourne all right, said she had come in around midnight, alone. She hadn't served her herself, but could recall the evening's menu – the contents of which matched what Spilsbury had found in the dead woman's stomach – a lot of beetroot.

As he started the motor, Greenaway thought of Evelyn Bourne's wristwatch, stopped at one o'clock. She must have taken nearly an hour to walk from the Three Arts to here. The label on the small case she had brought with her did not have an address, but Greenaway was sure his initial feelings about her were right. Even though getting around in the blackout was often arduous, slow progress, she couldn't have known London very well.

She didn't belong here.

The waitresses at Lyons weren't called Nippys for nothing; they would have had her fed and out of there within half an hour, forty minutes. She'd got back to Regent's Park a lot faster than she'd reached Lyons. Had almost made it . . .

But the killer had moved fast. Spilsbury's autopsy revealed that he had crushed the bones in her neck quickly and power-fully, perhaps before she could even have made a sound. Had he followed her out of the restaurant, tracked her until they came to terrain that suited his purpose best – the empty air-raid shelter, the deserted street? Then that would imply he knew the area much better than she did.

Greenaway parked around the corner from the station on Tottenham Court Road. Deep in his thoughts, he didn't reg-ister the Duty Sergeant's call until he was halfway towards the stairs and the man had left his desk and run up to him.

"Chief Inspector, sir! DCS Cherrill just called. He wants you immediately – he's at 153 Wardour Street. He said to tell you it's the Left-Hand Man again."

6

THERE'S SOMETHING WRONG WITH THE WEATHER

Tuesday, 10 February 1942

Sir Bernard Spilsbury looked every one of his sixty-five years as he stood over the single bed in the corner of the room in Wardour Street. There, beneath his frowning gaze, a woman lay stretched out diagonally; pale, white and naked, with great gashes of red across her neck and abdomen, from where her life had flowed away in a stream across the length of the room.

Next to her tangled blonde hair lay a safety razor blade and a pair of curling tongs, both encrusted in blood. In the middle of her open legs, a bloodied tin opener had been left, the business end pointing towards the handle of a torch that had been forced inside her, that had once been white but now was crimson.

So much blood.

"There was an attempt at manual strangulation before the throat was cut," the pathologist said, a waver in his voice. "Look at the abrasions on the front of the neck and the signs of haemorrhaging in the eyes and mouth."

Cherrill and Greenaway exchanged glances. Another freezing cold room, their breath hanging like ectoplasm on the dank air around them.

Spilsbury cleared his throat before he pointed to the puncture wounds dotted around the woman's pubic hair. "These bled a little," he said. "They were probably inflicted when she was on the verge of death, after the cut to the neck."

"Thank heavens for small mercies," said Cherrill softly.

Spilsbury gave a nod and rubbed his eyes. "I'll know more after a full post mortem, of course."

"That," said Greenaway, pointing to the tin-opener, "reminds me of the way he left the gloves on the last one. He thinks it's all one big joke, don't he?"

Neither of the other two men asked him which last one he meant.

"I think I'll be able to get some prints," was all Cherrill said. "I've found dabs on her mirror, and of course," he nodded at the implements arranged around the woman's body, "there's those, too."

He turned to Greenaway: "There's a detective next door with the woman who found her. She's not making much sense yet, but then, how could she? Poor old girl. At the very least, we know who this once was."

It was one of those peculiar coincidences that just became more commonplace the longer you worked for the law. This was a woman who had once been called Evelyn, too. Evelyn Bettencourt, alternatively known as Nina Oakley, a part-time actress who had fallen on hard times with the coming of the war and taken to supplementing her income with a few gentleman callers from time to time.

This much Greenaway was able to get from the detective attending to Ivy Poole, her neighbour. Ivy, a spinster, who as Cherrill had indicated was knocking on a bit herself, worked as an assistant at what they called the fun-fair in Leicester

Square, a tawdry assemblage of shooting ranges, slot machines and manky farm animals, where she was obliged to dress as an approximation of Calamity Jane, if the felt Stetson hat and shirt adorned with lampshade fringing that hung on the back of her door were anything to go by.

Greenaway felt the sadness of wasted years as he surveyed the single bed and one-ring stove of Ivy's little room, the solitary bowl and plate left in her sink when the meter men had roused her from her slumbers at 8am that morning to take a reading. Luckily it was the men from the Central Electric Company who had gone into her neighbour's room ahead of her and stopped her from seeing the full horror of what was in there. But Ivy had still seen the blood.

Now she sat on her bed wrapped in a candlewick dressing gown, clutching a long-cold mug of tea, red eyes staring into the distance. Letting the junior detective take his leave, Greenaway introduced himself and sat down next to her.

"All right, love?" he said, gently prising the mug from her hands. "D'you want me to make you a fresh one?"

For the first time in hours, Ivy heard something other than the Frenchwoman's words about servicemen. It was something about the size of the bogey sat next to her and the gentleness of his sleepy-lidded eyes that calmed her. Ivy's eyes regained their focus as she slowly took him in, her shoulders slumping, her mouth attempting the flicker of a smile. She shook her head.

"No, ta, dear," she said. "Ain't nothing another one of them's gonna make seem any better. Not after what he done in there. What he done to poor Nina. The *bastard*."

Greenaway leant down and opened his murder bag a fraction, enough so Ivy couldn't see inside of it, but so that he could extract the special extra item he always carried there. He poured her out a teacup full of Scotch and handed it to her, watched her pupils enlarge for a second before she took a hefty slug.

"Ta, ducks." Ivy wiped a hand across her mouth. "That was just what I did need, Inspector."

"So what can you tell me, Ivy," Greenaway flicked open his notebook, "that'll help me put a noose around a bastard's neck?"

Ivy straightened herself up. "I saw him," she said. "I saw the man what come in with her last night."

"Yeah?" Greenaway encouraged. "Tell me what he looked like, Ivy."

"He was a young man," she said. "Tall and handsome, I suppose – from a distance anyway."

"You saw him up close, then?"

"I did," said Ivy. "I heard her come in the front door about twenty to twelve. I went and turned the landing light on for her, like I always do. They was coming up the stairs, the pair of them."

"Good," Greenaway nodded. "So you saw them both come in together. You said he was a young man, how old would you say?"

Ivy pursed her lips. "'Bout twenty-four, twenty-five, something like that," she said.

"You remember what colour his hair was?"

"I do," said Ivy. "It was a sort of goldie-brown, wavy at the front, but going a bit frizzy at the back, like he ain't put enough Brylcreem on it." She squinted as she reached back into memory. "Parted on the left, I think. He had a moustache as well, just a small one."

"Nothing gets past you, does it, Ivy?" said Greenaway, taking it all down. "Good girl. You remember what he was wearing?"

"A uniform, by the looks of it," Ivy was still staring down her time-tunnel. "Big greatcoat, but not no ordinary one, this one looked like it was tailor-made. Had a belt around the waist. Blue. That's RAF, ain't it?"

Greenaway stopped writing. Reservist Constable Stokesby popped in his head, saying: "What people there was about were soldiers . . ."

Not perhaps as blind as he had first appeared.

"It could be, Ivy, it could be. Well remembered, love, that's a very important detail," Greenaway encouraged. "Now why did you say he seemed handsome, until you got close up?"

Ivy took another swig from her teacup. "Well," she said, dander now fully up, "when they passed my door, I had a good look at his face. It was all angles, you know, and he had these queer, light-coloured eyes that just seemed to see straight through you. He weren't handsome, but he thought he was. I think he fancied himself rotten."

"And Nina," Greenaway used the name Ivy called her neighbour, "how did she seem?"

"Oh, all right, her usual self, you know. She gave me a smile and said goodnight. She's a lovely girl, is Nina . . ."

Not wanting her to drift back away from him, Greenaway put his hand on Ivy's arm, made sure he had her full attention; that she was looking straight into his eyes.

"Then what happened, Ivy? Did you hear anything coming from the room?"

"Nina always puts the radio on when she gets in. Out of respect for me. I could hear the midnight news from the BBC coming on when I started to get ready for bed. It had finished by the time I'd turned in, there was just some music coming through the walls, dance bands, that sort of thing. Then, just as I was drifting off, it got turned up loud, real loud. Well, I should have known, shouldn't I, that he was up to no good? Nina wouldn't never be so rude . . ."

Ivy's eyes darted away from him, starting to look fearful again. "I should have gone to have a look, shouldn't I, Inspector? I should have tried to help her. Only . . ."

Greenaway gave her arm a gentle squeeze. "No you shouldn't, Ivy. There was nothing you could have done against that maniac. I wouldn't have wanted to find the two of you in there, now, would I?"

Tears welled in Ivy's eyes. "No, sir," she said, sounding like a child.

"Listen, Ivy," said Greenaway. "You done a good job here, girl, you can be proud of yourself. You've helped me and you've helped Nina, too."

Ivy shook her head again, but a momentary flicker of defiance returned to her face.

"You will get him, won't you, Inspector?"

"You got my word on it," said Greenaway, handing her the rest of the bottle.

– • –

The Archer Street joint was late-afternoon quiet. Just a couple of terminal old soaks snoozing over their plates of curled-up sandwiches and half-empty pint pots and a cleaner pushing a mop half-heartedly across the floor to the strains of 'Blues in the Night' coming out of the wireless, nodding her head sagely in time to the tune and the wisdom imparted by the lyrics.

Swaffer was not at the piano stool just yet, but lurking in the corner behind the stage, just visible behind a cloud of cigarette smoke, scribbling into his shorthand notebook.

"What do you know?" said Greenaway.

Swaffer looked up, blinked. "A couple of things," he said. "One: you've been busy. You've shrugged off that lugubrious air that's been haunting you since your onerous transfer. Two: the ladies of the parish are talking." He raised his eyebrows. "These things must be connected."

"What they talking about?" Greenaway pulled up the chair that was opposite the journalist and swung it round beside him, to sit where he could see but not be seen.

"An airman, I believe. Calls himself an officer. Am I getting warm yet?"

Greenaway nodded. "Here's one for your Ouija board, Swaff. There are two dead bodies in the morgue, both women called Evelyn. Miss Bourne and Mrs Bettencourt. Apart from their names, they couldn't be more different. Miss Bourne was a pharmacist from Newcastle. I've just been talking to her sister."

Greenaway's brow creased as he recalled the telephone conversation. Miss Kathleen Bourne was due in London tomorrow, entrusted with the ordeal of claiming her older sibling's body.

"A troubled woman," Greenaway said. "On the outside, intelligent and respectable. Qualified as a chemist from Edinburgh University in 1938, got a job as a shop manageress there soon after, stayed for nearly two years and then suddenly packed it all in. Told her sister she was bored stiff with it, wanted a change.

"Next she gets herself a job as a travelling saleswoman for a firm in Leicestershire, plugging new medicines to shops.

Sticks that for seven months before she goes back home to her Ma's in a state of depression. The sister persuades her to see a headshrinker she knows, who tells her she's suffering from overwork and needs some kind of tonic. So she takes it easy for a couple of months, not doing much except reading and going to the theatre. No sign of a boyfriend in all this time; in fact, her sister couldn't remember her ever having had one, or even having mentioned one."

"Ah," said Swaffer. "I'm getting a sort of a picture here. A well of loneliness, do you think?"

"Maybe." Greenaway shrugged. "Or she could have been one of those unfortunate women who only seem to be able to attract the attentions of married men. That would explain her secrecy, breaking her jobs off suddenly, the depression. Her sister described her as an intellectual and a socialist, who only ever wanted to improve her mind – maybe she was an admirer of yours and that's what sent her round the twist. Whatever's the case, she's not the type of woman who lets herself get picked up in the street by a soldier. Not even on the night of her birthday."

"Her birthday?" Swaffer echoed. "It was her birthday on Sunday?"

Greenaway nodded. "Yeah," he said. "She treated herself to a slap-up meal in the Lyons Corner House at Marble Arch. A plate of beetroot salad. Half an hour later she was dead."

Swaffer dropped his cigarette into the ashtray and reached for another. "Is that what brought her to London?" he asked, sparking up his Ronson.

Greenaway shook his head. "For the past few months she's been working at a chemist's shop in Hornchurch, living in digs nearby. Sunday last, out of the blue, she settles up with her landlady, tells her she's got a new job in Grimsby, but she's stopping off at London for the night on the way – to make a connection in the morning, I suppose. She had arranged for her luggage to be forwarded. But here's another funny thing: the booking clerk said she told him she was fed up with moving around and wanted to spend the rest of her days in peace. He said she had something wrong with her voice, and all, like her vocal cords were mangled."

Swaffer jolted, as if he had been given an electric shock. "Good Lord," he said. "As if she had a premonition . . ."

"Don't start with that," said Greenaway. "I don't want to hear it. But," he relented, "I know what you mean. And that ain't information I'm going to be sharing with the rest of the pack, neither. So, what else have you got for me?"

"He has a thing about blondes, apparently."

"Evelyn Bourne was about as dark as they come, her hair was almost black," said Greenaway. "But she did have the unfortunate habit of always carrying all her cash around with her. That's what got her killed. He watched her in the Corner House, I reckon, followed her from there. Evelyn Bettencourt, on the other hand, was a proper bombshell, just the type to get carried away by a fancy airman. So where's your snout, Swaff? You didn't find her hanging around here, did you?"

"Hereabouts," Swaffer withdrew the cigarette from his lips with a flourish. "I found her on her way back from her hair-dresser's in Shaftesbury Avenue actually, although I see her more often at Miss Moyes's. She is an old acquaintance of yours, too, I believe. I thought you might want to look her up."

Swaffer tore a page out of the back of his notebook and handed it across. "She was very concerned, you see, because at the moment she is working for the most strikingly blonde woman you have ever seen. They heard about this airman from a friend of theirs in the hairdresser's this morning, a lady who'd had a bit of a close shave with him last night. She was in the process of having her hair dyed brown."

Greenaway looked down at the given name and address and felt the hairs prickle up on his arms. He folded the paper carefully and swapped it for the envelope that was in his inside pocket.

"This friend of theirs was lucky. This," he handed his exchange across, "is Spilsbury's report on Mrs Bettencourt."

It disappeared into Swaffer's topcoat so swiftly it might never have even been there. "What more does no one else know yet?" the journalist asked.

"The man's left-handed," said Greenaway. "That's the main reason why I know it's him who done both of them. Fred Cherrill's working on dabs, but so far, he don't seem to be a known resident of any of his files. The airman thing fits with the information I got and the rest—" Greenaway looked up at the clock above the bar, "you'll have to deduce for yourself."

The detective got to his feet. "Do a good job, won't you, Swaff? For the sake of all the ladies of the parish. You know you're the only one they ever read."

7

I'LL BE AROUND

Tuesday, 10 February 1942

"And I told you – I ain't going with no bleedin' soldier!"

Twelve hours after leaving Gladys's salon with her freshly dyed locks waved and pinned securely under her favourite red pillbox hat, Lorna had found her voice again. It rang out shrill and hard in the ears of the Scots Guardsman who, approving of her new look, was flashing a wad of money at her, outside the New Eros cinema in Piccadilly Circus.

"What's wrong wi' ye, hen?" he said, alcohol-suffused blood rising. "Ye not ready ter help the fightin' man, eh? They's battleships comin' up the Channel, but ye's too good ter do yer bit, are ye?"

Lorna looked past him to the shadows under the awning of the tobacconist's next to the cinema. Molly stepped out into view.

"Ye's just wait," the Scotsman went on. "Ye'll ha' a fine auld time once the Russians get here. Oh aye . . ."

The cosh she had borrowed slipped down Molly's coat sleeve into her right palm.

Lorna felt a presence on her left-hand side, heard the hum of a familiar tune, the clack of shoes coming to a halt beside her. The Guardsman must have noticed, too, because he swung his head in the same direction.

A woman stood there, statuesque in a long black coat and matching felt hat, a cigarette in a long holder held poised in her right arm, smoke curving to wreath her face. She pointed in Lorna's direction.

"You tell him," she said, "you're thoroughly British and you'll stand no more of his nonsense."

She took a drag on her cigarette, regarding the Guardsman through narrowed eyes. In the glare of her basilisk stare, he appeared momentarily lost for words. He looked from the woman to Lorna and then turned on his heel, stalking off down Piccadilly, muttering darkly to himself. The woman winked at Lorna. She resumed her humming as she continued on her way.

Molly's hand touched Lorna's arm. "The *Lady*," she said.

The Lady afforded herself a smile. She was aware of how her fellow women of the street regarded her and how this was down to the way she projected herself, the attitude she kept at all times – she'd had a little training once, for the stage, and it had served her well. If only those two girls had known that the name on her ID card was Phyllis Rosemarie Lord.

There was nothing showing at the vast Deco picture house she had just passed that Phyllis was eager to see. *Next of Kin*, *One of Our Aircraft is Missing* – all those propaganda films left her cold. The figures that danced in her head belonged to the era that preceded the war, top hats and tails twirling under the Klieg lights to swooping strings orchestrated by Irving Berlin. That was where Phyllis had always pictured herself, dancing in the arms of Fred Astaire.

She took another long drag on her cigarette as her mind returned to more mundane concerns: the percentage of the night's earnings she would need to put by for her daughter's schooling at St Gabriel's in Southend-on-Sea, for clothing, food and other provisions, the rent on her small flat in Gosfield Street. Phyllis had been something of a businesswoman once, when she had run the Beach Bazaar, her husband Fred's fancy goods shop on the seafront. She had more nous for it, being an avid reader of *Vogue* and *The Queen*, and had always cut a stylish figure who knew exactly what cut-price copies of the goods displayed in those magazines would lure her customers into parting with their LSD.

But Fred had been stuck in his ways. Fred had his friends whom he always did business with, in the shop, and at their afterhours card games. Up to his neck in hock to them, Fred had popped his clogs from a massive heart attack by the time their little Jeanie was ten. The only way to keep herself afloat after that was for Phyllis to sell the shop and everything in it, enrol Jeanie in the best school she could afford on the proceeds and turn to the streets of London for a way of making money that she found less distasteful than scrubbing floors.

The one image she could not abide was that of herself on her knees in a pinafore, reflected in another woman's eyes.

Phyllis passed a couple of constables as she crossed into Shaftesbury Avenue. There were a lot of them about tonight and their presence brought briefly to her mind the headlines on the *Daily Herald*:

SEX MANIAC LOOSE IN LONDON!
NO WOMAN SAFE FROM LEFT-HANDED
KILLER, SAY SCOTLAND YARD
EXCLUSIVE REPORT BY HANNEN SWAFFER

Under her tailored coat and her freshly pressed skirt, her silk blouse and lambswool jumper, Phyllis bore the scars of the trade she had taken up. The Lady had come to Lorna's aid tonight precisely because she shared her views regarding servicemen. Those types always felt that there was something owed to them. Those types could rarely get aroused without becoming violent. After the last pounding she had taken from that Canadian, she wanted nothing more to do with them either.

It was funny, though, how they had all deferred to the sound of an upper-class voice, the Guardsman and those girls. Yes, she mused, as she stopped in a doorway, a safe distance from the bogeys, to light another cigarette. When it came down to it, all her life had been some kind of act or other. It was the only way she knew how to get through it, pretending it was all a dream.

"Pardon me," came a voice beside her in the dark. A voice that purred like a well-oiled Bentley. "But I can't help admiring your style. What say you join me for a drink?"

Phyllis turned her head slowly, parrying her torch towards a face with high cheekbones and light-coloured eyes, goldish-blond hair and a clipped moustache. She swept the beam down to take in the rest of him. He was tall and athletic-looking, he was the right age, but he wasn't wearing a uniform.

"Well," she said, offering him her arm. "I don't mind if I do."

– • –

Inside the Conway Hall in Red Lion Square, three hundred pairs of eyes rested on Swaffer. Not because of the headlines he had produced earlier in the day, nor because he was about to bring them news from the Other Side. Tonight, the pews of the austerely magnificent home of the Ethical Society were packed with people eager to hear him hold forth on another of his great passions: politics.

His age might have prevented him from the frontline reporting he had produced in the last war, and the coalition government had called an uneasy truce on party politicking for his beloved Labour Party, but Swaffer had not been idle on the Home Front. He had been the first national journalist to report from the East End when the Blitz began. He had seen the fire and carnage and had listened to the stories of the people who preferred to take refuge in the tube stations or under their own staircases than risk their lives in the flimsy shelters that the government provided. Then he had taken their concerns to his old friend Herbert Morrison, the Home Secretary, via a march from Bethnal Green to Whitehall. His efforts had brought about another coalition: of ministers, Trades Unionists and Communists, who continued to harangue MPs about the building of deep shelters and the bringing of relief to London's beleaguered communities. Tonight's meeting was both a progress report and a rallying of troops to keep the pressure on.

As Swaffer spoke, he became aware of one pair of eyes in particular, staring at him with a peculiar intensity. Throughout his address and that of the next speaker, through the question-and-answer session that followed, they continued to stare – but the mouth said nothing.

After the last cups of tea had been drunk, the cups washed up and the banners packed away, after the last hands had been shaken and the people dispersed, the owner of that pair of eyes lingered by the door like a shade. As Swaffer approached, she placed a hand on his arm and whispered a greeting.

"Mr Swaffer," she said, "my name is Daphne Maitland. We have never been introduced, but I have attended many of your rallies as a member of the CP and I am a great admirer of *all* your works."

Her appearance was that of an aesthete: tall and thin, encased in a dark grey suit and felt hat. The emphasis she placed on the last sentence sent a tingle up the arm where her hand still rested, to Swaffer's brain, which began to replay the conversation he had had with Greenaway the previous afternoon.

"I wondered," she continued, "if I may speak to you about a matter of great concern to me. I'm afraid it is to do with that article you wrote in today's paper."

"Of course, my dear," Swaffer said, indicating that they should sit down.

She shook her head. "No, not here, not in public." When she looked back up at him, tears were brimming in her eyes, but she kept her voice level. "Would you do me the favour of accompanying me home? I won't take much of your time, I promise, and I'll have my driver take you anywhere you wish to go afterwards."

Swaffer did not laugh at the idea of an avowed Communist ordering her driver to chauffeur him home. Nor did he look at his watch and inform her of the prior engagement he had at the Savoy, to which he really should have been heading.

"But of course," he said instead. He put his stovepipe hat down on top of his snow-white locks, gave the lady his arm and escorted her to her car.

– • –

Greenaway stood at the foot of the stairs, behind the unlocked door that the last careless punter had not bothered to close properly behind him. *Conduit Mews*, read the address on Swaffer's notepaper. A narrow, cobbled thoroughfare between

Paddington Station and Hyde Park, the ideal set-up for a prostitute and her maid – discreetly tucked away from the main thoroughfare and the fleapit hotels, public houses, illicit gaming rooms and bookies' joints that studded the warren of backstreets. The workshop beside the entrance, like most of its neighbours, had been a mechanic's garage that was now boarded up, the proprietor no doubt conscripted, the landlord not too choosey about whom he rented out the upstairs space to, under the circumstances.

Not that Greenaway would have expected the frontwoman of this operation to have presented herself in any manner other than such that suggested she really was some kind of down-on-her-luck dowager whose circumstances had reduced her to take rooms a little further away from Belgravia than she would have wished. And no doubt the property was being well maintained, whatever was going on in there. She was meticulous about making the right impression, whoever it was she was trying to cast her glamour over. Always had been. Despite their shared areas of interest, Greenaway wondered how much even Swaffer actually knew about her.

At the top of the stairs, a red bulb hung under a fringed shade. Greenaway could hear the muffled sound of voices and a jazz piano tinkling away. But what stopped him in his tracks was a scent that came wafting down to greet his nostrils, a perfume that brought back, in one synaptic rush, an entire world. A world of smog and dirt and deprivation, of clamorous hunger and noise. The smell of Greenaway's childhood: the smell of violets.

He took a deep breath, shook his head, and walked up the stairs.

8

WHY DON'T YOU DO RIGHT?

Wednesday, 11 February 1942

At the top of the stairs was a beaded curtain made from jet, hung to tinkle out a warning to those seated on the other side of it that fresh company had arrived. But in the pink glow of her table lamp, the Duchess waited alone. The voices and the jazz Greenaway had heard were all emanating from the radiogram beside her.

"Saw me coming in your crystal ball, did you?" he said, his eyes travelling around the room, taking in the gold- and red-striped wallpaper, the red velvet love seat, the walnut casing on the radiogram and the mahogany table behind which the Duchess sat, items that looked like they'd been salvaged from her previous employer on Dover Street. It was all very ostentatious for a one-woman set-up and obviously designed to convey a different class of service. Though the feeling Greenaway got was that he was standing in a gypsy caravan. The smoke left by the last visitor still hung in heavy trails on the air.

Finally, his gaze came to rest on the woman herself. She wasn't wearing a headscarf festooned with gold coins, as he had more than half expected. Instead, she looked serene, regal even, with her hair swept up into a roll at the front, cop-per-coloured ringlets snaking around her shoulders, a cameo brooch on a velvet ribbon around her neck, pearl teardrops hanging from each earlobe. One hand holding a bone china teacup halfway to her lips, the newspaper spread out on the table in front of her.

The Duchess arched one eyebrow. "Business is slack," she said, tapping an immaculately manicured and painted finger-nail on top of Swaffer's headline. "As well you know. Your firm seems to have frightened everyone off the streets tonight."

"My firm?" said Greenaway. "I thought there was a mad killer out there."

The flicker of a smile played across Duch's lips as she studied him.

"Lil!" she shouted. "Get yer knickers on. We got the law here."

At her bedroom sink, flannel and carbolic between her thighs, Lil yelled out: "Oh, bleedin' 'ell, not again!"

But when, hastily wrapped in her silk gown and slippers, she opened the bedroom door, the sight beyond surprised her. From the superior cut of his dark overcoat and the bashed-about look of his face, Lil would have assumed that the man standing in their parlour, twirling his trilby around in his right hand, was one of the lot her Tom was always on about, the racetrack hoodlums who hung about down Archer Street. As he nodded his head in greeting, she was sure that was where she had seen him before, at the bar of the *Entre Nous*.

"Lil," said her maid, "this is Detective Chief Inspector Greenaway. He's an old acquaintance of mine and a friend of Mr Swaffer's. The man who put the great Sammy Lehmann behind bars, no less. Ain't you, Ted?"

Lil frowned as her eyes flickered between Duch and the big detective.

"Well, what you after me for?" she asked him. "I ain't done no bank jobs lately."

"I think he wants to ask you about what you heard in the hairdresser's, love," said Duch. "That airman what attacked your pal Lorna. See, Ted's the head of the Murder Squad these days," Duch rolled her eyes. "He's out to catch a real villain."

"Oh," said Lil, sitting down. Greenaway did likewise, flicking open his notebook.

"All right," she turned towards him in a cloud of perfume that made his head swim. "Where d'you want me to start?"

– • –

Daphne Maitland stood in the first-floor sitting room of her Gloucester Place townhouse, arms clasped in front of her in a manner of penitence, eyes staring into the fire. Swaffer, sitting in a Regency armchair of a similar vintage to his surrounds, inhaled the contents of his brandy glass and waited for her to begin.

"One of the women you mentioned in your piece," she began. "One of the victims . . ." She drew in a breath and shuddered.

"Was known to you," Swaffer ended the sentence for her. "Miss Evelyn Bourne, I imagine. The lonely chemist from Newcastle."

His hostess turned her head sharply. "But how . . ." she began.

Swaffer put his glass down, opened his palms outwards. "It's not so hard to divine, my dear. Despite your concern for good works, I can't imagine how you would have come across the other unfortunate lady of the night. But Miss Bourne wasn't like that, was she? She was a socialist, an intellectual, so I was told. I expect you met her at a Party meeting," he picked up his glass again, eyes never leaving hers. This time it was Daphne who felt a curious intensity, as if the journalist was riffling through the contents of her mind. "Or some similar gathering."

Her eyes dropped back down to the carpet.

"Actually, I met her by complete coincidence," she said. "In the summer of 1940, in a tiny little village in Leicestershire called Appleby Magna. I was posted there by the Women's Land Army. Evelyn was a travelling saleswoman for a pharmaceutical firm; she had this hopeless old banger that conked out on the way to Burton-on-Trent one night. She got stranded at the village pub, where I was hiding from the ruddy-faced farmer who wanted me to do a little bit more than just milk his cows."

She reached for the cigarette case she had left on the mantelpiece.

"I could see she was as lost as I was," Daphne continued. "Sitting there in the corner, alone with her lemonade, trying to disappear into the furnishings." She lifted a jade table lighter to ignite her smoke.

"We got talking," she continued. "Well, I got talking. Evelyn seemed so terribly shy; she could barely say boo to a goose. But after a bit of prodding, I discovered we had a few things in common. As you say," her eyes briefly met Swaffer's again, "it was mainly politics. I told her I had joined the WLA because of Lady Denman and how I hoped I was going to be able to join her staff at Balcome Place – I was such an admirer of everything she did for the suffrage, you know."

"Indeed I do," Swaffer nodded gravely. "Lady Denman and I once attempted a raid on Parliament. Our plan was to float a suffragette over the House in a hot-air balloon, whereupon she would shower down leaflets about the plight of the ladies on hunger strike. Would have made a terrific front cover. Except that the wind was blowing in the wrong direction and she floated off down to Tilbury Docks instead." He shook his head. "Sorry," he said, "I digress."

For the first time, a tremor of a smile played on Daphne's lips.

– • –

"Gordon," said Lil, staring hard at the tablecloth as she summoned back the conversation at the salon. "Mol said the fella's name was Gordon. And his pal was called Felix." She looked back up at Greenaway, the pupils of her eyes so dark and dilated her irises looked totally black.

Greenaway felt a familiar tingle in his blood as she said it, as if he was back on the racetrack and a tip was coming good.

"Funny name, Felix," Lil went on. "Posh boys, I s'pose – they said they was training to be officers in the RAF, had some little white slips in their hats to prove it." Her frown deepened and her stare intensified. "They only take them sort to be officers, don't they? They don't take no commoners – nor Romans, neither."

The Duchess put her hand down softly on Lil's arm. "Well remembered, love," she said, patting her, "you never told us their names before."

"I only just remembered them," Lil turned her gaze on her companion. "You was late that morning, Duch, where d'you get to anyway? You never said . . ."

"Never mind that now," Duch's mothering fingers gave a sharp little squeeze before she let go. Greenaway noticed the smile tighten at the corners of her mouth. "Is there anything else you need to tell the Inspector you never thought of before?"

"No," Lil winced, pulling her arm away. "Oh," her features transformed, as quickly as the sun coming out behind clouds, the warmth of her smile resting on Greenaway. "One thing I'd like to know. If you're a friend of Mr Swaffer's, then you probably know my Tom – Tom Power, or Frank I should say – he was the crime reporter on the *Evening Sentinel* and he was always after Sammy Lehmann, too. I wondered if you'd heard from him at all, since he got the draft?"

Greenaway's mind shimmied like a tic-tac man calling the odds. Tom Power, that nosy little bastard? Had he been seeing this undoubtedly beautiful but at the same time fatally fallen woman while he was out chasing gangsters and then waxing moralistic in the linen drapers? What would Mrs Power think?

Mirroring this imagined countenance, the face of the Duchess flashed white.

"Course he don't, Lil," she said before he could reply. "And even if he does, he ain't got time for gossip now. He's got a killer to catch, ain't he?" She got to her feet. "I'll see you out, Ted, if there's nothing more we can help you with?"

Greenaway got to his feet. "No," he said, offering Lil his hand. "Except to say you've been very helpful, Miss, very helpful indeed. If you hear any more talk about this Gordon, then you'll be sure and let me know, won't you?"

Her hand was as light as chiffon in his big paw. There was something about her that went beyond how she looked and what she did for a living that turned all this into some grim kind of joke. Greenaway could see how easy it would have been for Tom Power to fall for Lil. Wondered what the Duchess was most afraid of – losing her to a murderer or to a hack.

"And if you see the bastard," he added, "run."

– • –

Daphne had almost come to the end of her tale. Swaffer had learned how it was membership of the CP that had brought the two women together – shared nights of intellectual discourse, rallying and sweating over pamphlets in the top room of a pub in Burton-on-Trent, owned by a sympathetic former miner. Of how Evelyn had shed her shyness amid their endeavours, while Daphne had found the purpose in life she had been seeking, the pair of them becoming so inseparable at one point that Daphne had even brought Evelyn back to London with her when she was given leave. And then, as summer had shaded into autumn, how the bloom had started to come off the red rose of their friendship.

"It was when I started to get friendly with some of the others in the group that it all started to change," Daphne recalled. "It was fine when I was the new girl and she was showing me off to everyone. But when others started taking an interest in me, well . . ." She rubbed her arms as if she was out in the cold, not standing in front of the fire.

"It started with a few snide comments here and there. I tried to ignore them, pass them off as my being too sensitive, mishearing what Evelyn had really said. But then, when she was driving me back to the farm one night, it turned into a full-scale row. She virtually accused me of being a prostitute because I had spent too long talking to this one other person.

Then I realised what it was. She didn't want me to talk to anyone else, have anyone else but her. I had thought it was she who was the shy one, when I met her that first time in The Black Horse, but in fact it was my own awkwardness she picked up on. And I think she read it as something else . . ."

She looked back at Swaffer, searching for the right words.

"She was in love with you," he said.

Daphne nodded. "Yes," she said. "Yes, I think she was. But she was so intense about it, so suffocating, it was frightening and I knew I couldn't go on seeing her. I'm not very good at that sort of conflict, I'm afraid, Mr Swaffer. So I rang Balcome Place and asked to be relieved of my duties. As you know, we're volunteers in the WLA, there's nothing to make us stay where we've been posted. I didn't tell Evelyn, I just went. And I never heard from her again until the night—" her eyes dropped back down to the fire in the grate, "she was murdered."

"What happened that night, Miss Maitland?" Swaffer asked.

Daphne lit another cigarette.

"She called me," she said, blowing smoke across the room, her eyes following the trail of it, into the distance. "At about half-past six in the evening. I don't remember having given her my number, but as I told you, she did stay here with me once and I suppose she was just cunning enough to have taken it down and stored it away. She said it was her birthday and that she was coming up to see me. Just as if we had never said a bad word to each other, just as if she was an old friend I would have been delighted to receive at such short notice. Well, I couldn't believe my ears. And I'm afraid I told her what I thought of her. I'll spare you the details, but suffice to say, there was this long silence and then she hung up the telephone. But that wasn't the end of it. I had a horrible feeling it wouldn't be.

"I told my housekeeper that if anyone should come calling later that evening she must tell them I was not in London and send them away. Sure enough, four hours later, there was Evelyn, standing on the doorstep."

Daphne's hand shook as she put the cigarette out, reached for her glass of brandy. "But, Mr Swaffer, if I had only known what was out there waiting for her, I would never have turned her away. I was so scared of her, but what was she, really? A lonely, frustrated woman, that's all. She didn't deserve to die like that. No one does. And that's why I wanted to see you. Because I know what you believe."

"My poor, dear girl," said Swaffer, rising to his feet to put his arms around her. "What a terrible burden you have carried."

Daphne could contain her tears no longer. "Please tell me," she said, "please tell me she's all right . . . Wherever she is now . . ."

– • –

Black pins in the map over Greenaway's desk marked the location of the two murder sites. Red pins mapped the killer's hunting grounds around Piccadilly and Soho. As he pushed in another one at the address of Lil's friend Lorna, Greenaway's eyes travelled in a circuit around his quarry's trails. A list in his hand of barracks and civilian buildings requisitioned for the duration of the conflict. Between Regent's Park and Marble Arch. Round in a sweep, clockwise. Green pins for the army, blue pins for the RAF. Round in a sweep anti-clockwise. Back to Regent's Park. Abbey Lodge: a mansion block taken by the RAF on St James Place, a crescent off Prince Albert Road that was mere strolling distance from the air-raid shelter on Montagu Place.

Greenaway checked his wristwatch. It was 1.15am.

– • –

Swaffer got back into the car outside on Gloucester Place.

"The Savoy," he told the driver, taking his fob watch out of his waistcoat pocket and speculating on how inebriated his intended dining companion, a young Labour firebrand, would have become over the course of the last hour.

Pissed to the point of impropriety, he gauged, as his eyes rested on the timepiece. It was 1.15am.

– • –

The click of the latch on the door of the flat opposite woke Mari Lambouri from her slumbers. Mari was not a good sleeper, her predicament made worse not just by the air raids, but the infrequent hours kept by the woman who lived across the hall from her, in Flat 4, 9–10 Gosfield Street. A woman that, good Catholic as she was, Mari would never dream of describing as any kind of lady.

Twice in the last two weeks Mari had been driven from her bed by screams of bloody murder emanating from Phyllis Lord's place. Twice she had been made to witness the purple bruises, freshly bloomed, across her neighbour's stomach and chest, the ripped clothes and smashed furniture. And twice the stupid woman had refused point blank to call the very police she had been yelling for only moments earlier.

So it was strange, on this night, that a mere click had been enough to rouse her. As her eyes adjusted to the darkness, Mari heard the sound of footsteps, a man walking away from Phyllis's flat and quietly opening and closing the front door. Whistling softly to himself a tune Mari vaguely recognised from an old Fred and Ginger film, she thought, although it was rendered flat and off-key.

The clock by her bedside read a quarter-past one.

9

DON'T FENCE ME IN

Thursday, 12 February 1942

"We've a man here who does answer to your description," the Corporal told Greenaway. The orderly in charge of RAF A Squadron, Abbey Lodge, looked just the way he'd sounded over the telephone: a black-haired Yorkshireman with a face the size and shape of a shovel and the demeanour of one who would use such an implement to dig graves.

"LAC Gordon Frederick Cummins," he went on, "training to be a pilot. Made an exemplary test, it says here." He had a form laid out on the table in front of him, beside the brown teapot and tin mugs with which he'd furnished Greenaway with an early morning brew. His office was in the foyer of a modern apartment block requisitioned by the RAF, where once a uniformed concierge would have served well-heeled residents. Now the marble and brass Deco fittings, the scalloped wall lights and parquet floors, had all been subsumed under layers of aerial maps and stacks of filing cabinets, overlaid by the smell of tobacco and boot polish.

"He's also six foot tall, has fair hair and wears one of them little pencil moustaches." He looked up at Greenaway with a steady, slate-grey stare. "Fancies himself as a bit of a ladies' man, so they say. Would that be . . . ?"

Greenaway cut him off with a nod. "It does have some bearing," he allowed. Though he'd introduced himself as a senior Yard detective acting on information received, he hadn't yet gone into the nature of the offence he was investigating, nor the department that he worked for. He didn't want rumours circulating round the barracks while he sniffed out a likely suspect.

"How long has he been here?" Greenaway asked, wondering how closely his interviewee read the linens. He looked like a *Herald* man, though one that would start with the sports pages and probably never had time to get much further.

The Corporal glanced back down at his form. "Not long," he said. "He were assigned his billet Monday, the second of February."

Greenaway felt the same prickling of his skin that had come when he was studying the map the night before.

"And did you manage to find out his whereabouts between midnight and dawn on the nights of Sunday, the eighth and Monday, the ninth of February?" he asked.

The Corporal raised one thick black eyebrow. "Aye, sir, that I did. And I'm afraid this is the point where all similarities end. I've the mess logbook here," he handed it across the table, "and as you can see, Cummins was here at the times you mention. Curfew's 22.30 hours sharp. The lads respect that."

Greenaway let his expression reflect mild surprise. "Do they?" he said. "Only it don't always look that way round Piccadilly Circus of an evening."

The Corporal grunted. "Be that as it may," he said, "I followed up on him for you. His four roommates swear blind he was in bed by ten-thirty both evenings and was still in his cot when they all got up."

Greenaway studied Cummins's handwriting. It sloped slightly to the right. Underneath the entry written on the night of the ninth of February, was one for an LAC F. R. Simpson. He passed the logbook back, pointed the name out. "*Felix* Simpson, is it?" he asked.

The Corporal frowned. "That's right, sir. How did you happen to know?"

Greenaway smiled. "I'm a detective, ain't I?" he said. "Now this Simpson . . . He wouldn't by any chance be one of the roommates who swear blind Cummins was safely tucked up for lights-out on both evenings, would he?"

"That he would," said the Corporal, his eyes narrowing for a moment, slate-grey glinting into steel. "But I've three others gave exactly the same story and none of them are quite so enamoured of Cummins as young Simpson is. They wouldn't be making up a cover story for him, if that's what you're getting at."

Greenaway raised his palms, smiling blandly. "Course not, Corporal, you know your men. You say so, I believe you. But you've got to admit it's interesting. My sources mentioned a Gordon and a Felix and here are these two, bunked up together. Course, it could all be coincidence . . ."

The Corporal kept his face straight. There was a reason why taciturn men like him were always put in charge of officer cadets.

"Why don't you call back later, when they're off duty?" he said. "Speak to them yourself, sir? I can always make sure their duties detain them here this evening."

"All right, Corporal," said Greenaway, getting to his feet. "I will. But I tell you what. Before I go, you wouldn't mind just showing me their kip, would you?"

– • –

The Duchess got to Holland Park at a quarter to ten, stepping through a swirl of sleet borne by a spiteful northeasterly wind as she made her way down Lansdowne Road. With a headscarf tied about her copper hair and a heavy tweed coat, she looked like any ordinary housewife burdened down with cares. The laundry bag she heaved over her right shoulder was her penance: heavy with offerings for Miss Moyes.

The iron railings outside number 3 had long since been taken away and smelted down for the war effort. The windows at the top of the stucco mansion were boarded up from the time incendiaries had got in and caused a fire on the third floor during heavy bombing the previous May. Once gleaming white, the outside walls were now crusted with soot, the paintwork below the fire-line torn and peeling. But still there was a smiling face to greet Duch at the front door.

"What a lovely surprise, dear." Winifred Moyes did not look like Madame Blavatsky, or the veiled, black-clad figures of ghost stories. She was square-shaped, mannish. Bobbed hair, which had once been auburn but now shot through with grey, crinkled around a long, equine face with round brown eyes set behind wire-rimmed spectacles. She dressed in sensible twinsets and tweeds and would not have looked out of place with a pair of Labradors, posing as a vicar's wife.

Miss Moyes had given up her job on the *Daily Telegraph* to form the Christian Spiritualist Greater World Association in 1931, at the behest of her spirit guide, Zodiac. Despite a singular lack of resources and bouts of ill-health that belied her robust appearance, everything she needed to aid her mission had been provided since she took her leap of faith – these premises and those for her women's night shelters, the funds to keep them afloat, a loyal band of women and men to assist her in raising money, printing weekly pamphlets and giving audiences to the needy up and down the country, which the war had not disrupted, despite all the privations of the Blitz and wartime rail travel.

Duch had herself been the recipient of charity once, at a crucial time in her life. Since she had taken up residence nearby, she had made regular attendances at Miss Moyes's circle and discreet donations to her funds. She handed over the bag and watched with satisfaction the expression of delight form across the other woman's face as she examined its contents.

"Sheets and blankets, just what we need." Miss Moyes held one neatly folded bed sheet up to the light. It had the initials CR monogrammed on the border. "Good as new," she considered, then winked. "I won't ask where you got them from."

Duch smiled. It was better Miss Moyes didn't know that the fine linen and blankets had furnished Carmen's boudoirs in Dover Street. She'd had more money than sense, had Carmen, and Duch had clocked Greenaway taking note of everything else that had come from that house the moment he'd arrived the night before – he never missed a thing. Which was why she'd felt it prudent to donate some of those gains to the bombed-out recipients of Miss Moyes's charity.

"Well," she said, shrugging, "I do what I can."

However, there was a more compelling reason for her visit. "Is there anybody else here at the minute?" she asked.

"As a matter of fact," Miss Moyes placed the neatly folded sheet back into the bag, "there is." She moderated her voice so that it couldn't be heard through the walls. "I've spent most of the night talking with a friend of yours, who's in a state of some distress. Shall we go through? I know she'll be glad to see you."

Duch nodded, followed her hostess through the door into the parlour, which now acted as both office and a waiting room for those who came for aid. Sitting there now was a woman of striking appearance, huddled in a black astrakhan coat, with a scarlet, feathered hat on the seat beside her. Despite the warmth of Miss Moyes's welcome, it was deathly cold in the high-ceilinged old house.

"Look who's here," said Miss Moyes.

"Madame Arcana," said the Duchess, her breath hanging on the air like smoke.

"Duchess!" the little Frenchwoman sprang to her feet. "You couldn't sleep either?"

— • —

"Present for you, Fred," Greenaway hefted a sack into Cherrill's office at Scotland Yard. The fingerprint man looked up from behind the stack of files that threatened to obscure him from view, his brows rising in a quizzical expression.

"Been holding up the postman, Ted?" he enquired.

"I just lifted this from an RAF billet on Regent's Park," said Greenaway. "It's the contents of the bin of LAC Gordon Cummins, who just happens to match the description Ivy Poole gave me of the man she saw with Evelyn Bettencourt the night she was murdered. The full-screw in charge of his gaff reckons he's got proof Cummins was tucked up in his bunk on the nights in question, but even so, he don't like him much. He let me have a rummage through his bin and if there's anything in here we can connect to the victims then I'm going back as soon as he's off duty for a parade of a different kind from what he's used to."

"You seem pretty sure of him, then?" said Cherrill, getting to his feet.

"Spoke to a snout last night with a matching description to Ivy's," said Greenaway, "who also knew the killer's name was Gordon. I had a shufti through all the RAF billets and Abbey Lodge is the closest to that shelter on Montagu Place. Cummins arrived there a week ago. Same snout told me this Gordon had a mate called Felix. Unusual name, I thought. Just so happens, one of Cummins's roommates is a Felix Simpson."

Cherrill nodded. "I see," he said. "Bring it over to this table by the window."

"There's more," Greenaway followed his colleague through the labyrinth of filing cabinets that made up Cherrill's domain, to a window overlooking the Thames. There was a long, metal-topped table in front of it. "The full-screw told me Cummins fancies himself rotten. I found a greatcoat in his locker that'd been altered by a tailor, a flash suit and a shirt that reeked of perfume."

"All right," said Cherrill, pulling on a pair of gloves. "You can tip it out now."

"Also," Greenaway upended his offering and let the contents slowly slide out, "Cummins's handwriting slopes to the right. Like he writes with his left hand."

"Got you," said Cherrill, poking a pen through the debris of tea leaves, newspapers, cigarette packets and the contents of several ashtrays. "Well, that's promising. I managed to lift some decent prints from the tin opener and the mirror I took from Mrs Bettencourt's room. One off the thumb of a left hand. If I can take anything from this that does correspond, then we could be in business. Did you say the fellow had an alibi?"

Greenaway grunted. "Yeah," he said. "The logbook says he was in quarters Sunday and Monday, between ten-thirty and dawn. And all his roommates swear to it." He looked over Cherrill's head, out of the window, visualising the billet. "Only there's a fire escape down the back of the building, goes underneath their kitchen window. If he was a stealthy bastard – which odds on, he is – he might have made use of that without any of them ever noticing. So I don't think it's bulletproof."

"Aha," said Cherrill, "what have we here?"

– • –

Madame Arcana's breath smelt of aniseed and her voice was husky from lack of sleep as she described to Duch the events that had brought her over to Miss Moyes's the night before.

"I tried to warn her, I did my best, but Nina would have none of it. Then I read in the paper yesterday . . ." she shook her head. "What good is this gift of ours if we can't make people see? The very people who come to us for help . . ."

"What did you see, Madame?" asked the Duchess. "What cards did she draw?"

Madame shook her head. "First of all," she said, "the five of Swords. Reversed."

"Ah," the Duchess nodded understanding. The first card was the one that set the tone for the whole reading, and this choice did not bode well.

"Secondly, the Knight of Swords."

Duch felt the blood drain from her cheeks. Lil had selected Swords from the pack last night. The Fool reversed, the ten of Swords and the six of Swords.

"And finally," Madame held the Duchess's green-eyed gaze. "The Tower."

"Couldn't get much worse than that, could it, dear?" Miss Moyes noted.

Duch gave a low whistle. She had wanted to talk about what she had seen, the aftermath of Ted's visit and the effect all of this was having on Lil's nerves. If she had had a fitful night, picturing her charge on the edge of peril, it was no wonder the Frenchwoman's had been entirely devoid of rest. Her client had picked a configuration that spelt out pure calamity.

"It's him, isn't it?" she said. "The Knight of Swords."

Madame nodded. "Nina had a boyfriend," she said, "in the services. A spiv, like they all are. He was making her do all sorts of stupid things, including trying to frighten her poor old husband away. I am sure it was him who murdered her."

"What sort of serviceman was he, do you know?" Duch sat forward. "RAF?"

"No," said Madame, "he was a Canadian. Nina dreamt he was going to take her away with him when the war is finally over." She gave a short, brittle laugh.

"Well, love," said Duch, trying to hide her disappointment, "you can stop punishing yourself for that, then. The fella they're after is English."

Her audience drew their breath in. Miss Moyes found her voice first. "And how did you come to know that?" she asked.

"An old friend of mine," Duch smiled grimly, "is in charge of the Murder Squad. He was round our gaff last night asking questions. See, Lil heard some talk down the hairdresser's Tuesday morning, about an RAF man with a kink for blondes, nearly done a girl in the night before. She was so frightened, she was having her hair dyed dark brown. The two of us ran into Mr Swaffer soon after, so I had Lil tell him what she heard and then give our address to send for Ted Greenaway."

Madame frowned. "I never knew you were friends with a policeman."

"Well," said Duch, "maybe 'friends' ain't quite the right word for it. But my point is I've known Ted for donkey's. I know exactly what kind of a man he is. If anyone can catch this maniac, he . . ."

The sharp trill of the doorbell made all three women jump.

"Oh," Miss Moyes's hand fluttered up to her chest. "Oh, I'd better see who that is."

Madame turned to the Duchess. "So it wasn't Nina's boyfriend," she said. "That is some kind of relief, I suppose. But do you really think your friend will catch the one who did this to her? It would mean a lot to me if he did."

"You know the old saying?" said Duch. "Send a bastard to catch a bastard."

The parlour door opened and Miss Moyes came back in, ushering a tall, nervous-looking woman in a grey coat and matching felt hat.

"Ladies, may I introduce Miss Maitland?" Miss Moyes said. "A friend of our dear Mr Swaffer's. She's come to offer her services to the refuge. Isn't that grand?"

$-\cdot-$

Mari Lambouri left her flat at eleven o'clock for her first cleaning job of the day. As she locked her front door and turned towards her neighbour's, she noticed the postman had been and left a parcel outside Phyllis Lord's front door. She tutted to herself, imagining the woman would have been too fast asleep to hear him call, after the night she had no doubt had. Shaking her head, she went on her way.

10

YOU ALWAYS HURT THE
ONE YOU LOVE

Thursday, 12 February 1942

The rest of the debris having been sifted through and discounted, Cherrill was left with a green propelling pencil and a pair of size-ten rubber-boot soles. He didn't hold out hope of the former being much use, but the latter were certainly of interest. Crammed into the tread were particles of dust and cement that brought his mind back in an instant to the scene of Evelyn Bourne's murder.

He rang Greenaway at Tottenham Court Road. "I'm sending them to the lab for analysis against the samples we took from the shelter at Montagu Place. If I remember rightly, the newspapers reported us finding footprints in the snow that morning, and if this fellow is as stealthy as you think he is . . ."

Greenaway, sat in front of a desk awash with statements taken from the prostitutes of Soho and Paddington, snapped the pencil he was holding clean in half.

"You beauty," he said. "How long will that take?"

"Hard to say," Cherrill glanced up at the clock on the wall in front of him. It was coming up to seven. "Even at top priority I'd be amazed if we got it back before the morning. There's just too few people with too many jobs to do."

"Don't worry," Greenaway's voice came back, "we can keep it up our sleeve for when I take the bastard in. Anything else?"

Cherrill picked up the propelling pencil and described it. "The sort of thing a sub-editor might use," he concluded, "or a draughtsman."

"Doubt Ivy'll recognise it, then," said Greenaway. "But keep hold of it, anyway."

The minute they had ended their conversation, another phone rang in Greenaway's office. This one wasn't a line from the Yard, but a private number he gave out to snouts, paid for out of his own pocket to ensure the confidence of his sources. The voice on the other end belonged to a member of a South London firm, who was not averse to a little cavort amongst the stalls of Berwick Street market when supply and demand required.

"Got some gen for you, Inspector," he came straight to the point. "A girl I know reckons she can put the finger on this sex maniac you're after."

"What," said Greenaway, "shopping you at last, is she?"

"Oh very droll, Inspector, very droll. Nah, but seriously, she had a run-in with him on Piccadilly, night before last."

"So did half the girls in London," said Greenaway, eyeing the mound of paperwork before him, his afternoon spent sifting witness reports that concurred with Ivy's description, and still only halfway done. "What's she got to add I ain't heard before?"

"He's an airman, ain't he? RAF?"

Greenaway picked up the remains of his pencil. "That's what she says, is it?"

"Yeah, reckons she could pick him out of any line-up," the voice went on. "She can even draw you a picture of him if you want. She's quite clever that way."

"All right," said Greenaway. "Send her down to Tottenham Court Road and I'll make sure I see her right away. What name she go by?"

"Ah, well, see . . . there's a bit of a problem with that."

"Oh, really?" Greenaway put the jagged half into his desk sharpener, began to turn the handle.

"Well, she's a bit shy, ain't she?" the voice wheedled on. "She don't want to come down the West End, not after what happened. She don't feel safe, like what you said yourself in the paper yesterday. She asked if you could meet her somewhere local, where I can introduce you to her proper."

"How local?" Greenaway's hand turned faster. "Your manor, I take it?"

"That's right, Inspector, the Effra Arms. You know it, dontcha?"

"Brixton," said Greenaway. "Ain't you heard of petrol rationing, son?"

"But that don't apply to you gentlemen of the Yard, surely?" the voice feigned wonder. "And anyway, I thought you wanted this maniac behind bars, pronto?"

Greenaway picked the pencil back out and examined the sharpened lead, thinking. He had been about to go back to Abbey Lodge, bring Cummins in to parade in front of Ivy. But, if he were to try to overturn the evidence of the Corporal's passbook, it would strengthen his case to have another good witness he could use, regardless of what Cherrill might come up with. It was seven now, but the Corporal had promised to detain his suspects until he called and surely this wouldn't take that long?

"All right," he said, "I'll be half an hour." He put the pencil back into his pocket. "Tell her to start drawing."

Duchess saw Lil's last client out and waited at the top of the stairs, making sure this one closed the door behind him. Then she went back to her empty parlour. Business was as dire tonight as it had been the evening before.

"It's like the *Marie Celeste* in here," she called out. "Want a cuppa char while we're waiting?"

Lil opened her bedroom door, wrapped in her robe without bothering to wash up after herself, her mascara smudged on her cheeks and her hair a tangled mess. She picked up an ashtray from the table, but instead of taking a seat there, she plonked herself down on the loveseat, swivelling sideways to stretch her bare feet onto the upholstery.

Duch tried not to look askance as Lil placed the ashtray on her belly and produced her cigarettes and lighter from the pocket of her robe. Instead, she busied herself filling the kettle and spooning tea leaves into the pot. Even so, she couldn't help cringing as she heard the click of the flame igniting and imagined a shower of embers falling.

"Well how many have I done today?" Lil finally asked. "Four or five? Ain't that enough to keep us ticking over?"

Duch kept her eyes on the crockery. "'Course it is, love," she said. "It's bitter out, and it's crawling with bogeys. That's what'll be keeping the regulars away."

"Maybe. Or maybe it ain't just Tom, eh?" Lil clicked the lid of her lighter open and shut. "Maybe they've all gone right off me."

"Oh, don't say that, love," Duch was forced to look over at her now, to try to keep the recrimination from her eyes. Lil was staring at her mutinously.

"Don't keep dwelling on it," Duch urged. "You don't know

what he's doing out there, do you? You know how clever he is with the undercover work. He probably got chosen to go on some secret mission and he ain't allowed to write to no one."

"So you keep saying," Lil snapped the lid of her lighter shut and screwed out her cigarette. "You think I'm a baby, don't you? Well, what do you know? You and your bleedin' cards and your bleedin' tea leaves, you can stuff the lot of it. You don't know nuffink about real life, that's for sure."

She stood up, smacked the ashtray back down on the table and stomped back to her room, slamming the door behind her.

– • –

Greenaway parked around the corner from the Effra Arms, on a residential street. The car pool at the station had been virtually empty and the Austin he had taken was not his usual marque, so he took the precaution of disabling the starting motor before he walked around the corner to the redbrick Victorian tavern on Kellett Road.

He found his contact with his arm around a young blonde in the otherwise empty snug. She was clutching a pink gin; with a similar fervour he was patting her shoulder, the pair of them putting on a fair performance of the concerned boyfriend comforting his moll. His snout's head shot up as Greenaway came through the door.

"This is him, Doris, love," he said, getting to his feet.

Greenaway walked over to their table, scanning the frosted glass behind it that separated them from the saloon, noting the hatch was up behind the bar. The landlord here was an old face from the track who had run with the Elephant Boys in his youth, before coming into the rights to this property via another type of gaming endeavour. No doubt he would be somewhere within listening distance.

"A pleasure, I'm sure," Doris raised her head demurely and offered him the hand that had been clutching her gin. It was cold and damp.

Greenaway ignored the snout's outstretched paw and sat down opposite the girl. She was done up in the approximation of a starlet, but her bleached hair and red lips could not disguise her spotty cheeks. These, coupled with the long teeth revealed by her nervous smile, had him wondering if she couldn't be more like a relative than a close friend of his informant. Still, the fact that she was blonde gave her credence.

"This is him." From the black handbag that sat on her knee Doris withdrew a crumpled betting slip, on which was sketched the face of a man with wide-spaced eyes and a pencil moustache, wearing a forage cap with a slip in the side of it. Greenaway had to admit the drawing did display a certain degree of skill. Better still, it adequately portrayed what Ivy had seen and what Lil had reported to him.

"You say you ran into him last night?" Greenaway looked back up at Doris. She nodded, her grey-brown eyes wide.

"On Piccadilly," she whispered.

"He come up to you, did he?" asked Greenaway. "What did he say?"

Her fearful gaze stole over to her boyfriend.

"That he liked blondes," she said. He nodded his approval.

"Piccadilly your usual beat, is it?" Greenaway asked. She looked back at him, startled.

"It's all right," her companion reassured, patting her knee. "He ain't gonna do you for it, Doris love. You're helping him, remember?"

"Well, yes," Doris said. "You got to go where business is good, ain't you?"

"So why d'you turn him down then?" Greenaway asked.

"Well," Doris shifted in her seat, playing with the clasp on her handbag. "I'd got to talking to some other girls, earlier on. They told me to be careful if anyone in an RAF uniform came up to me, on account of me being blonde. That's what this sex maniac wants, they said, blondes. And . . . well . . . I'm quite new to the bash, to be honest. When this fella comes up to me I got scared and went home."

"She done the right thing, didn't she?" the snout returned his protective arm to her shoulder. "She could be dead by now if she didn't, eh?"

"Yeah," Greenaway's sleepy eyes became hard as he stared at his informant. "Money ain't everything, is it, son?" He was wondering whether some other woman might not have taken Doris's place. All day long he had been expecting another summons to a murder site.

"What did he sound like, Doris, when he spoke to you?" he asked.

"Well," she said, "he was posh, weren't he?"

"I have to say, you got a good likeness from a few moments' conversation." Greenaway studied her drawing again and held it back up to her. "You'd know this face again as soon as you saw it, would you?"

"'Course," said Doris.

"That's good," said Greenaway, "'cos I'll need you for a line-up. There's no need to be worried, once I have this man in custody, he won't be going nowhere except the court and then the gallows. You got my word on that. And as your friend here knows," he nodded across the table, "I am a man of my word."

He smiled, patting his jacket pocket.

"Oh," said Doris, looking perplexed, "all right. When will that be, then?"

"Now," said Greenaway, getting to his feet. "If you don't mind?"

"Now?" Doris repeated. She turned to her boyfriend. "But you didn't say nuffink . . ."

He withdrew his arm from her shoulder rapidly. "Go on, Doris," he said. "You heard the man, he said you'll be all right. Go on and do your duty – for all the other girls on the bash."

"But," Doris got to her feet, clutching her handbag, "I . . ."

The snout's eyes narrowed just for a second, long enough for his meaning to be conferred to both people present. Greenaway picked up Doris's rabbit fur coat from the back of her chair and helped her into it.

As he steered her towards the door, he clocked the landlord hovering behind the hatch on the other side of the bar. His informant made no move from his seat.

Out on the street, Doris dragged her heels. "But mister," she started to whine, "Johnny didn't say nuffink about me coming with you now. I got places to go . . ."

"It won't take long," Greenaway's grip on her tightened and his own pace increased so that he was pushing her along beside him round the corner. "I'll make sure you get a lift home if that's what you're worried about . . ."

He stopped short of where he had parked the Austin.

The car was gone.

– • –

Duchess looked up, startled. Lil stood in her doorway now perfectly made-up, her hair teased into a roll and clipped under a black pillbox hat, blonde curls in a cloud around her shoulders. She wore her best beaver lamb coat and high-heeled black suede shoes and had a small, snakeskin clutch under her left arm.

"If they won't come to me . . ." she began.

"Aw c'mon, love." Duchess got to her feet. "It ain't that bad, surely? I don't want you out there this weather and with a bleedin' maniac about. Be sensible."

Lil waved a hand dismissively. "I am being sensible," she said. "I ain't got no work and we ain't got enough money. I've always been able to pull in a good crowd after a few minutes' stroll, you know that. All's I have to do is go down the train station, I won't be more than ten minutes."

Duchess walked tentatively towards her. Lil's voice had regained its usual matter-of-factness, all the insolence of their last exchange vanished along with the slutty appearance. Something else had changed, but you had to get close enough to see it. Her pupils were like pinpricks.

"Lil," Duchess said, mentally recapping all the men who had been up the stairs today, stopping on the face of a jazz drummer who played for the house band at the *Entre Nous*. "You ain't been back on the bennies, have you?"

"So what if I have?" Lil's top lip curled, the challenge back in a flash.

"'Cos you won't stop, will you? And it ain't safe, you know that . . ."

"Awww," Lil took Duchess's chin in her right hand as if she was talking to a child. "It ain't safe? Not without your big, friendly detective, is it, Duch? You know, you really got me wondering about him." Her fingers tightened, nails starting to dig into flesh. "Old friends, are you? Well why don't you give him a call," her hand dropped and she made for the front door with a rapid, darting movement, "and leave me to look after myself."

She clattered down the stairs and yanked the front door open, leaving her parting shot hanging ominously on the air. "Like I always used to!"

– • –

In the time it had taken to get back to the Effra Arms, Greenaway's snout had vanished. The landlord was standing behind the bar, polishing his just-washed glass.

"Need the blower, Inspector Greenaway?" were his greeting words.

– • –

Sleet was falling thick and fast in the cobbled mews, but Lil's need to escape the confines of the flat, fuelled by the drags on the inhaler the drummer had left her, was stronger than that. She had got to a point she had been to many times before in her short life. Her fuse had ignited. The soporific mental state that suffused most of her days had lifted like a veil before her eyes and she could suddenly see, all too clearly, that she had been kidding herself again.

Lil's beauty had marked her out, at an early age, from any wishes she might have had for a normal life. From the age of twelve, when the other kids on her road were still playing in the streets with dirty knees and broken nails, men had sidled up to her, asking her out for drinks, offering her pretty trinkets and baubles that she knew she was too young to take. She always knocked them back, for Mum had always warned her: "Never take money from a man."

It was a rubric she had abided by until the age of fourteen, when she had been indentured into service in a big house by the river in Chiswick, to two old dears and their deaf old brother. On her first day she had set out with purpose, starching sheets and scrubbing floors, washing down steps and making the meals the way her mother had shown her. The old girls had loved her, said she was a "treasure".

Pleased with herself, Lil had left for the evening to meet with a friend on Hammersmith Broadway, intending on a little promenade. A trio of young men in a sports car pulled up beside them. Lil had never met the sort of man who owned a sports car before, so she let herself be led into a public house for the first time and passed through a portal into another existence. Upon her first taste of gin, it had come to Lil with the force of revelation that only her looks stood between this tantalising taste of glamour and the lifetime of drudgery to which she had been assigned. She awoke in a hotel room in Paddington with a five-pound note on the pillow beside her, and neither the bereft old dears nor her poor mother had ever seen Lil again.

Along the way, there had been plenty of people who had promised her better – a career in modelling, the movies, and lately with the Duchess, the idea that once they had made enough capital they could set up their own legitimate business along the lines of Lil's latest fantasy, a dress shop in Mayfair. With Duch, whom she regarded as a kind of benevolent auntie better schooled in the ways of society than she had ever been, she had lasted longer than she had with any man.

Then Tom had come along, and Lil had dreamed of a different outcome. Of her very own house by the river, a loving husband and children who would never have to make the decisions she had, thanks to the money he earned.

All – she could see now – part of the delusion that had kept her the way she was: youthful, beautiful, eager to please, through all the years and the thousands of men there had been since that first sip of gin. And if Tom had let her down, Duch was no better; all she wanted was Lil flat on her back, earning money for a future that would never come. At that moment, Lil's Benzedrined mind pulsed with white-hot rage.

"If you're out there, you bastard," she said aloud, crossing through the mews and on to Praed Street, "come and get me. Go on, I bleedin' dare you!"

11

IN THE MOOD

Thursday, 12 February 1942

Madeline Harcourt looked at the clock hanging over the bar of the Universelle Brasserie in Piccadilly Circus. The second hand ticked past slowly, as if the fug of cigarette smoke that rose above the chatter and noise was obfuscating its purpose. It was eight and Madeline was early, couldn't bear to arrive late, a part of her nature which she could never seem to overcome, even though it left her frequently feeling like she did at present – nervous and uncomfortable.

She sat at a table close to the horseshoe-shaped cocktail bar from where she had as clear a view of the door as was possible. The place was packed with men in uniform – Canadians and Americans, most of them – picking up women as easily as children picking daisies. The British officer she awaited had yet to show.

Madeline had never been very lucky in love. At the age of thirty she was separated from her husband, the chief act of defiance in her life. She had met her Second Lieutenant in this very spot three months earlier and they had gone out for meals, drinks and the odd show ever since, according to the erratic schedule of his duties. What had impressed Madeline most about him were his manners. She had conveniently filed away, right to the back of her mind, the insight that it was precisely such refined traits that had led her into a loveless match with her estranged theatre director five years previously. As her eyes travelled around the tables, she had no idea that another had been studying her while she sat there alone.

"Are you waiting for somebody?"

Madeline looked round with a start. There was an airman standing behind her, tall and slender in his blue dress uniform, a wave of unruly hair, the colour of turning leaves, falling into his wide-spaced eyes.

"I'm sorry?" she said, having to make sure it was her he was addressing.

"I asked if you were waiting for someone?" His smile crinkled the corners of his eyes. His voice purred like a well-oiled Bentley.

"Yes," Madeline's voice came out in a gulp. "I have an . . . appointment."

Half of her hoped this would deter him. Her date could be here any minute and she didn't want any complications. Another half felt otherwise.

"Well," he said, "would you care for a drink while you wait?"

Madeline stared at him for a second. Should she? It was obvious what he was after. His type always were – they threw their money about with the reckless abandon that made them so irresistible to most of the women who clustered in the brasserie. But then, she had sat here for nearly fifteen minutes now with little in her own budget to cover the cost of another drink and no sign of the Second Lieutenant.

"Yes, please," she heard herself say. Even as he turned to fetch them, she admonished herself. Her date had told her he would arrive between eight and nine; she had only herself to blame for all this waiting, making herself a sitting target at the bar . . .

"Here's to you." A tumbler of Scotch was placed down in front of her before she had come to the end of her thoughts. He sat down opposite, raising his own glass in salute, before downing the contents of it in one gulp.

As Madeline began her first, tentative sip, the airman rolled his empty glass around in his hands, impatience rising off him in waves. She found herself staring into those strange, broad-set eyes, which, despite their pale hue drifting somewhere between blue and grey, burned with intensity.

"Why don't we go somewhere a little quieter," he said, "and have some dinner?"

"I told you," Madeline attempted to stand her ground, "I have an appointment."

He brushed his hand through the front of his hair, a boyish gesture, backed up by another of his crinkly smiles. "Oh, I'm sure we have plenty of time," he said. "In any case, I have to be back to my unit by ten-thirty."

It was as if somebody had taken a magnet and run it across Madeline's brain, erasing clean away all the thoughts about the Second Lieutenant and their possible future together that had previously been occupying her, so that all that remained was this handsome chap in front of her, willing her to agree. She nodded, put down her glass.

"Splendid!" He got to his feet. "I'll just get my coat."

– • –

He stayed inside his greatcoat, his gas mask slung over his shoulder, as they sat in another cocktail lounge, in the Trocadero, drinking more whisky. It was this seeming indifference to his surroundings, coupled with the fact that he had made no attempt at asking for a menu since they'd arrived, that made Madeline aware of how reckless she had just been.

"Where do you live?" he asked, fixing her with his mesmerist's eyes.

"Wembley," said Madeline, instantly regretting having said so.

"That's a long way out," he leaned across the table, smile not seeming so boyish any more, reminding her instead of something more animal. "Isn't there anywhere round here we can go?"

"No," said Madeline. *I ought to get out of here*, said a little voice in her head, barely more than a hum. But somehow she couldn't seem to rouse herself.

"Are you a naughty girl?" He raised one eyebrow, his leer widening, his eyes now curiously dull. Madeline noticed how pointed his teeth were.

"No, I am not," she said, cheeks reddening. "There's nothing like that about me."

He gave a gruff chuckle, went into his pocket and pulled out the most enormous roll of money Madeline had ever seen.

"I'm not broke, you know," he said. "Let me show you something."

He started to count out the bills in front of her, one by one, like a dealer laying out his cards across the table. Madeline counted to thirty before the hum in her head became a scream and she got to her feet.

"Well, thank you for the drinks," she said, pulling on her coat. "But I really must be going. You seem to have got entirely the wrong idea about me."

Equally as quickly, he gathered his wad back into his pocket, stood up beside her.

"Let me walk you back to your appointment," he said.

– · –

Madeline wanted to run as soon as they were back outside, but he placed a hand on her arm, steered her across the road.

"I'll take you to the Jermyn Street entrance, all right?" he said.

Madeline didn't answer. They crossed Piccadilly along the west side of the Haymarket, turned right towards Jermyn Street. Despite the foul weather, all around her she could hear music, laughter, people enjoying themselves just out of sight, hidden by the walls and the curtains of the blackout. Voices as disembodied as she felt herself at that moment, walking into the sleeting darkness with a stranger.

"Do you know, I knocked a girl out once?" He said it so pleasantly it took a second for his words to sink in.

"W-why would you do that?" she asked.

"Oh, her old man interfered," he went on cheerfully. "So I kicked him in the privates and then I knocked her out."

He had steered her down the wrong side of the road, Madeline realised. They were walking away from the Universelle, into St Alban's Street. She had a flash of her Second Lieutenant, waiting there for her, looking up at the clock the way she had . . . what? An hour previously?

"We're going the wrong way," she said, stopping.

"I just wanted to kiss you goodnight," he said, pulling her into a doorway. "Now come here . . ."

He took his gas mask off his shoulder and set it down on the floor, taking Madeline into his arms. Before she could think any more she was kissing him back, tasting the whisky on his tongue, feeling his arms moving up and down her body, around her waist and then under her skirt.

"No," she smacked his hands away, "I don't do things like that!"

He pushed her further back into the doorway, a low chuckle on his lips. His hands moved back up her torso, circling around her throat and then tightening there. Madeline tried to push him away, tried to beat him with her fists. But the harder she struggled, the tighter his embrace became, a ring of steel around her neck, closing in and in, his breathing heavy, her arms becoming heavier still, her heels scuffling on the concrete below her, a horrible gurgling sound coming out of her throat.

"You won't . . ." the airman whispered, his eyes huge now, saucer-like, and completely void of emotion. "You won't, you won't, you won't . . ."

Out of the corner of her eye, Madeline saw a flash, like the beam of a lighthouse, sweeping across her vision as everything slowed down and her legs buckled beneath her.

"You won't, you won't, you won't . . ."

The flash came again, and with it a man's voice, the sound of running feet.

"Oi! What's going on in there?"

Suddenly the pressure was gone. Madeline's head lolled back on the pavement as the dark shadow of a man flitted across St Alban's Street and was gone.

– • –

In the cells at Tottenham Court Road station, Doris began to cry. It was nearly half-past ten now, and there was still no sign of the big detective coming back for her. Her mother was going to have her guts for garters. How had she got herself into this mess?

That was something that Greenaway intended to find out, just as soon as he had discovered what had become of his car. It had taken the best part of an hour and a half to get from the

Effra Arms to Brixton nick and then back to the West End, where he had deposited his charge with the duty sergeant. He had spent the following thirty minutes burning up his private line talking to all the jokers in South London about the need for the missing Austin to be returned to Scotland Yard in haste and without a scratch.

Finally, one of them had told him what he needed to hear and now it was time to turn his attention to Doris. As he lifted the hatch on the cell door to peer in on her, he could see that her solitary confinement, listening to all the drunks of Soho ringing and singing out from the cells next door, had achieved the desired effect.

He opened the door and came straight to the point. "Tell me, Doris – I ain't had an entirely wasted evening, have I?"

Her face twisted with the effort of holding back more tears.

"I didn't really meet no airman in Piccadilly Circus," she confessed. "I heard some girls talking about him in the York Minster on Dean Street while I was waiting to meet Johnny for a drink last night. I had the paper, see, and Johnny saw your name in the *Herald.* He said he knew you personal like, and that there might be some kind of reward for that sort of information. Only, he reckoned it would go a lot better if I pretended I had actually seen this airman face to face."

"And this?" Greenaway dangled the portrait in front of her nose.

Doris took a loud gulp, scrubbed around her eyes with her hanky. "It's what they said he looked like," she said, "them girls. They was describing him to some friends of theirs and I started sketching while I was listening, on the back of some paper that was left on the table. I ain't really on the bash, see. I'm a student at St Martin's. But when Johnny saw what I'd done he thought it was perfect, that we were bound to get some reward money if you clocked it."

Greenaway rubbed his forehead. "So, you got brains enough to get into art school," he said, "but not to stop running about with a toerag like him?"

Her eyes filled with fresh tears. "That's just what me mum said," she blubbered. "What's going to happen to me now? Am I going to go to jail?"

Greenaway stood up. "I'm tempted," he said. "But I reckon it'll seem like punishment enough next time you pick up a paper and read about some girl getting murdered while you and your boyfriend send me off on a wild goose chase. I could have had my suspect in custody by now. Instead, he could be anywhere. Think on that while you spend the night safely tucked up in here."

He ran upstairs to his office. It was now three and a half hours beyond the time that the Corporal had suggested Greenaway could meet him back at Abbey Lodge for a little chat with Cummins. Knowing it was hopeless, the detective lifted the phone, asked the operator to put him through to the billet anyway.

"Oh, it's you, Inspector Greenaway," the Corporal answered on the second ring. "I was expecting your colleague from the Service Police. He must have got through to you fast enough, it's not five minutes since he called here."

Greenaway rubbed his temples. "Say that again," he said.

"Seems you were on the right track after all," the Corporal went on. "The number on that gas mask they found is the same as the one that was issued to Cummins. Soon as I had it, I sent an orderly up to his room. Seems he's disobeyed orders. He's not there. It's a shame you didn't pop by earlier, like I suggested . . ."

12

GOODBYE PICCADILLY, FAREWELL LEICESTER SQUARE

Thursday, 12 February 1942

Kate Molloy had read Swaffer's piece in the paper. She had heard what all the girls were talking about in Gladys's salon, Berlemont's pub and at the *Entre Nous*. That Jack the Ripper was raised from the dead and had taken the form of an airman.

The man that stood staring at her, outside Oddendino's in Piccadilly, was wearing an RAF greatcoat. He regarded her without speaking as he smoked his cigarette. The smile that played thinly around his lips didn't meet his widely spaced pale eyes, which seemed to look straight through her.

Kate had spent five years on the streets and liked to think she had developed a sixth sense for dangerous men. She knew she was looking at one now. But Kate had other problems pressing. Money worries. The sort that took the form of a man who wore padded shoulders and turn-ups in his suits and never went away.

As if reading her mind, the airman took two steps towards her, holding up the glowing end of his cigarette to view her face more clearly. Kate instinctively patted her hair. Another thing she'd been told. He went for blondes.

"Will you go with me?" He sounded posh. Like Jack the Airman was supposed to.

"It'll cost you two quid," said Kate, blood quickening.

"OK." Without blinking, he went into his pocket and handed the notes across. "Where do you live?"

Kate wasn't going to tell him that. She rented a room for business purposes, a room on which she was two weeks behind, owing to the crocodile in the pinstripe suit who would be round with his rent book tomorrow. For the moment, Kate was just one degree more frightened of him than she was of the man in front of her. The feel of money in her hands would do that to her.

"I got a place in Marble Arch," she said.

"I'll get us a cab," he replied.

– • –

"Madeline Harcourt's her name. Constable Skinner brought her in, just after nine," DS Tom Sheeney told Greenaway down the phone from West End Central station, Savile Row. "Found her staggering around the Haymarket with a young night porter who could barely keep her upright. First, he thought they was drunks. But it was the porter what broke up the fight between her and the airman, round the back of St James market, and picked up the gas mask the miscreant dropped. I had PC Skinner go back to the scene and retrieve her handbag while I took her statement."

"And where is Mrs Harcourt now?" asked Greenaway.

"St Mary's, Paddington," said Sheeney. "She was in obvious need of medical attention, but she insisted on giving her statement first. Brave woman."

"Yeah," said Greenaway, "and what did you tell them at Abbey Lodge?"

"That the owner of the gas mask RAF regimental number

525987 was wanted in connection with the assault of a woman in the West End." Sheeney looked down at his notes. "And that when he returns to his billet I want him detained."

"Right," Greenaway's voice sounded distant. "Thanks. That's very useful, Detective Sergeant."

"Why?" Sheeney asked. "You want him for something, too?"

But the line had gone dead.

– • –

Inside the cab, Kate tried to make small-talk. Her most pressing concern came spilling out instead. "I'd really like to make five quid tonight," she told the airman.

"Don't worry," he said. "Look what I've got."

He went into his pocket and pulled out a roll. Winking, he extracted two more one-pound notes and handed them over. Before she could stuff them into her handbag, he had got down onto the floor of the cab and began pushing up her skirt.

"No!" Kate saw the cabbie adjust his rear-view mirror, his eyes meeting hers for an instant as the airman buried his face between her thighs, rough stubble against tender skin, a worming, penetrating tongue and the feel of teeth behind it. "You mustn't!" she said, pushing his head away. "Not here."

Without saying a word, he pulled out from underneath and returned to the seat beside her. The cabbie kept his eyes on the road as he negotiated the roundabout and headed west down Hyde Park Lane.

"Then why don't we get out here and have some fun in the park?" Kate's companion suggested.

"Don't be silly." Kate's skin was beginning to crawl, knowing what went on in there, knowing that only a desperate woman would ever punt for business in that dark tangle of bushes and trees. "We'll be there any minute."

The cabbie looked at her once more in the rear-view mirror as he steered off the main road and into the little cobbled mews. He saw a woman afraid, biting her lip, but she didn't return his gaze until he was driving away and she was staring after his receding tail lights, the tall figure beside her taking her arm and steering her away.

– • –

Madeline Harcourt's eyes flickered open drowsily, the world around her morphine-blurred. There was a man sitting by the side of her bed, a big man in a black overcoat leaning towards her. As he swam into focus she discerned, to her relief, that he looked more like a pugilist than a priest.

"Mrs Harcourt, I'm sorry to disturb you," Greenaway, ignoring the frowning matron casting the evil eye from behind his shoulder, held out his warrant card. "I know you've already given your statement to my colleague at Savile Row, but I need to ask you one thing. It's very important."

Madeline found it impossible to read whatever it was he was showing her. The letters kept running down and off the side of the card. He put it back in his pocket and brought out something else.

"Is this the man what did this to you?"

The picture shocked her surroundings back into clear focus — the hospital bed, the dressings around her neck and head, the drip inserted in the vein on the back of her right hand. It was only a sketch, but those grey, flat eyes stared out of the piece of paper just as though she was back in their infernal gaze, back in that dark doorway on St Alban's Street. Her head jerked back and she gave a strangled little gasp, her hands involuntarily rising to her throat.

"It's all right," Matron darted between Greenaway and her patient, taking hold of Madeline's hands before she could manage to dislodge anything. "It's all right," she soothed, "you're quite safe now."

She turned her head and glared at Greenaway. "I trust that will be all, Inspector?"

"Thank you, Mrs Harcourt," he said, rising to his feet.

He stood outside the hospital, gulping in lungfuls of dank night air. Sleet enveloped him as he crossed Praed Street, his feet taking him around the corner before he even knew what he was really doing, stopping short at the corner of Conduit Mews.

He looked up at the room above the garage. The blackout was down. He caught a waft of scented violets and he closed his eyes, trying to shut out the memories of a little girl with copper hair who put on a headscarf and read fortunes in the tea leaves for everyone on the street, palming coppers instead of silver, back in the bad old days.

The hands on his wristwatch moved to eleven o'clock as he stood there, fighting the urge to press on the doorbell and ask her to look into her teacup and tell him why she had reappeared again now, in this time of madness, at the centre of his investigation. Then the visions sparked in front of his lids: of Madeleine Harcourt's terrified stare, of Ivy sat on her single bed with a room of blood behind her, of Evelyn Bourne stretched out on the cold concrete floor of an air-raid shelter and an elderly pathologist, dying in his eyes. Coming back to himself, he turned abruptly on his heel.

– • –

Kate lit the gas fire and turned the knob on her meter. The bare bulb above her head flickered, casting sickly yellow light across a single bed, a cabinet beside it and one moth-eaten armchair, then went out.

Kate swore under her breath. She looked back up at her client, standing in the middle of the room, a shadow only visible in the vague glow of the fire.

"Got a shilling for the meter, love?" she asked.

"No," he said, pale eyes boring through the gloom.

"Give me just one sec, will you?"

Her heart hammering, Kate stepped into the kitchenette and stashed the folding he had given her into a tin she kept beneath the sink. She took a saucepan from her one-ring stove and crumpled some newspaper into it, lighting it with a match.

"What are you doing?" he asked impatiently as she brought her improvised lamp back into the room with her. He had already peeled most of his clothes off.

"I just wanted a bit more light," said Kate, slowly unbuttoning the front of her jacket.

He watched, transfixed, as she peeled off the layers, his breathing became more distinct, more animal, until she was down to her lace-up boots and necklace.

The paper in the saucepan flared, crackled and extinguished.

"Stop there," he said. "Lie on the floor."

Kate scowled. "I don't do kinks, mister. It's the bed or nothing."

"As you like," he said. He smelt like an animal too, waves of him coming up at her; a smell of raw meat and dank earth suffused, making her think of foxes and the terrifying noises they made while coupling, banshee sounds she had heard as a child, back in the wilds of Ireland. His mask over her face now, grey eyes, pointed chin and goldie-blond hair completing the vulpine transformation. His hands on her; kneading and pulling, her skin crawling beneath his touch.

"D'you want to get on top, love?" she asked, hopeful of finishing him off quickly.

As he raised himself, Kate reached into the drawer of her bedside cabinet for a French letter. She was just tearing the packet open when he slammed himself into her, both knees to her stomach, the force of it sending her vision red and bringing a scream to her throat that was abruptly cut off as his hands flew to her necklace, twisting it into a noose around her neck. Panic, survival and the instincts of five years on the streets kicked in as Kate's fists connected with his wrists and she squirmed and bucked beneath him. The pressure on her windpipe grew stronger as he shifted his weight forwards, concentrating all his strength on snuffing her out.

Kate's head started to swim from lack of oxygen but there was something animal in her, too. As he tilted, she brought her booted foot up into his stomach, kicking with such force that he crashed headfirst off the top of her, landing on the floor with a startled yelp. Kate jumped to her feet, leapt from the bed over his sprawled form and made for the door.

"Murder! Police!" Kate screamed through the red-raw pain. She felt his fingertips brush her ankle as she pulled the door open, running straight across the hall to her neighbour opposite, a barmaid named Kitty O'Toole with whom she'd always been on friendly terms, hammering on the door. "Let me in! Let me in!"

Kitty, just in from her shift at the Duke of York, opened up in an instant.

"There's a man trying to kill me!"

She took in Kate's wild eyes and naked body and pulled her inside. Across the hall, her neighbour's flat was in darkness, but by the faint glow of the fire, she could make out the form of a tall man standing there. Another door opened along the hallway, an old woman stuck her head out, took one look and shut the door again, giving Kitty just enough illumination to see that the man in Kate's room had no clothes on.

"Could you give me a light, please?" he said.

"Call the police!" Kate's voice behind her was a harsh whisper. Kitty leant across her and picked up the vase from her occasional table, the first weapon that came to hand.

"Miss," the man repeated meekly, "could you please give me a light?"

There was a box of matches on the same table. Kitty used her spare hand to throw them towards him. They landed in the middle of the hall. As he bent down to retrieve them, she gripped the vase tighter, raising it up to smash it down on his head if he made a move towards them.

Instead he merely lit his smoke and turned back to Kate's room.

"Have you seen my boots?" he called out.

Kate crouched behind Kitty, beginning to hyperventilate. But neither of them could seem to tear their eyes away from the airman as he stumbled around the room opposite, picking up his clothes and putting them back on. He started to hum to himself, a discordant rendering of an old Fred and Ginger song.

He stepped back into the hallway. Kitty gave him her most venomous barmaid's stare, the vase raised high above her head. Kate's fingers dug into her shoulders.

"You're him," Kate hissed. "You're Jack."

He went into his pocket, pulled out a roll of money. Slowly, he counted out eight pound notes and threw them at her feet.

"I'm sorry," he said. "I think I've had rather too much to drink tonight."

Then he turned and walked away, picking up the refrain of his tune as he wove unsteadily down the corridor. Kitty and Kate waited for the door to slam behind him before they collapsed into each other's arms.

– • –

Claudette Coles stood under a shop awning across the road from Paddington Station. As she took down a lungful of smoke, she wondered for a brief instant what it was she thought she was doing here.

At seven o'clock that evening she had waved her husband, Herbert, off on his Circle Line train to Sloane Square and his job as a night manager at the Royal Court Hotel. Returning to the flat they shared in 187 Sussex Gardens, she had cleared the soup dishes from the dining table, letting water wash over them and her hands in the sink as she scrubbed methodically away, willing the mindless task to erase just as easily the banal platitudes she had shared with her old man over the consumption of their meagre meal, the routine they followed night after night after night.

The next time she had looked at a clock, it was the one in her bedroom, which told her an hour had passed. She sat down at her dressing table, stared at her face in the mirror, the cracks and lines that had appeared there over her seven long years of marriage. She began to plaster over the top of them, to powder and paint. Claudette had always looked more like a school-marm than a Windmill girl, but there was a certain sort of man, her husband included, that relished that sort of severity.

However, under the crouching gloom of the blackout, in the unrelenting sleet, there didn't seem to be any sorts of men except bogeys tramping the streets tonight. Claudette had walked a circular route, down to Hyde Park and along beside it to Marble Arch, where she had treated herself to a cup of tea in Lyons, hoping to find company there. When this proved futile she had come back up the Edgware Road to Praed Street, speculating that it might be possible to accost some late night travellers. She stopped for a cigarette first, holding the light from her match up to her wristwatch. It was now half-past eleven.

"Rotten night, ain't it?" a voice beside her startled Claudette. She turned to see a woman whose blonde hair framed the most beautiful, flawless face. A scent of violets, along with something altogether more human, drifted up to her nostrils. "How long you been out here, love?" she asked.

"Couple of hours, thereabouts," said Claudette, clocking the expensive coat her new companion was wrapped in. Despite the fact she had announced herself as a fellow professional, the woman looked more like a film star.

"Me and all," said Lil. "Thought I'd give the station a whirl, but the bleedin' porter wanted one on the house, the cheeky bastard."

"Ah," said Claudette, thinking even that would be better than nothing at all.

Lil, on the other hand, had exhausted her rage. She had found herself drifting back towards the scene of her youthful initiation to the game, the Norfolk Square Hotel. There she found a party of businessmen stranded for the night by the bad weather. The trouble she had taken with her appearance, coupled with the tip she palmed the barman, allowed her to pass from the saloon and up to one of the rooms they had taken, where she had found the oblivion she sought in sex.

"There ain't many trains running tonight, see," she went on to explain what she had learned during the course of her evening's endeavours. "The storms brought a load of trees down all along the line past Reading. I think I'm gonna call it a night. Maybe you should do the same."

"Maybe," said Claudette, still thinking about the porter. "But it's still so early. I don't like to go home empty-handed, you know."

"I *do* know," said Lil, giving a sympathetic smile. "Well, all right, love, ta ta." She started to walk back towards the mews, calling over her shoulder: "And good luck!"

Claudette watched her disappear around the corner, her heart sinking with every clack of Lil's receding footsteps as the brief glimmer of interesting conversation passed like a setting sun.

As she watched, a figure stepped out of the gloom. A man, in a military greatcoat and forage cap, tall and lean, shoulders hunched against the sleet. Claudette dropped the dregs of her cigarette and hastily found another, striking a match as he came close.

The flare lit up a face with high cheekbones and light-coloured eyes, goldish-blond hair and a clipped moustache. A cigarette hung out of the corner of his mouth, wreathing him in smoke and when he spoke he sounded almost apologetic.

"Will you take me home with you?" he asked. "I have two pounds."

He looked much better to Claudette than the porter she had been imagining and she liked the intelligent, educated sound of his voice.

"It's just around the corner, dear," she said.

– • –

Greenaway looked down at his wristwatch, the hands inching towards one o'clock. Above the snores of the three men in the bedrooms behind him, he could just discern other noises drifting up from beneath his post by the kitchen window in Abbey Lodge. The sound of footfalls on the metal fire escape that ran along the other side of the wall, and a song being whistled off-key. While Greenaway tried to place the tune, he watched fingers slide underneath the sill that had been left ajar by half an inch, presumably to allow such access upon the return of the one man who was still missing from his billet. From the opposite side of the sink unit, the Corporal likewise observed first-hand the trick his charge had employed to evade that evening's curfew. They had been waiting long enough by now for their eyes to grow accustomed to the dark.

The fingers flattened themselves out into an upturned palm, curled around the woodwork and heaved it up. Another hand came to join it, this one carrying a gas mask, which was tossed across the top of the sink and landed with a thud on the linoleum floor. From out of the darkness rose up a tousled head and with it, thick, entwined aromas of alcohol, tobacco and sex.

Neither Greenaway nor the Corporal moved as their quarry slid under the window, unfurling long legs out across the sink in careful, practised moves. He sat there for a moment, rubbing his eyes, then turned to close the window and lower himself onto the floor. Bending down, he fumbled for the gas mask, swaying slightly like a drunkard. Then his fingers located it, grasped it and brought it back up to his chest.

"*There may be trouble ahead . . .*" he whispered tunelessly.

"You got that right," said Greenaway, snapping on the light

and staring into a pair of wide-spaced eyes, a face that could perhaps have been considered handsome, if it wasn't for those cold grey lamps. "Gordon Frederick Cummins, you're fucking nicked, my son."

13

AFTER YOU'VE GONE

Friday, 13 February 1942

When Mari Lambouri opened her door on Friday morning, the brown paper package was still sitting there on her neighbour's doorstep. This time Mari didn't just carry on her way. She knew that Phyllis's young daughter, Jeannie, always came up from Southend on Friday afternoons to spend the weekend with her mother. It wasn't the fault of the girl – a solemn, studious looking fifteen-year-old – that Phyllis behaved the way she did. And by now it was abundantly clear to Mari that something very unusual – and perhaps very wrong – had occurred in the flat across the way from her. She had heard not a peep from the residence since the whistling man had departed in the early hours of Wednesday morning.

She had read the papers, too.

Taking her purse from her handbag, Mari went along the hall to see the landlord about making a telephone call.

– • –

West End Central was having the first crack at Cummins. It was protocol – DS Sheeney had called it in first, found the gas mask that positively identified the man – but it was also something of a relief for Greenaway. If he hadn't had the Corporal standing beside him when he made the arrest, Greenaway wasn't sure what he might have found himself doing. One look at that supercilious countenance and a tattoo had started up in his brain, the urge to redecorate the room in Cummins's blood surging with it, willing him to take his own justice into his own fists and to Hell with the rules he had sworn to abide by. Getting his suspect directly into custody at Savile Row had been safer for both of them. But the cold nerve of the trainee pilot lingered, prickling at the back of Greenaway's mind like blips from a half-remembered nightmare, snapshots of the carnage the killer had left in his wake mingling with other suppressed memories, of dark cold lumps in dark cold beds, back in the bad old days.

Cummins had shown no outwards concern at being confronted shinning his way into his billet, neither did he seem particularly perturbed to learn that he was wanted for the assault on Madeline Harcourt. He treated the whole situation like a prank that had backfired, offering the gas mask he'd thrown through the window as his evidence that it couldn't have been him that was up to anything naughty in St James market.

But then, neither he, the Corporal nor Sheeney knew what Greenaway was after him for. The DCI was content to let it stay that way, for now. He had deposited his quarry at West End Central at two in the morning and gone home for the first six hours of justified sleep he had managed since the case began.

Greenaway got to his desk freshly shaved and shined by ten o'clock. A pile of messages awaited him, amongst them one from Cherrill: *Results back from Forensics: dust in the boot soles from RAF bin a match for Montagu Place. Also a brown Austin Cambridge turned up at the Yard this morning.*

Then there was a copy of the log of the duty sergeant who had booked Cummins in last night. In the pockets of his RAF uniform he had found a wad of notes – fifty-six pounds in total, serial numbers all duly noted – a silver cigarette case, a woman's wristwatch with a strip of Elastoplast on the back of the face, some love letters and a revealing family snapshot: proud squiresman Cummins had a wife living in Barnes.

The label in the inside pocket of the smart suit Greenaway had extracted from his locker was from a tailors in that district. The shirt hanging underneath that suit had minute dark brown splashes on the cuffs. The smell of a woman's perfume still faintly lingered on it. All these items were now at the lab in Hendon.

He reached across to call Cherrill just as the phone began to ring.

Greenaway's sense of relief drained away as he listened to his summons. He hadn't got the bastard in time after all.

– · –

Numbers 9–11 Gosfield Street belonged to a block of flats only a few minutes around the corner from the station on Tottenham Court Road. A dark flock of constables guarded the entrance, blowing and stamping the cold away. Cherrill's car was already parked outside. At the door of the ground floor flat numbered 4, the divisional surgeon exited, looking like a man with a bad hangover.

"What we got here?" Greenaway asked.

"A woman, late thirties," the surgeon replied. "Name of Phyllis Lord. She's been strangled and then . . ." he shook his head, ". . . worse. Been dead about two days, I reckon, which ties in with what the witness called it in said. Her neighbour across the way, a Mrs Lambouri, says there's been a package left on her doormat since Wednesday morning. Mrs Lord's daughter apparently comes down to see her every Friday and Mrs Lambouri had read the papers, put two and two together. Didn't want to risk the girl walking in on anything. Thank Christ for nosy neighbours." He jerked a thumb behind him. "I've put everything back the way I found it."

Inside, Cherrill was setting up his lamps.

Phyllis Lord's front room was as still and cold as a mausoleum and held barely as much furniture – just a single bed pushed lengthwise against the wall with a black eiderdown thrown over it, an occasional table, a small square of carpet and a couple of wooden chairs. On the mantelpiece across the empty fireplace stood a glass candlestick and a tumbler half full of beer. There was a pile of clothing at the foot of the bed, discarded in obvious haste.

"Ted," said Cherrill.

"Fred," said Greenaway.

Greenaway put down his murder bag and pulled on his gloves. Cherrill picked up his magnifying glass and went straight to the mantelpiece. Greenaway felt bile rising in his throat as he walked the other way, towards the ominous lump hidden beneath the eiderdown. *Too late . . .*

The once handsome face of the Lady was now a livid mottling of brown and purple, pink froth around her nose and mouth, caused by her own silk stocking that had been pulled taut and tied around her throat. The rest of her was covered by two blankets and a sheet. Slowly, carefully, Greenaway folded them back.

It was even worse than Evelyn Bettencourt.

Phyllis had been attacked with an armoury of different weapons. By the side of her belly lay a breadknife, its saw-edge blade crusted with blood, pointed inwards and down. A black-handled table knife, smeared with gore, lay across the top of her left thigh. On the bedsheet to her right, a yellow-handled table knife and a vegetable peeler pointed dark brown blades across to the rest of the contents of her kitchen drawers. But even the butchery inflicted upon her by all these implements had not been enough. On the sheet between her open legs, a poker with its handle broken off. Protruding from inside her, a bloodied candle.

A scent lingered in the still air, the fragrance faint, but familiar enough to snap Greenaway's synapses back to the suit in Cummins's locker.

He turned his head to where Cherrill was examining the empty candlestick with his magnifying glass.

"There's latents on here, Ted," the fingerprint man said, "off the right hand. Which means," Cherrill mimed the actions of the attacker, "he used his left hand to take the candle out."

"I got him, Fred," said Greenaway. "He's in the cells at West End Central. I just didn't get him soon enough."

"Get him to sign something," said Cherrill, "see which hand he uses."

Greenaway lifted the blanket back to cover the scene already indelibly etched on each iris. "Spilsbury's on his way," he said. "I want him to talk me through exactly how this happened before I brace the bastard."

– • –

Herbert Coles stopped outside his flat at 187 Sussex Gardens. There was something wrong. The morning's milk delivery was still standing on the doorstep. Nervously, he looked up and down the street, a lump forming in his throat.

Herbert had spent the seven years since he had first encountered his wife on Oxford Street in a perpetual state of fear that she would one day leave him. He knew what she was and at first he had thought he could save her from that life. But perhaps that day had finally come.

He fumbled for his keys in his trouser pocket.

Twenty years older than Claudette, Herbert had been a man of comfortable means, having sold his hotel business for enough of a profit to see him through the rest of his days – or so he had thought. It had been enough to get his proposal of marriage accepted, two months after their first professional assignation in her old flat on the Edgware Road. Claudette had moved into his house on Bathurst Place and assumed the role of housewife, happily at first, but with steadily declining interest over the next three years.

It was as if Claudette sent out radio signals on a frequency Herbert could tune into, wherever he happened to be. When she started taking a little longer over the shopping of a morning, he knew it had started again. Afraid to confront his wandering wife, Herbert tried diversion tactics: he invested some of his capital to buy a café on one of the little backstreets between Paddington and the Edgware Road and gave Claudette the job as co-manager. It was a disaster. The backstreet was a customer cul-de-sac and in four months, Herbert had yet to recoup a fraction of his investment selling cups of tea and bread-and-scrapes to the elderly, while Claudette let the wide boys from every mechanics' shop, bookies and pool hall in the district run up a fortune on the slate. It was almost as if she was siding with them against him. Almost as if, the darkest voices in his head would insist, she was getting some other sort of payment for her bacon and eggs.

Herbert sold the café and relocated them to Eastbourne, where he spent hard on entertainments to keep Claudette out of the arms of other men. The change of scene worked while the summer and his funds lasted. When war was declared that September, a depleted Herbert packed his wife off to her mother's in Harrogate, while he returned to London and took a job as staff manager in Oddendino's, sending her an allowance each month, his comfy nest egg by now all but wiped out.

It wasn't long, however, before he bumped into his wife on Oxford Street again. Worse than the shock of this was the news she had found her own accommodation – right across the street from him in Sussex Gardens. Almost as if she was taunting him, almost as if she was rubbing his nose in it. Herbert pleaded with her to stay out of harm's way – meaning both Hitler's bombs and the attentions of those leering, pinstriped goons who had made his venture at the café such an unmitigated failure. Claudette laughed in his face. Herbert had never been man enough for her, she said. And if he wasn't up to the job, then what was she to do but find others who were?

Despite all his wife's cruelty and caprice, Herbert did not want to lose her. He pleaded and cried and demeaned himself before her until she gave up her flat and moved back in with him – on the condition that what she did with herself while he was at work was none of his affair. In order to turn a blind eye to her nocturnal activities, he found another job, as the night manager at the Royal Court in Sloane Square, far enough away from her stamping grounds that he didn't run the risk of stumbling across her hawking for business outside the establishment's front doors. He left every evening at seven and returned the next morning at eleven, to sleep until six, then have dinner with Claudette. That arid hour was all he had left of her, but to him, it was better than the alternative.

Herbert picked up the pint of milk, still icy cold, mind spinning back to the night before. Supper had felt even more strained than usual. All the way through his attempts to make conversation, she had stared straight through him, her mind far away, in a landscape he could not comprehend. Still, she had come to see him off on the tube, and from that he had taken crumbs of consolation, enough to see him through his shift.

He pushed the front door open, almost tripping over the morning paper that lay on the doormat.

"Claudette?" he called, kneeling to pick up the *Daily Herald*.

His own voice, high-pitched and strained, echoed back at him. Normally Claudette kept the wireless on while she was in the house.

"Claudette?"

Everything felt too still, too empty. He walked down the hallway, turning the doorknob into the lounge. The blackout was still down from the night before. He put a hand to the light switch, but the illumination of the electric bulb did not extend any clues to his wife's whereabouts. Everything was as meticulously tidy as it always was, not a hair out of place. Claudette was as obsessive about keeping the house clean as she was about rolling her own body in filth, he had always thought.

Herbert walked through the still life into the kitchen,

putting the milk down on the counter top. He unfurled the paper and the headlines hit him.

WEST END KILLER STILL AT LARGE!
SCOTLAND YARD URGE ALL WOMEN TO STAY
INSIDE AT NIGHT

Herbert turned on his heel, as if some unseen entity had a dagger pressed to the base of his spine, propelling him back down the hallway to the bedroom. He flung himself at the door, but it was no use. It was locked.

The dagger pressing harder, a dagger made of ice, Herbert began to pound on the door with his fists.

"Claudette!" His voice getting higher, shriller. "Claudette!"

Then, as if the dagger had penetrated, his blood began to chill and his panic subsided into an intuitive horror of the situation. He had tuned back into his wife's frequency and already knew what lay beyond the locked door.

He stepped backwards, turned the hall light off.

Sure enough, a band of glowing yellow at the bottom of the bedroom door told him Claudette was still at home.

Herbert walked backwards some more, into the front room. With shaking hands, he lifted the receiver of his telephone.

– • –

"Depending on whether she is breathing in or out when the murderer tightens his grip, it takes fifteen to thirty seconds to strangle a woman," Sir Bernard Spilsbury told Greenaway. "In this case," the pathologist dropped his gaze back down to the stricken visage of Phyllis Lord, "I would estimate she died in fifteen seconds. She was trying to scream when he pulled the stocking around her neck. Everything else came after."

"So let me get this straight," Greenaway's head was thumping so loudly he had to strain to keep his thoughts in order. "That," he pointed to the silken noose, "was for him. And this," his finger arced to the post-mortem butchery, "was for us."

Spilsbury raised his eyebrows. "I'm not a psychologist," he said. "But there's something in what you say. Are you thinking the same as I am?"

With a loud backfire from its exhaust pipe, a motorbike pulled up outside. Both men watched the dispatch rider enter the building, Spilsbury's question answered before Greenaway had even opened the message that was handed to him.

"Not another one?" the pathologist said.

"Yeah," said Greenaway. "Another one. At Sussex Gardens, Paddington." His stomach dropped as he read it. Sussex Gardens – so close to where he had been last night that it was entirely possible he could have missed Cummins on the street by only seconds.

"You coming?" he looked back up at Spilsbury.

Too late . . .

14

THE VERY THOUGHT OF YOU

Friday, 13 February 1942

Herbert Coles sat alone in his living room while the horde of policemen that had arrived within the past hour went about their business just down the corridor. The first of them to arrive, a constable from Paddington, hadn't been able to get through the outside window to the bedroom and in the end had seen no other way but to kick out the hinges of the locked door, warning – or advising, as he had put it – Herbert not to follow him in there. He had left Claudette's husband to pace the floor, tortuous thoughts ripping through his mind like the wood splintering from the doorframe.

That first constable had been very young. When he had finally come back, his face now pallid, he'd asked to use the telephone. Herbert heard him request Scotland Yard CID and the divisional surgeon to report to the flat immediately. He closed his eyes, seeing the newsprint headlines on the discarded paper in the kitchen next door. Pain like he had never known before flooded every cell of his body, every ending of his nerves. The nightmares that had tormented him through his whole married life were as nothing compared to the reality of Claudette leaving him this way: going from their marital bed to a place she could never come back from.

Tears began to leak out of the corners of Herbert's eyes.

He put one hand up to brush them away, while the other fell between the cushion and the back of the sofa. His fingers touched something soft.

It was one of Claudette's handkerchiefs, a piece of purple satin with red edging and an embossed red rose in the centre of the square she had folded and ironed it into. Herbert lifted it to his face, breathed in the scent of her perfume.

– • –

Jeannie Lord stopped at the top of the steps from Tottenham Court Road tube station. So far, it had not been a good day. Her train from Southend had been delayed by half an hour and then came to a halt on the tracks for another twenty minutes between Leigh-on-Sea and Benfleet. The carriage had been freezing, the view bleak – an eerie expanse of creeks and marshland, fringed by the black rolls of barbed wire that marked the edge of the Thames. Storm clouds chased across the grey sky, the estuary gazed sullenly back. Jeannie had put her head in her schoolbook, tried to concentrate on the words, even though she just wanted to scream: "Get a move on!"

She could never wait to leave the gloomy, gothic penury of her boarding school on a Friday afternoon and set out for London. Mother would always have a treat for them waiting: a trip to the cinema, a walk in Hyde Park or Kensington Gardens, window-shopping in the department stores that fringed those places, just occasionally a trip through the doors for a new handkerchief or gloves, a spray of perfume from the immaculately turned-out lady on the counter.

Best of all, though, would be dinner in Kettners. Jeannie loved Soho: the crowded bustle of it all, the street markets and spivs on Berwick Street, so many different types of people speaking all kinds of languages and wearing strange types of clothes. The food they had there she was sure you could get nowhere else, least of all Southend.

She wished she could just stay with Mother for the rest of the week and go to school in London, but Mother was adamant. It was too dangerous – and anyway, she had to pass her exams so that she would have a good job when she left school.

Jeannie had decided she would become a spy. She loved the way the Frenchwomen in Soho looked and spoke. If she could emulate them perfectly, she told herself, then she could become a secret agent, go to France and bring down a German general or two. Jeannie was always being teased at school for being a Plain Jane. None of her contemporaries would ever have guessed the reason why she always came top of the class in French, Greek and Latin. Which, of course, made her perfect spy material.

Such thoughts, along with analysis of all the people in the train carriage and then later, the tube, kept her occupied until she walked out on to Tottenham Court Road.

All the rubble and broken glass that had greeted her the week before had been cleared away from the half of the street where shops still stood and went about their business. Across the road, though, only a few fragments of blasted wall, standing out like blackened, broken teeth, remained from what had once been a row of houses. Jeannie's eyes alighted on a piece of rose-patterned wallpaper, still incongruously stuck to what must have been the inside of somebody's bedroom, and a horrible sense of foreboding descended. She hurried away, around the corner, towards Gosfield Street.

— • —

Like a macabre *pas de deux*, Greenaway arrived at the door of the ground floor flat in Paddington just as the divisional surgeon was leaving.

"Brace yourself." He nodded as they passed. "It's him again."

Greenaway turned to watch him go. Spilsbury hobbled across the forecourt towards him, waving him on with one of his walking sticks when he saw he was being observed. Cherrill, who had driven them there, carried both his own and the pathologist's bags from his car. Greenaway's mind flitted back for an instant to the last war and the things that he had seen there, the wraiths of the walking wounded. He shook his head and went through the door of 187 Sussex Gardens. A young constable greeted him, pointed him right down the corridor, lowering his voice as he told him: "She's in the bedroom down there. The husband's in the sitting room, I've told him to stay put." The PC put his hand over his stomach as he spoke, an involuntary indication of what Greenaway could expect to find.

— • —

The bad feeling increased when Jeannie saw two policemen standing outside the front door of Mother's block. What could they be doing there?

Hesitantly, she walked towards them, hoping they would part and let her pass. But instead they both moved in together, blocking the entrance, staring at her intently.

"Excuse me, Miss," one of them said. The older-looking of the pair, so old, in fact, he looked like he could have retired once before and then been sent back to work. "Would you mind telling me your name and business here?"

"Wh-Why?" Jeannie heard the tremble in her voice. "What's wrong?"

"I'm afraid there's been an incident, Miss," the old policeman said. "We're not letting anyone through here at the moment unless we know who they are."

Jeannie felt her stomach drop thirteen floors but she determined that she would show no fear. This was just a test, that was all.

"Miss Jean Louise Lord," she said, pulling herself up straight. "I'm here to see my mother, Mrs Phyllis Lord. She lives in Flat number 4."

The old policeman's eyes suddenly looked sad. "If you wouldn't mind just waiting here for a moment, Miss," he said. Then he turned to his companion. "Go and get the old dear," he said.

– • –

Like the other murder sites through which Greenaway had passed in the space of the last week, a stillness had settled in Claudette Coles's bedroom, as if an icy breath had frozen the scene. The feeling of déjà vu intensified as he crossed the threshold, the door leaning off its hinges at a woozy angle, and walked towards the lump on the right side of the bed. Another dark lump on another dark bed . . .

Greenaway pulled back the covers and saw white skin and fair hair, dilated pupils staring straight through him into infinity, mouth open in a silent scream. A black stocking made the ligature, the killer's finishing flourish to tie it up in a bow just under the left side of her chin.

Greenaway could feel his jaw tense as he heard the others enter the room behind him, the pounding beginning in his temples again. He made himself go on looking, take it all in, record exactly what he saw in his notebook with methodical detail.

A gash in her right cheek, made by clawing fingernails, wept congealed blood. Beneath her ruined face, her left breast had been cleaved away by a circular knife wound, four inches long. There was another half-inch knife wound on the right side of her nipple, as if the killer had tried to slice it off. Perpendicular to that, a deep slash six inches long carved her abdomen in two from her navel downwards, drawing the eyes down to the blood-encrusted ribbons he had made of her genitals, over which he had folded her left hand.

"You've got a madman on parade here," Greenaway heard Spilsbury say.

The pathologist had made the same mental leap as the women of the street. He had been nine in 1888, the year of Jack the Ripper; old enough to have those unsolved atrocities seared into his brain, the materials that would form the purpose of his life. As a young man, he had made his name on the case then considered the most gruesome of the twentieth century: that of John Hawley Harvey Crippen, who dismembered his wife in his Camden Town basement and tried to dissolve her existence with quicklime. A five-and-a-half inch by seven-inch piece of skin yielding an operation scar that Spilsbury proved to have belonged to the vanished Cora Crippen gave Scotland Yard the evidence to send the bad doctor to the gallows.

During the thirty-one years since, Spilsbury had never ceased learning the stories of the dead and speaking deeds of darkness into the light of a courtroom day. But his lifetime's service had taken its toll. Less than two years ago, he had suffered a stroke, standing at his dissection table, mid-autopsy.

It hadn't been severe enough to put him out of action, but it was the reason he now made his daily commute with the aid of two walking sticks. On top of that, he'd lost his doctor son Thomas in the Blitz, been bombed out of his home, his wife had gone back to her family in the country and he'd been left to barrack down with two elderly, unmarried sisters in Hampstead. His current caseload could not have been heavier, but still, he wouldn't give up the work.

Greenaway nodded, wondering how much longer the pathologist would still have the strength to go on with it.

– . –

Jeannie recognised the old lady who lived across the way from Mother. The Spanish Widow, as Mother called her, she always dressed in black, with a knitted shawl and a large crucifix around her neck. Jeannie had always been rather afraid of her stern appearance. But today the old lady approached her with an expression of grief in her dark brown eyes, and reached out to put a bony hand on her shoulder.

"Oh, Jeannie," she said. "I'm afraid we have to go with the policemen now."

"But why?" Jeannie replied. "Why won't anyone tell me what's going on?"

Mari Lambouri looked round at the two silent coppers and then back at her. Her other hand held rosary beads. "It's your mother," she said.

– . –

"Mr Coles?"

Herbert opened his eyes slowly, unwilling to break the spell that the perfume had cast, the feeling that a spectral Claudette had wrapped her arms around him. When he did, he saw a large plainclothes detective in a long black coat. His face looked like it had gone a few rounds, but the sleepy brown eyes showed sympathy.

"I'm Detective Chief Inspector Greenaway," he introduced himself. "I'm in charge of this investigation and I'm sorry to have to intrude on you like this. Is there anyone I can call for you? Anyone you could stay with, instead of waiting here?"

Herbert shook his head.

"N-no," he said, his voice sounding strange to his own ears, as if it was coming down a long tunnel. "There was no one else but Claudette." His watery eyes searched Greenaway's face for answers; then, finding none, dropped back down to the handkerchief he was holding.

"We're going to have to leave you for a while, Mr Coles," Greenaway knelt down beside him, "but I'll be back within the hour, I hope, to ask you some questions."

Herbert nodded without looking up. His finger traced the pattern of the red rose on the centre of the handkerchief.

"We'll have to take her with us," the detective went on. "Along with the bedroom door and the wardrobe door – for fingerprints, you see? But I'm going to leave this bright young constable with you until I come back, so he can . . ."

"Make sure I don't go in there," Herbert said.

"I was going to say, so he can make you a cup of tea," said Greenaway. "Look after you. But, yes. It would be for the best if you let us clean things up here."

"I understand," said Herbert. "Just do what you have to do, Detective Chief Inspector." He buried his face in the handkerchief.

– • –

Greenaway heaved his murder bag out of the door. Inside, bagged up for Forensics: two discarded French letters found on the floor by the bed, one containing fluid, and some crumpled, stained tissues. The butt of a Craven A cigarette left in the ashtray. A purse, containing Claudette Coles's identity card and some ration coupons, but devoid of any money. A Gillette safety razor, its blade encrusted in blood and a roll of Elastoplast with a thin strip neatly cut out of it.

He had one more stop to make, at West End Central, for the items found on Cummins at the time of his incarceration. The strip of Elastoplast on the back of the woman's watch they had found on the airman could be a match for that cut out of the roll of tape just recovered – and he would need to take it back to show to Herbert for identification. The silver cigarette case could have come from either or any of the women Cummins had been preying on. But there was nothing else that they had taken from her flat that he could possibly show to Phyllis Lord's young daughter.

– • –

Back at Tottenham Court Road station, Jeannie was waiting for him.

15

STRAIGHTEN UP AND FLY RIGHT

Saturday, 14 February 1942

Greenaway crossed Vauxhall Bridge, the events of the past twelve hours spooling through his mind as if he were viewing them all on a cinema screen. He felt the way he always did when he knew he was about to close a case: perfectly calm and still, running on the adrenaline surge that came from weaving all the strands together so tightly that the case had no weakness which could snap under the questioning of a clever barrister or KC. The long hours he, Cherrill, Spilsbury, DS Sheeney at West End Central, the Service Police and the Forensics team at Hendon had put in had forged a rope strong enough to take the weight of Gordon Frederick Cummins.

He could see Jeannie Lord's hazel eyes as if they were staring at him through the windscreen of the Wolseley, the way she had looked at him when he handed her the silver cigarette case.

"Oh yes," she said. "Mother always carries this about with her. If it isn't in her handbag, it'll be on the kitchen table. If you look inside," she said, opening it up, "there's a yellow band across the middle. You see?"

For a second, Jeannie had looked at him with an eagerness

that seemed to imply that she had passed a test. Then the full weight of her discovery and all that it meant bore down on her and she shut the case again.

"Why?" she had asked him. "Why would anyone do such a thing to Mother?"

There was no answer to that question that he could give.

But a further piece of evidence came his way shortly afterwards. A report made by a woman named Kate Molloy of an attack on her person on Thursday night by an airman she had picked up on Piccadilly – just fifteen minutes after Cummins had left Madeline Harcourt for dead around the back of St James's market. When Greenaway had interviewed her in her room so close to Sussex Gardens, not only did Kate's description tally, but she still also had the wad of money her thwarted Romeo had given her – and two of the notes had sequential serial numbers.

One more trip back to Abbey Lodge and Greenaway ascertained that these had been paid out of the five hundred brand new Bank of England notes dispensed to the cadet officers on Thursday the twelfth of February. The notes were given out consecutively as the men were paid, in alphabetical order. Greenaway found the man who had been in line directly before Cummins, who still had most of his pay packet on him, including the notes numbered 39806 and 39807. Kate Molloy's were 39808 and 39809.

Meanwhile, the Service Police had found the owner of the gas mask Cummins had brought back to barracks with him – another airman who had been drinking in the Captain's Cabin in Piccadilly, around midnight on Thursday. Despite everything he had inflicted upon Madeline Harcourt, Kate Molloy and Claudette Coles during the course of that night, once he had realised he was without it, Cummins had still had the wherewithal to get himself a replacement for the gas mask he had lost, and from a location just steps away from where he had mislaid it.

Greenaway drove through Clapham Common, pock-marked by craters of bomb blasts and the gaps of rubble amid the rows of tall houses that fringed its edges, barrage balloons swaying languorously overhead. Now it was Herbert Coles's watery eyes the detective could see staring back at him through the windscreen.

Herbert had identified the watch immediately, a present he had bought for his wife. He then had to face the ordeal of visiting her in the morgue. When Spilsbury turned back the sheet, Herbert had given a little cry, like a wounded bird, before turning his head away.

"Why did she have to . . ." he whispered, choking on fresh tears before he could get to the end of the sentence. Another question Greenaway had no answer to.

But the men that dealt in irrefutable facts had found their own indisputable solutions. Cherrill had made matches with the prints found at Evelyn Bettencourt's room with the ones taken from Phyllis Lord's flat and the doors they had removed from Claudette Coles's bedroom. They corre-sponded to the prints taken at West End Central at the time of Cummins's arrest. Further traces of rubble found inside the cadet officer's discarded gas mask were identical to those taken from the air-raid shelter where Evelyn Bourne had been murdered.

As Greenaway drove down Streatham Hill, he could pic-ture Cummins swinging from the gallows. The image car-ried him all the way to his destination, where the airman had been remanded following the charge of assault on Madeline Harcourt made by DS Sheeney, the detective who waited for him there. Justice to come for the orphan and the widower, who might still have a mother and a wife, if it wasn't for the last time he had travelled this way, on his doomed foray to the Effra Arms. His hands were steady on the steering wheel as he arrived at Brixton Prison.

– • –

"Chief Inspector," Cummins looked up with a bright smile, as if he was receiving an old comrade at the Officers' Mess and not the two detectives who stood before him. "Glad to see you. I've been trying to explain to your junior officers," he said, casting a sideways glance at Sheeney, "but I'm sorry to say, they haven't taken a blind bit of notice. I certainly hope we can sort this out now – between gentlemen."

Greenaway stood on the threshold of the interview room and took in the form of his phantom in the daylight. Cummins had made the most of the basic facilities to have a wash and comb back his wayward hair. Those strange, moonstone eyes were only slightly pink around the rims, suggesting that he had been sleeping well.

In short, nothing about the man's appearance would lead the casual observer to suspect he was responsible for the carnage Greenaway had witnessed during the past six days. Compared to the battle-scarred visages of the past roll-call of villains he had put away – all the racketeers, heisters, hoisters, petermen, kite-fliers and tweedlers – Cummins didn't look like much, least of all the worst of them.

Greenaway stepped inside the room. "I'm sure we can," he said, nodding at the guard to lock the door behind himself and Sheeney. "I think we've just about got everything sewn up. Only you have me at a disadvantage, Cummins." He sat down slowly, putting his murder bag on his knee. "I ain't exactly what you'd call a gentleman."

Cummins opened his palms. "Well, maybe I'm not so much of one either," he allowed. "Look, I know it was bad form sneaking in and out after curfew. But I'm not the only one guilty of that. After all, it's pretty remiss of the barracks, isn't it, to leave a fire escape outside the window like that?"

"It's gone a bit beyond that now," said Sheeney.

"Really?" Cummins leaned forwards eagerly. "Have you found the man who took my gas mask? The blighter that assaulted that woman?"

"Oh, we've found him all right," Greenaway said. He began to remove a set of crime scene photographs from a brown envelope. "The man whose gas mask you brought home with you was drinking in the Captain's Cabin Thursday night, too pissed to know his arse from his elbow. As I'm sure you recall."

Cummins raised his eyebrows. "Whatever do you mean?" he said. "Has your friend here not told you?" he cast another curt, meaningful glance at Sheeney. "I was at a party on Thursday night, in St John's Wood . . ."

"I'll give it to you officially," Greenaway cut him short. "My name is Detective Chief Inspector Edward Greenaway and I am conducting investigations relative to the murder of four women during the past week. One case at an air-raid shelter on Montagu Place, Regent's Park, on the night of Sunday the eighth of February."

He put down the black-and-white. Evelyn Bourne, her silk scarf cutting off her last breath, staring into infinity with her own pair of gloves pointing up at her in an inverted prayer.

"One case at 153 Wardour Street, W1, night of Monday, the ninth of February."

He added Evelyn Bettencourt, lying on a blood-saturated mattress, her torch protruding from between her thighs.

"Another at Flat 4, 9–10 Gosfield Street, near Tottenham Court Road, the night of Wednesday, eleventh of February."

Phyllis Lord with all her injuries and the knives that had made them placed in a ring around her thighs.

"And finally, the fourth, at a flat at 187 Sussex Gardens, Paddington, the night of Thursday, the twelfth of February, approximately one hour after the assault on Mrs Harcourt."

Claudette Coles, her stocking tied in a ghastly bow around her neck.

Greenaway straightened them out on the table in front of Cummins and sat back, watching for a reaction.

The calm grey eyes surveyed each scene for a few brief seconds. Cummins's pinprick pupils neither dilated nor contracted and not a muscle in his face moved until he raised his head to look back at Greenaway with a mildly quizzical expression.

"What has this got to do with me?" he said.

"Would you like to explain your whereabouts on those evenings?" Greenaway asked.

– · –

Lil sat at the table, the paper spread out before her.

"Duch," she said, as the door opened, "read this."

Duchess had been picking up some shopping from the market on Portobello Road. She put her basket down on the table and leaned over her companion's shoulder to see the headlines.

BLACKOUT RIPPER STRIKES AGAIN!
TWO MORE DEAD IN VALENTINE'S EVE MASSACRE

Her eyes ran further down the page, taking in the details and their implications.

"Oh my godfathers," she murmured.

"Yeah," said Lil. "Thursday night. You was right, I never should have gone out."

"He was here," Duch said. "Right here in Paddington."

"Not only that," Lil put a forefinger down on a photograph of a cross-looking woman wearing her fair hair up a chignon, "but I only just missed him. This lady was out on Praed Street, opposite the station. I said hello to her just before I come home."

"You never?"

"I did," Lil took Duch's arm, pulled her down on the chair beside her. "I said there was nothing doing out there, I told her to go home." Her eyes were filled with horror. "If only she had. If only she had. Oh my gawd, Duch – what have I done?"

Duch blinked out the memory of Madame Arcana with her hand on her arm saying more or less exactly the same thing to her on Thursday morning.

"What you talking about?" she said instead. "You ain't done nothing. You had a lucky escape, right enough, but you can't blame yourself for what happened to her. It was her bad luck, not yours."

Lil shook her head. "No, Duch, you don't understand. I was so angry that night. Angry with Tom, angry with you, angry with the whole bleedin' world. I made a dare with him – if he was there, he should come out and show his face." She glanced down at the newspaper then back at Duch. "I was high on them bennies, like you said, they turn me into a monster." Tears dropped out of the corners of her eyes, bounced in bright sparkles down her cheeks. "I brought this on her, Duch. I dared the Devil – but he got her instead."

"Oh, my darling," Duch took the sobbing Lil into her arms. She closed her eyes, feeling tears of her own prickling behind her lids. She knew it now. The time had finally come to say goodbye to her beautiful golden girl.

– • –

It seemed like Cummins had been talking for hours, etching out a fictitious account of his activities between Sunday night and the early hours of Friday morning. Sheeney was dutifully taking it all down.

"I've never been to a flat near Tottenham Court Road," he was saying. "I don't know Gosfield Street at all. Had I ever been there, I'm sure I would have remembered it. And I've never been with any woman in any flat in Sussex Gardens. I mean, I know the place, but . . ."

He frowned, patting at his shirt pocket for his cigarettes.

"Oh," said Greenaway, "how *remiss* of me. You want a smoke, don't you?"

Cummins put back what Greenaway could see was a packet of Craven A.

"Don't mind if I do," he said. "Getting pretty low on stocks in here."

"I'm sure you'll find a way around that," said Greenaway, offering his case. Cummins made his selection with his left hand, smiled as the detective lit him up.

"What was I saying?" He scratched his head, loosening an unruly lock from his carefully combed tonsure.

"You don't have to make a statement," Greenaway stared hard into the airman's eyes. "Anything you say may be taken down and submitted in evidence against you."

Cummins's pupils dilated by minuscule amounts as he waved the left hand that held the cigarette. "But I want to give an account of all my movements," he said. "I do know Wardour Street, I went to a flat somewhere around there with a blonde woman on Monday night, I already said as much. But I've never been in any other flat in the area with any other women."

Not entirely fictitious then, Greenaway realised. Cummins had also mentioned his friend Felix Simpson accompanying him on his rounds of Piccadilly and the blonde woman they met on Monday would be Lil's friend from the hairdresser's. Cummins was weaving fact with fiction, so as better to convince himself of the tale he was spinning. Perhaps the reason he remained so calm was that while he was talking, he actually believed it was the truth.

Greenaway went back into his murder bag. He took out the silver cigarette case and the wristwatch with the Elastoplast stuck to it.

"That cigarette case isn't mine," said Cummins immediately.

"And the watch?" Greenaway saw Herbert Coles in his mind's eye again.

"That isn't mine either," Cummins protested. "But both of those things were taken from the case of the gas mask that I had with me at West End Central Police Station." He was starting to look bored with the conversation now and Greenaway could see just how easily his phoney charm could curdle. "The one that wasn't mine. You said you'd found the other fellow," Cummins went on. "It's him you want to ask about those."

Greenaway looked down under the table that separated

them. When he looked up, it was his turn to smile at the man who sat across from him.

"Those your RAF-issue boots?" he asked.

"Yes," said Cummins, "naturally."

"Would you mind taking them off, please?"

Cummins rolled his eyes, stubbed his cigarette out in a final petulant gesture. Then he did as he was told, removing his boots and sliding them across the table.

"Thank you," said Greenaway, lifting them upside down and showing the soles to Sheeney. "What d'you reckon?" he asked his colleague.

"They look brand new," said Sheeney.

"Don't they just?" Greenaway agreed, returning to his murder bag for one last item.

"You don't think much of your corporal, do you, Cummins?" he asked. "He's an old man, ain't he? Don't see too much. That's how come it was so easy for you to pull the wool over, on your little trips up and down that fire escape. Thing is, he don't think all that much of you, neither. Which is how come he let me take a rummage through your billet Thursday morning, while you was on parade. And look what I found in your bin."

He took out the pair of boot soles that Forensics had examined, placed them over the top of the brand new pair attached to Cummins's boots.

"Look at that," he said to Sheeney.

"A perfect fit," the Detective Sergeant agreed.

"And what does that prove, exactly?" Cummins patted around his top pocket again. This time, Greenaway didn't come to his aid.

"That you wanted to get rid of these in a hurry, probably because you read in the newspaper that we had found a footprint in that air-raid shelter in Montagu Place. I think you also realised that all that dust and rubble that had got into the tread might be traceable to all that dust and rubble you walked over while you was in there. But what I don't think you did take into account was that it got into your gas mask and all—" Greenaway began to slowly count his fingers, "one, two, three, four . . . five whole days before you reckon you lost it at a party." He raised his eyebrows. "Anything you want to add?" he asked Cummins.

A shrug was all he was offered in return.

"We'll take these, then," said Greenaway, bagging up the boots.

"And you take these," Sheeney handed across a pair of prison-issue shoes that the Governor had provided before the interview.

Greenaway put back the cigarette case and the watch, cleared away the photographs.

"As a result of enquiries I have made," he told the prisoner, "you will be brought up at Bow Street Police Court on Monday morning and charged with murder."

Cummins looked mildly puzzled. "How many did you say again?" he asked.

"Four," said Greenaway, getting to his feet. "I don't somehow take you for a religious man, Cummins. But make the most of your day of rest, won't you?"

Cummins had nothing else to say.

– • –

"Listen," said Duch, "I've been doing a lot of thinking since Thursday night myself. All this just ain't fair on you, Lil. You don't need this life no more."

"But," Lil said and then hiccupped, "what else am I s'posed to do with meself? Tom ain't coming back for me, I can see that now. And I don't know no other way."

"I told you right at the start of our acquaintance," said Duch, "when we got enough money, you take your cut and set yourself up in business. Get yourself that little dress shop you was after. I've had a good look at our bank balance and, well—" she smiled hopefully, "there's enough in there now. You want to get out and give it a go?"

Lil's mouth fell open. She didn't know what to say.

"Here," Duch handed her a clean hanky. "Think about it, love. Only don't take too long about it."

Lil nodded solemnly. Then a smile crossed her face like a flash of sunlight.

"Ask the tea leaves for me, will you, Duch?"

Duchess stood up, shaking her head affectionately, turned on the radiogram and struck a match to boil the kettle.

"*Here is the news,*" the announcer's voice crackled into the room, "*for six o'clock on Saturday, the fourteenth of February . . .*"

"I'll miss your tea, you know," said Lil. "No one makes a cuppa like you do, Duch."

"You want to watch me sometime," said Duch, blowing out the match. "You might learn something."

"All right," Lil got to her feet. "Show me how you do it."

Neither of them listened much to the announcer as he intoned grave tidings about the imminent fall of Singapore. It wasn't until they had settled down with their cups in front of them that he finally managed to catch their attention.

"*. . . London and Scotland Yard announced today they have charged a man with the murders of four women which took place in the capital over the past week.*"

The two women stared at each other.

"Your old boyfriend," Lil spoke first. "That copper – he's got the bastard."

"*. . . the suspect has been remanded in custody at Brixton Prison to face magistrates on Monday morning . . .*" the announcer went on.

"So he has," said Duch, putting her cup back down in its saucer. "I knew he would."

Lil looked down at her own cup. "Did you see it in the leaves?" she asked.

"No." Duch's gaze went right through her companion, as for a moment she was drawn back to a different room in a different time, the air thick with the smell of blood and spilt perfume, an ominous dark lump on the bed in front of her. "I saw it when he solved his first murder, love," she said. "My Ted don't ever give up."

"Well," said Lil brightly, "this changes fings, don't it? I could be back on the bash tomorrow . . ."

"Don't you dare!" Duch's complexion turned white.

"Your face!" Lil said, breaking into a wild peal of laughter, relief tinged with hysteria. "Don't worry Duch, I'm only pullin' your leg. I've made up me mind now. I won't let you down. Still," her smile evaporated. "Thank God that's over, eh? Thank God they got him behind bars, where he belongs."

But the Duchess continued to stare into the middle distance, like an oracle ready to impart a vision. "It ain't over, Lil," she said, her voice sounding strangely emotionless. "That's just it, love. It ain't ever gonna be over. There's another one coming up, coming up right behind him . . ."

PART TWO

PEG O' MY HEART

16

AIN'T MISBEHAVIN'

Saturday, 14 February 1942

Over the rooftops, along the wide stretch of the Thames, rolling inky-black without the moon, across the scaffolding that encased the building works of the new Waterloo Bridge, down to the Port of London and north again to the other side of the city, in Bethnal Green, another woman waited.

Frances Feld tried not to keep looking up at the clock as she stood at the stove, stirring the pot. Seven chairs around her kitchen table, but only two places set for supper. Her husband was working lates this week, worked all the hours God sent. Her children had been evacuated, were all living on a farm, safe in the Welsh countryside – all except for one.

Her eldest, Bobby, couldn't take to the outdoor life. Kept running away and finding new routes back to the bomb-cratered mess of the East End, hitching rides with lorry drivers and sleeping in hedges. Did it so many times that her husband waved his hands in despair and told her: "Let him stay. He's in God's hands."

It was an argument she should have tried harder to win, she always thought at moments like this, remembered lines that revolved around her head like a stuck groove in a record. When she heard a tapping at the front door, her heart jolted.

"Bobby?" she said, as she turned off the gas ring, wiped her hands and headed up the hallway. Even though her head told her that the missing member of her household would simply have let himself in.

The face on the other side of the door was not one she had been expecting to see. It was framed dramatically in a red head-scarf, swept up and twisted in the manner of a turban. Beneath that, eyebrows plucked into crescents, arched over a pair of heavily made-up eyes, a countenance powdered and rouged in the imitation of youth and stardom, with red lips twitching up into an insouciant smile beside a painted-on beauty spot. A full-length rabbit fur coat swirled down to a pair of stockinged ankles set atop plum-coloured high-heeled shoes, a thin sliver of gold snaking around the left one.

"Mother of God," said Frances, her hand involuntarily flying to the cross around her neck. "Margaret."

"It's Peggy, these days, if you don't mind," replied her sister, her smile deepening. "Aren't you going to invite me in, dear?"

– • –

Not far around the terrace corner, beyond the craters that had been made of similar streets, on the lower reaches of Brick Lane, the cause of Frances's anxiety stood leaning on a broom in the corner of Soapy Larry Spielman's barbershop. Bobby Feld should have been home an hour ago. The blackout had gone down with the last dregs of the light at a quarter-past five, the sign on the door turned around to read: *Closed*. But still the big, black-framed, square-faced clock that hung above Bobby's head clicked away, unheeded by either himself, the man taking up the chair space, Soapy, who attended to him, or the figures who sat by the table near the window playing Klobbiotsch.

Bobby loved it in Soapy's. It was warm and smelt of good things: soap and leather, spices and musk – not like home, which reeked of cabbages and laundry on the boil. Here, the radio was always on, tuned to a station that played the best sounds. Negro Americans singing in a secret language Bobby longed to decipher, big-band swing laced with bittersweet traces of his father's favourite old records, of the singing in the synagogue that he infrequently attended, being a boy split between two worlds.

He loved watching Soapy practise his art to these soundtracks, the whole ritual of the hot towels and tongs, the foaming up of the soap with shaving brushes, the beautiful, pearl-handled razor the barber wielded with such delicate skill, the cologne and the Brilliantine that shined his customers up until they fairly sparkled.

But even that was not the main attraction. The main attraction were the customers – men who were free to stroll in and have their grooming attended to in the middle of the day, when Bobby's old man would either have been at work for six hours already, or round about now, when he would just be setting off. Men who could while away a whole afternoon just talking – and how. They had their own secret language, too.

The man in the chair was Moishe Abraham, known hereabouts as Bluebell. Not because he had the delicacy of spring's first bloom – far from it: Bluebell was a broad, thickset man with the neck of a bull and hair the colour of a raven's wing, a mass of curls close-cropped and glinting with pomade. He dressed in suits that went against all the fabric regulations – double-breasted, chalk-striped, with two-inch turn-ups at the bottom of the generously cut trousers. It was the shirts he customarily wore, in vivid shades of sapphire, augmented with silk ties and handkerchiefs, which were the source of Moishe's moniker. Bluebell smoked even as Soapy worked and when he went to retrieve a cigar from between the folds of pristine white towelling, gold rings caught the light.

The two men sitting by the window had their own names, too. The tall, thin man with the pencil moustache who was dealing the cards might be Raymond Parnell to his mother, but at Soapy's they called him Maestro. Sat across from him was the Bear – a logical name, considering Bobby would judge him to be about the size of one. He had a hard face set about with scars, wore modest suits of brown or black flannel and hardly spoke a word. He didn't have to – one glance from those amber slits of eyes that glittered beneath his protuberant forehead and bristling dark brows would be enough to silence a room. Those ursine eyes flicked upwards every so often, towards the door, over at Bluebell and back again. When his left arm moved forwards and his jacket slid open, Bobby caught a glimpse of the holster strapped under his armpit. Caught it and quickly looked away.

It was a gun that had first brought Bobby to Soapy's attention. A pistol he and Barney Newbiggin found in the bombsite on Swedenborg Gardens, back in the summer. Barney claimed it was a Luger, dropped by a German pilot. But he wouldn't give Bobby a good enough look to see for sure, had made off with it on his long whippet's legs too fast for Bobby to follow. Barney had made it as far as here before Bobby caught up with him, found him showing his bounty off to a gaggle of younger kids just outside Soapy's. The fight that ensued was loud enough to attract the barber's attention.

Soapy knew more about guns than Barney, that much was soon evident. It wasn't a Luger, it was a Colt .45, dropped by a Yank, most likely. It was, however, half loaded and could have blown their stupid heads off. As Soapy admonished them, twisting a lughole in each hand for emphasis, Bobby had stared at the gold ring in the barber's left ear, the tendrils of colour he could see escaping down his arms from where his shirtsleeves were rolled up. Bobby was fascinated – he had always been taught that such things were the marks of Cain. The sharp widow's peak, badger-striped grey hair and lines on Soapy's forehead all indicated that he was older even than Bobby's father, but he didn't much act like it.

After that day, Bobby kept coming back to stare into the barbershop, until Soapy took pity and let him in. He didn't give the gun back, but he did consider that maybe there were a few things Bobby could do for him that would "keep him out of bother" instead.

As far as his mother was concerned, Bobby was learning a trade on the weekends and evenings he spent at Soapy's. And so he was. He was learning the sorts of things Frances was most afraid of him ever finding out.

"Boychick," said Bluebell, clicking his fingers in Bobby's direction. "You want to hear a story? I ever tell you about how Sammy's luck ran out?"

– • –

Despite the pitch darkness of the evening, Frances cast an anxious glance up and down the street before she stood back and allowed entry. Once the door was closed, she ushered her visitor straight into the sitting room.

"Well, now," she said, "so you've found me. What is it that you want from me, Margaret?"

For a long minute, her sister didn't answer. Instead, her hazel eyes scanned appraisingly the modest room, taking in all the familiar hallmarks of Frances's endeavours – the neatly swept hearth, the afghan she would have knitted and the rug she would have woven, the cross on the wall and the pictures of her favourite saints, St Joseph and St Jude, the devotion to the latter no doubt inspired in no small part by herself. The things that weren't so familiar to her. That strangely shaped seven-branched candlestick in the middle of the mantelpiece: something to do with the husband, Margaret surmised.

The sisters had originally come over from Donegal to train as nurses. Frances, who had a deft brain and the ability to concentrate, had done well, steadily climbing the ladder of midwifery and then marrying a doctor. Fate had a different path mapped out for Margaret.

Margaret fixed a smile to her red lips. "Can I not drop by and see how my nieces and nephews are doing from time to time? Here, I've bought them some presents."

From under the folds of her voluminous coat, she retrieved a parcel she had tucked beneath her arm. "It's nothing much, just a few dollies for the girls and comics for the boys – you know, the sort of things they enjoy at that age. Plus, a little something for yourselves." She winked. "It's all legit, I promise."

Frances eyed the brown-papered lump as if it were an unexploded bomb and made no motion to take it. "You're doing all right for yourself these days, then?" she said.

– • –

Sammy Lehmann was the subject of a lot of the stories spun in Soapy's. Bobby had never met him, on account of the fact his liberty had been curtailed back in the summer of 1940. Sammy had been "sent down" by his nemesis from the Flying Squad, a man referred to as "that bastard Greenaway". But it was clear that up until then Sammy had been the leader of these men.

Bluebell puffed on his cigar, exhaled with satisfaction, and settled down to the telling. "There was a tickle he'd been perfecting since the blackout come in," he rolled his eyes to the ceiling, "which, might I say, was God's gift to the graft. No more lights blazing all night long, everything nicely tucked away behind the curtains. All a man like Sammy had to do in them days was wait 'til the coast was clear, go through the locks and have a shufti through all the tomfoolery he could unload. 'Course, these jewellers got wise after a while, started using a safe at night. But they weren't safe for long, not with Sammy around. He'd just wait for them to open up of a morning and have it away there and then."

Anticipating his customer's movements, Soapy withdrew his razor from Bluebell's cheek as the narrator's laugh cracked through the shop like a Tommy gun.

"What Sammy worked out was this," Bluebell went on. "You need two drags, two drivers, one block and tackle. One motor comes up the pavement, right up the front door, so no one in the shop can get out. The other one comes straight up the window, does out the glass with a sledgehammer, Sammy on the running board leans in for the grab and boom! You're off. Meanwhile, the other car pulls out into the road and blocks it off before the bogeys can get the scream on.

"Couple of jobs like this go off like clockwork. Sammy finesses it still further – he's a craftsman, ain't he? Instead of getting out of the motor, he finds one with a sunroof, so's he can pop up through that and have the windows and the trays all out in one fell swoop. So simple, it's beautiful. One of the boys even done him some special plates, for the benefit of that bastard Greenaway – MUG 999 they read."

Bluebell took another puff, savouring the chuckles this last detail provoked, even from those who had heard it many times before.

"Greenaway's as riled as a hornet at a picnic, but there's nishte he can do about it. Every time he pulls Sammy in and puts him on parade, no one's ever seen his handsome boat before – a man should be so lucky.

"But then, boychick, then the odds turn against him. He's been casing this joint in Conduit Street. Has a lovely little sports Alvis picked up from outside the Bath Club and a Bentley to bring up the rear, all beautifully ringed and repainted." Bluebell sighed and shook his head, regretful, allowed Soapy to douse his newly shorn countenance with cologne and then continued.

"The drag comes up Bond Street like planned, turns the corner and boom! Headfirst into a flatfoot. They swerve away from him, get up to the window, Sammy stands up with the sledgehammer – and the drag stalls dead. By now, the bogey's blown his whistle and there's a whole stampede of honest citizenry swarming towards them.

"Sammy makes for the Bentley but the bogey's already there. He throws his truncheon through the windshield; it rains down with glass and what do you know – that car stalls and all. Sammy does the only thing he can do – he legs it. All the way over Bond Street and down Bruton Street he goes, half of London on his tail. First doorway he finds, he's in and up the stairs, don't stop 'til he's on the roof. He takes a quick shufti and sees a hundred faces staring up at him from the street, all shouting: 'There he is, officer!'"

Leaning forwards in his seat, Bluebell went through the motions of his story like he was performing it on stage.

"Still Sammy don't give up," he said, drawing his arms wide. "He springs onto the next roof, nonchalant as you like, disappears down their stairs and out the back – only to find Lily Law waiting there in the doorway. Thinking on his feet, he points behind him and says: 'Quick, officer! He's in here!'"

Bear slapped his knee, shaking his head with silent mirth.

"Trouble was," Bluebell went on, "the half of London what had already seen him go up, calls back like bleedin' panto: 'Oh no he isn't! That's him!' And that was poor Sammy, bang to rights. The end of a beautiful caper."

Bluebell gave Bobby a rueful smile, then examined himself in the mirror Soapy proffered, nodded his satisfaction and stood up. This was Bobby's cue to remove the apron and rub down the pinstriped shoulders with a clothes brush.

"Two years in the Moor he got," Bluebell went on. "You know what he's doing in there?"

Bobby shook his head.

"He's the prison barber!" Bluebell exploded into laughter again, clapping Bobby round the shoulders. "As he was taught by Soapy hisself. So you watch out, my son. You never know where all this could lead you."

– • –

Margaret shrugged, put the parcel down on the nearest chair. "As you can see," she said, stroking the sleeve of her coat.

Then her expression changed, the sardonic mask slipped and a look of pleading came into her eyes, softening her features, reminding Frances for just one second of the girl her sister had been, tickling trout in the burn under Muckish mountain, mud on her face and tangles in her hair.

"Francie," Margaret said, "I know it's asking a lot, but could I not just say hello to them?"

Frances stiffened, the shutters clanging down on her memories.

"There's no point," she said, wondering if for once, Bobby's absence counted as a blessing. "They're not here. They're on a farm in Wales, out of harm's way. Do you think I would let my children stay here, with the bombs raining down on them every single night?"

It was clear from Margaret's face that the finer details of motherhood and responsibility had not once crossed her mind.

Aware that at any moment, the one component of this white lie that could cause its undoing could present himself and expose her falsehood, Frances moved in for the kill. "Now, we made a deal long ago and it was for everyone's sake that we did. If there's nothing more I can help you with, then you'd best be on your way."

She was only a thin, slight willow of a woman, but at that moment Frances stood as hard and unbending as steel. Margaret knew that it was better not to argue. Frances held the winning cards in this hand of the game and maybe she always would.

On the doorstep, Frances pushed the parcel back into Margaret's arms. "And you can take this with you," she said, shutting the door before there was a chance to say another word.

– • –

Bobby held tightly to the coin Bluebell had given him as he was leaving, clasped it in the centre of his fist as he ran all the way home. Half a crown! It was imperative that he kept this safe from the disapproving eyes of his parents.

He didn't get back soon enough to glimpse the departing figure in the fur coat. But when he reached his front doorstep, he found a parcel sitting there, wrapped in brown paper and tied up with string. Lifting it up curiously, Bobby breathed in the scent of violets.

17

JEEPERS CREEPERS

Monday, 16 February 1942

"What kind of a man is he?"

Daphne Maitland looked down from the public gallery in Bow Street Magistrates' Court at the figure in the dock, this stranger who had snuffed out Evelyn's life as easily as another might swat a fly. His appearance came as a shock to her – here was neither the drooling demon of her imagination, nor an echo of the top-hatted wraith from Victorian Whitechapel that the papers had conjured. Instead, an ordinary, almost pleasant-looking young man with his wavy, golden hair, standing to attention in his RAF uniform while the magistrate read out the charges. It was only when he began to smile at the list of outrages he stood accused of that the question flew from her mouth.

Madame Arcana gripped her handbag tightly as she leant forward for a better look. "The Knight of Swords," she replied in a whisper, dark eyes glued to the same insouciant countenance, the smirk that danced beneath his pencil moustache.

Daphne's other neighbour gave a mirthless grunt. "He don't exactly look the part, do he?" The Duchess put her hand over Daphne's and gave it a squeeze. Daphne did her best to return a smile. They had been so kind to her, Miss Moyes and her circle, just as Mr Swaffer had predicted. It had given her the courage to come here, knowing that her new friends would be with her; there was no one from her own circle she could possibly have asked. Though, she was surprised just how familiar her new friends had been with the processes of a court – when to arrive, where to go and what to do – not to mention the number of other women they knew who had all turned up with the same purpose in mind: of seeing a Ripper, if not in chains, then held captive at least.

"But I s'pose he knows what he's doing," Duchess nodded down towards Greenaway as the detective was called to take the stand.

– • –

Placing his hand on the Bible, Greenaway swore his oath, eyes travelling around the courtroom. Aside from the officials, police officers and journalists present, Cummins's audience consisted of women. Up in the gallery, the amassed ladies of the parish were doing their best to make their grievances palpable, staring down all the curses known to them with their glittering eyes. Behind the dock where Cummins stood sat two others whose lives had been ruined by the man: his wife, Marjorie, and her sister, Freda Stevens – though the rigid pose of the former and the scowling visage of the latter did not radiate hatred like the others – with them, it was more like fear.

Greenaway had visited these two women the previous day in the flat they shared in Barnes. He'd been hoping to discover something more about the airman's motivations, work out how he had successfully kept his murderous impulses under wraps for so long. He had certainly hidden his domestic situation well, in an unremarkable street between the common and the river that even the Luftwaffe seemed to have overlooked.

Marjorie Cummins was a good-looking woman, as attested by the photo found in her husband's wallet. The thick, almost black hair which clouded around her shoulders in that image was now hoisted up into a bun, but her arresting, pale-blue eyes needed no making up, despite the puffy redness of the skin around them. She dressed demurely, in a tweed suit that did not disguise the elegance of her long legs and slim ankles.

Cummins had got himself a trophy wife all right, and then had been content to leave her on the shelf, along with all the other items in the overstuffed front room that seemed to chime with his conceited view of himself: the claret leather armchair on which Marjorie bade Greenaway sit; the oil painting of aircraft ascending over cornfields that hung inside a rococo frame worth more than its contents; the abundance of brass knick-knacks and the grandfather clock in the corner that Greenaway wouldn't have minded running past Stolen Property.

But no doubt it was Marjorie who had paid for all these things. She worked as an assistant to a theatre producer, earning a decent wage, though she still had need to take a lodger, in the stout, plain form of her sister, who sat on the sofa, smoking and sizing up Greenaway with eyes that displayed all of the guile her sibling lacked. Looks and sense must have been doled out straight down the middle of that family, he thought.

Marjorie went through the motions of making him some tea, though most of it was in the saucer by the time her trembling hand had passed it across. Then she shrank back onto her end of the sofa as if trying to disappear into the fabric, wringing her hands while she hesitatingly sketched out a life of marital bliss with her heroic other half. That she refused to believe the charges was only natural – what woman would want to admit she had been married to such a man? But it was the reason she clung to that rang false – that her beloved would never do anything that could jeopardise his chances of qualifying as a pilot. That was why, she insisted, Gordon had refused to come home during the previous week – he wanted to be sure to be back in his billet each evening at a decent hour, to be well rested for the next day's training.

Throughout the interview, Freda leaned over to pat Marjorie's shoulder each time her voice started to break, reminding her that she didn't have to answer if she didn't want to, while at the same time, flashing Greenaway knowing glances. When it became clear there was nothing else he could learn from Marjorie, it was Freda who stood up to show Greenaway out, taking her cigarette with her and pointedly closing the door on the tragedy behind them.

In the hallway, she spoke. "As my sister told you, we've not seen Gordon since Sunday," she said, keeping her voice low. "And that was his first visit home since he got his new billet."

"Which was Monday, the second of February," Greenaway said, making a note of it. The date the Corporal had said Cummins arrived at Abbey Lodge.

"That's right." Freda curled her upper lip. Though she shared the same well-modulated tones as Marjorie, Greenaway could imagine her language soon turning earthier. "I'm afraid I do count the days, Chief Inspector. He came for lunch so he could cadge some more money out of her. I didn't catch the full performance; I only came in at about five o'clock myself, by which time I was hoping he'd be gone. They were standing where we are now and she had her hand in her purse, as usual."

"You're not fond of your brother-in-law, I take it?" Greenaway enquired.

Freda exhaled smoke. "I don't know how I came by such a word, but our Gordon is what you would probably call a ponce," she said. "He's taken every penny Marjorie earns and has given her absolutely nothing in return."

Her eyes travelled from Greenaway's to rest on a framed poster of one of her sister's employer's productions. One that depicted the silhouette of a man in a top hat and a stylised drawing of flickering flame emitting zig-zagged yellow rays. The words GAS LIGHT fell in a diagonal line between the two images, trailing a red drop-shadow.

"You would have thought," she said, "that with all her education, she might have seen through a rank poseur like him. But no," she stubbed her cigarette out with some force in a brass ashtray on the telephone table. "As you can see by her line of work, Marjorie is a cursed romantic. Gordon swept her off her feet at an air display on Empire Day in 1936, badgered her to marry him for seven months and took off again the moment the ring was on her finger. No, I never did like him much."

"All the same, this must have come as a shock to you?" Greenaway asked.

Freda looked away from the poster and down at the floor. "Of course it did, Chief Inspector. However much I detested Gordon and the effect he had on my sister, I never thought him capable of such . . ." She looked back up at him. "Well, if it is true, what you say."

"Believe me," Greenaway told her, "I wouldn't be here if it wasn't. I'll be honest with you, Miss Stevens. I've never worked a case like this before. I mean, I've done my time in the navy and on the Flying Squad, I thought I'd seen every kind of crook there was to know. But not like him. It keeps me up at night trying to work out what kind of a man he really is."

Freda lit another cigarette. "One who is different things to different people, I suppose," she offered. "Not so very far from an actor, when you think about it."

"And did you ever see him acting violently towards your sister?" Greenaway asked.

Freda went silent, weighing up her response, or perhaps, the reflection it would have on the woman silently weeping in the next room. "No," she eventually said, looking away.

– • –

Freda didn't look at Greenaway as he detailed to the magistrate how he had charged Cummins at Brixton and submitted his formal application that the prisoner be remanded without bail. To the end of his careful testimony, she kept her eyes on the magistrate, who peered above his half-moon spectacles at the man in the dock.

"How do you plead?" he asked the accused.

Cummins smiled back at him. "Not guilty."

– • –

Before Greenaway was halfway across the lobby, he felt a hand on his arm.

"You sure you got the right man, Ted?" the Duchess

demanded. "Only that little ponce up there didn't look like much to me. We want to know if it's safe for us to go out at night. That's really him, is it?"

Greenaway looked at her, and the women grouped around her, all batting their painted lashes at him. Amongst them was a face that didn't belong, though it only took him a second to place the connection. Lady Daphne Maitland was the woman Swaffer had brought in to see him, a friend of Evelyn Bourne, who had been able to identify the green propelling pencil found in Cummins's bin as the type the lonely chemist habitually carried around with her.

"It's him. You got my word on it," he said, his eyes lingering on Lady Daphne.

"Strange company you're keeping, ma'am," he added, just as the Assistant Commissioner passed close enough to hear the exchange.

"DCI Greenaway," he said. "A word."

– • –

"Got a bollocking for that," Greenaway explained to Swaffer later in the bar of the *Entre Nous*. "Apparently, reassuring your snout, or should I say snouts, outside a magistrates' court that we had the right man in custody could be construed by the gentlemen of the press as giving my permission to go out soliciting."

Swaffer raised a hand to his heart in mock horror. "Perish the thought!" he said.

"Yeah, and perish the thought of getting any credit for taking a madman off the streets," Greenaway lifted his glass, noting the lack of liquid inside with surprise.

"Allow me," Swaffer caught the barman's eye.

Greenaway's countenance radiated ill-humour. Swaffer had previous experience of the DCI in his cups and decided the judicious imparting of information might raise his spirits more effectively than the fresh glass of stout being placed on the beer mat in front of him.

"I've done some more digging," he said, handing the barman some coins. "Shall we retire to my table?" Greenaway shrugged, but followed Swaffer to his usual lugubrious corner and watched him pull out his notebook, extracting several sheets to scribble on as he talked, to translate his shorthand into names and numbers.

"Miss Stevens' summation of events to you seems accurate," Swaffer said. "When Cummins was first married he was stationed with the Marine Aircraft Experimental Establishment at Felixtowe in Suffolk. The unit moved to Scotland in 1936 and he was with them for a further three years, during which time he earned himself the nickname 'the Count'—" Swaffer's eyebrows rose as he peered over the top of his pad, "owing to the decadent lifestyle he maintained, with the help of the local ladies. In the October of 1939, he transferred as a rigger to 600 Squadron at Helensburgh, Dumbartonshire, where not only did his carnal escapades continue apace, but his rendering of those exploits to the other cadets earned him a promotion – at Helensburgh, they called him 'the Duke'."

Greenaway swallowed half a pint in one gulp. "Go on," he said, wiping his mouth.

"It seems our illustrious braggart began to believe his own press," Swaffer continued. "By the time he was posted to Colerne near Bath in 1941, he was referring to himself as the Honourable Gordon Cummins. I spoke to a friend of his there, Flight Lieutenant Alfred Peters," Swaffer scribbled the name and a telephone number down, "who is the PR man for the RAF in Wiltshire. He believed Cummins to be the son of a peer. He was always flush, drank only the most expensive Canadian rye whisky and was forever boasting of the swathe he was cutting through the ladies of Bath."

"What, literally?" Greenaway's eyes narrowed.

"Sorry, unfortunate turn of phrase." Swaffer hastily returned to his notes. "But here's where we get the measure of his audacity. Cummins was billeted off-barracks in Colerne and made himself at home with the farmer, a man appropriately named Fields, who seems to have a very accommodating wife. The Honourable Cummins became a bit of a celebrity at the local pub, thanks in part to his generosity, and also because he took to riding down there on one of the farmer's horses. To the manor born, indeed – he even had Lieutenant Peters's wife doing his laundry for him. His mastery of illusion only really started to crumble when he was transferred to Predannack in November 1941."

"Yeah?" Swaffer detected a glint of interest return to Greenaway's eyes. "In what way?"

"Cummins's charms didn't wash quite so well down in Cornwall," Swaffer reported. "The men at this posting apparently found his ceaseless boasting a bore, so he tried to find other ways to appeal to them. He became good friends with the landlady of the Blue Peter club in Falmouth, who gave him a part-time job behind the bar and access to her flat above it. It all went sour when she caught him serving free drinks to the rest of his squadron. After she gave him the boot, she realised a lot of her jewellery had gone missing. She called the police and Cummins was investigated, but unfortunately they couldn't prove anything. From there, Cummins requested a transfer to train as a pilot, he passed the selection and was transferred to Regent's Park, as you know."

Greenaway nodded slowly, regarding the journalist with narrowed eyes through the veil of smoke from their cigarettes.

"Well," he said, "I have to commend the industry of the press. That'll make a good scoop for you when he goes down. Your friends at the Ministry help you with that?"

Ignoring the jibe, Swaffer pushed his annotations across the table. "These are the names and numbers of everyone I've spoken to so far. I'm sure they can be of further use to you." He tapped the side of Greenaway's empty glass. "Another?"

"In a minute." Greenaway folded the paper in his right hand and tucked it away in his pocket. He leant across the table, his voice a low rumble. "There's a few other things I want to know before I go on drinking with you. First off, what's Lady Daphne doing mixing with your snouts?"

"Daphne Maitland?" said Swaffer. "But I told you. I sent her to Miss Moyes to help her through the trauma of losing her friend."

"What?" Greenaway looked incredulous. "They done a séance for her, did they?"

Swaffer shook his head. "No, dear boy, you misunderstand. There are many other strands to Miss Moyes's work and charity is the chief of them. Since the Blitz began she has been finding refuges for women and children made homeless, as well as providing clothes, food and comfort for them. It is a commitment that requires many kinds of skills, one of which is the production of pamphlets each week for publicity. Daphne knows how to write, and how to use a printing press. She is also very useful at helping to distribute these pamphlets and knowing into which hands to put them to achieve more funding. In helping others, she helps herself, do you see?"

Greenaway looked slightly mollified by Swaffer's speech, but he hadn't finished yet. "What about the other one?" he said. "You know, the one that got me into trouble with the AC this morning? The one who goes all the way back to Dover Street." He stared at Swaffer meaningfully. "How much do you know about her?"

"You mean the Duchess, as she is known colloquially?" Swaffer said.

"You don't know her real name, then?"

The journalist shrugged, a plume of ash dropping from his cigarette, "I don't believe she has ever formally introduced herself. Again, Miss Moyes is the connection and this time it is with the esoteric that our shared interests lie. Which, of course, would be of no interest to you."

"I didn't see her blonde friend at the arraignment," said Greenaway. "What's happened to her?"

"I believe she has taken early retirement," replied Swaffer, "in order to take up dressmaking. Which is one less for your Assistant Commissioner to worry about . . ."

Greenaway began to rub at his temples. "All right," he said. "Enough. Go and get me another pint."

18

OH, LADY BE GOOD

Tuesday, 17 February 1942

Peggy Richards did not care to read the details of the fall of Singapore that spread across the front pages of the paper. She had already sat through Churchill's speech about it on the wireless Sunday night, but only because her old man had wanted to listen. Where Peggy came from, the Prime Minister was not regarded in quite the same light as he was here, and the memories stirred by the sound of his portentous drone flickered like ghosts around the edges of her mind.

"What's up with you?" Charlie had asked her.

Peggy looked around their room as if waking from a dream, no longer pleased with the Woolworths' prints she'd arranged around the fireplace, the highly polished mirror or the vases of fake flowers she had ornamented the mantelpiece with. Now all she saw were the damp patches coming through the walls, the shabby, mismatched patchwork of cut-offs that made up the carpet. The laundry strung across the fire, shirt collars, string vests and baggy underpants drooping mournfully towards the grate were spectres of the time she had been living here, playing the housewife in a two-room flat in Deptford.

She didn't have the words to explain it to him, how this life she had been happy with for the past two years had all come crashing down on her last Saturday night, leaving her feeling rootless and alone, a restless shade of herself.

"I don't know," she finally replied. "Maybe I've a touch of indigestion."

Charlie looked hard at her, his eyes narrowing for a second. "Hmmm," he grunted through his teeth and the stem of his pipe, before retreating back behind his Sunday paper with a loud rustling of pages. Peggy felt the word "sorry" rising to her lips, but bit it back down. Hadn't she learned anything? It was no good giving in to sentiment now. Look where it had got her before . . .

Which was how she came to find herself now, on a tube train heading west through the remains of Tuesday night, her best possessions on her back, the bank book, ID card, ration book, coupons and purse in her handbag all she dared take with her.

Someone had left behind a copy of the *Daily Herald* on her seat and she began to flick through it, mainly to avoid thinking than to actually learn more about Singapore or anything else to do with it. Until she came to a photograph of a woman – a marcel-waved blonde, looking over her shoulder and smiling out of a carefully lit studio pose. Peggy's eyes moved across to the headline: MAN CHARGED WITH FOUR MURDERS.

It had been a while since Peggy had last worked in the West End and, as she drank in the dreadful details of the story, a force of habit deeply ingrained within her made her cross herself. Which in turn made her think of her sister, Frances.

Peggy folded the newspaper and put it back down on the seat, shaking her head to be rid of the vision of a door shutting in her face as the train rattled into Charing Cross. Stepping out onto the platform, she left Deptford Peggy Richards behind, the same way she had once shed a girl named Margaret McArthur on the shores of Donegal.

The woman who snapped smartly up the concourse on her plum-coloured heels, fur coat swishing down to her ankles, red turban and matching lipstick, was known by other names in the cluster of pubs around Villiers Street and the Strand, and to the Beat Bobbies who patrolled the streets around them. She might have been Kitten Prine, Kitty Wordsworth, Peggy Time or Shelley Coleridge, depending on how her mood took her. But tonight she didn't feel she fitted inside any of them either. Though she might have use of them shortly, her priority was to find some old pal who might help her get digs for the night.

The Hero of Waterloo was the sort of place she would likely run into someone she knew. The noise that greeted her as she stepped inside the saloon bar came as a comfort: the raucous plinking of a piano and the roar of song and chatter through the cigarette smoke afforded her the perfect cover to lose herself. A couple of pink gins would make the transformation complete.

As she ordered the first of them, she scanned the room, breaking down the mass of faces into individuals to be assessed for probabilities. Her eyes honed in on a woman standing along the counter from her, a redhead in a green suit, rabbit fur draped over her arm. The name Mina came back to Peggy, a woman of similar background to herself, although perhaps the three soldiers she was entertaining with her raucous laugh might have been introduced to someone different.

Peggy watched them as the barman placed her drink on

the mat before her and she handed him some coins. She had enough to keep herself going for a week or so, she judged, by which time she felt sure she would have sorted herself out with a place to live. Running into Mina seemed a good omen. Maybe she'd even have a room to spare herself, if the look of her suit, matching heels and freshly set hair was anything to go by. Raising her glass, Peggy caught the redhead's eye over the tam o'shantered heads of the three servicemen.

"Sláinte," she said, holding up her glass.

"Sláinte!" Mina's green eyes lit up in recognition. "Peggy! It is you, isn't it? By God, it's been some time. Won't you come and join us? Fellers," she turned to her companions, "meet an old pal of mine."

Peggy shook hands first with fair-haired Frankie, then broad-shouldered Dennis and finally, swarthy Joe, who held onto her hand a beat longer than the others, locking her into the gaze of his eyes, so dark as to look almost entirely black.

"Ma'am," he said, "you sure do remind me of a dame I used to know." The aroma of an exotic, musky aftershave surrounded him. He had a hooked nose that looked as if it had been broken in a fight and the unruly curls that sprouted from under his cap all added to the sort of raffish appearance Peggy had always found hard to resist.

But she hadn't expected the accent. From the back, with their tartan caps, she had thought these men would belong to a Scottish regiment. But the word CANADA was stitched to the front of their battledress and, as Mina was quick to explain, this particular branch of the Cameron Highlanders came from a land of plenty.

"You need any nylons, cigarettes, coupons," she whispered into Peggy's ear, "they're your men. Don't know how they come by such fortune, but your man Joe seems to be the well-spring of it. Looks like he's taken a bit of a shine to you, eh?"

Peggy nodded. "Actually, what I really could do with is a place to stay the night," she said. "Would you be able to help me out there?"

"'Course," Mina nodded, "if you don't mind giving me a hand with these first?"

"For sure," said Peggy, feeling the magic of the gin start to work.

– • –

A couple more drinks later and the landlord was ringing last orders.

"Tell me, fair lady," said Joe, "could you be persuaded to take a little promenade?"

Peggy looked up from the rim of her glass. Since they'd found a table to settle down at, the room beyond her Highlander had become a little blurry, the lights sliding off bevelled panes behind the counter and flickering around the optics.

"I believe I could do with a little air," she said. She looked across at Mina, now sitting on Frankie's lap. Dennis had fallen asleep, his head amongst the empties on the table.

Mina winked, taking hold of Peggy's hand and pulling her down to ear-level. "Let's meet back at the tube in half an hour," she whispered. "Should be time enough . . ."

Outside in the night, Joe put his arm through Peggy's. "Did you just tell your pal there you were looking for a place to stay?" he asked.

"Well now, you have got sharp ears. But," Peggy admitted, "I've no room of my own right now. Still, there are plenty of places around here . . ." She indicated the warren of little streets to their right, darkened doorways she had known well enough in the past.

Joe laughed, flicking his torch beam around and then bringing it to rest on her face. "No," he said, shaking his head. "This is no place for a lady. I have something a little better in mind for you."

"Oh?" Ludicrous visions of grand hotels swam into Peggy's head, borne by Mina's assertions of Joe's black-market dealings. But the Highlander continued to lead her down the Strand until they turned towards the new Waterloo Bridge which, although it spanned the river, was still a work-in-progress, surrounded by scaffolding, cranes and a huddle of huts for the construction workers.

Peggy stopped in her tracks, squinting into the darkness. "What?" she said. "You don't mean *that*, surely?"

"I got a pal who works here," Joe explained, "one of the night watchmen. In exchange for this," he pulled out a bottle from his jacket, "superior Canadian whisky, we'll get the use of his suite for a while."

"You mean one of those huts?" said Peggy.

He shrugged. "Better than a doorway, ain't it? It's OK," he put his arm around her shoulder, ruffling the fur of her coat. "I know my way around the place. You'll be safe with me."

But Peggy had stalled. The wind was coming up the river from the direction of the rooms she had left behind, bringing little stinging tears of sleet in its wake. She felt herself sobering up too fast. "You must be joking," she said.

"Well, how about this?" Joe went into another pocket, this time coming up with three pound notes. He shone his torch on them so she could see exactly how much he was offering.

"Enough to keep you around for a while?"

It was enough to call it a night afterwards and pay for a bed for the night, without Mina's help. Peggy curled her hand over the notes.

"There'll be more of that," he added, "after I see my pal the night watchman. C'mon. Let me show you the view. It'll take your breath away."

She let him lead her onto the bridge. Sure enough he did seem to know his way, picking a route between the huts, his torch shining a pathway before their feet to avoid the pot-holes and planks, until they had broken the cover of the scaffolding and stood only feet from the parapet.

"Now," said Joe, looking out towards the river, "ain't that something?"

Peggy glanced about her, struggling to catch her breath. Above, the beams of searchlights moved across the clouds, criss-crossing the skyline behind the dome of St Paul's Cathedral. Below her, deep and dark, swirled the onwards rush of the Thames. It made her feel dizzy. Unbidden, an image of Frances blipped into her mind, Frances underneath Muckish mountain, standing in the burn with mud on her face saying: "You've not lost your sense of adventure, Margaret?"

"Will you give me a ciggie?" she asked her Highlander.

"Sure." She heard the soft click of his lighter behind her. He put both arms around her, his left hand placing the cigarette between her lips.

"Do you like the movies?" he said, his breath warm against her ear, the smell of him surrounding her. "You look so much like a film star, you know. Nina Oakley – that's who you remind me of. Do you know who I mean?"

"I don't think so," said Peggy, enjoying the warmth of him beside her. She thought that she might have heard that name before, but though she had spent most afternoons in the picture palaces of Deptford High Street, she couldn't bring a face to mind.

"Well," said Joe, "you might not have caught her latest drama. It only came out last week. You know, I had the honour of meeting her once." His left hand travelled down the length of Peggy's coat and found its way inside.

"Hadn't you better be seeing about our suite?" said Peggy, smacking it away with a giggle, "before you get too carried away."

"Of course, ma'am," he said. "We have a call sign, like they teach you in the army. Listen." He turned, facing back towards the bridge, and cupped his hands around his mouth to make the hooting call of a barn owl. As the wind carried the sound away, Peggy strained to hear a reply.

"Wait here a minute," said Joe, "maybe he's not in range."

Peggy tried to keep sight of him, but in the dark, with all the strange shapes made by the planks and metal poles around her, it was impossible. She turned back towards the river. "Nina Oakley," she said to herself. "Where did I hear that name before?"

It came to her in the same second that his fist connected with the underside of her jaw, in the same second that she turned to run. It flashed in front of her eyes before her head snapped back, in black-and-white newsprint:

The second victim, Miss Evelyn Bettencourt, was also known by her stage name, Nina Oakley . . . A picture of a marcel-waved blonde looking over her shoulder and smiling out of a carefully lit studio pose . . .

Peggy toppled sideways, glancing the edge of the parapet before she hit the floor. The pain had scarcely registered before he was on top of her, his legs straddling her torso, pulling her handbag away from her shoulder.

"No!" she screamed, grabbing it back. "No, no, no, no, no!" Everything she had left in the world now was contained within those black leather dimensions and the thought of what it would mean to lose it overrode even the fiery rush of pain that came streaming down the side of her face.

"Shut up, lady!" Joe yelled back, his voice rising octaves as he scrabbled to remove the straps from her fingers, pushing each digit backwards until the pain forced her to recoil. He threw the bag from her reach and leant forwards over her, pushing down onto her diaphragm so that every struggle she made would rob her of breath.

"I said shut up!" he hissed, his hands going over her mouth, pinching her nostrils shut. "Don't make this any more difficult than it needs to be. Just be good, lady. Be good."

The world swam in front of Peggy's eyes and she made one last attempt to throw him off. She heard a sickening crack and then the darkness rushed in.

– • –

Mina looked at her watch for the second time. It was gone midnight now, twenty minutes past the time she had agreed to meet here with Peggy. Maybe her friend had already found a place to spend the night, she thought, flashing her torch up and down Villiers Street, for there was no sign of her here.

Another soldier, caught at the end of her beam, walked towards her, a hopeful expression on his face. Mina was too cold and too tired to wait any longer.

"All right, dear?" she addressed her new punter. "Looking for a good time?"

No doubt she would hear all about it in the pub tomorrow night.

— • —

Visions swam in front of Peggy's eyes. Frances in her nurse's uniform, staring at her with disapproving eyes. A baby wrapped in a white sheet, his eyes like the deep blue sea. The sea breaking against the white sands of an Atlantic shore, shrouded by a crest of blue mountains, in the far away haze of summer . . .

She became aware of breathing, laboured and intense. There was something tight around her neck and something heavy, pinning her down against a cold, hard floor, so she realised that the breathing could not be her own. She couldn't seem to move a muscle of her body either. Maybe she was already dead, being planted in the ground? Back into the Donegal earth . . .

As the thought occurred, she heard the sound of footsteps running across boards, a man's voice shouting: "Hello? Who's there?"

Abruptly, the weight was lifted from her. Breath streamed in through her open mouth with a piercing whistle and with it returned a rush of pain so intense she began to black out again, hovering between one world and the next as a pair of arms lifted her up from where she lay, pushing her against concrete, pushing her over the edge of the parapet. She opened her eyes and the dark swirl of the Thames rushed to greet her.

Then her head caught the side of a scaffolding pole and the woman who once was Margaret McArthur, once was Peggy Richards, knew and felt no more.

19

CRUISING DOWN THE RIVER

Wednesday, 18 February 1942

Greenaway's feet crunched over shingle, dirty with Thames mud, towards the tangle of limbs and fur that lay beneath Waterloo Bridge. The man at his side was a GPO cableman who was sure he had witnessed a murder the night before.

"Just gone midnight, I heard it," Alf Simmons told the DCI. "I'd been over the supplies' shop, the other end of the bridge, to get some more batteries for me torch and I was just about halfway back across. Sounded like a couple having a right old ding-dong. It all goes quiet and then she let out this bloodcurdling scream – God's truth, it made me hair stand on end."

Alf had covered these few, previously electrified strands of hair with a flat cap. Leading Greenaway down the steps beneath the scaffolding that surrounded each flank of the vast Peter Lind construction site, he continued, "Only, by the time I got to the place I could hear it all coming from," he nodded up at the first arch on the northeast face of the bridge, "there weren't no sign of her. There was just this man standing there. A soldier – he had a sort of tartan cap and the word CANADA on the front of his jacket." Alf scratched under the rim of his cap. "Tell yer the truth, I ain't sure what regiment that is."

"Don't worry about it," said Greenaway, "just tell me what you do know."

Closer to the stricken body, he could make out a peculiar detail: one of her legs was encased in a black stocking, the other one was bare. A familiar thrumming tattoo started up at the back of his brain, the feeling he was walking back into a nightmare that he thought he'd just woken from.

"'What you doing here?' I asks him," Alf went on. "'Oh, I'm all right, don't worry about me,' he says, 'I've just lost me friends somewhere.' Too right you have, I think, you just pushed her over the side. So I have a bit of a recce, flash the torch about and that, but there's nothing on the bridge itself. Beyond that, you can't see far enough with the blackout. By now he's weaving about a bit, either pissed as a parrot or making out he is; I can't leave him on the bridge like that. So I bring him down the steps, trying to keep an eye on him and still have a shufti as we get closer to the shore. Only, once we hit dry land he's out of the traps like a rabbit. I couldn't have kept up with him in the dark."

"No point you trying," said Greenaway. "Go on, Alf, what happened next."

"Well, after he'd gone, I had another look for her. Crawled along a gantry up there," Alf pointed upwards at the scaffolding, "as far as I dare go. That's where I found her headscarf, flapping round the end of the trestle. Must have hit it on the way down. I knew there weren't no more I could do then, so I waited until first light when I could actually see her – right underneath where I found him. And that's when I got on the blower to you, Mr Greenaway."

By now they had reached her. She was face down on the foreshore, her arms flung up over her head, which lay in the direction of the bridge. The tide had risen to the point where it was lapping against the side of her head, the long, chestnut-coloured hair that had spilt out of her turban floating like seaweed, the blood that had congealed around the wound on the back of her skull now diluting and colouring the grey waters pink. Her stockinged right leg, crossed over the top of the left one, still had a plum-coloured shoe attached to the foot, the other shoe was nowhere in sight.

"You done right, Alf," said Greenaway, wondering how long the tide would take to claim her, "but this ain't an ideal situation. I should really have some pictures of her here, but if we leave her any longer it'll mess up the forensics. Can you get some kind of stretcher to help move her back upstairs? I'll give you a hand with it, soon as I've made some notes."

"Right you are, guv," Alf turned and crunched his way back to the bridge.

Kneeling beside her, Greenaway sketched the position of the body, filling in details with words. Only when he had finished that did he lean across to move her sodden hair away from her neck, to where his gut was telling him he would find the other stocking without even knowing why, except for the fact that he had seen women killed this way too many times of late.

He took his hand away, sat back on his heels, returning his notebook to his murder bag. His fingers brushed on the as yet unopened bottle of Scotch he had put in there to replace the one he'd given Ivy Poole just over a week ago, a week that felt more like a year. Greenaway bit back the urge. He hadn't even had a proper breakfast yet.

Instead, he looked up at the archway above his head made of cool, grey Portland stone, the rows of supporting beams beneath the bridge that, despite their modernist intentions, suggested the vaulted ceiling of a medieval cathedral. What a thing it was to build a bridge in the middle of a war, he thought. He got to his feet, stepping backwards to scan the scaffold. Clumps of fur from the woman's shredded coat flapped off the corners of poles, a trail of the trajectory of her descent.

There was a sound of boots on gravel behind him: Alf and two more pallbearers in blue boiler suits, with a six-by-four piece of planking to receive this fallen angel.

– • –

"What was they doing up here in the first place?" Greenaway asked, gripping the tin mug of tea Alf had brewed up for him to keep his thoughts away from the contents of his murder bag. "You get much of that going on here, do you?"

"What, brasses?" said Alf. "Pubs round the Strand are full of 'em, but we don't usually get no bother from them up here. Nah—" he lowered his voice, not watching the Divisional Surgeon or the PCs now congregated around the corpse, "which ain't to say you don't find other sorts of people hanging about the place what shouldn't be."

"D'you want to step outside a minute?" Greenaway said, catching his drift. "Ain't too pleasant watching the doctor at work, is it? Take me back to the spot where you heard the argument, Alf, I'd like to take a better look at that."

Alf retraced the route. Up on the bridge, the wind was strong, the air full of the booming of ships moving up and down the river. In the daylight, London looked as shattered as the woman's corpse, great gaps of rubble surrounding St Paul's Cathedral in every direction, everything the colour of rust. Once they got to the spot where Alf had found the Canadian it was plain to see how easy it would have been to push the woman over – the parapet stood at barely three feet six. Greenaway put his bag down, began to examine the stonework.

"So tell me," he said, "about these other sorts of people?"

"Well," said Alf, "there's one of the night watchmen you might mistake for a fence. I seen people going in and out of his hut of an evening who ain't got no business up here. Sometimes it's soldiers. Other times," kneeling close to Greenaway, he whispered, "faces from back East."

Greenaway turned his eyes away from the scuff marks he had found on the parapet to look at Alf. "Anyone specific?" he asked.

Alf looked at the ground. Greenaway sighed, put his hand in his jacket pocket and withdrew his wallet. A pound note passed between his hand and Alf's before the cableman found his voice again.

"Bluebell," he said. "Bear. There must be a game going on in there, at the least."

"The Lehmann firm," said Greenaway. "It'll be more than just cards, Alf."

Alf nodded, his Adam's apple bobbing up and down as he swallowed. He'd said enough, Greenaway judged, putting a hand down on the other man's shoulder as he stood back up. "And," he said in a voice loud enough for any passer-by to hear, "let's see that gantry where you found her scarf from up here."

"Right," said Alf, rising to lean over the parapet. "Straight down there. See it?"

"You were right," said Greenaway. "Looks like that is what killed her." The two men stood in silence for a moment, eyes on the smashed trestle, before the detective spoke again. "When's the bridge supposed to be opening to the public?" he asked.

"Fortnight's time," said Alf. "They want to let two lanes of traffic through by then."

"Well," said Greenaway, "you've still got some work to do, ain't you? I won't hold you up no longer. Thanks, Alf."

"Thank you, Mr Greenaway." The cableman gave a little bow and edged himself away. Greenaway knelt back down to his examination of the low wall in front of him. The scratches in the stone told him there had been a fight here, that the woman had been pushed and not fallen.

"'Scuse me, sir," a uniformed copper appeared in Alf's place. "Surgeon told me to let you know they're ready to take her to the morgue."

– • –

Under the harsh lights the woman's body was a stark collision of blue, black, purple and white. Her kneecaps were shattered, both thighs fractured and the right side of her chest was smashed in, puncturing the lung and crushing her liver and right kidney. But there were other marks of violence that spoke of the desperate prelude to her fall: a blue, oval bruise underneath her jaw and a ring of spot bruises around her nose and mouth, ligature marks on her neck from where her assailant had tried to strangle her. A fracture in her lower back, where the rib met the spine, attested to the ferocity of the fight she had put up on the bridge.

"It wasn't caused by her hitting the scaffold," Spilsbury explained. "This would have been her struggling to release herself from where he had her pinned down."

"He was sitting on top of her." It was easy for Greenaway to picture. "Knees on her chest, straddling her, as he tried to strangle her." It gave him the cold chills to think about it. Cummins might be safely under lock and key in Brixton but here was yet another Allied serviceman, apparently carrying on his work for him. "Seen a bit too much of this kind of thing lately, ain't we?" he thought aloud.

"How did you come by this one?" the pathologist asked.

"I got a snout works on Waterloo Bridge who was the first one to find her. It ain't the usual sort of tip I get from him, but he's got a guilty conscience. He reckons he could have saved her if he got there sooner and he thinks he let the murderer get away."

Spilsbury raised his eyebrows. "He saw the assailant?" he said.

Greenaway nodded. "A drunk Canadian soldier, he says. D'you reckon it's catching?"

Spilsbury stared down at the corpse. "There are more things in heaven and earth than are dreamt of in your philosophy," he said. "But what we can safely establish is that, despite all these injuries, she was alive when she fell. It was probably the blow to the head that killed her, but the injuries sustained on the impact of landing would have done that, too. I would rule out self-precipitation or accident and there's no possibility that she drowned. Another thing you'll find interesting, given the circumstances," he looked back up at Greenaway. "There are no signs of sexual intercourse."

Greenaway's mind flashed back to Kate Molloy, putting a hand up to the bruise marks around her neck, to Madeline Harcourt in her hospital bed. Sex, or seduction, had only been Cummins's premise with them. Once he had them where he thought he was safe, he had tried to kill them immediately – it was the act of strangulation that actually aroused him. If Cummins's twisted mind was anything to go by, this killer had assumed he was secure enough where he was not to even make the pretence of a straightforward transaction with a working girl. Which meant he was every bit as dangerous as the man Greenaway had just put away.

"Right," he said, "I'll call a press conference. Try and find out who she was."

— • —

"Why do they call you Maestro?" Bobby Feld asked the man in the pinstriped suit who sat at the table by the window in Soapy's. Bobby had been watching him out of the corner of his eye for the past hour, shuffling, cutting and dealing out a pack of cards, muttering to himself in a voice too soft to catch.

Raymond Parnell looked up slowly, as if the ritual he was performing with the cards was indeed some kind of spell that Bobby was breaking. Oval brown eyes with long lashes blinked twice, transporting him back to the reality of the barbershop in late afternoon and the boy leaning on his broom, an earnest expression on his face.

"Is it something to do with magic?" Bobby persisted.

Parnell smiled, scooped the deck up off the table and in one deft flick of his wrist, fanned it out in a semicircle.

"Pick a card," he said. "Any card. Take a good look at it, but don't show it me."

The Maestro looked so much like one of the hoodlums in a Cagney film it was always a surprise to hear his Northern accent. A flicker of a smile spread across Bobby's face as he snatched up a card.

"Right," said Parnell. "Now remember what it was and give it back – only be careful I don't see it, or it won't work."

Bobby held his palm over the Jack of Spades as he handed it over.

"Good lad," said Parnell, slipping it back between the other cards. "Now," he said, scooping them back up into the deck and handing them over. "You give that a good shuffle now. Be as crafty as you like."

Bobby turned away from him, partly to appear as if he was indeed being crafty, but mainly to hide the fact he was no expert when it came to handling a pack of cards. When he had slowly cut and separated it five times, he judged he had messed up the order of the cards well enough to hand them back.

"Right," said Parnell, turning the pack face side up and fanning them back out across the table. "Now then," his brow furrowed in concentration as he hovered his right hand over them. Fingers lingered for a moment, above the Two of Clubs. "No," Parnell shook his head, "that's not it." His hand wafted on in a circular motion, pausing over the Eight of Hearts. "No," he said again, "not that one neither. Am I getting warm, though?"

"No," said Bobby, his smile now spreading right the way across his face.

"Oh dear," said Parnell. "Think I'll have to use some magic words to help me, then. Abracadabra!" He swooped the hand from left to right, "Alacazam!" He brought it down on the Jack of Spades, flicking it up for Bobby's approval. "Am I right?"

"Yes!" said Bobby, his face a picture. "How d'you do that?"

"What's the sudden interest?" Parnell asked.

Bobby's mouth went into a straight line and he swivelled his eyes about the shop to make sure Soapy was otherwise occupied. Then he rummaged in the pocket of his shorts and brought out a piece of paper that he slowly unfolded and handed across.

"*Learn the art of magic,*" Parnell read aloud. "*Everything you need to amaze and astound your friends!*" The advert showed a top hat, a cane, a pack of cards and a handkerchief. "*For only*

3/6." He looked up at Bobby. "Where d'you get this from, one of your comics?"

Bobby nodded. The Maestro was right again – the advert was from one of the comics inside the brown paper parcel he had found on his doorstep last Saturday night – which was a mystery in itself. When he'd brought it in to show his mother, she had gone very pale and sat down at the kitchen table with her hand on her forehead, the way she looked when she had one of her headaches. Yet the moment he suggested opening it, she jumped straight back to her feet and started shouting. Snatching the parcel out of his hands, she told him that since it wasn't addressed to him he had no business taking it, it must have been left at their house by mistake and she would see that it was handed in to the Post Office in the morning for redelivery.

Once she'd put it up on her highest shelf, another strange mood had overtaken her. Instead of tearing another strip off him for staying out late like she normally did, she dished him up a huge portion of stew and started asking him how he was enjoying his job. Bobby answered as best as he could, sticking only to what Soapy had taught him about keeping the place clean and tidy. He didn't ask her how she could get the parcel redelivered when it had no address written on it. He didn't give her any cheek at all. He ate up all his food like a good boy and asked if he could be excused to go up to his room and read. She dismissed him with an air of relief.

Keeping vigil from his darkened room, Bobby peered down the side of the blackout curtain into the back yard where he observed his mother taking the parcel down to the dustbin. He waited until she had been in her own bed for an hour before he crept downstairs to retrieve it.

Back in his room he'd opened it slowly, by torchlight, under the cover of his bedclothes.

There were enough presents inside it for everybody in the house, if everybody had been there. Alongside some more babyish fare was a copy of *Ace Comics*, its cover illustrated with the same spade symbol as the card he'd just picked from the Maestro's deck, surrounded by drawings of cowboys, pirates and soldiers. There were also three rag dolls and a bottle of French brandy. But as hard as Bobby examined these items, and the paper that had covered them, he couldn't find anything to say who had sent them, which deepened his dilemma still further.

If his mother would rather have thrown the parcel out unopened than let him have it, he couldn't go back and tell her it was she who had made the mistake, that it must have been meant for them after all. Should he tell his father, or would that only get him into trouble for taking it out of the dustbin? Who was the mystery benefactor and why had their gift made his mother so angry? Bobby fell asleep with unanswered questions revolving round in his head, illicit bounty under his mattress.

First thing Monday morning he put it all inside his school satchel and transported it to the nearest bombsite, hiding everything amid the rubble except for his comic, which he had since read from cover to cover, and the brandy. He had a feeling that bottle could come in useful and now he knew that instinct was right.

"I can afford it," he told the Maestro. "I been saving up my tips for months. Only, it's got to be delivered, ain't it?"

Parnell looked at the small print on the ad. "That a problem?" he asked.

Bobby nodded. "My mum would send it straight back."

"Ah," said Parnell. "She don't approve, eh? Religious, is she?"

"Yeah," said Bobby, frowning. "She's a Roman Catholic."

Parnell's eyes registered surprise.

"My dad isn't," Bobby added quickly. "He's Jewish, like Soapy and Bluebell." Then he shrugged. "Don't know what that makes me."

"Only half-kosher," the Maestro's face lit up in a dazzling smile, "same as me. Listen, Bobby," he said as he handed the advert back, "what you've got there, that's not magic, that's more like extortion, that is."

"Well, if you can teach me instead," Bobby said, his voice lowering to a barely discernible whisper, "I can give you a bottle of French brandy."

Parnell looked at the solemn little face in front of him. "A whole bottle?" he asked. "Not one fell out of Bluebell's back pocket?"

"No," said Bobby. "This is proper French brandy."

Parnell laughed. "Well, I won't ask you where you came by that then, but all right, son, you've got yourself a deal."

"Really?" this was a much better result than Bobby had dared dream of.

"Really," the Maestro handed the boy the deck of cards, catching Soapy's eye with a wink. "From now on, you can be *my* apprentice, too."

20

I GET ALONG WITHOUT
YOU VERY WELL

Thursday, 19 February 1942

"So, let me get this straight, son," Greenaway sounded calm, almost reasonable as he read back from his notes. "You came across a Canadian solider rummaging inside a lady's handbag on Platform 15 of Waterloo Station at one o'clock Wednesday morning. Can you describe him to me?"

The young PC tried to meet the dark brown eyes beneath the heavy lids of the man sat opposite, but found that he couldn't; they didn't match the tenor of the voice. He flicked his gaze up at the clock on the wall behind him instead. "He was about five foot ten," he replied, "quite broadly built and with a swarthy complexion. One of them pencil moustaches. Wearing the uniform of the Cameron Highlanders."

"Aha," said Greenaway. "A regiment, at last. And apart from what he was up to, did you notice anything unusual about his appearance?"

"Well," said the PC, "he was sweating quite heavily and seemed to be drunk. When I took the handbag from him, I saw there was a scratch mark on his left hand."

"So you took the handbag from him. What did it look like?"

"Quite small, maybe four inches by two. Black leather, with a tortoiseshell clasp. I'm no expert but I'd say it cost a few quid."

"And naturally, you asked him what he was doing with it?"

"Yes, sir," the PC made eye contact for less than a second before looking back at the clock. "He told me it belonged to his girlfriend, and that she must have dropped it on the bench behind him when they were saying their goodbyes before she got her train. He said they were both a bit the worse for wear and he did smell very strongly of perfume. I noticed that there was a ration book in the middle compartment of the bag, so I asked him what her name was. He told me it was Peggy."

"And the name on the ration book was?" asked Greenaway.

"Peggy Richards."

Greenaway wrote it down. "What else was in the bag?" he asked.

"A powder compact and a lipstick, that was all. He told me she always carried her purse and her door keys about her person, that she'd be OK getting home, but he'd make sure he got it back to her first thing in the morning. I didn't think there was anything she couldn't do without for one night."

"And did you ask him to turn out his pockets? To make sure he hadn't actually siphoned off her purse and anything else of value already?"

The PC bit his lip. "No, sir," he said.

"You gave him the bag back instead," said Greenaway, shaking his head. "Well, son, you might never make a detective. But you did get his name and regiment, at least?"

"Yes, sir," the PC's fingers fumbled over his notebook, "it's Private Joseph Muldoon of the Cameron Highlanders. They're stationed in Ewshot, in Hampshire."

"Well, well," said Greenaway. "There's hope for you yet."

— • —

The description of the soldier tallied with witness reports that had been given to Greenaway the previous evening, following his pub crawl around the Strand. Not being as familiar with the locale as he was with Soho, he had taken along an old timer PC from Charing Cross station, who reckoned he knew this Peggy a few years back.

"There was one just like her used to be a regular on this beat," he told Greenaway. "An older lady, Irish, took better care of her looks than most of the others. Seemed to be fairly well educated, too. Used to have an unusual repertoire of names, if I'm right. She liked to name herself after poets."

It was the barman in the Hero of Waterloo who had seen three soldiers with Balmoral caps entertaining a couple of brasses in his saloon on Tuesday night. One he described as "swarthy and quite athletic-looking" had left with an older woman wearing a red turban. The cellar man backed up his story. They had reason to remember the troop, as they'd both had to help one of the soldiers off the premises when the others had left him there, face down on the table.

Added to this, the green PC's bag-snatcher looked like a fit. Greenaway picked up the phone.

— • —

Frances Feld saw the sketch of the dead woman while she was on the bus, on the front page of the *Daily Herald* that was being read by the man sitting opposite. STOCKING WOMAN'S FIGHT FOR LIFE ON WATERLOO BRIDGE read the headline above it.

Frances looked back at the image. It was only a drawing, a

police artist's impression. But her sister's eyes stared back at her accusingly.

"Mary, Mother of God," Frances breathed, her fingers seeking out the crucifix around her neck as she leaned forward in her seat, straining to read the newsprint beneath the headline. POLICE SEEK INFORMATION announced a smaller subheading. The man turned the page before she could see any more.

"Are you all right, love?" asked the woman sitting next to her.

Frances turned, her eyes not quite focused. "Yes, thank you," she said in a high, quavering voice. "This is my stop," she added, and though it was nothing of the sort, she stood up and rang the bell. The other woman continued to look at her with concern as she hurried away, the weight of so much human company around too much to bear.

The bus set her down on a wet, congested pavement full of people and, as it left her, sent up a wave of rainwater in its wake to splatter down the front of her coat.

– • –

Set on a meandering road that traced the course of the river after which it was named, Mole Cottage was a vision of rustic idyll: all faux wattle and daub, red-brick chimney stacks and a low, shingled roof with a gabled porch, net curtains at the diamond-paned windows, a sign hanging at eye level reading: VACANCIES. Not the sort of place you'd take for the hideout of a killer on the run.

Yet, as Greenaway had earlier learned from his Regimental Sergeant Major, it was to this address that Private Muldoon had been headed for his week's leave. It seemed he was a regular guest at the boarding house, in the Surrey town of Leatherhead, some distance from his barracks in Ewshot. There was a suggestion amongst the men that he had some sort of arrangement with the landlady. Yes, the RSM had opined, in tones very similar to those of Cummins's corporal before him, Muldoon did have a bit of a reputation with the ladies.

Once their conversation had concluded, Greenaway had rung the local police to find out more about the landlady from a friendly sergeant he'd had cause to work with once before. Mrs Edith Cavendish-Field was in her early fifties, he learned, the widow of a colonel. She was also something of a local celebrity, with a host of admirers drawn to both her reputedly glamorous appearance and perceived bank balance. Not the sort who would seem likely to fall for a twenty-one-year-old spiv in a private's uniform.

There had been no reports of suspicious behaviour at her establishment over the past three days, but the Sergeant advised Greenaway against announcing his arrival in advance. Mrs Cavendish-Field would likely turn unhelpful if she caught a whiff of any impending scandal. When Greenaway explained exactly what kind of danger she might be getting herself into with her lodger, the Sergeant offered to keep a discreet eye on things himself until the Yard could get there.

Driving out of London through the evening dusk, Greenaway turned over the information the RSM had given him, wondering how much trouble Muldoon might give him. The young Canadian had not set his sights on a career in the military; he'd been working as a bartender when he had been drafted, from Hull in Quebec, and his introduction to the army was as brutal as it came. Though thousands of frontline troops had arrived in Britain from the Empire since War was declared, the Cameron Highlanders was one of the few Canadian regiments that had seen any actual fighting – and Muldoon had been deployed in the very worst of it.

During the retreat from Dunkirk in May 1940, he was part of a reserve company of forty-five men who had led a counter-attack to drive the enemy back over the Lys Canal at La Bassée. They had fought with utter, bloody determination for five solid hours before ten Churchills'-worth of the Royal Tank Regiment came to their aid. Between them, the Allies managed to take down twenty-one enemy tanks and force the Germans into retreat – by which time there were only seven Highlanders left standing. It was just the sort of battle that had destroyed so many young men of Greenaway's generation, if not in body then in soul.

On his return from France, Muldoon had been given a couple of weeks' leave before a medical board assessed him fit to continue service. The CO, a decorated veteran who had fought for the 16th Canadian Scottish at the second Battle of Ypres, was of the mind that it was better for a man to get straight back in the saddle if he wasn't to lose his nerve. However, an Allied agreement that precluded Canadian troops from the campaign in North Africa meant there was little for them to actually do but make their own entertainments. Muldoon had already served time in the company slammer for running card games and books on the dog races at White City.

In all, it appeared he was a damaged and dangerous young man – but was Edith Cavendish-Field as unaware of this fact as Cummins's own wife had been? And was Muldoon as adept as the airman had been at being able to kill, steal and still turn up behaving as if nothing untoward had ever happened?

Night had fallen by the time Greenaway locked up the Wolseley on the road outside Mole Cottage. Before he had even reached the front door it was opened and a woman stood framed in the light. She was as striking as the Sergeant had suggested. Thick chestnut hair coiled into a high coiffure framed an angular face. A slim figure in a well-cut tweed suit, cashmere jumper and a string of ancestral pearls – almost like an older, just as well-bred version of Marjorie Cummins. Only her wide, green eyes belied the air of authority she would usually have conveyed, as, with a flash of wild panic, they met with Greenaway's and floundered for recognition.

"Oh," she said, putting a hand up to her throat. "I was expecting someone else." The hand came back down quickly, and with it the pitch of her voice, modulating to its usual, deeper tones as she gave his face a rapid assessment. "Sorry, can I help you?"

Greenaway showed her his warrant card as he gave her his name. "I'm looking for a soldier I believe you've got staying with you," he said, "a certain Joseph Muldoon of the Cameron Highlanders."

The hand went back up, this time further, to land on a strand of curl around her right earlobe. Her forefinger snaked around it, tugging at it, and the panic flared again in her eyes as she glanced beyond Greenaway into the darkness.

"That's just who I thought you were going to be," she said, dragging her gaze back. "He took the dog out over two hours ago, I don't know what's keeping him."

"Well," said Greenaway, taking a step forward, "shall we wait for him inside?"

"Oh yes, of course," Mrs Cavendish-Field opened the door to him, manners instilled in childhood taking over, though she hesitated before shutting it again behind them. Her green searchlight eyes once more strafed the garden path. Only then did the implication of Greenaway's job title seem to sink in. "Oh my word," she said, leaning back against the woodwork. "Whatever do you want with him?"

– • –

Bobby Feld was concentrating so hard on perfecting the trick that it took a while for the sound of voices coming from downstairs to permeate his consciousness. He had found it hard to believe, at first, that it could be so easy, but the Maestro had shown him it was. All you had to do was remember the card underneath the one that had been picked. It didn't matter how many times the pack was then reshuffled, you couldn't take odds on those two cards being separated. So when you fanned them out again, you just picked the card to the right of the one you had memorised.

He had repeated the sequence over twenty times already, and each time it worked. Tomorrow he would be ready to try it out on Barney Newbiggin and all the other gulls at school. He was just picturing his friend's face when his mother's raised voice broke through the wanderings of his imagination.

"What was I supposed to do, Harry? Should I have asked her to stay, introduced her to him as his auntie? She might have been earning enough to wear a fur coat but she looked exactly what she was – a woman of the night!"

"Calm down, Frances, be quiet," he heard his worried father reply. "You don't want the boy to hear you."

Bobby put the deck of cards down on the bed.

"Did I do so wrong?" his mother's voice was cracking into tears. Bobby slipped his shoes off and walked softly to the door.

"Of course not, bubbala, you did what any good woman would have done in your place," his father replied. "You did more than enough for that one already."

Bobby turned the door handle softly, stepped out onto the landing. He could hear his father whistle between his teeth the way he always did when words were about to fail him. "Families," he said. And then, "Are you sure it was her?"

There was a brief silence as Bobby set himself stomach-down on the landing, cocking his ear beside the stair rail. The rustling of paper and then his mother's voice again.

"Take another look, Harry, and tell me I'm wrong."

Bobby heard his father make another whistling sound. "It looks like her, all right," he said. "But it's not a photograph. What makes you so sure of it, my dear?"

"The clothes," his mother's voice was steadier now. "Everything they describe is identical to the outfit she was wearing that night. No, Harry, there's no mistake about it. You know the life she was leading. Is it any surprise where it took her?"

There was another long silence, during which time Bobby could feel his heart beating through the floorboards. Who was this woman of the night they were talking about – and what was a woman of the night, anyway? A strange sense of dread overcame him, though he couldn't understand why.

"What are you going to do?" his father spoke again.

"Do my duty, I suppose. Go to the police, identify the body, if I have to. Lord knows who else will be able to do it." The calmness in his mother's voice as she said these words chilled Bobby still further.

"If you're sure it's her, then you must," his father agreed. "Do you want me to come with you?"

"No, Harry, this is my burden. It was me who started it by not listening to my own father all those years ago and now it's up to me to see it through to the finish. God forgive me for saying so, but at least now he'll never have to know. There's no risk of her ever turning up out of the blue like that again."

"Frances," his father sounded shocked, "are you sure you know what you're saying? Don't you think there will ever come a time when he should know?"

"Why?" the voice that replied was icier still. "What do you think it would do for him if he did know? Isn't he trouble enough as it is?"

Bobby heard his father's chair scraping back from the kitchen table.

"All right, all right. You wouldn't listen to your father, so why should you listen to me? Have it your own way. But you remember, as hard as you try to keep them, secrets have their own way of finding you out."

Bobby got up, ran back to his bedroom. Dived onto the bed with his heart pounding, feeling for the *Ace Comic* under his pillow and breathing in the faintest scent of violets.

21

I'VE HEARD THAT SONG BEFORE

Thursday, 19 February 1942

"I'm hoping Private Muldoon can help me with a little enquiry." Greenaway took in the layout of his surroundings as he spoke. The dining room was off to the right; he could see the tables and chairs through the half-open door, so the sounds of a radiogram coming from the left suggested that was the lounge where the guests spent their evenings. Mrs Cavendish-Field must have been lingering in the hallway, where a cigarette smouldered in an ashtray on the table next to a half-drunk glass of sherry, waiting for sounds of Muldoon's return.

"But you've come all the way from London," she said.

"That's right. Can you remember what Private Muldoon was up to this past Tuesday night? Was he here with you all evening or did he go up to town for the night?"

"I-I don't keep tabs on my guests at all times," the pitch of her voice started to rise again. "I was out myself on Tuesday night. Can you please tell me . . ." She put a restraining hand on his arm.

"But he was here for breakfast Wednesday morning?" Greenaway scrutinised her face. The landlady took her hand away and her eyes fell along with it. "Well, yes, yes he was," she began to twist her fingers together, rubbing at her wedding ring.

"You're certain of that?"

"Yes!" Her face coloured as she looked back up at him. "Look, do you mind if we go somewhere more private to talk about this?" she hissed. "I have other guests to consider." She motioned her head back towards the sounds of the radiogram.

"Not at all," said Greenaway. "In fact, I was hoping you might be able to show me Private Muldoon's room. You've got a spare key for it, haven't you?"

"But he'll be back any minute. Can't you talk to him first?"

"Mrs Cavendish-Field, how well do you actually know Private Muldoon?"

The landlady frowned, her attention drawn back to the cigarette she had previously discarded. She lifted its smouldering remains and took a deep drag before answering. "Not as well as I perhaps should," she admitted.

"Has he ever given you a reason to feel afraid of him?"

Her green eyes shot him a look that said he had her bang to rights. She crushed the cigarette out in the ashtray, took from her jacket pocket the set of keys that she herself had been on the verge of using just before her unexpected visitor arrived.

"Follow me, please," she said.

– • –

Muldoon's room was right at the top of the staircase. Mrs Cavendish-Field hovered nervously outside, knocking on the door despite the fact she knew the room was empty and waiting a couple of seconds before putting the key in the lock.

"You can go back downstairs to your guests if you want," Greenaway told her.

The landlady shook her head, folding her arms. "No, I'll wait here. Only I don't know if he put the blackout down before he went out . . ."

Greenaway stepped past her into the room. A lingering, musky scent of aftershave and sweat hung heavily in the air, exactly the odours the PC on Waterloo Station had remembered. The curtains had not been drawn before Muldoon went for his constitutional, and in the glow cast from the hallway, Greenaway could see a room in disarray. He strode over and took a look through the window, to scan for any signs of life below, before pulling down the blackout and turning on the light.

It illuminated a bed left unmade, sheets and a feather eiderdown in a tangle, a kitbag spewing out its contents in the middle of it. A bottle of NAAFI Canadian rye whisky on the table by the bed, only a dribble inside the smeared glass that had left rings over the polished surface it sat on. Boxes of Lucky Strike cigarettes on the bed and on the table, an ashtray overflowing with fag ends. Papers everywhere, pages of old newspapers and a thick wad of what looked suspiciously like petrol coupons. Muldoon was a deviator all right, and murder was clearly not his only transgression.

Greenaway put down his murder bag and took out a pair of gloves. Snapping them on, he stepped in for a closer examination.

"Can you tell me something?" he asked Mrs Cavendish-Field as he lifted the wad of coupons. There was at least a score of them and they looked pretty good forgeries. He had come across the like before. "How did you first become acquainted with Muldoon? Was he introduced to you socially or did he just turn up one day, looking for a room?"

The landlady's memory needed no prompting. "I met Joe in the Running Horse – that is to say, our local pub," she said. "I was seeing a friend there for lunch, only I'd got there a bit early. I wouldn't naturally go talking to strangers, but I had the dog with me and he started to make a fuss of her." She cast her eyes back down the stairs, waiting for the sound of the door. "He was in uniform, so naturally, we began to chat about the war. But he soon digressed from that rather tiresome subject. You probably won't believe this, but he was an interesting conversationalist."

Greenaway grunted. "He must have had something going for him," he conceded.

The comment, and its implication, stung Mrs Cavendish-Field and she moved forward from the doorway into the room. "Well, you wouldn't have thought so from his rank or his age, but he seemed very well educated, keen to know all about the local history. He told me he was waiting for a friend from London who had suggested meeting at the Running Horse because of its history. Good Queen Bess is said to have stayed the night there, you know."

She realised that, in the state of panic she found herself in, she was rambling. But it was imperative that this oaf of a policeman believed her.

"Anyway," she reined herself in, "it turned out to be the funniest thing. When his friend did eventually turn up, it was one of the guests I already had staying with me. They hadn't decided whether to remain here for the weekend or to go down to London, but, since I had a vacancy, they found it convivial to stay."

Greenaway stared at her. "And when was this, can you remember?" All sorts of angles had started clicking together in his mind as she spoke; separate threads suddenly pulling together to link his conversation with Alf Simmons on Waterloo Bridge to the Squad business that had brought him to Leatherhead the year before. Two lorries of NAAFI cigarettes bound for army bases in the area, hijacked a week apart, on the outskirts of the town.

"I have a good memory for dates," said Mrs Cavendish-Field. Though it was true, this one was etched on her mind for other reasons. "It was the first of March last year."

"And the friend's name?"

"Mr Parnell," the landlady said, her voice lowering to a whisper, "Raymond."

A grim smile spread over Greenaway's face. "Well, well . . ." he began.

"Don't say any more, Edie," the voice came from outside the room: a Canadian accent mouthing a line like it came out of a Cagney film. Both pairs of eyes snapped towards the door. Neither had heard him creep his way up the stairs.

Now he stood framed in the doorway: a swarthy man with a tangled mop of jet-black, curly hair. A face dominated by thick eyebrows and dark, glittering eyes, set over a boxer's nose and underscored with a pencil moustache. His hands out front, waving a Smith & Wesson Military & Police model revolver from side to side between them.

"Who is this?" he jerked the barrel in Greenaway's direction, while his wild stare locked onto the landlady. "What's he doing in my room?"

"Chief Inspector Greenaway, Scotland Yard," Greenaway said, opening his palms to show Muldoon he was unarmed. "I just want a little chat, son."

Muldoon's pupils were so enlarged that his entire irises

seemed black. He took a step towards Greenaway, the strong, musky scent of his aftershave advancing before him.

"What are you doing with my things?" His voice rose into an unattractive whine. Greenaway kept a beady eye on the revolver.

"Your things, are they?" he said. "That's very helpful. Bootleg coupons and hijacked NAAFI supplies – not what I expected to find here, but a bonus, all the same."

"What you talking about, man? Bootleg? Hijacked? Get out of here!" Muldoon did what Greenaway wanted, came closer to him, leaving Mrs Cavendish-Field temporarily out of range. Greenaway had used that type of gun often enough himself to be able to see that the safety catch was still on, and it would only take another step for him to get close enough to knock it out of the Canadian's grip with the side of his hand.

But the landlady had other ideas.

"Joseph," Mrs Cavendish-Field's voice trembled as it lowered. But she did not speak in fear now. It was rage that boomed the next lines from her lips. "What the hell have you been up to?" she demanded. "And what have you done with my Chocolate?"

Muldoon lurched round in her direction. For a second, Greenaway had the notion that it was the landlady who was actually running the black market ops here and that she was missing the confectionery constituent of her order.

"Shut up, Edie, I said, shut up!" Muldoon raged, waving the gun at her.

"How dare you?" Before Greenaway could even make his move, she slapped Muldoon around the face so hard and so loudly that he dropped his weapon involuntarily. Deftly, Mrs Cavendish-Field dived forwards to snatch it up.

"I wasn't married to a colonel for thirty years for nothing, you fool," she hissed. Setting her jaw in a grim line, she unclicked the safety catch. "You're supposed to do this before you threaten someone," she told Muldoon, placing him firmly in her sights. "Now," she said, "what the bloody hell have you done with my dog?"

As if to answer her, the doorbell sounded in a furious jangle and with it came the muffled sound of barking.

"Inspector Greenaway," said Mrs Cavenish-Field, breathing heavily, "perhaps you would like to take this gun from me while I go and answer the door?"

– • –

"Sorry I couldn't get here no earlier, Ted," the Sergeant said. "Only he did lead me a bit of a merry dance."

Two reservists had arrived shortly after the Sergeant, called by him from the local pub after he had lost his tail on Muldoon. They were now sat guarding the prisoner in the back of Greenaway's car while the DCI finished gathering up evidence at Mole Cottage and learning what his counterpart in Leatherhead had been up to all evening.

Good as his word, the Sergeant had kept watch on the cottage until he'd seen Muldoon come out with Mrs Cavendish-Field's springer spaniel. Recognising the uniform, he'd tailed him down to the Running Horse, where Muldoon took himself off to a corner by the fire, ostensibly reading the paper over his pint, but keeping an eye on the door. When he saw a couple of young women come in, he rapidly became animated. Just as he had once done to ingratiate himself to her owner, he used the dog as an ice-breaker, to initiate conversation with the pair. The Sergeant watched him buy drinks and settle them down at his table. Then, after a few minutes of chatter, Muldoon produced something from the pocket of his greatcoat – a small, black leather handbag with a tortoiseshell clasp.

As the girls passed it between them, the Sergeant recognised the description Greenaway had given him of the bag the PC had seen Muldoon with at Waterloo Station. It was evident he was trying to sell it and one of them readily agreed – such a pretty little thing, they both considered. As soon as he had money in his hands, Muldoon excused himself, making for the Gents and leaving the spaniel still tied by her lead to the table leg.

At this point, the Sergeant was forced to move in and get back what he knew to be a piece of crucial evidence. In the time it had taken to explain himself to them, he presumed Muldoon must have seen him talking to the girls, panicked and run back to Mole Cottage, forgetting the dog completely. Once the Sergeant had ascertained the Canadian was no longer on the premises, he had called up reinforcements and hot-footed it back himself, bringing the spaniel with him.

"Two quid that cost me," he said, handing the black leather bag to Greenaway. "And I still don't think she believed a word I said. Right put out about it she were."

"Well," said Greenaway, "it would have cost a lot more than that to begin with. She thought she had a nice little bargain in her grasp." He sealed it inside an evidence bag, adding it to the mound he had culled from Muldoon's room, before taking two pound notes from his own wallet to reimburse the Sergeant.

"Hopefully it'll still have some of his prints on it," he said. "If not, we've got the ration book." Greenaway had found the document, made out to Peggy Richards, stuffed inside Muldoon's kit bag. "Like to see him talk his way out of that."

"Oh, he'll think of something," said the Sergeant, raising an eyebrow. "He likes a good jaw, from what I just seen of him."

Greenaway pointed to the cartons of fags. "And what about all this?" he said. "Puts you in mind of those NAAFI lorries last year, don't it?"

The Sergeant stroked his moustache thoughtfully. "That is the same cargo as what went missing back then. Makes you wonder, don't it? Still, I expect you'll get to the bottom of it, Ted. Anything else I can help you with, you know?"

"I won't keep you much longer. I just need a last word with Mrs C-F before I go."

The Sergeant allowed himself a smile. "What d'you make of her, then, Ted? Bit of a one-off, in't she?"

– • –

"Come in," the landlady bade him enter.

She was in what she called her den, a small room at the back of the house where she ran the business that the sudden death of her husband five years ago had prompted her into undertaking. The den had a window at which, in daytime, she could look out onto her favourite part of the garden, but apart from this aspect, it was a very masculine room, crammed full of parchment lampshades depicting ships' charts and naval scenes. A photograph of the late Colonel stared out of a black frame on the shelf over the roll-top desk, surveying his former domain from between two model galleons.

Standing on the threshold, Greenaway had another flash of Marjorie Cummins in the front room that had so clearly been furnished to her husband's taste, and instinctively he knew that this was part of what Muldoon had been doing here: finding out how the other half lives.

Mrs Cavendish-Field sat beside the fire, clutching a glass of brandy. The brown spaniel lying at her feet raised her head and gave an inquisitive whine.

"You asked me earlier if Joseph had ever given me a reason to feel afraid," she said, staring into the flames. "Well, he hadn't. Not until Wednesday morning."

"That so?" Greenaway moved cautiously towards her, wondering if she kept any of her own firearms tucked away about the place. "What happened then?"

"He woke me at five in the morning, throwing stones at my window. I'd never seen him in such a state – hair standing on end, utterly reeking of booze and, when I let him in to stop him waking up the rest of the house, I could see he had scratches all over his hands. I asked him whatever had he been up to," her eyes finally rolled up to meet Greenaway's, "and he said he'd had some bad news from home, something about his sister. He'd gone drinking to drown his sorrows, apparently. Fallen asleep in a field somewhere and got injured trying to find his keys after they'd rolled underneath a barbed wire fence." Her expression told him she did not believe it.

"His sister?" Greenaway frowned. The dog got to her feet and bustled towards him, her whine getting more insistent as she pushed her head underneath his right hand.

"I thought I'd get it out of him once he'd slept it off," Mrs Cavendish-Field continued. "But he stayed in his foxhole until late this afternoon. I went up to see if everything was all right, I had really started to get worried by then. But he was still in a foul mood – hung over, of course. Wanted to be left alone, he said. He offered to take the dog out for a walk, so he could go straight to the pub, I suppose." She shot the animal in question a look of disdain. "Look at her," she said, "wanton beast. Some guard dog you turned out to be, eh, Chocolate? She's never got over the loss of my husband, you see. She's like this with every man she meets."

The spaniel stared up at Greenaway with love in her eyes, her stump of a tail thrashing from side to side. "Ah," he smiled, trying not to marvel at how closely her words mirrored what the Sergeant had already opined of the landlady herself. "So *you're* Chocolate, are you?" He ruffled the top of the animal's head. "Don't seem to me like you're in much need of a guard dog, Mrs Cavendish-Field. I must say I'm impressed by how well you can look after yourself."

"Chief Inspector," the landlady's voice turned sharper, "you still haven't told me what it is you wanted to see Joseph for."

Greenaway looked into her green eyes, straightening up to stand to attention. "There's a few more things I need to ask you," he said, taking out his notebook. "If I remember rightly, you told me Muldoon first stayed here on the first of March last year."

"That's right," she held his stare, her expression opaque.

"After that, did he come back here on a regular basis?"

"Well," Mrs Cavendish-Field looked back towards the fire, "I suppose he did. Every couple of months he'd be back for a weekend and then, last summer, he spent two weeks of his leave here. That was the longest he ever stayed." Her hands searched out her packet of Pall Malls and lighter.

"And what about his friend, Mr Parnell? Did they always visit at the same time?"

Mrs Cavendish-Field lit up. "No, not after that first time.

Mr Parnell is a businessman, he travels a lot, so his visits were always fairly sporadic. After that first time, they were only here together once more and—" she found herself looking above Greenaway's head to the photograph of her late husband. "And I'm afraid I don't think they parted here the best of friends. They had some kind of a falling-out after they'd been to the pub one night. But don't ask me what about," she continued swiftly, her eyes dancing away. "Neither of them would tell me. Mr Parnell never came here again and this past week Joseph really hasn't been himself at all."

He could hear the cracks start to form in her voice. It had been a long night already, and suddenly he felt sorry for her, as capable as she undoubtedly was.

"During this past week," he asked, "he didn't mention the case of Gordon Cummins to you, did he? Or the Blackout Ripper, as the papers liked to call him?"

Mrs Cavendish-Field shook her head. When she turned back to him, he could see that her eyes were beginning to glisten. "No, no, I can't say he did." The adrenaline provoked by her earlier confrontation with Muldoon having left her system, she had come over feeling very tired, very old and very stupid indeed. "Look, Inspector—" her eyes were pleading, "just tell me – what has he done?"

Greenaway decided against mentioning the newspaper pages, annotated with Muldoon's ramblings, that he had also recovered from the room. The Canadian's little commentary on the Blackout Ripper's progress could wait for the interview room.

"I'm afraid it's murder," Greenaway said, putting his notebook away.

22

DRY BONES

Friday, 20 February 1942

"What you doin' there, son? Lost something besides your marbles?"

Bobby put the dustbin lid down and turned to face Soapy. "You still got any of yesterday's papers?" he asked.

Soapy shook his head, chewing thoughtfully on the tooth-pick that habitually protruded from between his canines as he took in the shadows under the boy's eyes, the tousled mop of hair. "You know how it works, son, they all go in the boiler at the end of the day. You helped me clear them up yourself last night, if you can remember that far back. What you doing here at this hour anyway? Shouldn't you be in school?"

Bobby shrugged, rubbed his eyes. He couldn't find any easy excuses to explain himself. "Soapy, what's a woman of the night?" he asked instead.

"Not something you want to be losing sleep over at your age," said Soapy. "Now go on, clear off to school. And comb your hair while you're about it."

– • –

Greenaway drained the last dregs of the chicory grounds being passed off as coffee from the station canteen while he typed up his notes on Muldoon. The bitter taste went with the picture he was formulating of the man he had left in the cells at Bow Street court prison the night before, adding to the report he had taken from the Canadian's RSM to what he had found in the room in Mole Cottage.

Muldoon, it appeared, had been taking a keen interest in the story of Gordon Cummins. He had collected cuttings of every murder – preferring the *Daily Mail*'s coverage, but with a few *Heralds*, *Daily Mirror*s and an *Evening Standard* thrown in – underlining the words "strangle", "stockings" and the myriad allusions to "working girls", "ladies of the night" and "ladies of easy virtue" in red pen throughout the copy. Evelyn Bettencourt's murder seemed to have excited him the most, but perhaps that was because all the papers had managed to get hold of glamorous publicity pictures she'd had taken in her actress days, her hair in marcel waves. WHORE he had written across her forehead, adding a drawing of a bow tied around her neck and further amateur cartoonist's attempts at splurges of blood and flying daggers. A further SOCK IT TO HER, BUDDY!!!! in the margin.

On the one hand, this was evidence that could lead a jury to believe that Muldoon had been an admirer of Cummins, and had set out to murder a prostitute in imitation of the techniques he had been poring over in the papers, by strangling her with her own stocking – perhaps even in tribute to his now captured hero. But, on the other, it could equally well convince them that Muldoon was stark raving mad.

The crux of Greenaway's dilemma was how easily a clever barrister could apply the M'Naghten Rule as defence of temporary insanity – which, should it be accepted, would mean

Muldoon avoided a date with the gallows. The script for this practically wrote itself: the aftershock of the carnage Muldoon witnessed in France unhinging his mind, the lack of any subsequent action in the field leaving those horrors to fester in the bad company he kept in barrooms – the drunks, the prostitutes, the smooth-talking likes of Raymond "the Maestro" Parnell – all taking advantage of a man not in his right mind. In this scenario, the jury would be invited to consider Muldoon as a war hero, the killer himself a victim of cruel and capricious circumstance.

A hat Muldoon seemed to have already tried on. He hadn't invented his sister in Quebec; shortly after his return from France, his CO had received a petitioning letter from her, begging for Muldoon's discharge on grounds of his delicate mental health. She referred obliquely to an incident in his youth for which "he should have received proper treatment" without actually stating what this was. But it had, she said, caused previous "temporary lapses" from his "normally kind and gentle nature".

Muldoon's CO was having none of it. Twenty-mile runs in full pack and nights in solitary in the barracks' slammer were his way of dealing with the pernicious Private's regular post-France acts of insubordination. That none of these measures seemed to have had much effect on him would only strengthen a defence barrister's argument in favour of M'Naghten, Greenaway feared – especially if that barrister were to get his hands on the sister's letter.

His defence against that line took the form of a six-foot-two pinstriped spiv. Raymond Parnell might not initially play well for a jury, but if Greenaway could get his testimony that Muldoon had tipped him off about the cigarette lorries in

Leatherhead then Muldoon could be shown to have a well-hinged criminal mind that acted at all times entirely out of calculated self-interest.

The handsome, saturnine face of Sammy Lehmann flashed through Greenaway's mind as he formulated his plan, giving him a cocksure little wink: "I might be in the Moor thanks to you," the gesture seemed to imply, "but my boys are still running things nicely, you mug . . ." Greenaway batted him away with the return of his typewriter carriage. Before getting to that, he first had to make sure the murder charge stuck. It was time to meet Muldoon in the cold light of day.

– • –

"How's he spent the night?" Greenaway enquired of the Duty Sergeant at Bow Street.

"Quietly," the other man replied. "Didn't ask for anything, other than a paper. I was finished with mine so I give it him. Thought it'd be nice for him to see his handiwork splashed all over the front page."

"You're right about that," said Greenaway. "Give him something to add to his collection. I found quite a pile of Penny Dreadfuls in his kitbag already." The clippings were stowed in his murder bag, awaiting further discussion.

Arriving at Muldoon's cell door, he opened the hatch. The noise was enough to send the prisoner up from the bunk that took up half the width of his place of confinement and onto his feet. He stepped sideways towards the door and saluted as it opened.

Greenaway and the Duty Sergeant exchanged glances.

"At ease, Muldoon," said Greenaway. The Canadian dropped his hand but not his gaze. In contrast to their previous meeting, his expression had altered from hostility to something approaching deference – though he hadn't been so mindful of the rest of his appearance. The pencil moustache was now virtually indistinguishable from the rest of the thick stubble that shadowed the lower half of his face, and the cloying smell of his cologne seemed to intensify with the underlying musk of unwashed hair.

"Had a good night's sleep?" Greenaway enquired.

"Sir," Muldoon said.

"Ready to have that little chat now, son?"

"Sir," Muldoon repeated, "are you the same Detective Inspector Greenaway who caught the Blackout Ripper, sir?"

Greenaway moved closer to the Canadian, looking hard into his dark eyes. "Why?" he asked. "Do you fancy him or something?"

Muldoon flinched, took a step backwards. "Say what?" he said, frowning.

"Cummins," said Greenaway. "I found all those clippings you kept in your room at Mole Cottage. Bit of an unhealthy interest you were taking in him, don't you think? Or do you find him as dashing as those poor, unfortunate women did?"

The furrows deepened on Muldoon's forehead and he gave a little laugh. "Gee, I don't know what you mean, sir. I always take an interest in murder mysteries. I read all the Edgar Wallace and Sherlock Holmes books in the barracks library, got a big collection back home. Everybody loves that stuff, don't they? And you took a real life Ripper down. Man, you're a hero. It's an honour to be arrested by you."

It was Greenaway's turn to frown. "*Me* the hero? Funny, I had the idea it was Cummins you were looking up to. Thought maybe it was him who gave you the idea. I mean, Peggy

Richards was strangled with her own stocking, just the way Cummins liked to do it."

"Peggy Richards?" Muldoon maintained his expression of incomprehension. "Who's she?"

"The woman you threw off Waterloo Bridge," said Greenaway. "The woman whose handbag you stole and tried to fence in the Running Horse last night."

Muldoon laughed as if Greenaway was telling him a joke. But his cheek twitched and his eyes shifted their focus from Greenaway's to a space a few inches above his head.

"You're telling me I killed somebody?" he said. "What, are you nuts?"

"I've got her body down the morgue and her ration book in your kitbag," said Greenaway. "You're such a murder-mystery fan, you tell me what it looks like."

Muldoon's eyes came back to him, narrowed. "You've got her body at the morgue?" he said. "Well I guess then you should show her to me."

Greenaway's eyebrows shot up and nearly didn't come back down. "You what, son?"

"I want to see her." Muldoon stared defiance. The twitch in his cheek grew more pronounced and beads of sweat started to form on his forehead. "I want to see the body."

Greenaway turned to the Duty Sergeant so he didn't have to look at this unsavoury show of mounting excitement before he'd had more chance to gather his thoughts.

"Now there's a request you don't hear every day," he said.

"Indeed," said the Duty Sergeant, looking like he'd caught a bad smell. Something worse, even, than Muldoon's aftershave.

"Let's see what we can do about that, shall we?"

– • –

Twenty minutes and one phone call to Chief Commander Peter Beverley later, Greenaway and Muldoon were handcuffed together in the back of a car, travelling towards Southwark Morgue. Having discussed Muldoon's behaviour with his superior officer and oldest ally in the force, Greenaway had decided not to engage his prisoner in any small talk, just observe his actions. He was convinced the Canadian was putting on an act. The formal autopsy was due to take place that morning. He wanted to see how much of that Muldoon could stomach.

He was also sure, as they walked the short journey from the pavement to the room where Spilsbury was preparing for his task, that Muldoon was getting a kick out of attracting attention to himself this way. His demeanour had brightened considerably since they had left Bow Street with all eyes following the pair of them. It was the same at the morgue. While Greenaway manoeuvred them past the front desk and down the corridors, he could feel Muldoon puffing himself out, his stride becoming a swagger, as if in his head he was a film star walking down a red carpet. When they entered the autopsy room, perhaps he mistook the bright lighting for the Klieg lamps of his vivid imagination, the stern form of the pathologist standing by the body on the gurney for somebody about to give him an Oscar for his canny portrayal of a Chicago hood – or maybe even a Blackout Ripper. But when Spilsbury stood aside to let him witness the outcome of his last date, all Muldoon's talent suddenly seemed to desert him.

Greenaway watched his prisoner's face as he contemplated reality. The smile fell away from his lips and the colour drained from his face as his eyes took in the livid hues of blue, black, purple and yellow that adorned the smashed contours of the body before him. Then wandered across to the row of instruments laid out ready to dissect the damage in minute detail: the saws, scalpels, tongs, blades and receptacles. Involuntarily, he raised his left hand, the one that wasn't handcuffed to Greenaway's, to shield his eyes. Then he turned away.

"Seen enough already?" asked Greenaway. "Don't you want to stay for the autopsy? It starts in ten minutes and I've got permission for you to be here. That's if you don't have any objections, Dr Spilsbury?"

"No, indeed," said the pathologist. "Be my guest."

Muldoon shook his head furiously but didn't say a word. He kept his thoughts to himself all the way back to Bow Street, where Greenaway left him in his cell with a bit more information to chew on.

"I'll be getting the fingerprint tests back this afternoon from the lady's handbag," he let Muldoon know. "Then I expect I'll be back to see you. With my charge sheet."

Muldoon stood facing the wall. "You'll get nothing from me," he muttered, without turning around.

– • –

Greenaway had only just reached his office at Tottenham Court Road before one of his brighter detective sergeants stuck his head around the door. "That sketch in the papers has done the trick," he said. "We've had two people come in this morning claim to know the Waterloo Bridge woman. A dockworker from Deptford says he's been living with her the past two years, and an Irish nurse from Bethnal Green thinks it's her sister."

"Bethnal Green?" Greenaway turned over the information in his mind. All roads seemed to be leading back to the place. An Irishwoman, too – the old PC from Charing Cross he'd done his pub crawl round the Strand with had said Peggy Richards was Irish. "Well, well."

"They both seem genuine to me," the DS went on. "Who would you like to see first?"

"The man," Greenaway decided. If the woman from Bethnal Green really was the sister of the deceased, then she would need to identify the body. Which had better wait until after Spilsbury had finished his work in the morgue.

– . –

He looked to be in his late thirties, had a wide, ruddy face dotted with the open pores and thick lines that come with long years of working outdoors, a thatch of thick, curly hair that once had been dark brown but was now all but frosted over. He wore a donkey jacket over blue overalls and a pair of steel-capped work boots, and he was twisting the peaked cap he carried between his hands in an anxious fashion.

"Inspector Greenaway here is in charge of the investigation, Charlie," the DS said. "Will you tell him everything you've just told me?"

"'Spector Greenaway," the man's bloodshot brown eyes travelled around the patchwork of maps, mugshots and paperwork that crowded the wall behind Greenaway's desk, lingering uneasily on the sketch of Gordon Cummins before finally meeting Greenaway's gaze. "Charles Beattie," he said, raising his rough paw to briefly grip the DCI's. "Call me Charlie."

The man spoke with a slight undercurrent of wheeziness that was the hallmark of a Thames dockside worker. "Charlie," said Greenaway, "please take a seat, make yourself comfortable." He nodded to the DS, who bowed out, closing the door behind him.

Charlie Beattie sat down slowly, taking from the pocket of his jacket a folded copy of the previous day's *Herald*, which he unfurled on the table top between them, smoothing his hand over the creases across the police sketch on the front page.

"She was my missus," he said, looking back up at Greenaway. "My Peg." Then he leant forwards, putting his head in his hands in an attempt to hold back his tears.

The DCI took out his cigarette case, offered it across.

"Here," he said. "Take your time, Charlie." The docker fumbled out a smoke, the hand that had gripped Greenaway's own with assured strength only moments earlier now racked with tremors. Greenaway lit him up, watched him throw his head back and gulp down a lungful. Another three drags and he had composed himself.

"Least I thought she was," he said. "Two years we been living together like man and wife. I thought we was happy. Thought I'd got her away from all that . . ."

Through Greenaway's mind, a re-run of Herbert Coles, sitting on his sofa, breathing in the perfume that lingered on his wife's handkerchief. The wife whom he also thought he had got away from all that lying in pieces in the room next door.

Charlie took another hefty drag.

"Where do you live, Charlie?" Greenaway asked.

"Number twenty-three Castell House, Deptford Church Street."

"And you work on the docks?"

"That's right."

"And when was the last time you saw Peggy?"

"Tuesday morning," Charlie said. "But things ain't been right since last Saturday. Since Valentine's Day." He shook his head, exhaling clouds. "She's a bit of a romantic, see, my Peg. Gets these ideas in her head and there's no stopping her. That was one of them times. She was planning something, I dunno what, but Saturday morning she was full of herself, Saturday night it was like she'd lost a quid and found a ha'penny. I couldn't get it out of her what went on, we ended up having a right old row about it. She was still sulking Sunday and Monday, then Tuesday night, she never come home. She has done that sort of thing before, mind. Only this time . . . This time I got the feeling she'd blown the gaff for good."

"What made you think that?" Greenaway asked.

Charlie rubbed at his eyes with his cuff. "The things she took. She had all her paperwork with her, and all the coupons we had in the house. Put her best clothes on and all . . ." Seeing the cigarette burning down to the filter, Greenaway pushed the ashtray towards his interviewee and opened his case again. Charlie stubbed the end of the old fag out and took a new one without losing his composure.

"But she didn't think it through properly, did she? Whatever went on Saturday got her so riled up she didn't know what she was doing. Else," he fished into the other pocket of his jacket, "she'd have took this, wouldn't she?"

Greenaway took the green passport the docker held out to him. The name on it was that of Margaret Theresa McArthur. The photo was of the woman he had last seen in the morgue, only taken twelve years earlier, when she was fresh-faced and beautiful. The address given was the Halls of Residence at the London Hospital, the occupation a trainee nurse.

Greenaway shook his head.

"I never even knew that was her name," Charlie said, staring straight through Greenaway, to a place where the detective could not follow. "She never told me nothing about her past, her family. She never wanted to talk about it at all. I always thought she must have run away from home, some terrible old man she had over there, which was why she wouldn't never marry me. I thought it was because perhaps she couldn't. The only thing she brought with her 'sides her clothes and her hand-bag was all these books she kept. Romantic poetry, she called it, Wordsworth and that. Used to quote it at me sometimes, when she was in a good mood, which like I say, she was, most of the time. Only she went and left all them behind," he said, his eyes filling up. "All them books she loved so much. Oh, Peg. What d'you have to do it for, eh, girl?"

23

WHAT WOULD HAPPEN TO ME IF SOMETHING HAPPENED TO YOU?

Friday, 20 February 1942

Frances sat in the CID room, eyes darting around like a nervous bird's. The officer who had taken her details had given her the seat at his desk and even made her a cup of tea while Chief Inspector Greenaway was busy interviewing another witness who had arrived before her. Frances had no idea there could be so many detectives all in one place, talking across each other, taking telephone calls, banging away at their typewriters and generally making such a noise it was a wonder that any of them could think. The grim visages on the many WANTED posters adorning the walls stared down at her, with expressions that ranged from moody to outright demented. Frances took another sip of her cooling tea, made too weak and too sweet for her liking. It was all she could do to keep seated and not make a last-minute bolt for the exit.

Finally, the door to the Chief Inspector's office opened and a man in dock-worker's clothes came out, shuffling his cap between fidgeting fingers. Frances had never laid eyes on him before in her life, but this nervous tic, together with his hollow-eyed expression, told her that if he was also here because he had known her sister, then at least he must have cared for her.

The telephone on the desk beside her jangled to life. The officer lifted the receiver and spoke a few words of confirmation. Frances watched the docker walk away with his eyes downcast. Under his arm he was carrying a rolled-up copy of the same *Daily Herald* she'd purchased as soon as she'd stepped off the bus yesterday.

"Mrs Feld," said the officer, "the Chief Inspector is ready for you now, if you'd kindly follow me."

If Frances thought the docker a large man, then DCI Greenaway stood a foot taller, with an abundance of thick dark hair, greased away from his forehead, and heavily lidded eyes. Frances found herself fretting at the handles of her bag, the way the docker had with his cap, as she took in her surroundings, her eyes drawn to a sketch of a man with wavy hair and staring, pale eyes that she recognised at once from the reports she had read in the paper as the face of the Blackout Ripper.

"Mrs Feld," Greenaway offered his hand, catching where her eyes rested, the same as Charlie Beattie's had. "Do take a seat. My men been looking after you?"

"Yes, thank you," Frances said, taking the proffered hand and then lowering herself uneasily into her seat.

"Glad to hear it. Now then," Greenaway clasped his hands on the desk in front of him. Frances took in the nicotine stains, the bitten-down nails on his big, blunt fingertips. There was something curiously reassuring about those hands, she thought, they were indicative of honest toil. "You've got some information about the Waterloo Bridge woman, I believe?"

"Yes," Frances came straight out with it, "I believe she was my sister, Margaret McArthur."

"Oh?" said Greenaway, scanning the face in front of him. Frances Feld was a slender woman who sat ramrod straight in her smart navy coat and hat, clearly mindful of her appearance. Her face had an austere beauty, made more intense by the intelligence of her dark blue eyes and the curly, chestnut hair that surrounded it – the same colour tresses as the woman who had floated in the Thames. Though he couldn't imagine a more outwardly different type of woman, the resemblance was clear.

"That's not the name she was going by," he said. "Nor the name on the ration book we recovered from the deceased woman's handbag. We have her down as Peggy Richards. Ever heard that one before?"

"I'm sorry to say deceit was second nature to my sister." Even now, Frances couldn't stop the bitter words from tumbling out. "But the last time I saw her she did inform me that she was going by the name of Peggy."

"And when was that, Mrs Feld?" Greenaway picked up a pencil.

"Last Saturday," said Frances, and gave a little sigh. "Saint Valentine's Day."

"Did you see a lot of your sister?" Greenaway asked.

Frances shook her head. She was trying so hard to stay detached, to tell the policeman what he needed to know and not let her feelings get in the way. But it was much harder than she had anticipated. She felt as though she was sitting in front of a priest and must now make full confession.

"I'm afraid I didn't, no," she said, looking down at the handbag in her lap, her shoulders slumping. "Saturday was the first time I'd seen Margaret for nearly five years, Chief Inspector. We had a falling out, a long time ago, and I told her I never wanted to see her again. Yet she'd track me down again every few years and attempt to make reconciliation. That's what she was up to on Saturday, but I did what I always do and sent her away."

Greenaway could see her eyes begin to glitter. He resisted the urge to solve another mystery and ask her what they had fallen out over and instead watched her open up her handbag.

"Then," she went on, "when I saw the report in the *Herald* about the woman at Waterloo Bridge, the clothing matched the outfit Margaret had on last Saturday – a rabbit fur coat, red turban and purple shoes. The sketch that went with it," she extracted a bundle from the depths of her bag, "matches the face you'll see on these pictures. There's some official paperwork here, too, what I have of it – certificates for passing our nurses' exams at the London Hospital in 1930 with Margaret's real name and my maiden name on them. I hope that's proof enough for you."

Greenaway saw black-and-white photographs: two girls with long, wild hair playing in a stream under a mountain, turning into more sophisticated young women wearing cloche hats over their smart bobs, then starched and prim in their nurses' uniforms. As far back in time as the pictures went, Frances looked aloof while there was something about Margaret's smile that hinted that the sisters were already on divergent paths.

"We came here from Dunfanaghy in 1928, to try and lead a better life than we could in Ireland," said Frances. "There were enough of our brothers to look after the farm there. Nursing was the one way we had to better ourselves . . . Or so I thought."

Greenaway felt the weight of passing lives, the expectations and thwarted dreams that spoke from each item he had been given. All the proof that Frances could find of Margaret's existence and their familial ties that she was willing to show to a stranger.

"But," she went on, "as you've no doubt gathered from your own investigations, once we got here, Margaret formed a different idea of what constitutes a better life than I did. Which is why we went our separate ways and how she would have come to be in such a place as she ended up. God rest her soul."

Greenaway looked from the young Frances in the photo to the woman sitting opposite. She was right, the arrest sheet he'd seen at Charing Cross station had illustrated precisely what had been occupying her sister for most of the ten years before she had met Charlie. The expired Irish passport completed as much of this picture as Greenaway needed to know. That families had their secrets, extreme differences of opinion that could cause rifts as wide as the former McArthur sisters', was not news to him. He had no desire to intrude on Frances any further than the one onerous question he was now obliged to pose.

"So, Mrs Feld," he said, handing her memento mori back to her, "as her nearest next-of-kin, would you be prepared to identify Margaret's body?"

Frances felt a sudden sense of calm, as if she had passed this test and now God was giving her back the strength she needed to see it all through. "I would," she said.

– . –

Still, she gripped her rosary tightly as Dr Spilsbury rolled back the sheet. Frances had seen death close up before and, with the carnage that the Blitz had wreaked upon East London, with more voracity than she could have believed possible when she first donned her uniform. She was well aware of the sort of injuries she would see on her sister, and how a body would appear after autopsy, stitched up like a rag doll. What she hadn't been prepared for was the very waxy stillness of her, the total absence of life in one who had always been so full of it.

She looked from Margaret's empty, ruined face to the sad eyes of the detective.

"This is her," she said.

Greenaway nodded and Spilsbury replaced the shroud, nodding respectfully.

"I'm very sorry," he said.

Frances closed her eyes. "Thank you," she replied, feeling her strength deserting her, leaving her as empty, cold and vulnerable as her sister's corpse.

"Can I run you home, Mrs Feld?" asked Greenaway.

– • –

As he stopped his car outside her door, Frances turned to look at the big detective. There was only one more question she wanted to ask him, the one thing that preoccupied her thoughts during their silent journey to Bethnal Green.

"The man who you saw before me today. Was he a friend of my sister's?" she said.

Greenaway nodded. "He was a good friend, Mrs Feld," he said. "Someone who cared a lot for her."

"I thought so," said Frances, nodding. "He looked as if he did. Did he tell you anything that bears repeating?"

Greenaway thought about it. "Your sister loved poetry," he said.

"Well," Frances's irises widened, "so she did. When we were young, she could declaim books of it by heart. It was always the Romantics she liked best – Shelley and Wordsworth and Keats." A sad smile crossed her face. "I suppose that speaks volumes, doesn't it?"

Greenaway thought of Muldoon, locked in the cells, awaiting his charge. "I will get justice for your sister, Mrs Feld," he promised. "Poetic, or otherwise."

She nodded, turned away and let herself out of the passenger seat. He watched her make her way back into her small, terraced house, waited until the front door had closed behind her before he slowly drove on.

Half of the street was in ruins. All about him were piles of bricks, jagged, shattered walls, the impromptu revealing of the insides of rooms where buildings had been blown in half, basements caved back into the ground, chimney pots above swaying at drunken angles. Though he knew precisely where he was going, Greenaway could no longer recognise large swathes of the route to Brick Lane; the war had changed the geography almost irrevocably. Except that, when he left his car to walk the remainder of the way, tucked behind the canopies of the market, the heady smells of rotting vegetables and the cries of the barrow boys, Soapy Larry's barbershop was still exactly as it had always been.

– · –

"You see, you got the hang of it all right," the Maestro nodded approvingly as Bobby picked the card he had chosen from the deck. "And you showed them that at school today, eh? Good lad."

Bobby recalled the look of amazement on Barney Newbiggin's face, acknowledgement that he had finally managed to get one over on his bigger, tougher pal – the one highlight of a day racked with exhaustion and confusion.

"Suppose you'll be wanting me to show you another? Sit down then, lad, take a gander at this . . ." The Maestro began to reshuffle the deck. As Bobby watched, a question burst from the back of his mind straight out of his mouth.

"You know you said you was half-kosher – I mean, that *we* was half-kosher? Well, which half of you is the kosher one? Is it from your mum or your dad?"

Parnell raised his eyebrows. "It was my dad," he said, "which means I can't technically be called kosher at all. It's supposed to come down your mother's side to make you proper Jewish. But I'm the spitting image of my old man. He was Russian, with the black hair and dark eyes, like I got. He could sing and charm the birds down off the trees with his stories." With a flourish, Parnell fanned the deck out in a horseshoe across the table. "Mind, he were a proper wandering Jew and all. Wandered off when I was seven with a fancy piece, left me at the mercy of me staunch Roman Catholic Ma. Sound familiar, does it?"

Bobby shook his head and whistled. How could the Maestro know so much? He was about to ask something else when the bell over the door began to tinkle.

The atmosphere in the barber's changed as quickly as if a black cloud had blotted out the sun. Soapy froze, his razor poised in mid-air above Bluebell's lathered face. Bear's eyes narrowed to amber slits and a sneer lifted his top lip up to reveal short, pointed teeth. The Maestro's smile drained away as he looked up at the figure that filled the doorway.

Bobby had never seen him before. Though he was the same age and general appearance as the rest of them, in a long black coat and trilby that spoke of money to spare, he also wore a seriousness that marked him apart. He hadn't come to lose his troubles here. He'd come to bring them.

"Greenaway," hissed Bear. "The fuck you want?"

A thin smile crossed the lips of the man in the doorway as he took in the tableau in front of him. "Corrupting minors, are we, Parnell?" he said, hooking an index finger towards the Maestro. "Looks like I got here just in time."

He strode forwards into the room, eyes fixed on his prey. Bear moved his hand inside his jacket as he came nearer, but

Greenaway ignored the gesture.

"Forget about it, all of you," he said. "This ain't a social call. This is Murder Squad business." He reached the table, put a hand on Bobby's shoulder. "Out of the way, son," he said softly, "I need to have a word with your friend here." Petrified, Bobby shot from underneath him, not wanting to see or hear any more.

– • –

Walking towards the synagogue, Harry Feld had to stop in his tracks, wipe his glasses and put them back on before he could verify that the sight before him was real and had not sprung from the places where his troubled conscience had been taking him all day. Sitting on the steps, his arms wrapped around his knees, looking morosely up from beneath his thick wedge of fringe, was Bobby.

"Dad!" the small figure uncurled to his full height and streaked towards him, flinging his arms around Harry's waist in a show of affection that was as rare and unexpected as his presence here.

"What's all this?" said Harry, ruffling the boy's hair, going over many possibilities in his mind and none of them good ones. "What are you doing here, Bobby? Has something happened at home?"

"No," said Bobby, burying his head in his father's waistcoat, breathing in the reassuring smell of peppermint and tobacco and screwing up his eyes to stop the tears that threatened to spill. "I just wanted to see you, that's all."

Harry put his arms about the boy and hugged him close, while a great wave of sadness broke over him. He wondered how much Bobby had heard Frances say last night, and what of it that he would have properly understood.

"And you knew where to find me, huh?" he said.

Bobby raised his head and nodded. "I want to hear the singing, Dad," he said. "Is it all right to come in with you?"

"Of course it is, my boy," Harry said, wondering even as he said the words if there had ever been anything he could have done better for this stubborn, stray child that could have made him turn out more like one of his other siblings. Whether anything could ever really alter God's plans.

– • –

Frances sat at the kitchen table, asleep and dreaming. She was back at the burn, underneath Muckish mountain, the smell of earth and water in her nostrils.

"Oh, thank God," she said, looking around her, taking in the fluffy white seed heads of the bog cotton and the star-shaped yellow flowers of the asphodel that told her it was finally summer. "I thought I'd never know that smell again." The sun was warm on her face, sparkling off the surface of the burn, where Margaret crouched, bare feet planted on stones, skirt pulled up around her knees, staring intently into the water.

"Shhh!" her sister murmured. "There's one coming now. Ah, and he's a beauty."

Frances watched Margaret slip her hands under the surface, while she ran her own fingers through the thick, fragrant grass, wanting to make sure that all this was real. "I never thought I could come here again," she whispered to herself in wonder, "and that it would all be just the same as it was."

She looked back up at Margaret. She was young and thin, stray tendrils of her chestnut hair escaping from her attempts to corral them into a ponytail, rising and falling on the breeze. The rest of her was stock still, concentration etched all over her face, which was free from the pretence of make-up, free of the lines of care. Margaret had always been brilliant at tickling out the trout. In a silvery flash, her hands came up above the surface, grappling the twisting body she had brought up from the burn into the embrace of her arms. Frances rose to her feet, moved towards her to help, realising as she did that her own legs were bare, her skirt pulled up and tied to one side, so that she could wade into the cool slipstream beside her sister.

Margaret turned to face her. "Look!" she said, happiness catching her face like the glow of the sun. "Did I not tell you he was a beauty?"

Frances looked down into her sister's arms. It wasn't a fish that she held there, but a baby, the darkness of his thick black hair a stark contrast to the white swaddling in which he was wrapped, staring up at her with the bluest of blue eyes.

"I want you to take him," said Margaret, offering the bundle towards her. "Take him and look after him. Will you do that for me, Francie?"

"But . . ." Frances began, wondering why it was so familiar, wondering how she knew that all of this had already happened before, but in another time and place.

"Only—" Margaret looked round across her shoulder, back towards the mountain. A cloud was moving across the sun, sending a dark shadow travelling fast across the land towards them. "I can't stay here much longer. Will you do it for me, Francie?"

Frances took the baby in her arms, his blue eyes holding her gaze for a second's worth of eternity, time enough for the shadow to fall across Margaret. When Frances looked back up, her sister was gone.

"Margaret!" she said, tears in her eyes. Said it loud enough for the veil to lift between the world she had left and the world she was now in: suppertime in the London blackout, the smell of fish in her nostrils coming from the stove behind her, where supper bubbled in the oven. Blinking in the light that came from the electric bulb overhead, illuminating the pages of the book she had been reading while she waited for her husband to come home, a book of verse open on a page of Wordsworth:

> *A slumber did my spirit seal*
> *I had no human fears*
> *She seemed a thing that could not feel*
> *The touch of earthly years.*
> *No motion has she now, no force*
> *She neither hears nor sees*
> *Rolled round in earth's diurnal course*
> *With rocks, and stones, and trees.*

Frances looked up from the page and wiped her eyes as she heard the front door go and the sounds of talk and laughter proceeding up the hallway. The kitchen door opened and Harry came in with Bobby right behind him, rubbing his hands and asking: "Is that supper ready, my dear? It smells a treat, doesn't it, Bobby?"

She closed the book and stood up, forcing a smile to greet this unexpected sight of familial solidarity.

"Not half," Bobby agreed, his blue eyes catching hers and a tentative smile forming there. "I'm starving, Mum," he added.

"Well, we'd better get you fed then," Frances said, smiling back at him.

She scooped the book off the table, put it back up on the shelf where she had put the package her sister left on Saint Valentine's Day. Now she knew exactly what words to use in parting when she took Margaret's body home.

24

KILLIN' JIVE

Friday, 20 February 1942

He feigned outrage at first, the way his sort always did.

"What murder enquiry?" Parnell asked as Greenaway walked him to his car. "What you talking about? You must have run out of ideas, picking on me."

Scores of children playing amongst the debris at the end of the market day stopped their games and stared at the pair of them, round eyes in mucky faces reflecting a mixture of curiosity and awe. The one little sentinel Greenaway had singled out to keep an eye on the motor for him was still at his post, standing guard like a good soldier. Greenaway ruffled his curly head and slipped him a shilling.

"Well done, son," he said. "Come and see me when you're out of short trousers, I'll make a good copper of you yet."

"Wow!" The boy eyed his bounty with delight. Parnell gave him a venomous stare.

"That's all bogeys are about, you know, bribing off decent folk," he hissed. "You want to watch yourself, sonny Jim."

"Up yours!" the child replied, sticking two fingers up and running away, laughing.

Greenaway afforded himself a chuckle. "He's got your

number, Parnell. Now shut up and get in the car."

The Maestro spent the journey brooding in silence. He had never had a face-to-face with Greenaway on his own before, but he had been forewarned that there was no dealing with the DCI. If he seemed to be being reasonable, it was because he was working an angle on you and getting you to help him discover exactly what he wasn't sure of – making you knit your own noose, as Bluebell would put it. Parnell wasn't sure that was what was happening here – so far Greenaway had been much less than friendly. All he knew was that he'd had nothing to do with any murder. Not that the fact was any comfort where he was being taken.

Greenaway, meanwhile, was whistling "The Camptown Races", getting the feeling he was on to a winner all the way back to Tottenham Court Road, past the Duty Sergeant to the door of the cell in which he deposited his witness to collect his thoughts while he cleared up a few other pertinent matters.

"You've still not told me what this is all about," Parnell protested as the door was closed on him.

Greenaway smiled back through the hatch. "An old friend of yours," he said. "Private Joseph Muldoon of the Cameron Highlanders. He threw a woman off of Waterloo Bridge Tuesday night and ran off with her handbag to a certain little boarding house in Leatherhead. That's my murder enquiry and that's what you're going to be assisting me with. So, make yourself comfortable while you cast your mind back a year or so and remember everything you can think of about lorries full of cigarettes, the landlady of Mole Cottage and the Canadian toerag in question. I'll see you later."

He closed the hatch on Parnell's yelps of protest.

Since he'd been out of the office, a courier had brought over a couple of documents Greenaway needed to read. First, Cherrill's forensic report on the handbag. With his usual meticulous attention to detail, the fingerprint man had established a match for two thumbprints found on the tortoiseshell clasp and the ration book made out to Peggy Richards with the dabs that had been taken upon Muldoon's arrival at Bow Street. It was exactly what Greenaway needed.

These would form the basis of the physical evidence against the Private, along with Alf Simmons's report of the encounter on the bridge and the testimony of the landlord and cellarman from the Hero of Waterloo – Muldoon's movements tracked by witnesses from the time he left the pub with Peggy/Margaret to the moments just after he threw her to her death. The strands of the rope were starting to weave themselves together. But there was still contingency work to do, starting with the second document. Greenaway found something interesting on that one, too.

He picked up the phone to the Chief Commander. Once he had brought Peter Beverley up to speed with Muldoon's performance in the morgue and Cherrill's report on the fingerprints, Greenaway had a theory to expound to his old boss.

"Some old unfinished business of ours ties into this," he said. "The landlady at the boarding house where Muldoon was picked up told me that the first time he stayed with her was in March last year. He was introduced to her by a mate of his who's another one of her loyal customers – one Raymond Parnell."

"Not the same one that we know?" said Beverley.

"I doubt they made two like him," said Greenaway. "Now, you might recall a couple of NAAFI cigarette lorries got hijacked in the vicinity of Leatherhead around the time, one on the first and one on the eighth of March. I've brought Parnell in for questioning this afternoon, made sure I pinched him in plain sight of the rest of his firm, at Soapy Spielman's barbers. See, I've got a hunch there's more to Muldoon being on Waterloo Bridge than meets the eye."

"Go on," said Beverley.

"My snout who found the body," said Greenaway, "also tipped me off there's a night watchman on the site hosting little parties in his hut of an evening. Said he'd seen some faces from back East dropping in on him, namely Moishe Abraham and his pet Bear, associates of our dear friend Parnell. Which signals to me, it ain't some simple game of Klobbiotsch going on in there. So, I got a list of all the night watchmen employed by Peter Lind Construction sent to me," Greenaway consulted the document, "and the name Morris Spence comes up on there."

"The plot thickens," said Beverley. "Morrie the Tipster, I take it?"

"If it ain't too much of a coincidence that this Morrie's been working on the site for as long as that Morrie got out of his last stretch at the Ville, then we are talking the very same gentleman I once nicked with a portable press, rigging the Tote for the Lehmann firm at Sandown," Greenaway confirmed. "Exactly the sort of press that could very easily be adapted to manufacture the same kind of bootleg petrol coupons I found in quantity in Muldoon's kitbag. I must say, there was something familiar about them."

"How very interesting," said Beverley.

"That's what I hoped you'd say, sir. See, I've been having these horrible premonitions that if Muldoon gets some clever barrister, he might try the M'Naghten defence, on account of his war record in France. He might come across as a bit of a hero, being only one of seven men to come back from his squad alive; destroying twenty-one Jerry tanks in the process and so on. But if we can prove he's spent most of his leave ever since at work for the Lehmann firm, he ain't going to look quite so sweet, is he?"

Greenaway could hear the Chief Commander's teeth chomping against the side of his pipe. "I rather like your thinking, Ted," Beverley told him. "What you proposing?"

"Well," said Greenaway, "when I picked Parnell up, I told him and the rest of his firm that this was Murder Squad business. They've probably all read about Cummins in the linens, but I'm not so sure they'll have been so interested in the Waterloo Bridge woman, or have half a clue how it could connect back to them – yet. I'm aiming to keep the Maestro sweating overnight, let him out bright and early and see how quickly things move when news gets back to the rest of his clan. In the meantime, I was hoping you might be able to spare an officer or two to keep an eye on the huts along the north entrance to the Waterloo Bridge site between now and then?"

"I see," said Beverley. "What's the hurry, if you have Parnell locked up already?"

"His firm get itchy fast," said Greenaway. "I don't want to leave nothing to chance. The press don't have Muldoon's name yet, but I intend to charge him this evening and you know how leaky even the walls of Bow Street can be. If Moishe Abraham gets wind of any of this, he'll be straight over there to sort out any outstanding business he might have with Morrie the Tipster, believe me."

"All right," said Beverley. "I'll see what I can muster. And I'll expect to hear back from you in due course."

"Thank you, sir," said Greenaway. He resumed the whistling

of his favourite sporting ditty while he made his next telephone call to Charing Cross station.

− • −

Parnell sat down on the bunk, looked down at his long, manicured hands to make sure they weren't shaking, then took the pack from where he had concealed it in his sock and began to shuffle. Feeling the cards flying through his fingers had a calming effect on the Maestro, putting him back in control of a system of logical thinking that would stop the narrow walls from bearing down on him and his mind from straying into panic.

Parnell had been keeping his mind agile this way for almost as long as his call-up to the RAF had been served on him − currently three years and counting. The morning those papers had landed on his mother's doorstep was the same day he had left his hometown of Preston for good, putting the full width of the Ridings between them before he stopped in Bridlington.

There, Parnell had tried his luck fulfilling his dearest ambition, playing drums in a show band at the Spa Pavilion. He had displayed enough of an aptitude for hitting things with some sort of rhythm to earn himself a place in his school orchestra and was therefore competent enough to pass the audition. What he hadn't realised was quite how desperate his fellow Long Shore Swingers had become for someone to fill their vacant stool before they ended up hiring him.

Parnell's education in the music business over that first summer season was one long, slow and bitter realisation that he was never really going to be up to the task of playing big-band swing. No matter how hard he practised, he could never get to the stage he had always dreamed of − to lose himself within the rhythm and merge with the music he loved. It was a bitter pill to swallow.

Luckily, he found a sympathetic friend in the kindly old duffer who did the magic turn in the same summer show. In Parnell, this ageing Maestro saw a glimpse of his younger self and, following a few commiserating after-show drinks one night, set about schooling him in the arts of illusion, card sharpery and mesmerism, techniques that, to his delight, Parnell found much easier to master. Once his benefactor was convinced a new Maestro had been born, he offered some sage advice.

"You want to get yourself down to London, my dear. Don't waste your life like I have in these provincial dives. There are many more opportunities for a clever boy like yourself in the Smoke than you'll ever find on the end of a pier."

He supplied his protégé with the phone numbers of his remaining contacts before he waved him off on the train down south and, by the summer of 1939, Parnell had joined a variety troupe making their way around London and the Home Counties. For two weeks that June, they were booked at the Victoria Hall in Leatherhead – which was how he had first made the acquaintance of Edith Cavendish-Field.

A sudden barrage of shouting broke Parnell's concentration. A drunk-and-disorderly was being manhandled into the cell next door, letting his captors know his frank opinion of their parentage and choice of careers. Parnell rolled a finger around the neck of his shirt. Edith and Joe. It had all started off as a joke to him. But it hadn't turned out very funny.

– • –

As Margaret McArthur's body had been found on Charing Cross turf, it was with one of their senior detectives that

Greenaway made his return visit to Bow Street. DI William Bright was exactly the sort of dedicated connoisseur of villains who would be useful on a trickster like Muldoon. Ten years younger than Greenaway, he had been spared the call-up thanks to an injury sustained while pursuing a suspect over a warehouse roof and falling through the ceiling, which had left him minus three toes on his left foot. Bright's limp only served to enhance a formidable presence, built like a blacksmith with a thatch of hair the colour of barley and unnervingly pale-blue eyes.

Greenaway outlined his angle on Muldoon to DI Bright as they waited for him to be brought up from the cells to the interview room. "Let me take the lead," he said, "but if anything occurs to you, adjust your tie and I'll let you make your presence felt. In the meantime, you've got a good pair of eyes on you, see if you can't sus him out."

Their prisoner was back to playing his insolent act, with a constable on either side needed to manoeuvre him up from the cells and deposit him in the chair opposite the two detectives. Greenaway began with the formalities.

"My name is Detective Chief Inspector Edward Greenaway and this is Detective Inspector William Bright. I am conducting investigations relative to the murder of the woman now known to have been Margaret Theresa McArthur on Waterloo Bridge on the night of Tuesday, the seventeenth of February." He paused to stare hard at his suspect. "I did tell you I'd be back, Muldoon. Couldn't you be bothered to even have a shave? We do allow it here, you know."

Slumped in his chair, Muldoon stared back with all the hostility he could muster. "Can I have a cigarette?" he asked.

Greenaway gave his jacket pocket a cursory pat. "Oh dear," he said, "I've run out."

"Here," Bright picked up his cue, offered his own case across. "Have one of mine."

Muldoon accepted the smoke and a light, exhaling his first drag in Greenaway's direction. Greenaway took Cherrill's report out of his murder bag.

"Your fingerprints are all over that handbag you tried to flog in Leatherhead," he told his suspect. "Margaret McArthur's handbag. That's irrefutable evidence, Muldoon."

"It don't mean I killed her," Muldoon said, his dark eyes shifting between the two detectives and finally settling on Bright.

"Then explain what happened between the hours of eleven o'clock and midnight on the evening of Tuesday, the seventeenth of February," said Greenaway. "We know you were in the Hero of Waterloo pub on the Strand until closing time, and we know you left with the deceased. We have witnesses to all of that. We have a further witness who places you on the northeast side of Waterloo Bridge at midnight. All you need to do is fill in the missing details of how you ended up with Miss McArthur's handbag in a pub in Leatherhead and how she ended up lying dead underneath the exact spot on the bridge where our witness found you." He spread his hands out. "It's simple, really."

"Look," Muldoon kept his eyes locked on Bright, "I'll level with you guys. I paid that dame three dollars, up front, for a service *she* offered *me*. I even found us a nice, out-of-the-way spot to do it in, instead of the doorway she tried to drag me into. But when it came down to it, she wouldn't put out. I asked for my money back, but she wouldn't give that up either, instead she started yelling the place down like she was drunk or mad or something. You know what those Irish broads can get like." Muldoon pointed an index finger towards his temple and spun it around in a circle. Bright smiled encouragement back at him.

"They're crazy, yeah? I had to get my money back so I pushed her around a little bit – but who wouldn't, in those circumstances? I got the bag off her and then I took off. And that's all there is to it."

"Really, Muldoon," said Greenaway. "I've left you here all afternoon and that's the best you can come up with? You were seen, remember? That man who helped you down off the bridge? He heard you both arguing, but by the time he got to where you were, there was no sign of the woman. He thought there was something a bit strange about that, so he hung about 'til daybreak, when he found her dead body."

Muldoon shrugged, kept his eyes on Bright. "How should I know what she did with herself after I took off?" he said. "She was mad as hell, mad enough to throw herself off the bridge for all I know. Or maybe she was so drunk she tripped over her own feet – I mean, Christ, she was only a whore. What do you care if she did herself in?"

Bright put his hand up to loosen the knot of his tie. "Tricky creatures, ain't they, women?" he said. "Do you mind telling me, at what point during your transaction did you realise that this one wasn't going to play the game?"

"Soon as the folding was in her purse," Muldoon said. "I shoulda known better."

"What happened then?" Bright looked puzzled. "Did she try to run off or did she just start shouting at you?"

Muldoon's brow furrowed. "She tried to run off," he said, "so I caught hold of her arm." He nodded, satisfied with his explanation. "And that was when she started screaming."

"Right," Bright said, scratching his head. "So then at what point, between you giving her the money and her trying to run off, did her right stocking come off and tie itself around her neck? Or did that happen when she tripped over her own feet?"

Muldoon's expression soured. "I don't get it," he said.

"The stocking," repeated Greenaway. "How did it get around her neck, Muldoon? Some sort of a magic trick, perhaps?"

Muldoon's cheek began to twitch the way Greenaway had come to expect when he'd run out of smart things to say. "How should I know?" the Private said. "You're just trying to pin something on me I had nothing to do with."

Greenaway shook his head. "None of you can ever think of an original line to say, can you?" He leant across the table. "I know you couldn't bring yourself to take a very good look in the end, but all those injuries you witnessed today at the morgue, they weren't just caused by her fall from the bridge, as well you know and as the autopsy makes clear. In addition to the ligature marks caused by your little homage to Cummins, she was punched on the lower jaw and had fractured her spine struggling with an assailant prior to smashing her head in on the scaffold on the way down. Or are you trying to tell us she managed to do all that to herself, too? You're a useless liar, Muldoon, on top of the rest of your failings."

Muldoon slapped himself hard on the giveaway cheek. For a moment he maintained eye contact with Greenaway, putting everything he had left into that wild-eyed stare.

"Anything more to add?" Greenaway kept his own face neutral as he stared back, looked deep into those black-hole eyes until he could see gravestones appearing there.

"No? Well, then, as a result of enquiries I have made you will be brought up at Bow Street Police Court on Monday morning and charged with murder." Greenaway stood up. "Do yourself a favour, son. Have a shave before then."

25

HAUNTED NIGHTS

Friday, 20 February 1942

"My dear, may I present another newcomer to our circle tonight?"

Miss Moyes had brought her best grey moiré gown out of mothballs, augmented it with black lace and a solid silver cross at her throat. The parlour of the Christian Spiritualist Greater World Association had been dusted from top to bottom, best silver and Wedgwood laid out and all rations put to the service of the largest gathering the Duchess had ever witnessed at Lansdowne Road.

All to honour a singularly unremarkable guest, as far as Duch could see.

Mrs Helen Duncan was a stout, plain-looking woman with a flat black bob, dressed in a floor-length black gown and Paisley shawl. She could barely dislodge her cigarette from between her stumpy fingers before they shook hands. Her husband Henry, a similarly barrel-shaped man, had narrow, watery eyes and an equally moist handshake that did not inspire any further conviction in Duch that she was in the presence of elevated beings. However, their fame within Spiritualist circles had quadrupled the attendance of the regular Friday night meetings. Duch could count the heads of almost everybody she had ever met through the Association, alongside a fair smattering of strangers, like the tall, red-headed gentleman Miss Moyes was beckoning her to meet.

"This is Mr Ross Spooner," her hostess informed her. "He's a journalist from *Two Worlds* magazine."

"A pleasure to meet you," he said. Like the Duncans, he spoke with a Scottish accent, but whereas Duch had struggled with their dialect, Spooner's voice had a rippling cadence she found immediately engaging.

"A journalist?" said Duch. "How interesting. Have you been writing for this magazine for long?"

"Tell you the truth, it's the first time I've been trusted with a story," he said, a slight colour rising in his cheeks, which, along with his unruly shock of hair and the wire-rimmed spectacles that did not sit quite straight across the bridge of his nose, gave him the look of a naughty schoolboy. "I hope I won't make a hash of it."

"And it's Mrs Duncan you'll be writing about?" enquired Duch.

"Aye, that's right," said Spooner. "She's quite a fearsome reputation with the ectoplasm, hasn't she?"

Duch raised her eyebrows. "I don't doubt she's full of it," she said. "Do you know of her from Scotland, then? I'm afraid to say I'm not so familiar with her talents myself. I'm only really what you could call a dabbler, you see."

"Oh aye, yes, well," Spooner's face got redder still. "Mrs Duncan's from Callander, she's a Highland lassie, whereas I'm from Aberdeen. We've no' actually met before, but I have been taking a keen interest in her career for a wee while now."

"Well, I'm sure your story will turn out fine," Duchess

tried to sound more encouraging than she felt. "It's a shame Mr Swaffer isn't here," she added, sweeping the room for any sign of his snowy-white head. Strange that everyone else had turned out for Mrs Duncan except for him, she realised, although this guest spot had been a somewhat impromptu affair, arranged only in the last couple of days, so perhaps the news had just not got through to Fleet Street's finest. "He would have been able to give you some tips on getting a scoop, no doubt."

"Mr Swaffer?" Spooner spilt drops of his sherry down the front of his waistcoat without noticing. "Hannen Swaffer, you mean? *The* Hannen Swaffer?"

"That's right," said Duch. Her eyes stopped on the figure of Daphne Maitland, who was bending awkwardly over a vintage supporter of Miss Moyes who sat in a bath chair, holding up an ear trumpet for her to talk into. Daphne was trying hard, as she always did, thought Duch – despite her attempts to dress as dowdily as possible, in the plain grey or brown suits her Communist principles dictated, those suits still came from Derry & Toms and she still looked like a fashion plate from *Vogue*. A quality which, Duch suspected, would not be lost on young Spooner.

"Though we have got another of his protégées with us. That lady there," she pointed, "Daphne Maitland her name is. She does the in-house magazine for Miss Moyes. Puts the whole thing together and then prints it in the basement here. Would you like to meet her?"

The green-brown eyes behind Spooner's spectacles widened with interest as he followed the line of the Duchess's finger.

"Oh aye," he said, and cleared his throat. "I mean, yes, please."

Hannen Swaffer was not happy. For a start, he was on the other side of the river, where he never felt entirely safe. The squat, redbrick pub to which he had been despatched to meet with the group who addressed themselves as the Campaign Against Capital Punishment in the letters sent to the *Herald* offices, was clearly a hive of villains. The landlord, Swaffer recalled, was once a member of the infamous Elephant Boys racetrack gang, with whom Greenaway had frequent skirmishes in the past decade. The proximity of the Effra Arms to Brixton Prison was no coincidence either.

Inside the snug bar sat the deputation. Miss Olive Bracewell had been known to Swaffer since April 1935, when she had begun her campaign outside Wandsworth Prison, where the murderer Leonard Brigstock was due to be hanged. There, dressed and made-up like a film star, she had put on as much of a show as her wealth could command, hiring a choir to sing "Abide With Me" and men with sandwich boards protesting that "A murderer is no different from a madman" to march about distributing leaflets urging the abolition of capital punishment. Her arrest for obstruction in the glare of the flash-bulbs of the press was taken as a personal challenge. She had taken up her cry at every major murder trial that was likely to afford her maximum press coverage ever since. In turn, Swaffer had done his own share of digging on her.

Miss Bracewell was the industrious only daughter of a coal porter and a washerwoman from Birmingham, who had amassed a fortune in her youth by inventing the first brushless shaving cream, enabling her escape from the Midlands and relocation to a gothic pile in Hampstead. There she mixed with the kind of people who, if they found her eccentric, were not unsympathetic to her cause. Indeed, she had even been encouraged by one or two of them in an ill-fated attempt at standing as an abolitionist Labour MP in the doldrums of the Thirties. But the longer her activities went on, the more she seemed to gain a grudging kind of acknowledgement, the result, Swaffer thought, due more to her sheer tenacity than to the actual public mood.

It was therefore no surprise that she began to bombard him with letters about Gordon Cummins the moment the ink was fresh on the paper that proclaimed his murder charge. What was new was this title she was now giving herself, as if she had finally become an organisation, rather than a one-woman campaign. This was not the impression Swaffer garnered from those gathered around her: a bunch of meaty-armed Brixton housewives with headscarves over their curlers – and cleavers in their overalls, no doubt – a greasy-haired young man wearing an expensive camel coat with padded shoulders and a bleached blonde in a rabbit fur. It was only the threat implied in her latest missive and his editor's reaction to it that had brought him to meet her.

"Miss Bracewell," Swaffer took a deep breath and doffed his stovepipe hat.

"About time." Even in matronly middle-age, she still retained a certain glamour, thanks to a highly skilled paint job, diamonds that flashed in her earlobes, a pillbox hat with an ostrich feather bobbing on its crown and a fox-fur collar to her coat. The only thing she had never managed to iron out was the accent of her youth, still ending each word she pronounced with an upward whine. "We've been sat here twenty minutes waiting for yow."

Swaffer gave her his most charming smile and took the

chair opposite that had pointedly not been offered to him. "Well," he said, "there is a war on."

Miss Bracewell pointed a pudgy finger, encased in black-lace gloves, accusingly. "Yow'd better take note of what I have to say this time, Mr Swaffer," she said. "This time it's not just the abhorrence of the death sentence we will be protesting against. It's the evidence that has come to my attention that yower friend, Chief Inspector Greenaway, did not act properly during the course of his investigations."

Now she was getting to it. Pulling his notepad from his frock coat, Swaffer flicked it open and then reached for his pen. He sat, poised and cross-legged in an exaggeratedly theatrical pose.

"Go on then, my dear," he encouraged. "I'm all ears."

Miss Bracewell sat back, turned her head towards the tarty blonde in the rabbit fur. "Go on, Doris," she ordered imperiously. "Yow tell him."

– • –

"Is this how it normally goes?" Spooner hissed in Duch's ear.

The room had been arranged so that the rows of seats faced towards the specially constructed cabinet in which Mrs Duncan sat in an armchair, curtains draped on either side of her. The sitters blinked in the gloom of a single red bulb, from a lamp behind them. Mrs Duncan, her eyes shut, slumped backwards, arms lolling over the arms of the chair, head lowered on her chest. Groans rose up from her throat, getting louder as the air gradually became infused with a briny, bodily aroma.

"No," Duch admitted, wrinkling her nose. "I can't say I've ever seen it done quite this way before. Leastways, not here."

A white cloud began to manifest itself around the dark form of the medium, first floating around her head while it grew more substantial, then spilling down to the floor in front of her in a cascade. The room was filled with sharp intakes of breath, murmurings of astonishment. Then, billowing, tremulous, the cloud began to rise up in front of the sitters and take on a human form, filling out into the shape of a man – but with a black hole where the face should be.

"What a pleasure it is to see so many of you gathered here." The voice that floated forth from this apparition also seemed to tremble between two worlds, those of male and female. The being hovered for a moment in the centre of the front row, then moved closer towards where Daphne, Duch and Spooner were seated.

"And some have travelled far to be here, seeking answers to their woes."

A ghostly arm reached out in the half-light, a hand touched Spooner's knee.

– • –

"Well," said Doris, "what happened was, I had some information that I thought could help the police catch the Blackout Ripper. Only I didn't know what to do about it."

"Go to your nearest police station, I should have thought," said Swaffer.

One of the Brixton housewives thumped a fist down on the table. "That ain't the way fings is done round here," she informed him. "We don't just go running to the bogeys with our business. We sort it aht between ourselves first."

The youth in the camel coat put a comforting arm around Doris's shoulder. "It was a delicate situation," he explained in a more reasonable tone. "Doris come to me to ask what she should do. She wants to tell the bogeys what she knows, 'cos she's scared for her life of this Ripper. But on the other hand, she don't want to end up getting pinched herself for how she come to know what she knows, if you see what I mean."

"She was afraid of being judged on her profession and not being taken seriously?" Swaffer divined.

"Yeah," said the youth, "somefink like that. Any road up, I tell Doris that we all know Chief Inspector Greenaway round here, and if there's anyone who she can trust to tell this information to, then it's him, right?"

Doris's bottom lip trembled. "That's right," she echoed, looking down at her gin.

"And what was this information, my dear?" Swaffer asked her gently. She looked back up at him, her eyes moist and hesitant between the caked-on layers of mascara.

"Some friends of mine," she said, "had a run-in with this airman on Piccadilly. One of them took him back with her but it didn't go quite right. He paid her up front but then he couldn't do nuffink." Though she had gone through this part over and over again, Doris still found her memory of the overheard conversation in the York Minster pub disintegrating as she attempted to put it into words. "So she tried to chivvy him along and then he . . ."

She stopped, looked up at Swaffer helplessly, the words dying on her tongue. Her companion came swiftly to her aid.

"He started to strangle her," he said, leaning forward in a confidential, man-to-man gesture, "and that's when he spent his load." He winked at Swaffer. "That's the bit what gets to her, see. She don't like talking about it."

"And when did this happen?" Swaffer asked him.

"It was Monday the ninth," the youth replied smoothly. "Ain't that right, love?"

"That's right," said Doris, rolling her frightened eyes back up at Swaffer. "Though I didn't actually see my friends until the Wednesday."

"And they asked you to tell the police for them?" Swaffer could not easily discern where this was going, only that the girl's story had many similarities to the one the Duchess's friend Lil had told him on Tuesday the tenth, after she had heard it from the mouth of the woman who was attacked. The date tallied, if not the precise details.

"No, it weren't that exactly," said Doris. "They asked me to draw a picture of him for them and then go to the police, so they could use it to warn all the other girls."

"She's very good at drawing, see," the youth put in helpfully.

"So I had a couple of goes at it, got it to how they said he looked," said Doris. "Then I come and see Johnny and he arranged this meeting with me and Inspector Greenaway."

"And then what happened?" Swaffer enquired.

"Police brutality, that's what happened!" Miss Bracewell reared back up. "Instead of passing on this piece of very useful information in confidence, Inspector Greenaway marched this poor girl back to his station and made her spend the night in the cells, while he went out and arrested Cummins on the strength of her drawing!"

Swaffer ignored her. "In what way was Inspector Greenaway brutal to you, dear?" he asked Doris.

The witness shrank into her seat. "He took my picture," she said, her voice little more than a whisper, "and used it to get Cummins. But I never saw Cummins, did I?"

"Which tends to rather cast doubt on the veracity of his arrest, wouldn't you think?" Miss Bracewell parried. "How can we be sure he even got the right man, and not just the first person he saw wearing a moustache and an RAF forage cap?"

"That is a somewhat perilous accusation to make, Miss Bracewell," said Swaffer. "Especially to someone who knows a lot more about the facts than you do." He turned back to Doris. "And where is it you really work, my dear?" he pressed on. "Gladys's Hairdressing Salon of Piccadilly, is it? Or the York Minster, somewhere like that?"

"What d'you mean by that?" the youth's face curdled into a hostile sneer even as Doris's open-mouthed stare gave her game away.

"Miss Bracewell," said Swaffer, closing his notebook and putting it away. "Where did you first learn of this injustice? These people came to you, did they?"

"They certainly did," she replied, puffing herself out. "They knew I could be relied upon. I told them yow wouldn't have it, that yow'd only stick up for him, I know yow're all in it together. But this time, so are we."

"Hence this new name you're trading under," Swaffer concluded. "And did you, by any chance, pay these people for their information?" He looked firmly at the greasy youth as he said this, received a smirk in reply. Miss Bracewell ignored the question.

"Know this, Mr Swaffer," she said. "I've filed a petition to the Home Secretary and the moment we leave here, we will be starting a vigil outside Brixton Prison that'll last for as long as Gordon Cummins remains incarcerated."

"Oh dear," said Swaffer, getting to his feet.

The Campaign Against Capital Punishment rose as one,

two of the Brixton housewives reaching for the banner pro-claiming Cummins's innocence that had, until now, been concealed behind their united front.

"Stick this up yer front page," one of them challenged him as they unfurled it.

"He hasn't got the guts," said Miss Bracewell. "He likes to call himself a socialist, but just listen to him! He's a lackey of the state like they all are!"

"Madam," Swaffer drew himself up to his full height, "I will have you know the Home Secretary is a very dear friend of mine and I have no doubt he will treat your petition in exactly the same way as I will treat this story. By showing it the door!" With that, he turned on his heel and made his exit. Thankfully, he had asked his driver to wait for him.

"Take me to Archer Street," Swaffer said. "As fast as is humanly possible."

26

RIPTIDE

Saturday, 21 February 1942

As the night drew on and the pubs emptied, all the cells around Parnell filled up, four- or five-men deep by the sound of it, although he had obviously been singled out for the solitary treatment. The clamour cut through his attempts to keep distracting himself with the cards. As the witching hour struck, spectres came back to haunt him, images of faces swirling around the confines of his tiny, locked room.

Edith Cavendish-Field. Joseph Muldoon. Ken 'Snakehips' Johnson.

It was the latter of these three that had inadvertently brought the other two together. Parnell's mind travelled back to the beginning of the previous year, down Old Compton Street to a green-painted door with a Judas hole. A winking of an eyeball and through that portal, down a set of stairs into a crowded, smoke-filled basement, where the greatest performer he had ever seen in his life was on stage in full flight.

Ken Johnson, from British Guiana, taught to move by Buddy Bradley who had coached Fred Astaire. All six-foot-four-inches of him, all lithe and beautiful: black suit, white shirt, black skin, white carnation in his lapel. Tails flying from his hips and honey dripping from his lips.

Another voice beside him as the first set ended, cutting through the applause, bringing Parnell's mind back from the faraway flights he'd been riding on.

". . . somethin' else, ain't he? Buddy, thought I'd seen the best of them, you know, Calloway and Henderson, but this guy steals the lick on all of those cats. How the heck does he move like that?" The speaker looked like a Mediterranean pirate with his hooked nose, thick lips, olive skin and black curls snaking out of the tartan cap that perched sideways on his head.

"You look like you know a thing or two about jazz," he went on, his eyes glittering as they travelled up and down Parnell's pinstriped suit, taking in the wide shoulders and lapels, the generous turn-ups on his trousers and the pointed, shiny shoes beneath. "And a lot of other things, I'll bet." He took his cap off, ran long fingers through his hair. A waft of his cologne, all pirate's rum and spices, reached Parnell's nose.

"Joe Muldoon," he said and stuck his hand out. "'S'cuse the uniform. Ain't really my regular style, you dig?"

Parnell finally remembered how to say his own name, laughed and returned the handshake. "So, you're not over here on your holidays, then?" Cringing inwardly as he said it, the sort of thing his granddad would have come out with. Muldoon didn't seem to mind, responded with an equally corny line.

"Yeah, some vacation this turned out to be. Still, there's fun to be had if you know where to look for it, right? Hey, you want a cigarette?" Offering him a packet of Lucky Strike, then lighting him up with a brand new Zippo, he added: "There's plenty more where that came from . . ."

The thought of cigarettes snapped Parnell out of his reverie.

He patted his pockets in what he knew was a futile gesture: he may have kept his cards safe from the Duty Sergeant but that was all. He got up from the bunk, stretched himself, walked up and down the cell a few times to try to shake off the craving. In the cells beyond, someone started singing 'Danny Boy' in a voice that had not been made for such delicate work. A couple of other barroom crooners joined in, raising the feel of the place to that of an alleyway full of stray hounds. Parnell sat back down on his bunk, reshuffled his deck of cards.

Edith's face replaced Muldoon's in his mind, the backdrop shifting from the New Harlem bottle party in January 1941 to the dining room of Mole Cottage in the summer of 1939, the night still warm although the moon was high in the blue velvet sky beyond the diamond-hatched windows. Edith was putting his post-theatre dinner down on the table in front of him, a thick slice of game pie, mashed potatoes, carrots and green beans, all covered in a simmering lake of gravy.

"You're early tonight," she noted, lingering by the table as he tucked in. She knew she was a good cook and she liked to see a man enjoy her work.

"The others went off carousing," he told her, "but I couldn't wait no longer for this."

"Good." Edith's smile lit up her handsome face. "Would you like a beer to go with that?" she offered. "Or a glass of wine, perhaps? I keep a few good bottles to share with those who appreciate the finer things."

Parnell had known she had her eye on him, had deliberately left the others to it that evening precisely to see what would happen when he was alone with her.

"You do the magic act, don't you?" she asked, when she had cleared away his empty plate and settled down on the chair opposite, pouring them both another glass from the already half-empty decanter.

"That's right," Parnell dabbed his face with the crisp, white napkin before he took another sip, savouring the richness of both the drink and his surrounds.

"Is it all an act?" she asked, rolling the stem of her goblet around in her fingers and studying him carefully.

"How d'you mean?" Parnell noting the growing intensity in her gaze, wanted to carefully gauge where this was leading.

She smiled, shrugged. "I wonder if you'll think I'm being silly," she said, "but I've always wanted to know. Is everything you do in your act just a trick that anyone can learn, given the time, or do you have to have some sort of . . . I don't quite know how to put it . . . a gift for it?"

"You mean," Parnell read the signals of her hesitation, "a gift like how the Spiritualists mean it? Sort of a sixth sense?"

He saw colour rise in her cheeks. "I knew you'd think I was being silly," she said, looking away from him and raising her glass to her lips.

"Not at all," said Parnell. "It's a question a lot of people ask. But did you know that magicians are forbidden to reveal their secrets?"

Edith raised her perfectly plucked eyebrows. "Is that so?" she said, smile returning.

"Aye," said Parnell, "it is. You'll have me drummed out of the Magic Circle if you press me on the subject. What I can tell you is that what I do up on stage is like an art form that needs constant working on, it's got nowt to do with the supernatural. But what drew me towards wanting to learn this art form in the first place," he lowered his tone to a whisper, "was experiences I've had in life that have seemed to suggest I do have some sort of a gift for the other."

Edith's pupils widened. This was what she wanted to hear. "Is that so?" she said. "What kind of experiences do you mean?"

Parnell focused the full beam of his saucer-shaped brown eyes on her and lifted her right hand up off the table. Pressing it gently, he told her: "Seeing people who aren't really there. Like the man I can see standing behind you now, wearing his colonel's uniform."

Edith jerked her hand away. "My husband!" she cried, turning to scour the empty room behind her as if she expected him to have crept up on them. "Oh, my!" she turned back to Parnell, covering her mouth with her hand. "Is he really there?"

Parnell looked into the empty space behind her, summoning all the details he had memorised from the photograph in her study and the conversations he'd had in the pub down the road, where Edith and her intrigues were a major topic of conversation. "He's about six-foot-two, with dark, wavy hair and blue eyes. Very powerfully built, could have been a heavyweight boxer, but when he smiles you can see what kind of a man he really is, there's laughter lines all over his face. That sound like him to you?"

"Oh, I say," said Edith. "Oh, it does."

"See, I don't pick when this kind of thing happens to me," Parnell returned his gaze to Edith's. "It's more like they choose me. He's been waiting for a long time to have this conversation. Three years now, in't it, since he passed away?"

Edith nodded, her fingers still trembling by her lips.

"Well, your husband wants me to let you know that you don't have to go on worrying for him any more. It were sudden, like, how he left, and he knows it were a shock for you, but he's found himself in a much better place now and he'll be waiting there for you when your time comes."

Edith's smile drooped a little at this information. Parnell gave a chuckle, nodding and winking at the space above her head. "Right you are, sir," he said, looking back at Edith. "He's just said he knows that happy day is still going to be some while off yet, love. He wants you to get on and enjoy your life as best you can until then, and not to spend any more of your time in mourning."

"Does he really?" Edith's smile returned. This was more than she had dared hope.

"Aye," Parnell said, his smile on equally full wattage. "You have his blessing."

"Mr Parnell," tears sparkled in Edith's eyes as she reached for his hand across the table. "How can I ever thank you?"

– • –

Free board and lodgings, best steak, the odd bottle from the Colonel's cellar and his collection of cigars were amongst the tokens of Edith's gratitude Parnell received for that night and the subsequent "readings" he was to give her each time business took him back to Leatherhead, though the magic act tailed off after he made the acquaintance of Sammy Lehmann and Bluebell at the *Entre Nous* in the winter of that year. In exchange for them sorting out his problem with the RAF, he put his skills to other uses for them. The work that they sent him out to do still often involved out-of-town driving at anti-social hours, making Mole Cottage a convenient bolthole. He had some business cards made up to present himself as a travelling salesman and told Edith that, valued private clients like herself aside, he could make better money this way while the war was on, further enhancing the illusion by slipping her the odd item of contraband on his visits.

For Parnell genuinely liked Edith. He enjoyed her company and the ongoing saga of her liaisons at the Running Horse that she would confide in him over another bottle of the Colonel's wine, or a couple of Gin-and-Its, when the rest of the household was asleep. So when Muldoon tipped him the wink about the consignments of cigarettes due for his army base and the roads along which they'd be travelling before they could get there, it seemed the ideal set-up.

The cards now in disarray across the grubby, grey blanket that covered his bunk, Parnell slumped against the wall. It felt as clammy as he was, and once more he felt the need to loosen his tie and undo another button on his shirt, forcing down the memories he knew he would have to find some way of confronting when Greenaway came knocking at the door, the question he would have to answer himself before that moment came, in order to be ready for it.

Despite everything that went down in Leatherhead, could he really help Greenaway send Joe to the gallows?

– • –

"I was hoping you'd be here, dear boy," Swaffer's eyes alighted on Greenaway at the bar of the *Entre Nous*. "Might I have a word?"

"Swaff," Greenaway turned from his companion, an equally robust plainclothes detective with thick, fair hair, and greeted the journalist with more enthusiasm than Swaffer had seen since all this Murder Squad business first began. "Can I introduce DI Bill Bright from Charing Cross? We're just drinking to our chances of getting another sinner bang to rights."

"Delighted," said Swaffer, taking Bright's massive paw in his long, nicotine-stained fingers. "Am I to surmise you have the culprit from Waterloo Bridge?"

"On the nose as ever, Swaff," said Greenaway, exuding bonhomie and something more, a sparkle of excitement in his eyes that had been missing for a long time. Swaffer swallowed, hoping his own news wouldn't do too much to quash it.

"Charged the bastard this evening, the arraignment's first thing Monday morning, if you want to put that in your social diary." Greenaway waggled his eyebrows and then leaned back on the counter to survey the room with a satisfied air.

Swaffer followed his gaze to a familiar-looking group clustered around the table nearest to the stage. There he discerned the menacing bulk of Moishe 'Bluebell' Abraham and his accomplice the Bear, in contrasting sapphire-glinting pinstripes and business brown worsted, their brilliantined heads locked together over the glass ashtray at the centre of their table as they telegraphed malevolence back in Greenaway's direction with every flick of ash and muttered curse. Sitting with them, but slightly apart, was a woman whose raven-black hair was sculpted upwards into gravity-defying rolls, dressed in a blue satin gown straight out of a Parisian couturier's and a mink stole. She was leaning back in her chair, blowing smoke rings to the ceiling in an exaggerated show of boredom, her long false eyelashes batting slowly and insolently as her manicured fingers played around the stem of a champagne glass. She took occasional glances towards her two companions then exhaled again. As lean and angular as her husband was heavy and rotund, this was Ava, Bluebell's wife.

At once Swaffer realised why his old friend appeared so

chipper. "Ah," he said. "This has something to do with the Lehmann firm."

"It might," said Greenaway. "But they don't know what yet. All they know is I've got one of theirs spending a sweaty night down the cells in connection with a murder they currently know nishte of. I'm just wondering how long it'll take those two to puzzle it out, 'cos I'm laying two to one on that they ain't gonna get there before morning." He smiled, winked and turned back round to face Swaffer. "Anyway, you wanted to tell me something."

"It would be better said in private." Swaffer looked apologetically towards Bright.

"I see," said Greenaway, "protecting your sources at all times, eh, Swaff?"

Bright looked down, checked his wristwatch. "About time I pushed off anyway," he said. "Nice to meet you, Mr Swaffer, and Ted, good luck, I'll see you Monday."

– • –

"What did you make of Mrs Duncan then, Daph?"

The Duchess and Daphne stood at the sink in Miss Moyes's kitchen. There was a mountain of the night's crockery and cutlery to be breached, but Duch had volunteered on the basis that clearing it up was the best way to circulate the room and hear what everybody had made of the extraordinary night's entertainment.

Ross Spooner had needed the assistance of several more glasses of sherry to come to terms with being on the receiving end of the first manifestation of the evening. It had been one of Mrs Duncan's spirit guides, a little girl called Peggy, who assured him that the spirits knew he had chosen the right path and sung him an encouraging verse of 'Loch Lomond' before melting back into the ether.

Others had been delighted by what Mrs Duncan had brought for them. Old Mr Worth, the man in the bath chair, had a visitation from his aunt, who'd recently died from bowel trouble. Mr Hillyard, the caretaker, had his brother come through, speaking in a Yorkshire accent, to tell him he didn't think much of the medium, she was too fat – which proved beyond all doubt that it was him. A lady whose son was missing in action, received a soldier killed in an explosion in Singapore, telling her that he would always remain by her side, for which she wept in gratitude.

Once the human spirits had exhausted themselves, animals had come through. Duch had learned that the parrot who'd appeared to screech: "Pretty Polly!" at them was another of Mrs Duncan's regular spirit guides, who went by the name of Bronco. This evening, he had been joined by a cat and a rabbit – actually rather shapeless, white oblongs, Duch had thought – before the show came to a dramatic climax with Mrs Duncan lurching out of her cabinet, flailing her arms and crashing down next to her husband. After being revived by him, with the help of a lit cigarette, the lights went back up and the Duncans themselves melted away into the night, leaving a lot of excited chatter in their wake.

Daphne, who was on wiping duty, picked up a glass. "Well, you know I'm not an expert in these matters," she said. "When I was first introduced to her, I'm afraid I found her somewhat menacing – and her husband. I was surprised Miss Moyes had asked such people to come here. Of course, I had no idea that such an extraordinary reputation preceded her."

"And does it?" Duch held another glass up to the light.

"That's news to me and all."

"Apparently so," said Daphne. "Miss Moyes told me that Mrs Duncan rarely comes to London any more, though she caused rather a stir here in the Thirties – made herself some powerful enemies as well as friends, apparently."

"Oh yeah?" said Duch. "Like who?"

"There's a fellow from the National Laboratory of Psychical Research, if you know what that is?" said Daphne. "Harry Price. He's one of them. Keeps trying to expose her as a fraud, even though she's been examined God knows how many times by experts before she gives her exhibitions. So she's set up a new circle at a church in Portsmouth, where she's apparently doing tremendously well."

"Portsmouth?" The glasses were flying through Duch's fingers now, her interest in their condition waning in direct proportion to her attention to Daphne's story. "What would you want to go there for?"

"Our biggest naval base," said Daphne, "in the middle of a war? Of course she's going to get an audience there – think about it. All those families whose nearest and dearest are in daily peril from the sea . . ." She raised her eyebrows.

"'Course," said Duch. "So," she shot Daphne an appraising look, "you think her doubters might have a point, then?"

"Miss Moyes is adamant in her support for Mrs Duncan and I don't want to be disloyal. You know how much it means to me, working here." Daphne lowered her voice to a whisper. "But just between you and me, after tonight's showing I rather think they might."

Duch chuckled, shook her head. "I hope you didn't say anything of the sort to poor Mr Spooner. Would have broken his heart. I must make sure I get hold of a copy of this magazine he works for, 'cos I can't wait to read his report on meeting little Peggy on the bonnie, bonnie banks of Loch Lomond."

Daphne snorted with laughter. "Oh God!" she said. "I thought he was going to jump through the roof when that thing touched him! Honestly, though, what on earth do you think it actually was?"

"I wouldn't like to say," said Duch, recalling the odour that had permeated the parlour during the séance. "But I don't think I'd have wanted it touching me either."

"No," said Daphne, her expression turning sterner. "And I'm not altogether sure what you were up to with that man either, but I could swear you were encouraging Mr Spooner to be more than a little friendly towards me."

Duch batted her lashes. "What, me?" she said. "Whatever gave you that idea?"

27

SING, SING, SING

Saturday, 21 February 1942

Long after the drunks had exhausted their repertoire and loud snores became the soundtrack of the cells, the man in solitary could not find oblivion. Parnell could only lie on his bunk, scenes flickering behind his closed eyelids of the nights he'd spent with Joe.

Upstairs in his office, Greenaway had given up on the idea of sleep, too. Swaffer's news about Olive Bracewell had sent him back through his files on Cummins to double-check there was not a hair out of place. By the time he was satisfied that he could hang the killer four times over with his evidence it was too late to go home. Greenaway had never had much trouble catching a nap at his desk, but now, each time he shut his eyes, he was back in the old nightmare that had resurfaced from his childhood on the night he caught Cummins. Back in that dark cold room, with the dark cold lump on the bed in front of him. Only now there was a new twist to it. As always, he moved towards the bed against his will, as if he was a puppet that someone else was manipulating. He felt his hands close on the dirty grey blanket, tried to turn his head away as he lifted it up but found he could not move his neck. His eyes were locked in close-up, and in full-colour, to the entire oeuvre of Cummins's crimes as the woman on the bed changed from Evelyn Bourne to Evelyn Bettencourt, to Phyllis Law, to Claudette Coles and finally to Margaret McArthur, who, lying on the hospital trolley in the morgue, opened her eyes, but they were not her eyes they were green eyes, and said in a familiar voice: "You took your bleedin' time, Ted. How many more of us do there have to be, eh?"

He gave up after thirty minutes, went out to catch the morning's papers being delivered to the newsstands and brought a sheaf of them back to the canteen for inspection.

Though Swaff had immediately seen through the story he was being peddled in the Effra Arms, his editor was keen on Bracewell as an eccentric character and so likely to send him back to Brixton to report on her protest, as well as follow up on the progress of her petition. Leafing through the rest of the linens, Greenaway could catch no further scent of her works yet. But there was still plenty of time for more mischief-making; Cummins didn't come to trial for another month.

Five chicory coffees and one plate of watery eggs and toast later, Greenaway made his way down to the cells. His mind rested briefly on Doris, and how he had hoped her night behind bars would have put her off having anything more to do with the lowlife she was flirting with. But she was clearly up to her neck in it now. The only thing he couldn't adequately explain to Swaff about the whole set-up was Madeline Harcourt's reaction to Doris's drawing – how the seemingly witless art student had managed to forge such a potent likeness of Cummins from her eavesdropping.

Swaff would have to consult with the spirits on that one.

– • –

Parnell, his memory having returned to a bedroom in Mole Cottage, could almost smell rum and spices when the hatch on his door clanged open and a voice announced: "Rise and shine!"

Greenaway was at least reassured that his interviewee had had an even worse night of it than he had as he observed the shaky, sallow figure that tottered off his bunk, gathering up his pack of cards and the tie that he'd flung to the corner of the room.

"What time is it?" asked Parnell.

"Half-past seven," Greenaway replied. "I hope that's given you long enough to collect your thoughts."

"Half-past seven?" Parnell repeated. "But you've not even charged us yet!"

"It might not come to that, Parnell," Greenaway said, tapping the side of his nose. "Depends on how much I like what I hear."

"You got any smokes?" asked Parnell.

– • –

In the interview room, Greenaway lit two cigarettes. "Start at the beginning, Parnell," he instructed, passing one over. "How did you first meet Private Joseph Muldoon?"

Parnell inhaled, the nicotine racing through him, returning his mind to a more even keel. If this was an official grilling, he realised, then Greenaway was supposed to have another officer present.

"What's in it for me to tell you owt?" he asked. "I mean, I know you could beat the shit out of me if I don't talk, and that you'd probably enjoy it. But then again," he raised his eyebrows, "so might I. You never know, do you?"

Greenaway returned his smile and cracked his knuckles. "I'll tell you what you enjoy, Parnell, and that's your liberty. You want to go on enjoying it, don't you? Only, thanks to that nice

Mrs Cavendish-Field, I now have the evidence to link you and Muldoon to a couple of NAAFI cigarette hijackings that took place near Leatherhead in March 1941. You want me to overlook these new leads," Greenaway spread his hands, the gesture of a reasonable broker, "then I would have thought that was good enough reason to co-operate. But," the fingers moved back together, forming a steeple as the detective shifted forwards, "if you need another, it's quite simple. Muldoon's a nasty bastard and I want him to swing. As such, I'm prepared to overlook more minor misdemeanours in my quest to take him to the gallows. As you can see," the palms opened once more, "there's no one else listening."

Parnell weighed up the value of these words in the greater scheme of his life and the question he had been struggling with all night. He had never thought himself capable of grassing. But after what had gone down in Leatherhead, there was a part of him that wanted to assist Greenaway in his not unreasonable aim. After all – and this was what he kept coming back to – it could so easily have been Edith's neck on the receiving end of those murderous hands of Joe's. And whose fault would that have been?

"On the level?" he said. "If I tell you all I know about Muldoon then I walk away from here like we never met?"

"You make it sound so romantic, Parnell," said Greenaway. "But that's about the gist of it, yeah. So if we've got the niceties out of the way . . . ?"

"OK," Parnell looked down, imagined a spread of cards fanning out before him, the Jack of Diamonds face up. "I was at the New Harlem bottle party, back in January last year, to see Snakehips Johnson. Soldier-boy sparked up a conversation with us. It were about the music, like, but he was sussing us out at the same time. Comparing British swing to what they've got in North America; Snakehips and Hutch with Fletcher Henderson and Cab Calloway. Dropping hints that he come from a land of plenty and had access to the spoils. He wasn't green to the graft, if I got his drift."

"He was touting for business, then?" said Greenaway.

Parnell nodded. "Yeah. And Joe weren't interested in any smalltime pilfering. He needed help with what he had in mind."

"The cigarette lorries," said Greenaway.

Parnell shrugged. Talking about Muldoon was one thing, the business he did for the firm another matter. Even if no one else was listening.

Greenaway divined his hesitation. "So you set up a meet in Leatherhead. And how exactly did Mrs Cavendish-Field fit into this rosy picture?"

"Good old Edith." Parnell smiled, picturing the Queen of Hearts, face up on the pack. "I've known her for years."

"Is that so?" said Greenaway. "Convince a cynical old man how that unlikely statement might prove to be true."

"Like this," said Parnell. He closed his fist over his cigarette, raised his right arm and opened it again. His palm was empty. Then leaned forward, put his left hand behind Greenaway's ear and appeared to produce the still-smoking fag from behind it. "Magic," he said, snapping his fingers.

For a second, Greenaway was back in his nightmare, flashing back to the bubbles of blood around Claudette Coles's mouth, and he slapped his neck in reflex. Parnell read it as a nervous reaction.

"I were in this variety act, see," he said, a grin extending across his face. "Played her local fleapit the summer before the war. Edith were one of the few landladies who'd take in theatricals.

She didn't mind doing the late meals and, in fact, she loved it – looked on it as her chance to get in on all the gossip."

"Found you amusing, did she?" said Greenaway, grimacing, annoyed at his own momentary loss of control.

"When she found out I did the magic turn, she did, aye." Parnell winked. "Took it to mean I was some sort of medium – she were not long widowed back then, see. Wanted me to tell her what her old Colonel was up to on the Other Side. And, not being one to disappoint, I made up some old spiel about him being happy and wanting her to enjoy the life she had left. You know, the sort of thing them Spiritualists go in for." Parnell smirked. "And it seemed to do the trick."

"Very considerate of you," said Greenaway. "So, you gained her trust with your sleight of hand and then what? Some kind of long game? You and Muldoon was out to fleece her on top of the other job you were pulling?"

To Greenaway's relief, the smile fell from Parnell's face. "No," the Maestro said. "Not at all. I was just having a bit of fun with the pair of them, at his expense, mainly. I never expected her to fall for him."

"What, respectable Mrs Cavendish-Field and a lowlife like Muldoon?" Happier still, Greenaway feigned surprise at his own conclusions being confirmed. "How did that happen?"

"Don't seem likely, does it?" Parnell admitted. "But you want to try and understand Edith, you start with her natural habitat. There's this pub near her house called the Running Horse. Ha! Phoney Pony, more like. That's where all the proper gentry mix it up with those with an eye for the main chance. And Edith acts like a honeypot. Every fake general and dodgy vicar in Surrey come buzzing around her, vying for her hand, 'cos they think the Colonel left her a fortune. She wouldn't be renting her house out if he did, like, but she knows how to deal with them sort. Had a pack of the buggers on a string, paying for her social life and getting nowt in return but a nudge and a wink." Parnell sighed. "It were only with Joe that she didn't have a clue."

"Seeing as you're such a keen student of psychology," Greenaway offered his cigarette case a second time, "how d'you work out he done it?"

Parnell gladly accepted another smoke. Despite his surroundings – and his listener – he found a curious relief in being able to recount the tale. "I set him a task, didn't I?" he explained. "Joe was due to meet us in Leatherhead one Friday lunchtime. I sent him to the Phoney Pony, knowing that Edith would already have a date lined up with one of her drooling admirers, but she always turned up early to see if there was owt better going on. Gave him half an hour to see how far he'd get." Parnell raised his eyebrows. "Thought I'd see him outside, head first in the water trough. But, I totally underestimated him."

"Why, what did he do to her?" Greenaway asked.

"Well, according to him . . ." Parnell leaned in closer. "He's got there first, so while he waits for Edith to show, he practises his chat-up lines on the barmaid. She tells him all the pub folklore, including the nice little detail that it were once the centre of an Elizabethan smuggling ring. Then Edith appears. Joe starts off making a fuss of her dog. He's in his uniform, so straight off she can see he's just a lowly private, but she can hardly refuse to talk to him. And with what he's just learned from the barmaid, he seems quite clever, like he's really interested in the local surroundings. He does a bit of forelock tugging about discovering his roots – he's in a Highland regiment after all, and Edith knows all about grouse shooting in the Cairngorms. So she goes on talking to him, trying to work him out. By the time I get there, she's so intrigued she's virtually horizontal. Meanwhile, the rest of her would-be suitors can only look on aghast while this strip of a lad swans off with all their pension plans. I got to hand it to him. He were better than Laurence Olivier that day."

Greenaway's mind shifted again, back to Freda Stevens in her sister's hallway, talking about Cummins: "*Not so very far from an actor, when you think about it.*"

"Muldoon ever tell you about his time in France?" he asked.

Parnell frowned. "Not that I recall. Why, did he see some action out there?"

"A bit," said Greenaway. "He was at Dunkirk. Him and forty-four others of his outfit held the line at La Bassée canal for five hours until the tank regiment got through. By which time, there was only seven of them left."

Parnell's stare intensified as Greenaway relayed this information, his head shaking from side to side, as if something that had up until then been a mystery to him was finally being explained. He ran a finger around his collar, loosening the careful knot he had put in his tie between the cells and the interview room.

"That'll account for it, then," he finally said. "Bloody hell."

"Mrs Cavendish-Field told me you'd had a falling out," Greenaway pressed on. "What was it about?"

The shaky, sickly expression Greenaway had noted in the cells stole back over Parnell's face. Greenaway opened his cigarette case on the desk between them.

"Have as many as you like," he said.

Parnell nodded. "A week after that," he said, "we're back in the Phoney Pony, making out like any door-to-door salesman and off-duty soldier would do of a Friday night." His mind spun backwards, to an oak-panelled snug, thick with smoke and the plummy chatter of Surrey voices exchanging the price of hay.

Louder still was the sound of Muldoon wheedling at him, drawing unwanted attention their way.

"Only, Joe was getting a bit excitable," he recalled, "on account of the fact that Edith had let slip to him what I did when I first met her. He was like a little kid, demanding a demonstration of me magical powers. So, to shut him up, I promised to show him a few card tricks back in me room." An image of Bobby's eager face snapped into Parnell's mind as he spoke. With an effort, he pushed it away. "But it weren't card tricks he were after, was it? No, he had this bee in his bonnet about mesmerism. Reckoned his mind was so strong that no one had ever been able to put him under."

"What?" Greenaway thought of the sister's letter, the "unfortunate incident" in Muldoon's youth. "Does he make a habit of trying to get hypnotised?" he wondered aloud. Or could he have been psychoanalysed before?

"Dunno," Parnell conceded. "But he were taking it all so serious. I told him what I did was just an act I learnt off some old fella in Brid, but he were having none of it. He bet me five quid I couldn't hypnotise him. So . . ."

Parnell was back in Mole Cottage, Muldoon sitting down on his bed, his stubble blue on his chin, his pirate's aftershave permeating every humid molecule of air in the room. An occasional table strewn with glasses of whisky, an overflowing ashtray and the Ace of Spades face up on the deck between them.

"I get out me pocket watch, dangle it in front of him and tell him to sit still and follow the motion with his eyes."

He heard once more the sonorous ticking of the grandfather clock in the hall outside, Muldoon's breathing getting louder and deeper.

"I tell him he's going under. Either he's more pissed than I thought or he's having me on, 'cos I can see his eyelids start to flutter. I tell him he's out and under my control and what d'you bet? He slumps like a sack of potatoes. I prod him a few times, check he's not having me on, but no, I've really put him under – and in no time at all. Never mind his superior mind control, soldier boy's totally susceptible. So, I start to think, how I can use this to my advantage? I tell him that when I click my fingers he's going to come round, go straight to his room and get to sleep."

"What happened?" Greenaway watched as Parnell lit another cigarette with shaking hands. The Maestro looked past his inquisitor and into the shadows beyond.

"I click my fingers," he mimicked the action. "And he rises up off the bed like King-fucking-Kong. I start laughing, tell him his act's definitely better than mine and he can stop doing it now. But his face don't change, he's all dead-eyed and breathing heavy. Then he says something really weird. He says: 'Just be good now, laddie, just be good,' puts his hands around me neck and lifts me up with a strength that don't seem human."

Greenaway saw Margaret McArthur's body lying in the morgue, an abstract in black and blue. "Sounds like what he did to the woman on Waterloo Bridge," he said. "How did you get out of it?"

"Well," said Parnell, pulling his tie loose, "this is it, I didn't. He's choking the life out of me and I'm starting to black out, when I hear all this commotion, the dog barking, someone knocking at the door – only it sounds like it's coming down a tunnel, from far away . . ."

Parnell had seen his life in that moment unfurl before his eyes: the terraced house in Preston under a skyline of belching chimneys and frowning moors. His father in the pub, laughing and singing. His mother in the parlour, a rod in one hand and a rosary in the other. Lessons at the day school she inveigled him into after Dad left, the punishments for not paying attention, playing the drums his only release. Going on the lam to Brid, the frustration of the show band, the consolation to be found at the old Maestro's knee. Meeting Bluebell in the *Entre Nous*, a flash of familiarity in his smile, Parnell seeing the old man reflected in his face. Soapy in his barbershop, seeing something else, another kind of recognition there. Snakehips Johnson up on the stage, singing "It's Only Make Believe" through the smoke of a crowded ballroom, the whole of the moon in his dazzling smile . . .

Had Parnell not been in Leatherhead that night he would have been at the Café de Paris on the eighth of March 1941, when the German bomb fell and killed his hero. Afterwards, he'd heard tell, they found Snakehips without a mark on him, his white carnation still perfect in his buttonhole.

"He must have let go of me then, dropped me on the bed," Parnell resumed his tale. "'Cos next thing I know, I'm lying face down on the pillows and Edith's dog's licking me face. I'm not quite fully there, but I can hear Joe telling Edith that I'm a bit the worse for wear with the drink and he's putting me to bed. Next thing I know, he's left and closed the door and I'm lying there in the dark like I'm coming out of a bad dream. I get up and start retching something chronic. When I look in the mirror, there's bright red marks all round me neck."

Parnell blinked away the memory of his own stark white face. "He would have fucking killed me," he concluded, "if it weren't for that dog."

Greenaway studied the afterglow of fear in the other man's eyes. "But you still got up the next day and did the job with him?" he asked.

"We're not talking about that," said Parnell, snapping back to his surroundings. "Though I'll tell you summat else you will find interesting. The next day, Joe acted like none of it had ever happened. Were even joking with us over the breakfast table about the hangover I must have after all I'd put away. So, I don't know whether it *is* all some act with him, or whether he genuinely goes somewhere else when he flips that he don't remember in the cold light of day." Parnell gave Greenaway a thoughtful look. "When you arrested him, did he act like he couldn't remember none of what he'd done then, too?"

"He did," said Greenaway. "But he overlooked the fact that he did remember to steal his victim's handbag and bring it back to Mrs Cavendish-Field's with him to try and sell on. In my book, that makes him bad and not mad."

"Mebbe he's both?" offered Parnell.

Greenaway shook his head. "In a court of law, you're either one or the other, and I'm saying Muldoon's bad. If he uses the defence of temporary insanity, he might convince a jury to let him off his all-important date with Mr Pierrepoint. Which is where you come in."

"What?" Parnell assumed the same expression of outrage he had when he was arrested. "But I've told you all I know. You said . . ."

"I said, what happens next depends on how much I liked what I heard. And I liked most of it, so here's the deal. You appear as a witness for the prosecution. You tell the nice ladies and gentlemen of the jury how Muldoon approached you in the less than salubrious surrounds of the bottle party and asked you to engage in some criminal activity with him," Greenaway lifted his hand before Parnell could protest. "No mention needs to be made of any cigarette lorries, Mrs

Cavendish-Field or any of that. I give you my word."

Parnell swallowed. "Then what?" he asked.

"Coupons," Greenaway suggested, "Canadian whisky, rations from his mess – something he'd already had away himself. You try telling him you're only there for the music, but he's persistent. So you explain you're not really the villain that you appear to be, you're actually a magician, which is why you spend your time hanging round dodgy spielers with showbiz types. That seems to satisfy him, though he still asks you if there's anyone else in the room might be interested in his nefarious scheme. You tell him nishte, you say goodnight and that's where it ends. This way, Mrs Cavendish-Field stays out of it, you've got no explaining to do to Bluebell, and best of all, I get to prove my point about Muldoon and there's nothing his barrister can do about it."

At the mention of Bluebell, the fear returned to Parnell's eyes. "What if I say no?" he asked.

Greenaway's eyelids lowered. "Then I tell the chief of the Flying Squad all I know about the cigarette lorries and I summon Mrs Cavendish-Field to appear in court," he said. "If it would help to make up your mind, I can take you to the morgue. Have a look at Muldoon's handiwork up close and imagine it's good old Edith lying there instead. Which would you prefer?"

28

IT'S A SIN TO TELL A LIE

Saturday, 21 February 1942

Soapy's was open for business by the time Parnell got back to Brick Lane, Bear keeping guard at the window, Bluebell having his morning shave three hours earlier than usual. Only Bobby was nowhere to be seen.

"Maestro!" Bluebell waved from under his towels as the bell above the opening door rang out Parnell's arrival. The room smelled of fresh bread and coffee, it made the Maestro's stomach yawn. "Here at last. I knew that bastard Greenaway could have nishte on you, my boy. Sit down, have a beigel, tell your Uncle Blue what kept you all night."

Bear shook a brown paper bag in his direction. Parnell lowered himself down beside him, rummaged inside. The beigels were still warm from the oven. As his fingers closed over one, he felt quite sick from hunger and couldn't stop himself from wolfing down a huge mouthful.

"Coffee?" Bear lifted the red coffee pot from the table between them and poured into a cup that had obviously been set aside for the Maestro's return.

"How long you all been here?" Parnell asked.

"We followed you up West, hung about Archer Street until it

became evident you was in shtuck for the night," said Bluebell. "And, since my old lady couldn't lay off with the yammer, we come back here to get some peace and quiet."

Bear made the alarming grunting noise that was actually his laugh.

"I'm sorry." Parnell dunked his beigel in the coffee, chased down another mouthful.

"Don't worry yourself," Bluebell said. "Finish your breakfast." He started to hum along to the radio while Soapy applied the razor to his cheeks. For a few minutes, the sound of Parnell's munching jaws battled with Benny Goodman's orchestra to be the loudest noises in the shop. Then, having worked off his hunger, the grateful Maestro took a final swig of coffee, wiped his mouth and dusted the crumbs away.

"Remember my old Canadian connection," he said. "Mr Lucky Strike?"

Bluebell frowned. "The army kid?" he said, leaning forwards to let Soapy remove the towels from round his neck. "What, he's gone and got you in lumber?"

"No," said Parnell, "he's gone and killed a woman, chucked her off Waterloo Bridge. Told you he was a maniac."

"What?" Bluebell repeated. "When was this?"

"Tuesday just gone," Parnell informed him. "Greenaway picked him up in Leatherhead, at a place I used to stay back when I were doing me magic act. He took a shufti at the register while he was there, saw my name on it and tried to put two and two together."

"Oh yeah?" Bluebell examined himself in the mirror. "How far d'he get?"

"Far enough for me to realise whatever hole Joe's got himself into, he's not grassed on us. Greenaway knows nishte." As he spoke, Parnell offered a silent prayer that Greenaway would keep his word and his companions would never find out about his court date. "He were just trying to put the frighteners on, 'cos it seems to me, this whole business of catching murderers has got to him." Warming to a diversionary theme, he tapped the side of his head. "He's starting to lose his grip."

Bluebell projected his bottom lip. "I heard something like that," he said, nodding thoughtfully. "All this Blackout Ripper grief he didn't take so well, maybe it brought up some bad memories for him. That and him being on the Murder Squad instead of the Heavy Mob, it fucks with the bastard's digestive system. You think he's starting to fray at the edges, Maestro?"

"Oh aye," nodded Parnell, lips curling into a smile. "Happen I showed him one of me tricks during the course of our conversation – nowt special, just made me cigarette vanish and then reappear again behind his left lughole. Kids' stuff, really, but it made the bugger jump about ten foot in the air."

"Mazel tov!" Bluebell clapped his hands. Bear made a noise like a Lancaster bomber starting up its engines. "You're a mensch, Maestro." He got down off his stool, put a fresh cigar in his mouth and lit up. "Why don't you take the rest of the day off," he suggested, "recuperate your energies? Seems to me you earned it. Meet us back over Archer Street later on, after you had some proper shluff."

Parnell got to his feet, still wobbly, but thanks to the thoughtfully provided breakfast, now only weak from relief. "Thanks, Blue, think I'll take you up on that," he said, shaking the big man's proffered hand. "Good job we ditched him when we did, eh?"

"That's right," said Bluebell, clapping him on the back, watching him make his way out of the shop. It wasn't until

Parnell had disappeared into the throng around the market stalls that Bluebell turned around to speak.

"Did you know about this thing with the woman?"

Bear shook his head. "Not me, boss."

Bluebell scowled and spat. "We got a month before Sammy gets parole and now all this. What are we paying that gonef Morrie for?"

"Not his tips, that's for sure," said Bear.

"OK." Bluebell's eyes narrowed as his mind raced at the problem in hand. "I can't be having this mishegas. We better think what to do next . . ."

- • -

Despite an overnight drop in attendance, as the murky Brixton afternoon made its gloomy process into night, the ranks of the Campaign Against Capital Punishment began to swell afresh, their singing and chants assisted by the recent arrival of a brass band. Having run the gauntlet of their ringleader's harangues while his photographer captured the scene on film, Swaffer had retreated to the safe distance of the Governor's office for a personal lowdown on Miss Bracewell's tactics.

"About half-past three, a mobile canteen appears on the High Street and makes its way up to our gates, stopping to recruit every shopper in its path," the Governor told him. "By four o'clock I made fifty-seven recruits to the cause, all familiar faces."

"What was she feeding them?" Swaffer asked.

"Fish suppers, brown ale and chocolates from Fortnum & Mason, apparently. All paid for by Miss Bracewell, of course, but I suspect she had help with the menu. She's suddenly getting much better at all this."

"I think I met her new PR man in the Effra Arms last night," said Swaffer. "A young chap in a camelhair coat who certainly did seem much more in touch with the tastes and concerns of the local population. What time did the band get here?"

"Four o'clock," the Governor said. "Along with the second consignment of brown ale. Don't quote me, but I'd wager that came straight from the cellar of the Effra, too. By then there was about eighty of them out there, looked like a bleeding Hogarth etching. Still, it won't last. I give it until the siren goes or until the beer runs out, whatever comes first. I doubt she'll do a repeat performance. Beer or no beer, people round here just don't stay that interested for long."

"She's got what she came for, her face in every paper." Swaffer stopped scribbling for a minute. "And what of Cummins – does he have any idea all of this is being done in his honour?"

"Oh, Cummins is still playing his Good Chap role to the hilt," said the Governor. "Spends his days playing gin rummy, telling the guards all about his aerial exploits and trying to convince them he's some form of minor royalty. Way he's charmed most of them, I wouldn't be surprised if word hadn't been passed along." The Governor shook his head. "Makes you sick, don't it?"

"Miss Bracewell once asked me why, as a good socialist, I didn't support her cause," said Swaffer. "I told her it was because, unlike her, I had seen the bodies. I wonder how much she would like to be left alone in a room with the people she tries to save."

"Don't tempt me," said the Governor.

– • –

Greenaway was back in the old street, back in the bad old days. Past all the costermongers shouting out their wares, the pens of livestock bawling just as loudly, the air thick with their stink and clamour. It felt as if his feet weren't touching the ground, he was hovering inches above the cobbles like a ghost. He saw a little girl, aged about nine, her copper hair hidden under a gypsy headscarf, reading palms for ha'pennies. He saw a little boy, aged about six, deftly removing her customers' wallets from their pockets while they were so distracted. He carried on past both of them, back to the soot-dark slum of a house at the end of the street, the house that had once been his home, passed through the front door without having to open it and glided up the stairs. Greenaway knew where this was leading, to which room and which vistas of horror. "No!" he said in his sleep and rolled over. The vision cleared. He was back on the bridge of the SS *Kalomo,* in the middle of the last war, the roar and hiss of the waves in his ears.

A hand came down on his shoulder. "You won't find him there, Inspector." It was Mrs Cavendish-Field's voice, plummy and condescending, with a little trace of amusement. "He'll be on Waterloo Bridge, won't he?" Greenaway turned his head as her voice changed. It wasn't Mrs Cavendish-Field after all, it was the same little girl as before, but all grown up and wearing the landlady's expensive tweeds, mocking him with those same green eyes. At her feet, a brown springer spaniel gave a little whine. "You want to get yourself down there, Ted," she said, raising an eyebrow. "Before there's any more . . ."

"Inspector Greenaway, sir," a man's voice cut through her. "It's seven o'clock."

Greenaway's eyelids flickered, then opened on a curtained cubicle in the Turkish Baths. Last night's work sweated out of his system by a series of saunas, massages and icy plummets, he had at last managed seven hours' straight kip in the Moorish netherworld of Tottenham Court Road.

"Thanks, Ali," he said to the attendant, sitting up on his bunk. It was the sound of gurgling waters and hissing stones that had guided the latter part of his reverie, mirroring the feel of the ocean rising and falling as he had once known as he worked the ship's radio. He took his time dressing, breathing in the smells of amber and musk that permeated the air along with the other, comfortingly male aromas of the baths.

According to Peter Lind Construction's rota, Morris Spence didn't start work for another two hours, which gave Greenaway plenty of time to get properly fed before he returned to Waterloo Bridge.

He checked his reflection in the mirror before he left. Despite his restful afternoon, the face that stared back looked huge and strangely white, compared to the mauve smudges under his eyes. Greenaway felt the ground shift beneath his feet, as if he really was back on board his old ship, and wondered for a moment if he was starting to go mad. No, it was just the vibration of a tube train passing close by. The seal was still unbroken on the new bottle he'd put in his murder bag. Despite every provocation of the past two weeks, he hadn't got there yet.

– • –

Peter Beverley had put a sergeant on watch at the construction site. Greenaway met him amid the huddle of huts on the northeast side of the bridge, about ten feet away from the parapet where Margaret McArthur had dropped to her death. After arranging a signal, they took up flanking positions on either side of the night watchman's hut. Though they were prepared for a long night, instinct told Greenaway someone would be here as soon as Morris's shift started.

He checked his watch and sure enough, a familiar, burly figure appeared in his sights, glancing around as he made his way onto the bridge, then proceeded on a direct course to the night watchman's door.

Two minutes, they had agreed, before they went in after him. Give them the time to catch whatever act was going on in there. As Bluebell began to knock on the door, Greenaway made his signal to the sergeant, turning his torch on and off three times just as his quarry was given entrance. Then he stole forwards into the night.

– • –

"Morrie," said Bluebell, placing a Gladstone bag on top of the night watchman's table. "However many of them coupons you still got, put them in here now. And give me the plates while you're about it."

"Why?" Morris Spence put down his glass of rye whisky. "What's going on?"

Bluebell cocked his head, scrutinised the other man with astonishment. "Remind me how you got this job, Morrie," he said. "Did someone tell your boss here that you was a good lookout?" He leaned forward, across the table. "There's been a murder on the bridge involving someone we know and you don't think to tell me?"

Morris opened his mouth to protest and then shut it again as he registered the little, snub-nosed pistol that extended from the sleeve of Bluebell's coat, pointing in his direction. He opened the drawer of his desk instead. "The petrol coupons?" he asked.

"What do you think?" said Bluebell. "Of course, the petrol coupons. The ones that came from the same place as this did, you gonef." He tapped the top of the tumbler with the object in his hand. "Stopped by to see you before he chucked her over the side, did he?"

The night watchman looked perplexed. "I don't know what you're talking about, Blue," he said. "I swear to God, I ain't seen that one in weeks."

"Well, that bastard Greenaway has." Bluebell swiped the tumbler off the table, sent it smashing to the floor. "He's got him down the nick."

Morrie jumped in his seat. "You mean – he was the one what done that tart in?" he said, beads of sweat breaking out on his forehead. "Him? The Canadian?"

"Yes! The Canadian!" Bluebell shook his hands in a gesture of exasperation that made his companion fear he might accidentally blow his brains out.

"All right already," Morris ducked beneath his desk to produce the plates for the portable press he had adapted for the forgery of betting slips to petrol coupons that Muldoon and others had brought him. Bluebell dropped them into his bag, waved the pistol about a bit more.

"The petrol coupons," Morris muttered, burrowing in his drawers. Sweat rolled down his forehead as he began extracting sheaves of paper and flinging them on the table.

"In the bag, Morrie," Bluebell ordered.

"I don't know if . . ." Morris began and then thought better of it. In his scramble to do Bluebell's bidding, his nervous, fumbling fingers sent the paperwork flying. He knelt down to pick spilt coupons up from the floor just as the door crashed open and the hut was flooded with shouting.

"What the . . ." Bluebell spun round and was confronted again by a face from the past.

"What's going on here, then?" the expression on Greenaway's face developed into a shark-like grin as he took in the chaos spread around Morrie and the forgers' plates protruding from Bluebell's bag, enough evidence for at least two years' hard labour. He even gave his old adversary a wink before his gaze alighted on the weapon in Bluebell's trigger hand. It was then that something finally clicked in his head.

"Don't point that thing at me, you toerag!" he roared and let fly with his right fist.

It had come at last, the madness that had been lurking, waiting for its chance. Along with the rush of blood that felt like the roaring of wind in his ears, a movie reel of images unspooled before his eyes. The smirking visage of Gordon Cummins; the arrogant sneer of Joseph Muldoon. Knuckle connected with bone and Bluebell fell backwards, spitting teeth.

"Give it up!" Greenaway shouted, aware that he was putting on a performance so the sergeant could cover up for him as he wrenched the gun out of his opponent's hand. But he couldn't stop the stream of images, the broken bodies of Evelyn Bourne in the frozen air-raid shelter; Evelyn Bettencourt in a room saturated with her own blood; a white candle bathed in the red gore of Phyllis Lord carved up with knives; Claudette Coles with her insides out and Margaret McArthur's hair floating in the Thames, colouring the dirty old river pink with her blood. Down came the hand that gripped the gun each time, down on the head that Bluebell tried to protect with his arm as he shrank back against the wall. Still Greenaway couldn't stop. Before him swam the bewildered faces of Ivy Poole, Herbert Coles and poor little Jean Lord, uncomprehending of how life could have dealt them so brutal a personal blow even amid all the random carnage of war, why they had been singled out, what they could possibly have done to deserve this, too?

Then, like the movie reel jamming, his mind stopped on a black-and-white photograph of Margaret and Frances McArthur, sunlight gleaming off the surface of a stream in which they stood, so far from the murky Thames below. He dropped his hand.

Gradually, Bluebell's whimpering replaced the roaring noise in his ears and the room came back into focus, blood plastered halfway across the walls. Greenaway turned slowly to face the night watchman and Beverley's sergeant staring back at him, their mouths open in shock. He looked down at his own red hands and felt the ground shift under his feet.

"You saw him," he said, his voice sounding ragged to his own ears, holding out Bluebell's pistol for inspection. "He came at me with this in his hand."

The sergeant snapped out of it, showed some initiative.

"Flew at you, sir," he said, nodding. "Must have thought he was going to kill you."

Sitting on the floor, surrounded by coupons, his face splattered with red, Morris Spence could only hope his meek acquiescence would spare him the same treatment.

Greenaway nodded, wiped his forehead with the sleeve of his jacket. "That's right," he said, his voice sounding more normal now. "So, if you don't mind lending a hand, let's get these miscreants out of here and back where they belong."

29

JACK, YOU'RE DEAD

Tuesday, 21 April 1942

"RIPPER" TRIAL DRAMA read the front page of the *Herald*. Parnell examined the photograph of a rotund, middle-aged woman with what looked like almost an entire pheasant sitting on her head, being barrelled by four uniforms through a seething mass of people down the steps of the Old Bailey.

As record crowds gathered around the Central Criminal Court yesterday morning, Miss Olive Bracewell, leader of the Campaign Against Capital Punishment, was arrested for obstruction. Miss Bracewell has for years protested against the death penalty outside the trials of Britain's most notorious murderers, but has upped the ante in the case of Gordon Cummins by alleging wrongful arrest and police brutality. See our profile, by Hannen Swaffer, on page 3.

With proceedings off to a dramatic start, the trial was halted and the jury dismissed following a procedural error. Judge Justice Asquith appealed for press discretion over the matter and in the interests of fairness and justice we are happy to comply with his request. "The full truth will be published later," Judge Asquith directed, "but not until this trial is over."

A new jury will be sworn in and the trial reopened today. Our man-on-the-spot will be there to bring you all the facts – and any further mishaps – on this most controversial of cases.

"You intend paying for that?" the newsagent's voice cut through Parnell's perusal. "This ain't a bleeding library, you know."

Parnell flashed him a smile. "I'll take a copy of *The Stage* as well," he said, handing over a pound note.

"Ain't you got nothing smaller?" The vendor's scowl deepened as Parnell shook his head. "I won't ask where the likes of you got money like that to flash about, but I can take a good guess," he went on, handing him his change and his papers. "Bloody iron hoof," Parnell heard as he got to the door.

He turned on the step, about to give the old bastard a piece of his mind, when a man making his way into the shop cannoned into him. As Parnell's arms went out to grab the doorframe and stop himself from falling, he let his cargo drop.

"Oh, I am sorry, sir," said the man with whom he had collided. "Please, let me."

Winded, Parnell watched the man scoop down to retrieve his papers from the pavement. He wasn't anyone he recognised, he didn't think.

"There you go, sir," the man placed the bundle of papers back into Parnell's arms, patted him on the shoulder. Parnell registered a moth-eaten trilby and gaberdine mac. Then he looked at his papers and saw something else there.

"You ain't the only one who can make things appear out of thin air," said the man in the mac with a smile. Parnell stepped away from him onto the pavement. The man winked and walked swiftly away.

Parnell looked down at the court summons he had just been served.

Duchess sat in the public gallery, the theatre of the Old Bailey spread out before her. Mr Justice Asquith presiding at the centre, the barristers in their wigs at either side. Mr Christmas Humphreys and Mr G. B. McClure for the Crown, Mr Harold Flowers and Mr Victor Durand for the defence. The accused, all shaved and shined and dressed in an immaculately tailored dark-blue suit, looking even more pleased with himself than he had the day before. Things appeared to be going his way.

Cummins's defence had taken a line similar to Miss Bracewell's – the Metropolitan Police were a bumbling load of crooks and bullies who had framed the wrong man for expediency's sake. An impression that was only reinforced when Fred Cherrill took the stand to explain the points of similarity between crime scene fingerprints and those taken from Cummins at his arraignment. Even from the distance between them, he could see the jury had been handed the wrong photographic enlargements to study. No wonder his Lordship had appealed for press silence over that little matter.

It now fell upon Humphreys to outline the case for the Crown to the new jury. In compliance with standard practice in cases of multiple killings, Cummins was being charged on only one count of murder, that of Evelyn Bettencourt. The evidence they had heard from Sir Bernard Spilsbury the day before had been strong enough to see off Madame Arcana and Daphne, who had begun the day at Duch's side. But it hadn't had the same impact on Cummins's wife Majorie, who sat at the other end of the front row, shielded from her neighbours by the stalwart bulk of her sister.

As Humphreys spoke, the accused looked up to the gallery to smile and wave. Duch watched willowy Marjorie return his gesture with a flickering ripple of her gloved hand and the faintest ghost of a smile. The gesture wasn't lost on Humphreys. Having summarised the finding of Mrs Bettencourt's body by the meter readers on the morning of the tenth of February, he took Cummins squarely in his sights as he launched into the details.

"She had her throat cut – a deep cut right across the side of her neck, causing tremendous loss of blood and shortly after, death. Just before she died, the person who had done this had also inflicted a series of jagged stab wounds in the pubic hair and around the entrance to the vagina."

Duch watched the jury wince and shift uncomfortably in their seats. She looked back towards Marjorie Cummins and caught instead her sister's despairing gaze.

– • –

Parnell read the document one more time before folding it inside *The Stage* and then both inside the *Herald*, tucking the paper under his arm before he came into view of Soapy's. Bear was staring out of the window like a dog without his master.

Bluebell was cooling his heels in Wandsworth, facing two years or worse, considering his previous. Parnell had no idea what had been going on at Waterloo Bridge; the news had come as yet another nasty surprise. But when the knowledge that Bluebell and Bear had not, in fact, severed their connections with Muldoon did sink in, so, too, did the enormity of the situation he faced. Now that Bear would be taking an interest in Muldoon's trial, there was no way he could hope to get away with appearing unnoticed as a witness next Monday, as the Summons demanded. That bastard Greenaway had him over a barrel and the only option that seemed open to him now was to go back on the lam, as far away from Bethnal Green as possible.

While he considered how best to go about that, it was essential to keep up appearances – despite the fact that nothing was now the same. Inside Soapy's, the wireless continued to play, but there were no chattering voices to compete with the good-time sounds, just the steady scraping of razor against chin.

"Morning," Parnell nodded to the barber. Bear didn't have any coffee or beigels to offer the Maestro today, just the glint of his eyes as they ran him up and down, the expression behind them opaque. Parnell put his carefully folded papers into his coat pocket and hung it up on the peg, extracted his cards from inside his jacket.

"How's tricks?" he said, taking a seat next to the brooding form in brown and starting to shuffle the pack. Bear grunted non-committally, turned his gaze back to the street.

Parnell flicked over the top card. The Jack of Spades: the card that Bobby had chosen when he'd showed him his first trick. Another thing that had changed, he realised. There was no sign of the kid about the place any more. He looked up, frowning.

"Where's your apprentice got to?" he asked Soapy. "I've not seen him for a while."

"No, well you wouldn't have," the barber replied, not taking his eyes off the chin he was shaving. "His old man come round to see me. Said Bobby's Mum's gone back to Ireland, sort out a problem in her family or something, and he wants the kid at home while she's away." Soapy flicked foam into the basin, wiped the edge of his razor on his apron. "Well, you know what an impressionable boy he is." The barber's eyes finally rose to meet Parnell's. "His old man ain't stupid."

Parnell swallowed. "When was this?" he asked.

Soapy looked at Bear. "Day after you got nicked," he said.

"Oh," said Parnell, his stomach hollowing out.

"Yeah," said Bear, slowly turning his head. "About that. You and me need to have a little chat."

"Wh-what? Why, what's up?"

Bear gave Parnell a smile that didn't reach his amber eyes. "Not here," he said, scooping up Parnell's cards and putting them in his inside pocket, opening his jacket far enough to let Parnell see the gun in its holster. "We're going to take a drive, you and me. A nice, long one."

– • –

On the witness stand, Fred Cherrill faced Harold Flowers for the second time.

"My learned colleague Mr Humphreys described you as one of the greatest experts in the country upon fingerprints," the defence barrister began, in unctuous tones. "I suppose it is difficult for anybody, in a way, to challenge your specific knowledge of this branch of science, is it not? Have other people quite the same knowledge of fingerprints as you, or are you alone in the country on this?"

"Oh no." Cherrill wore his customary expression of a downcast bloodhound.

"It is limited, I suppose, to the police force?"

"I think there are a few amateurs about."

"I suppose you would not put the opinion of an amateur as being anywhere near as worthy of credence as yours?" Flowers raised a quizzical eyebrow.

Cherrill shook his head. "Hardly, sir," he said.

"I must challenge you a little with regard to this matter," Flowers went on. "This fingerprint you lifted from the handle of the tin opener. It's a very imperfect mark."

"Not for a mark that's been put on metal," Cherrill said.

"But it's very faint," Flowers's smile was that of an adult indulging a daydreaming child. "Would you, with regard to that mark, stake your reputation, knowing that a man is being tried for his life?"

Cherrill did not hesitate. "Yes," he said.

– • –

From the press gallery, Swaffer rapidly constructed a pen-portrait of Cherrill's unflappable professional demeanour. It would be followed by the report of Sir Bernard Spilsbury, next up for cross-examination, who had to face Flowers's inference that he had mucked up the victim's time of death as thoroughly as Cherrill had his prints. Aided by the testimony of Cummins's comrade in carnal activities, Felix Simpson, he sought to prove the story that Cummins had been weaving from his jail cell – he could not have been at the scene of the crime at the time the Crown said he was.

Despite Flowers's needling, Spilsbury's distinguished bearing, his long and brilliant career and his personal knowledge of the man, all helped the words to flow easily from Swaffer's pen. The only problem the *Herald*'s man-on-the-spot was going to have in convincing his readers of the infallibility of the Crown's case was, he considered, with Greenaway.

As the DCI had feared, plenty of mischief had been made during the past month by Miss Bracewell and her supporters with this pair of defence barristers who had, naturally, made the short journey from Brixton Prison to the Effra Arms in the course of their evidence-gathering. Now knowing that part of the case against Cummins revolved around the identification of his gas mask, Miss Bracewell was convinced that the hapless drunkard with whom Cummins had attempted to pull the switch on was the real Blackout Ripper, but that brutal, vindictive Greenaway had refused to consider questioning him.

It was the image of the DCI as a truncheon-wielding Neanderthal that swirled most darkly around these proceedings and one that Swaffer feared Greenaway could not easily shake off. Especially not if any other reporters picked up on rumours that, buckling under the strain of his two consecutive murder cases, Greenaway had taken his frustrations out on a suspect in a fraud case, a gangland enemy of old, who was currently eating through a straw at Wandsworth Prison hospital. Nor that this incident had taken place on Waterloo Bridge, mere steps away from the scene of the murder Greenaway had just been investigating.

Cigarette ash cascading down the front of his jacket, Swaffer's pen hovered nervously over his notepad as Greenaway's name was called.

– · –

"Do you remember," said Flowers, "just before your interview with the accused on the fourteenth of February, that you told him he could not consider you to be a gentleman?"

Greenaway stared back at the barrister. "Does the record show me saying that?" he asked. Flowers smiled. "I was asking you if you remembered saying that," he said.

Greenaway's face remained blank. "No," he said. "*Sir.*"

"Well," Flowers went on, "do you remember that the accused volunteered to you the information that he had been in a flat in Wardour Street with a blonde woman on the night of Monday the ninth of February?"

"Yes." Greenaway knew he could recall every word of Cummins's statement. He also knew Cummins had worked hard on his lines as he lay in his cell, utilising all his aptitude for twisting the truth with fiction. But he could disprove every lie that fell from the airman's lips. He only had to keep his cool while doing it.

"I put it to you that when he said he had gone off with a woman, you thought that you had got an admission from him that he had gone off with Evelyn Bettencourt."

"I thought no such thing." Greenaway's tone was perfectly calm.

"But did you not say to him at this point, 'Now I've got my rope around your neck,' or words to that effect?"

"Certainly not," said Greenaway, allowing a trace of indignation to surface. He didn't quite know how Cummins had drawn down his thoughts at the time so accurately, but as he had never actually said them aloud, the words did not appear in the statement.

Nonetheless, Flowers clearly felt he was on a roll. "I put it to you that you frightened the life out of him after he told you about going off with this woman," he persisted.

"I did no such thing," Greenaway flattened his voice out again. "No such thing."

Swaffer scribbled: *Stoic in the face of the defence's barrage of insinuation, Edward Greenaway proved to the jury the qualities that have earned him the rank of Detective Chief Inspector. He is the tower of strength we require to uphold the truth.*

– • –

Flowers called Cummins himself to the dock next. During Greenaway's testimony, the airman had assumed an air of nervous bewilderment, which he persisted with in the witness box, his hands clasped tremulously together in front of him.

"Would you tell My Lord and the jury, what, if anything, had been said to you by Mr Greenaway just before you made your statement?" Flowers asked.

Casting a brief look of terror in the DCI's direction, Cummins proceeded in his best King's English. "I told him I was very glad to see him, because I had every confidence we could sort out this misunderstanding he had of me like gentlemen. To which Inspector Greenaway replied that I had him at a disadvantage for he was no gentleman."

"And then, what did Mr Greenaway say to you when you told him you had been with a woman in Wardour Street on the night of the ninth of February?"

"That it gave him rope enough to hang me with," said Cummins. "Or words to that effect."

"Did that frighten you?" his barrister asked him.

Cummins nodded, loosening his tie for emphasis. "It did," he said.

"Remembering where you stand and the oath you have taken, did you have anything to do with the murder of that unfortunate woman, Mrs Bettencourt?" Flowers said.

Cummins shook his head. "No, I did not."

"Bastard," hissed Duch from the public gallery. She turned her head again to look at Marjorie Cummins, who had leaned forwards to the very edge of her seat. Her sister, by comparison, had slumped back in hers, arms folded across her chest. She looked as if she believed Cummins could trick the jury the way he obviously had her sibling.

But now it was McClure's turn to cross-examine the accused for the Crown.

"You were frightened by Mr Greenaway?" he asked with a doubtful frown.

Cummins nodded. "Yes," he said.

"Will you tell the jury why you were frightened?"

"Quite naturally," Cummins's hand went up to his tie again. "I was frightened because Inspector Greenaway made that remark with reference to murder and hanging and well, he frightened me." He cast another fretful glance in the DCI's direction.

But McClure did not look convinced. "I want you to tell the jury more about why you were frightened," he said. "Were you frightened because you told a lie?"

Cummins's head jerked. It looked like a nod.

"Would you please speak so the jury can hear your response?"

"Yes, sir," said Cummins.

"It is quite untrue that you met Simpson again that night," McClure waved his copy of Simpson's statement for emphasis. "We have his testimony that he left you at Piccadilly Circus at ten-thirty and did not see you again until the morning. You told him that you had arrived back at your barracks via the fire escape at the back of the building at three-thirty in the morning, while he was asleep. Between those hours, is there any living soul who knows what you did?"

Cummins moved from one leg to the other. A strand of hair broke loose from his carefully groomed forelock. "I saw no one else," he said.

"The mistake you made – so you call it – was to say in your statement that you got back to Piccadilly Circus and met Simpson there at about ten pm," McClure now read from Cummins's statement. "A mistake that you made before you were, as you say, *frightened*?" The prosecutor's eyes narrowed.

"Yes," Cummins said. "I was very vague as to times. In my statement, all my times were probably wrong like that. It's because of the blackout, you see, sir. I had not a watch myself, and of course, in the dark, one cannot see public clocks."

McClure sighed. He and the jury, his expression suggested, had had enough of Cummins's fabrications.

"Can you explain," he stepped his questioning up a gear, "that if you had never been to Mrs Bettencourt's flat in Wardour Street, why your fingerprints were found there? And how her neighbour, Mrs Poole, managed to identify you as the last man she saw go to Mrs Bettencourt's room with her on that same evening?"

Cummins's pale eyes, the mesmerist's stare he had used so powerfully on his victims, seemed to fail him in the sepulchral Old Bailey. The expression they currently held, as they rolled around the courtroom, was that of a man going under a wave.

"I'm afraid I can't recall," he said. "I'd had rather a lot to drink at the time . . ."

Duch looked back at Marjorie Cummins's sister. Freda Stevens stared down on her brother-in-law, a grim smile of triumph on her face.

– • –

"A sadistic sexual murder has been committed here of a ghoulish and horrible type," Justice Asquith summed the case up for the jury while keeping his eyes on Cummins. "But of a type which is not at all uncommon. What you have to determine is whether, upon the evidence, it has been proved beyond reasonable doubt that the murderer is the man who stands in the dock. His life and liberty are in your hands. But in your hands are also the interests of society."

– • –

The jury took only thirty-five minutes to make their deliberations. As they filed back into the courtroom, none of them looked towards the defendant.

"How do you find the accused?" asked the court clerk.

The foreman stood. "Guilty of murder," he said.

Freda Stevens closed her eyes in relief.

The clerk turned to face Cummins. "Prisoner at the bar," he said, "you stand convicted of murder. Have you anything to say why the court should not give you judgement of death according to the law?"

Cummins's veneer was broken. He was ashen, shocked to the core. "I am completely innocent," he said, struggling to keep his voice from breaking.

Freda Stevens put her arms around her sobbing sister as the court chaplain approached the Justice's bench and placed the black cap on Asquith's head.

"Gordon Frederick Cummins," the Justice said, "after a fair trial, you have been found guilty, and on a charge of murder, as you know, there is only one sentence which the law permits me to pronounce, and that is that you be taken from this place to a lawful prison, and thence to a place of execution, and that you be there hanged by the neck until you are dead. And may the Lord have mercy upon your soul."

Duch got to her feet and looked down on Greenaway's head and the tangle of grey hairs that had sprouted on his crown since the last time they had met. She made one last scan of the rows around her, vainly searching out a cloud of white-blonde curls amid the throng. But it seemed Lil had not returned to see justice served today.

Duch sighed, cast her parting glance on Greenaway. "You done us a mitzvah, Ted," she said.

30

GUILTY

Monday, 27 April 1942

It was Madame Arcana who dragged the Duchess back to the Old Bailey a week later. The Frenchwoman had recovered from the harrowing testimony on the fate of her former client and was glad Cummins had got what he deserved. Yet, she worried Nina was not at peace. There was a matter that still troubled her, that could only be resolved by a trip to the trial of Private Joseph Muldoon.

There were no crowds gathered about the court steps on this morning, no Miss Bracewell being forcibly removed from the railings and only two others waiting to be let into the public gallery: a middle-aged woman in a dark-blue coat and hat and a broad, battered looking man in a threadbare black suit. Entering in silence, they took up seats apart from each other. Below, the snowy-white head of Swaffer mingled with a smattering of reporters in a similarly depleted press gallery. Once more, Judge Asquith presided and G. B. McClure prosecuted. Muldoon's defence counsel was the state-appointed Mr Stephen Lincoln.

As the jury was being sworn in, one last straggler arrived in the public gallery. While Madame's eyes remained fixed on the dock for her first glimpse of the prisoner, Duch turned her head in time to see Bear take a seat behind them.

Madame jumped in her seat. "I knew it!" she said. "Look!" The prisoner had arrived.

"What?" Duch turned her eyes towards the swarthy service-man. "You know him?"

Muldoon had made sure to have a decent shave and haircut before he appeared in public. Unlike Cummins before him, he did not swagger his way into the courtroom, but kept his curly head down, his expression a mix of fear and apparent bewilder-ment that he should find himself in such a situation.

"It's *him*," hissed Madame. "Nina's old boyfriend, the Canadian. *Mon Dieu*," she shook her head, "what an unfortu-nate woman she was. The Knight of Swords was determined to have her for his bride."

She had only met him once before, in Berlemont's with Nina, during the full flush of her former client's infatuation. Madame had felt him to be malignant then, draining the room of life with his repertoire of crude jokes and stories, which that night had been mainly at the expense of the First French Army and expressly for her benefit, she felt. So when she heard of a Canadian soldier called Joe being tried for the murder of a woman on Waterloo Bridge, she had to ride her hunch. The fact that he belonged to a Highland regiment sharpened her certainty – as well as the tartan Balmoral cap he had worn when she met him, all his talk that night had been of how the cowardice of the French had cost the lives of his comrades at Dunkirk.

"Things *have* got peculiar all of a sudden," said Duch.

– • –

At his place in front of the witness bench, Greenaway was quietly seething. Despite the trouble he had taken to make sure Parnell received his Summons while alone, it appeared his witness had done a flit the moment it was served. The plainclothesman from Leman Street station who had done the necessary for Greenaway reported seeing Parnell being driven away from Brick Lane by Bear within ten minutes of their encounter and not one of the DCI's snouts or fellow officers in the whole of London had seen hide nor hair since. The magician had vanished.

Greenaway was disgusted, but not altogether surprised: Parnell was a weakling hiding behind his bag of tricks, who would have found it easier to go running to Bear with his troubles than to turn up like a man today. He pondered briefly how permanently the Maestro's misdemeanours might have been punished by his firm. Right now, that mattered little compared to losing a crucial witness. It was a bad omen.

In the press gallery, Swaffer felt it, too. He was tired – of the constant bombing of letters from Miss Bracewell, who was getting up a new petition to try to prove Cummins's innocence; and from the events in the world that had shifted his editor's focus far away from courtroom concerns. The raids on the historic German towns of Lübeck and Rostock that had been reciprocated last night by the bombardment of Bath and Exeter; the repercussions of the raid on Tokyo that had resulted in public beheadings of their ARP wardens. Even the bizarre story of a man sketching the ruins of St Clement Danes and finding the five farthings of "Oranges and Lemons" fame on the floor had been given more space than he had been promised for the coverage of Muldoon's case. Swaffer wondered if the jury would share his editor's feeling, that the successful conclusion to Cummins's outrages had drawn a premature curtain over the activities of his fellow stocking-strangler serviceman.

Greenaway heard his name called and rose with a heavy heart.

Though logic told him that the evidence stacked up high enough against Muldoon even without his gangland connections being taken into account; that his defence was a state-acquired hack who rarely roused himself to make an effort; and that no honest British jury could sympathise with such an obvious delinquent as this Canadian, Greenaway still couldn't shake his feeling of imminent doom.

– • –

"How does the jury find the accused?" the clerk asked the foreman, seven hours later.

The man rose. Madame gripped Duch's hand tightly.

"Not guilty," came the reply.

"No!" Madame hissed. Duch turned her head. The woman in the blue coat sat with her hands together, rosary beads between her fingers, her face disbelieving. The man in the funeral suit buried his head in his hands and gave out a low moan. Bear got straight to his feet and made swiftly for the exit, not looking behind him.

"I don't believe it," Madame went on. "How could they?"

"How indeed . . .?" Duch said to Bear's departing back, before turning to her friend. Muldoon had stuck stubbornly to the line that he had not been there when Margaret McArthur, or Peggy Richards, as she had introduced herself to him, fell from the bridge. Instead, he said, they had been arguing when she refused to provide the services he had already paid her three quid for. The Crown's witness, GPO cableman Alf Simmons, had heard them, but crucially, his defence argued, never actually seen them together. Her stocking had come off as Muldoon attempted to retrieve his money from where she had hidden it, he had no idea how it wound itself around her neck, it was dark and the struggle chaotic. Finally, and most ludicrously in Duch's opinion, he had snatched her handbag in self-defence after she hit him over the head with it. Then, he said, she must have either fallen or thrown herself off the parapet in her drunken rage – despite all the evidence Spilsbury and Greenaway had supplied to the contrary.

In all, it was a load of old pony that would not have fooled a child, let alone twelve grown men. Only, as they were dismissed, the jury didn't look too pleased with their unanimous verdict either, just eager to get away from the whole stinking business.

"C'mon," said Duch, catching Swaffer's weary eye below and then Madame's elbow. "Let's not hang about here. Let's go down Archer Street, talk about it there."

– • –

On the steps outside, Muldoon stood triumphant, talking to a reporter from *The News of the World*. A couple of his friends from his regiment had come to greet him.

"Gee boys, it's good to be free!" he exclaimed.

"Were you never afraid you would go down for murder, then?" the reporter asked.

"Hell no, I never worried," Muldoon lit a cigarette, caught sight of Greenaway coming down the steps beside them and tossed the match in his direction. "Why should a guy worry when he's innocent? Now if you'll excuse me . . ." He broke free of the little group, in pursuit of his former pursuer.

Greenaway felt a hand on his back. He turned around, came face to face with the first man he had ever arrested not to have been found guilty at a court of law.

"Say, Inspector." Muldoon fixed him with a twisted smile. "Seeing as you're all done with it, can I take that handbag back with me now?"

– • –

When Swaffer arrived at the *Entre Nous* he went straight to the piano, began banging out a sombre version of 'St James Infirmary'. He had filed his copy, all sixteen lines of it, and now he wanted to rid the whole ghastly affair from his system. But not before he had made some kind of requiem for the poor woman McArthur, who had received no justice in this world today.

"That's all I need," Madame put her hands up to her ears. "I think I'm going to call it a night. You coming?"

Duch shook her head. She welcomed the gloomy dirge, it matched her own mood. Part of the reason she had wanted so much to come down to the Archer Street club was to see if, just maybe, Lil might have wandered back here yet. She'd still heard nothing from her since their parting, and that weighed heavily upon her heart.

"No, I'll stay here a bit," she said. "I want to talk to Swaff."

– • –

"C'mon," Frankie got up from the table at which he, Dennis and Muldoon sat in the Hero of Waterloo and jerked his thumb towards the bar. "One more for the road."

Muldoon stubbed out his cigarette in the ashtray. "OK," he said. "But let me go take a piss first." He stumbled as he rose to his feet, the effect of all the hours of celebratory drinking taking its toll on his head as well as his bladder. The pub was packed to the rafters with servicemen and tarts and it took him a while to fight his way through them to get to the doorway that led to the downstairs lavatories. It was worth it for the relief that came when he emptied himself in one long, gushing stream, a satisfaction similar to seeing the outraged look on that detective's face outside the Old Bailey.

He still felt a bit dizzy as he made his way back up the steps. There was a woman standing at the top of them, a blonde.

"Hello, soldier," she said, as he drew level with her. Muldoon's jaw gaped a little as he took her in. She was stunning: flawless, creamy skin, red lips and dark-brown eyes fringed by thick lashes, her hair a shimmering cloud around her shoulders.

"Am I dreaming?" he asked her.

She chuckled. "D'you want to find out?" She motioned towards the door with her head, crooked a red-painted finger-nail. Muldoon wavered for a second, thinking of his loyal friends on the other side of the wall of bodies that were clustered around the bar. Then he looked back at the blonde. They would do the same in his place, wouldn't they? It wouldn't take more than a few minutes and after all he'd been through, surely he deserved it . . .

She smiled as he lurched towards her, got hold of his collar and tugged him out into the street, the door closing on the lights and music inside the bar, back out into the blackout. "This way," she said, taking hold of his hand, pulling him past the front of the pub and around the corner into the little alleyway beside it, where he'd stopped with a woman once before. This time, Muldoon was too drunk to reach for his torch and suggest a different location nearby.

"Now then, soldier," there was laughter in her voice as she pushed him up against the wall, pressed herself against him until he shut his eyes, breathed in the heady smell of violets. "You *are* a naughty boy," she said.

"Oh, he's that all right," said a familiar voice beside them. "A right little trickster is our Joe. Thank you, love, I can take over from here."

Muldoon opened his eyes. The girl had melted away and

there instead was Parnell, holding a six-inch-long blade to his throat.

– · –

"You got any idea," Duch asked Swaffer, "what Bear was doing there today?"

"Bear?" Swaffer's eyes widened and a fresh torrent of ash cascaded from his cigarette. "He was there, at the trial?"

Duch nodded. "Left a bit sharpish, mind; soon as they'd given the verdict. Have you ever seen such a miserable-looking jury in your life?"

Swaffer's mouth opened and the fag dropped into the ashtray between them. "You've heard about Bluebell, haven't you?" he said.

Duch frowned, shook her head.

"Ah," Swaffer leant forward conspiratorially, ready to tell her, when he caught sight of Ava Abraham throwing her expensive stole over the back of a seat near the stage.

"*Cavé*," he said. "His wife's just arrived."

– · –

Greenaway stood on Waterloo Bridge, leaning against the parapet where Margaret McArthur had fallen. He stared out into the night at the searchlights criss-crossing the sky behind St Paul's Cathedral, while below his feet the Thames roiled and hissed. On his tongue, along with the acrid sting of too many cigarettes, was the bitter taste of defeat. He had failed Margaret McArthur and the worst of it was, he knew why. Because he hadn't played straight, because he had bent the rules to fuel his own personal vendettas and blinded himself to the dangers such corruption would bring. This was his comeuppance; he knew it and could not bear it.

Peter Beverley had given him two weeks' leave, suggested he spent it at the races and forget all about it. He had caught the Blackout Ripper and that's what he should be proud of. But Greenaway could not be proud of anything. Muldoon's words on his heroics came back to mock him, as if the Canadian had shared a secret about their true identities. He had let his madness out and now he had blood on his hands.

Which was what had brought him back here. If Greenaway knew anything about the criminal mind, it was that its greatest weakness was the same as a gambler's – not to give up when the going was good, but to chance everything gained on one reckless last punt. Muldoon was out there, somewhere in the city, with plenty more victims to choose from. The fact that he had got away with the killing of Margaret McArthur would likely make him think he could pull off the same stroke again. Bring him straight back here. The only thing Greenaway hadn't worked out was what would happen then. He looked down at his hands, rubbed them together. As he did, he caught something out of the corner of his eye. A thin beam of light from a torch bouncing a trail along the side of the bridge. A figure behind it, coming towards him.

It was then that realisation dawned.

There was something he had forgotten, something that should have been at the very forefront of his mind: the date that Bear and Parnell had disappeared was also the date Sammy Lehmann came up for parole.

"Thought I'd find you here, Greenaway, you mug."

– • –

"All right, here's something I've been meaning to ask you," said

Duch, changing the subject for him. "D'you know of a magazine called *Two Worlds*?"

"Certainly," Swaffer replied. "It's rather a good Spiritualist publication, I'm surprised you haven't come across it before."

"I met a journalist who works for them at Miss Moyes's a few weeks back. He was writing a story about the séance Mrs Duncan done."

"Oh yes," said Swaffer. "I would have been there myself if it wasn't for that blasted Bracewell woman and her damned petition. What happened, was she good?"

Duch cocked her head to one side. "Is she supposed to be?" she asked.

Swaffer nodded vigorously. "One of the best Materialism Mediums there has ever been. Didn't she bring about many manifestations at Miss Moyes's, then?"

"She certainly did," said Duch. "That's what was so funny about it. This geezer was telling me how nervous he was about writing a feature, it was the first time they'd let him do it, he said. Then, as soon as the lights went down, this thing appeared right in front of him and tapped him on the knee. He almost shot through the ceiling! God, it was funny, me and Daph didn't half laugh about it later. Ever since then, I been meaning to get hold of an issue to read up what he said, only I ain't sure if I've gone and missed the right one. Do you keep any copies of it, Swaff?"

The journalist nodded. "I've probably got the one you need in my pile at home, unread. Now all this is over, I'll have time to go through them and look it out for you. What did you say this fellow's name was?" Over Duch's shoulder, Swaffer saw Ava notice them, pick up her mink and begin threading her way through the tables.

"Now let me see . . . He was a Scottish bloke himself," said Duch. "I got it. Ross, his name was, Ross Spooner."

"Duch, me old China, long time no see. What brings you here?" Ava clapped her hand down on his companion's shoulder just in time for Swaffer to disguise his expression. Without waiting for an answer, she pulled out a chair and plonked herself down beside them. "You heard about my woes, I take it?"

– • –

"Don't look at me like that. For once, you might just be pleased to see me."

"Now, why would that be?" Greenaway stepped back a pace. Two years on the inside of Dartmoor Prison didn't seem to have affected his nemesis in any way. Sammy Lehmann looked as handsome as ever, Brilliantine shining in his abundant black hair, polish on his handmade shoes and nothing but Savile Row in between.

Registering the expression in Greenaway's eyes, Sammy smiled. "'Cos the moment I got out, I was thinking only of you. You and your outstanding business, that little matter what you couldn't take care of yourself. Look . . ."

Sammy opened his palm, shined his torch on what he held there.

– • –

Swaffer had no desire to hear about Mrs Abraham's compromised domestic arrangements, especially not now he had the answer to the question he had posed to Greenaway in this same room, back in the previous December. Ross Spooner was pursuing Helen Duncan in his new guise as a hapless amateur journalist. Now he knew for sure the Ministry had the medium in their sights.

"If you'll excuse me, ladies," he said, raising his stovepipe hat. "I must away."

"He's a funny one." Ava followed his departing figure with her eyes.

"He's a good man is Swaff," Duch considered. "Always looking out for other people. If it weren't for him knowing all what he does, and who he does, they might not have caught that Blackout Ripper so quickly."

Ava turned her face back to Duch's. "What, you're saying he done all that bastard Greenaway's work for him there and all? Don't surprise me." She downed the contents of her glass in one gulp, grimaced as she surveyed the empty vessel. "I'd better go easy on this," she said. "Keep forgetting I got to pay for it myself now."

"I'll get you another," offered Duch. She hadn't really noticed before, but Ava Abraham was quite a stunning-looking woman, in a severe kind of way.

"Oh, thanks, Duch," said Ava. "Here, what happened to that lovely girl you used to be with? That blonde one, looked like a film star, she did."

Duch shrugged. "Me and Lil parted company," she said. "It's a long story. But I ain't half bored without her. Been doing all sorts of silly things lately. Found myself only lately trying to set up one of Swaff's higher-class friends with some stranger we met, just to see which way she'd swing." She shook her head. "I think I need a distraction, get back to some real work. Start making some proper gelt and all."

Ava looked at her steadily over the top of her empty glass. "So do I," she said.

– • –

Greenaway picked up the chain from Sammy's open palm. It was an identity disc, the sort that soldiers wore around their necks to identify themselves, in case the rest of them got blown to pieces on a battlefield.

MULDOON, JOSEPH, R A POS, HQ43-21-97562, CCH, RC

He looked up. "What's this? One of Parnell's party tricks?"

Sammy chuckled. "You underestimate the boy. I know what you're thinking, Greenaway, 'cos I always do, but he's got a lot more bottle than you give him credit. He brought me this to give you as a peace offering."

Greenaway felt the ground shift beneath his feet. "What d'you mean, a peace offering?" he echoed.

"The reason I knew you'd be here," said Sammy. "Raymond should have been in court for you like you wanted him today. But he found himself between a rock and a hard place. Without Bluebell, someone had to help the Bear get everything in order for when I come out of the Moor. You put away my best lieutenant, Greenaway, and I will not tell a lie, that didn't half get me riled. But, on the other hand, I can see your position. What happened here was bang out of order and merited the punishment. Only, I can't have my dirty washing done in public. Therefore, Raymond owes us both. I had him personally call this one in, in the hope that this will also cancel his debt with you."

Sammy tapped the identity disc on Greenaway's palm, let the weight of his words sink in along with it.

"Now you've seen the proof of it," he went on, "you have my word, nothing else is traceable. Here," he closed Greenaway's hand into a fist and put his own over the top of it. "That's your insurance against me. Call it a goodwill gesture on my part."

Greenaway stared at him. "Let me get this straight," he said. "You nobbled the jury so that Muldoon would walk. Then you had your boy Parnell dispose of him anyway. Is this really what you're telling me?"

Sammy put his hand back in his coat pocket. "I'm just saying, God works in mysterious ways. Ain't that what they always taught us?" he said.

Greenaway shook his head. He felt as if it was he who was falling from Waterloo Bridge now, into the swirling waters below. He opened his fist, stared down at the identity disc, trying to clear the rushing noise in his head.

Sammy gave a little bow and turned his torch back on. "Be seeing you, Greenaway." Greenaway opened his mouth to call after him, but found no words would come. His hand closed around the identity disc as he watched the torch's trail, bouncing away over the bridge and into the night. He lifted his shoulder back, ready to hurl his tainted gift into the water, to throw it after Margaret McArthur – her retribution in blood, given by a gangster.

Then he stopped. This was no justice for Margaret. This was his penance, a reminder of failure that he needed to keep close, of the crooked world around him that he could never stop from operating, no matter how hard he tried to fight against it.

Because he was a part of it, too. Despite the oath he had sworn when he joined the police, if he could have traded places with Parnell tonight and put Muldoon in the grave for Margaret, he would have done. That was why he came to be standing here. He understood only too well.

"Insurance," he said, putting it back in his pocket. "For a better day to come."

Greenaway walked back across the bridge.

EPILOGUE

Thursday, 25 June 1942

Weights and measures: that was what mattered to Mr Albert Pierrepoint. In order to do his job properly, he had to know the weight and height of the condemned man, which necessitated a trip to the scales for Gordon Frederick Cummins every day that he remained in his temporary lodgings at Wandsworth Prison. Chipper to the last, Cummins had faced each reminder of time running out with a nonchalant smile, a joke on his lips for the warder taking notes.

Only yesterday things had been different. Yesterday, Pierrepoint had set eyes on the Blackout Ripper for the first time, mentally applying the ratio of his height and weight to the length of rope he would need and the corresponding drop from the trapdoor. Nothing else concerned him. Nothing else appeared to trouble Cummins either. After the hangman had left, he went on with his game of cards.

His equipment having arrived from Pentonville, Pierrepoint tested his calculations with a bag of sand. The same piece of rope that would go around Cummins's neck was tied to the sandbag, which would be left overnight to remove any stretch from it. The rope itself was special – ten foot of Italian silk hemp, smooth but strong, with a chamois leather binding to prevent any chafing. Pierrepoint liked to despatch his duties with the minimum of discomfort, even if his charges had shown little in the way of such consideration along the course of their journey to meet with him.

At seven in the morning, the rope was coiled and ready.

Cummins dressed in his cell, the same smart suit he had worn in court, and a freshly laundered white shirt, the same calmness in his demeanour as he fastened his buttons for the last time. Only when the prison doctor came to give him his final checkup and offered him a glass of brandy to steady his nerves did the nervousness show in his face.

"Best get it over with quickly," was his summation of forthcoming events, a sentiment with which Pierrepoint would have concurred.

Just before eight o'clock came the last theatrical flourish: the wardrobe against the wall of Cummins's cell was slid aside, revealing the entrance to the room of execution right behind it. From therein came Pierrepoint, two warders beside him, ready to take up their positions on either side of the condemned man. Cummins's hands betrayed a shake as they were placed behind his back and secured with a leather strap.

In silence, the hangman led the way out of the cell and into the room beyond. Cummins's warders guided him to the trapdoor, on which a large white "T" had been chalked, indicating the position on which he should stand. Above him hung the noose.

For the last time, Cummins's strange, pale eyes looked out upon the world. Then Pierrepoint pulled a white execution hood over his head and placed the noose around his neck, while the warders secured his ankles with another leather strap. Finally, the noose's brass eyelet was placed below his jaw and secured in place.

Pierrepoint moved quickly to remove the safety pin from the base of the trapdoor release lever. With a pull of the wooden handle, the floor gave way beneath Cummins's feet and he was falling, through the door into the cell below, the free length of rope uncoiling for all ten feet until it sprang tight and snapped his neck with an audible click. Cummins's legs jerked and twisted in a last, violent dance.

Then the Blackout Ripper was gone.

Greenaway watched with grim satisfaction. He had been up all night again, thanks to Miss Bracewell and her latest petition, claiming that the man with whom Cummins had switched gas masks was the real killer. He had enjoyed writing the report that thoroughly answered all her charges and was ready to hand it to the coroner once Cummins was taken down, swear his testimony over the dead body of the mass murderer Gordon Frederick Cummins. Call it a job well and thoroughly done.

The prison doctor approached the dangling man with his stethoscope. He steadied the body and listened for a while and then nodded his affirmation.

When the orderlies entered the death chamber, an hour later, the body had stopped swinging. One man grabbed his legs, the other climbed up a stepladder to remove the noose from his neck.

As they did, high above them in the skies, a formation of aircraft amassed. Not Cummins's former brethren in the RAF, but a squadron of German bombers on their first mission to London since the night of February the seventh – the night before the Blackout Ripper claimed his first victim. His brief reign bookmarked by air raids.

Cummins's body dropped from the end of the rope to the mournful wail of sirens.

GLOSSARY

Bang to rights – apprehended by the constabulary with positive proof of guilt.

Beat Bobby – a uniformed police constable, "Bobby" deriving from Sir Robert Peel, British Prime Minister and founder of the Metropolitan Police. See also: Flatfoot.

Block and tackle – a sledgehammer, used to break the windows of a jewellery shop and initiate high-speed robbery from the seat of a car; and a bag to catch the spoils, collected while standing on the running board. An audacious technique perfected by the Billy Hill gang in London during the early days of WWII.

Blower, the – telephone. From the 12th-century Old English *blaware*, horn-blowers.

Boat – boat race = face. Cockney rhyming slang.

Bogeys, the – police. In common use in London from the 1930s–1960s, it has its origin in the term the "bogey-man" invoked to frighten children. See also: Lily Law.

Bottle party – in the instance of clubs in London during WWII, a bottle party was a club that offered legal all-night drinking by way of a loophole in the law. Customers would sign order forms in advance of their arrival which were sent to all-night wine retailers, the drink being bought in the customer's name and therefore, in theory, never belonging to the club.

Boychick – affectionate term for a boy or young man. Yiddish.

Brasses – prostitutes. From the Cockney rhyming slang: brass nail = tail. See also: On the bash, Working girls.

Bubbala – sweetheart, darling: an affectionate term for someone close. Yiddish.

Caper – a scheme, a wheeze, a criminal enterprise. See also: Tickle, a.

Clock, to – to notice. According to Eric Partridge, compiler of the *Dictionary of Slang*, this is prison parlance dating back to the 1930s. To "clock" someone can also mean to hit them, "clock" itself also meaning "face".

Dodgy – dishonest or unreliable, liable to dodge responsibility.

Drags – cars. Dealers in the second-hand variety of which are liable to be dodgy.

Elephant Boys, the – a racecourse gang, originating from the Elephant and Castle area of London in the late Victorian era, whose influence lasted until the 1930s. Their rivals, the Italian Sabini clan from Clerkenwell, were interned during WWII.

Fag – cigarette, originally especially the butt of a smoked cigarette, common from the late 19th century and deriving from a 15th-century term for a loose piece of fabric, geographically linked to the traditional weaving and clothing industries of London's East End. In British usage it is not a derogatory term for a homosexual.

Fence – the middleman in a criminal transaction who sells on the stolen goods. Thieves' cant from the 17th century onwards, popularised by Charles Dickens' Fagin.

Flatfoot – a uniformed Police Constable or Beat Bobby.

Full-screw – a Corporal in the British Army.

Gaff – living quarters. In usage since the 19th century.

Gelt – money. Yiddish.

Get nicked – be arrested. As opposed to doing the nicking – stealing; or the nick – prison. An expression curious to Britain, it derives from a 1530s term meaning to put a notch into something. The shuttling between sides of the law indicates the irony inherent in British slang.

Get the scream on – pursue a fleeing villain.

Gonef – thief. Yiddish.

Graft, the – the work of thieving. Corruption of "hard graft", the sentences given to criminals deported from Britain in the 19th century. Eric Partridge believes the word came to be used in the sense of obtaining money corruptly via the penal colonies of Australia and New Zealand.

Grass or grass up/on – to inform on a fellow criminal to the police. The *OED* thinks it is derived from 19th-century slang: grasshopper = tell a copper. Also used as a noun. See also: Shop, to.

Half-cut – drunk. Before 1800 the phrase was "half-shaved" but meant the same thing: a customer too incapacitated to receive the complete treatment from his barber.

Have it away – steal. See also: Heist/hoist, Hooky.

Heavy Mob, the – the Flying Squad, the division of the Metropolitan Police set up in 1919 to tackle armed robberies and other serious crime. Originally known as the Mobile Patrol Experiment, the Squad's nickname came about in 1920 when they purchased two Crossley Tender cars that had previously been the property of the Royal Flying Corps. Latterly, the Heavy Mob would be known as The Sweeney, from the Cockney rhyming slang: Sweeney Todd = Flying Squad.

Heist or hoist – to lift or steal. From the Naval term "hoisting", to raise [a flag].

Hooky – stolen. From the verb hook, euphemistically meaning "to steal".

Hostess club – during the 1940s, a drinking establishment in which mugs are encouraged to buy their hostesses non-alcoholic drinks at extortionate prices, the bill then being settled under the threat of violence. Later known as clip joints.

I can't be having this mishegas – I must deal with this madness. Yiddish.

I should cocoa – certainly, I agree. From the Cockney rhyming slang: coffee and cocoa = I should think so.

In hock – in debt. From the Dutch *hok*, meaning jail or doghouse.

In shtuck – in trouble. Eric Partridge defines it thus: "Not Yiddish despite appearances, although probably formed on the Yiddish model of a reduplicated word commencing with a 'sh' sound, in which case 'shtuck' is a variant of 'stuck' (in a difficult situation) UK, 1936." Perhaps, then, another word of East End origin.

Iron hoof – male homosexual. From the Cockney rhyming slang, iron hoof = poof.

Judas hole – the eye-hatch in the door of a spieler or similar illegal establishment.

Kip – sleep, or a place where one goes to sleep. The *OED* has it as "mid-18th century (in the sense 'brothel'), perhaps related to Danish *kippe*: a tavern". See also: Shluff.

Kite – a fraudulent cheque, passed by a kite-flier.

Klobbiotsch – a card game.

Knocking shop – brothel. From "knock" meaning to copulate with, from which we also get "knocked-up" meaning pregnant.

Lamps – eyes, as in the headlamps of cars.

Lily Law – police. From Polari.

Linens, the – newspapers. From the Cockney rhyming slang: linen draper = paper.

Long game – a confidence trick that unfolds over several weeks and involves a team of swindlers working like actors in employing props, costumes and scripted lines. Can also be used analogously to refer to espionage, diplomacy and statecraft.

LSD – pounds (l.), shillings (s.) and pence (d.) in Old British Money. After the Norman Conquest, the pound was divided into 20 shillings, or 240d. Shillings, commonly individually referred to as "one bob" were further sub-divided into halfpennies and farthings, thruppence bits, sixpence or "a tanner". Two shillings or a florin was known as a "two-bob bit", two shillings and sixpence "half a crown" and five shillings "a crown". This system remained until decimalisation in February 1971. It has nothing to do with Lysergic Acid Diethylamide.

Lughole – ear. From the Cockney rhyming slang: Toby jugs = lugs.

Lumbered, in lumber – in debt to the police, liable to be sent to prison. Possibly originates from the Lombard family of pawnbrokers, who set up business in London in the 13th century. A "lumber-house" is slang for a pawnbroker's shop.

Mazel tov! – Congratulations, good luck. Yiddish.

Mensch – a good fellow. Yiddish, cognate with German for a human being.

Mitzvah, a – an act of human kindness. From the Hebrew word for a commandment.

Moor, the – Dartmoor Prison.

Mug – a gullible fool. Thieves' slang dating back to the 19th century.

Murder bag – a forensics kit used by detectives at crime scenes that was developed by Sir Bernard Spilsbury, in conjunction with Scotland Yard, for his work on the John Hawley Harvey Crippen case in 1910. The kit contained rubber gloves, tweezers, evidence bags, a magnifying glass, compass, ruler and swabs.

Nippy – a waitress in a Lyons Tea or Corner House, a popular chain of low-cost eateries with stylish interiors that existed in London from 1894 to 1981. The nickname derived from the fast service offered by the female staff.

Nishte – nothing.

Nobble – disable, tamper, put the fix in. Often applied to jury tampering, it derives from the expression to nobble a racehorse, i.e. incapacitate it, usually by drugging.

Old China – friend. From the Cockney rhyming slang: old China plate = mate.

On the bash – working as a prostitute. A combination of "on a bash", early 20th century term for a drunken spree, and "getting bashed", i.e. being beaten up. An expression from the 1930s–1950s that surmises the trials of a working girl's life.

On the lam – on the run. From an Old Norse word *lamja*, meaning to make lame, which when it first appeared in English in the 16th century meant "to beat something soundly", transmuting into "beating it" meaning making a hasty exit. Its popularity in 20th-century US slang was exported via Hollywood back to its source in Britain.

On the level – true. Derived from Freemasonry and the tools of stone-cutting, from which we also get "fair and square", "a square deal" and the allusion "on the square".

Peterman – a safe-cracker. The origin of "Peter" as a safe comes from thieves cant as far back as the 17th century, when it meant a trunk or any kind of parcel that required a lock to be broken in order to access its contents – after St Peter, "the rock".

Polari – slang used in Britain by show folk, market traders, criminals and the gay subculture. A mash-up of Italian, Lingua Franca, Yiddish, Cockney back-slang and rhyming slang and sailors' terms, possibly dating back to the 16th century. Strongly associated with Punch and Judy shows and the 1960s BBC radio comedy *Round the Horne*, which featured Kenneth Williams and Hugh Paddick as Julian and Sandy, "two barristers involved in a criminal practice".

Ponce – a man who makes his earnings from a woman. In the 1940s it meant the same as "pimp" means now. A ponce was considered the lowest form of lowlife by the criminals themselves, therefore the word was often used as an insult. From Polari.

Pony – nonsense, rubbish. From the Cockney rhyming slang: pony and trap = crap.

Popped his clogs – died. Originating from the north of England, where clogs were working men's footwear. To "pop" as Anthony Newley fans will know, first meant to pawn, something the working man of the 19th century could ill-afford to do with his shoes, therefore the phrase is imbued with grim irony.

Put the finger on – identify a felon.

Put the frighteners on – threaten or intimidate.

Rabbit – talk incessantly. From Cockney rhyming slang: rabbit and pork = talk.

Ringed and repainted – the disguise of a stolen car with new number plates and a colour respray.

Rosie/Rosie Lee – tea. Cockney rhyming slang.

Scrubs, the – Wormwood Scrubs Prison, which was partially seconded by MI5 at the beginning of WWII.

Sent down – sent to prison. Originates from the Old Bailey in London, where the remand cells were underneath the court itself.

Shluff – sleep. Yiddish.

Shop, to – inform on. The earliest use can be dated to a British police report of 1898. Believed to be derived from the same source as "grass".

Shufti, a – look around, reconnoitre. From the Arabic *šāfa* "try to see", the word was brought to London in the 1940s by WWII servicemen who had encountered Middle Eastern spivs drawing attention to illicit wares by using the phrase: "Shufti, shufti".

Snout – a police informant. Also prison slang for tobacco.

Spiel – a glib, plausible style of talk, associated with conmen and salesmen. From the German word for a game or play, an actor being a "Schauspieler", literally a show-player putting on a show for the punters.

Spieler – a place where an illegal card game is held.

Spiv – a dealer in black market goods, whose appearance is an affront to the strict clothing regulations imposed in 1940s rationing. A typical spiv would wear a drape jacket, turned up trousers, shiny pointed shoes, a DA (duck's arse) haircut and a pencil moustache. According to Eric Partridge, its origins are in racetrack slang and certainly our image of the "spiv" concurs with that of the 1930s racetrack gangs such as the Sabinis and the Elephant Boys. See also: Wide boy.

Steal a lick – appropriate an idea, from the musical meaning

of "lick" as a short solo in improvised jazz. The *OED*'s first
usage is from *Melody Maker* in 1932.

Sus – to work out a suspect's motive, or simply to suspect.

Swell – a fashionably dressed person, first recorded in 1810. By
the 1930s, having crossed the Atlantic, it had become an
expression of satisfaction to Americans.

Take stoppo – leave.

Tic-tac man – a man who calls the odds at a racecourse, via
a language of hand signals emphasised by the wearing of
white gloves. A common sight at British meets until mobile
technology rendered them redundant.

Tickle, a – a scheme, a wheeze, a criminal enterprise.

Toerag – a contemptible person. Mid-19th century, originally
denoting a rag wrapped around the foot of a tramp or
itinerant, coming to mean the person themselves.

Tomfoolery – jewellery. Cockney rhyming slang.

Tweedler – a conman working a specific three-man graft known
as "The Tweedle", in which a mug punter is persuaded to
spend a lot of gelt on a dodgy diamond ring.

Ville, the – Pentonville Prison.

Wide boy – a black-market dealer, a spiv. Robert Westerby's
1937 novel *Wide Boys Never Work* first brought the term to
the British public's attention.

Windmill girls – performers at the Windmill Theatre in Great
Windmill Street, Soho, which hit upon the unique formula
of presenting nude *tableaux vivants* – naked, but motionless
girls – to escape the rules of the censor between 1932 and
1964. Many prominent British comedians began their
careers in this venue, which stayed open throughout WWII
and the worst of the Blitz.

Working girls – prostitutes.

AUTHOR'S NOTE ON SOURCES AND ACKNOWLEDGEMENTS

The events in this book are based on two real cases which happened within the stated fortnight's timeframe in February 1942: the crimes of Gordon Frederick Cummins, aka "the Blackout Ripper", and the unsolved murder of Margaret McArthur on Waterloo Bridge, both of which also came to trial within days of each other in the April of that year. Because this is a fictitious account and I have taken liberties with some of the facts and persons involved, not everybody in the book shares the same names as their counterparts did in real life. As in my previous novel, *Bad Penny Blues*, based on the unsolved "Jack the Stripper" murders of 1959–65, I think of this rendering as taking place in a parallel universe.

It was due to the recurring themes of *Bad Penny Blues* that I began to research the crimes of earlier London "Ripper" Cummins; and also the strange case of medium Helen Duncan, the so-called "Blitz Witch", who was incarcerated under an obscure seventeenth-century law during WWII. The novel I originally envisioned would have taken place over several years. But an unexpected gift narrowed that focus down to two bloody and bizarre weeks in February 1942.

Historian Nick Pelling had been gathering information on the Waterloo Bridge murder with the intent of writing an historical account. However, his efforts to find out what had become of the Canadian Cameron Highlander who was tried and acquitted of the murder of Margaret McArthur at the Old Bailey in April 1942 hit a brick wall and stymied his quest. Having read and approved of *Bad Penny Blues*, thanks to his friendship with my brother, Matthew Unsworth, he generously gave me all he had unearthed in the National Archive and the National Newspaper Archive.

Nick's researches had begun with his fascination with the fact that the second Waterloo Bridge, designed by Gilbert Scott, had been under construction for the duration of the war, an undertaking that seems bewildering in hindsight. But John Rennie's previous Georgian structure had been found to be severely unstable, so London County Council decreed its demolition and the rebuilding of a new bridge in 1937 – and once that was set in motion, they weren't going to let a little thing like the Luftwaffe halt progress. Despite being hit by bombs, the new bridge was completed in March 1942, two weeks after it had been baptised in Margaret McArthur's blood.

Many resonances echoed as I read Nick's notes: the lyrics to the traditional "London Bridge is Falling Down" and their allusion to "my fair lady" that some claim represents a female sacrifice planted beneath the structure to guarantee its continued stability; the tales told to tourists by Thames river boatmen that Waterloo Bridge is known as The Ladies Bridge because a predominantly female workforce built it during WWII. And the haunting, fictional *Waterloo Bridge*, Robert E Sherwood's 1930 play set during WWI that was remade as a film by Mervyn LeRoy in 1940, on a set that resembles Gilbert's bridge, with Vivien Leigh as the tragic, streetwalking heroine who meets her death so close to where the real Margaret McArthur fell.

Like Nick, I became haunted by the question: who was the real Margaret McArthur? Little is revealed in the archives, besides that she was Irish, apparently well educated, and her arrest record for soliciting around pubs on the Strand revealed a taste for poetic noms de plume. Charles Beattie, her common-law husband, did come forward to talk to the police, but his interview indicated she had kept much of her previous life hidden from him, too. I have stuck to the facts that are known about the murder – that Margaret was last seen alive in the Hero of Waterloo pub on the Strand, that a GPO cableman heard a furious argument on the bridge and found a drunken Canadian solider whom he escorted off the site. That the Canadian was then seen by a PC rummaging through a woman's handbag at Waterloo Station and was subsequently picked up in a boarding house in Surrey. Once under arrest, the Canadian requested to see Margaret's body at the post-mortem and then reacted in horror to it; and when acquitted of her murder, he asked for her handbag back. But the backstory I have fashioned for my fictional Margaret is conjured from my own imagination, inspired by stories told to me by my grandmother-in-law, Frances Meekin, of her home in Donegal and work as a midwife during WWII. My further explanations as to why the man tried for Margaret's murder was absolved by the jury, despite the police having what appeared to be a strong case against him (and why it may have been that Nick could not follow his trail any further), also come purely from my imagination.

The sensational case of trainee RAF pilot Gordon Cummins, who savagely despatched four women and attempted to kill at least two more in the week preceding the Waterloo Bridge murder, was successfully solved and the perpetrator hanged by Albert Pierrepoint just prior to an air raid on the given date. I have stuck to the facts of Cummins's murders, including the airman's frenzied last night in Piccadilly and Paddington, but I have altered the names of his victims, their friends and family members, as I have imagined backstories for some of them in lieu of recorded fact.

Simon Read's *In the Dark* (Berkley Books, 2006) is an excellent source of the known facts of the Cummins case, taken again from the National Archive and also from the memoirs of the detectives who caught the Blackout Ripper: Edward Greeno's *War on the Underworld* (Long John Limited, 1960) and Fred Cherrill's *Cherrill of the Yard* (The Popular Book Club, 1955). I also consulted Colin Evans' *The Father of Forensics* (Icon Books, 2007) for background on Sir Bernard Spilsbury, who was also essential in bringing Cummins to justice.

Brilliant men though Cherrill and Spilsbury undoubtedly were, of the three, it was the more wayward Greeno who most fascinated me. Seemingly born on a racecourse, he showed uncommon sympathy for the women killed by Cummins and intuitive understanding of the criminal mind. His memoirs obfuscated his background; I made him into my fictional Ted Greenaway to invent a plausible backstory for an imaginary detective that might help me to better learn the motivations of the man he was based on. The real Greeno did not work on the Margaret McArthur case, though strangely enough, he did bring to justice another murderous Canadian soldier, August Sangret, who killed his girlfriend Pearl Wolfe and buried her body on Hankley Common, Surrey, in October 1942. Greeno's memoir is further interwoven with one of my favourite sources, Charles Raven's *Underworld Nights* (Hulton Press, 1956), often telling what appear to be the same tales from the angle of the criminals Greeno put away. Many of the slang terms used in this novel and its glossary come from these sources.

Donald Thomas' *An Underworld at War* (John Murray, 2003) was the most authoritative and comprehensive book on the subject of criminals, deserters, spivs, racketeers, police, press and civilians in WWII, and how these various factions interconnected. *Few Eggs and No Oranges: The Diaries of Vere Hodgson 1940-45* (Persephone Books, 1999), who worked with Winifred Moyes providing assistance to the bombed-out women and children of the capital throughout WWII, was an invaluable daily account of the madness endured by Londoners, as well as an insight into Miss Moyes and her organisation. Barbara Tate's wonderful *West End Girls* (Orion, 2010) was a similarly illuminating story of the working girls of 1940s Soho.

Malcolm Gaskill's definitive study of Helen Duncan, *Hellish Nell: Last of Britain's Witches* (4th Estate, 2001), provided all the details about the ill-fated medium and led me in turn to the formidable form of Hannen Swaffer, the erstwhile Pope of Fleet Street, to whom no biographer has yet to do justice, least of all his sole representative Tom Driberg, whose *Swaff: The Life and Times of Hannen Swaffer* (Macdonald and Jane's, 1974) did at least provide a chronology. Readers may find it hardest to believe that a committed Spiritualist and ardent socialist was once Britain's most popular journalist, but the celebrated status of this Anti-Richard Littlejohn is by no means made up or exaggerated. Similarly, Swaff's adversary, Olive Bracewell, is based on the astonishing Violet Van Der Elst, whose campaigns against capital punishment were of the scale described and would eventually rob her of her self-accrued fortune. *The Incredible Mrs Van Der Elst* by

Charles Neilson Gattey (Leslie Frewin, 1972) was my source on an audacious life that I have, if anything, toned down for fear of defying credulity. Meanwhile, James Morton and Gerry Packer's *Gangland Bosses*, together with James Morton's *Gangland Soho*, provided further connections between Swaffer and his police and underworld pals.

Julian Maclaren-Ross' *Memoirs of the Forties*, taken from the 2004 Black Spring Press edition of his *Collected Memoirs,* was a peerless time-tunnel trip to the Turkish baths and bohemian Soho. Thanks to Maclaren-Ross' biographer Paul Willetts for bringing those tracts back to life and for the many other kindnesses with research he has shown me during the writing of this book. Similarly wonderful were Joan Wyndham's war diaries *Love Lessons* and *Love is Blue* (Virago 1985, 1986, respectively). Thanks to Max Décharné for putting them my way, as well as many other helpful comments and suggestions, and for a mastermind's knowledge of slang.

Maclaren-Ross' works of fiction, together with those of Patrick Hamilton, Gerald Kersh, Simon Blumenthal, Alexander Baron, Norman Collins, James Curtis, Robert Westerby, Nigel Balchin and Graham Greene, were massive influences and I am grateful to publishers who have kept the least-known of these masters in print, especially John King and Martin Knight of London Books, Robert Hastings of Black Spring Press and Ross Bradshaw of Five Leaves Press, whose editions are presented with such loving care.

Once more, I owe a special debt of thanks to Ruth Bayer for her help on magical matters; and to Emma Murphy for her supernatural gift of the Duchess. The Sohemian Society's Marc Glendening took me on a spooky tour of the Blackout Ripper's haunts that will not be easily forgotten. For lessons in the correct use of London Yiddish, I dunk a beigel to Marc Fireman, and for military manners, I salute Sohemian RSM Dave Fogarty.

As well as all of the above, my thanks and love as always to my family: Phil and Brenda Unsworth, Yvette, William, Tommy and Sophie Rose Unsworth, Cathy Meekin, Danny Meekin, Eva Snee, Danny and Elaine Snee, Mick and Maureen Snee.

More champagne for my real friends: Ann Scanlon, Pete Woodhead, Joe McNally and Dierdre Rusling, Benedict Newbery, Richard and Sarah Newson, Raphael, Lucia and Leo Abraham, Predrag and Damjana Finci, Doreen Montgomery, Fenris Oswin, Dave Knight, Chris Simmons, Paul Murphy, Katja Klier, Meg Davis, Hel, Luke and Adam Cox, Kriss and Lynn Knights, Sal Pittman and Mark Stripling, Mark Pilkington, Syd Moore, Travis Elborough; The Cesarians: Justine Armatage, Charlie Finke, Suzi Owen, Budge McGraw, Bev Crome, Christine Lehlett and Ed Grimshaw; Debbie Voller, Duncan Bolt, Anna Pattenden, Abby Taylor, Margaret Nichols, Claudia Woodward, Lynn, Nick and James Taylor-Haslam, Tom Vague, Ross McFarlane and Phoebe Harkins, David Collard, Lydia Lunch, Jake Arnott, David Peace, Andrew Whitehead, Ken Worpole, Iain Sinclair, Chris Petit, Ronnie Hackston, Anna Whitwham, Julian Ibbotson, Mari Mansfield, Jay Clifton and Vanessa Lawrence, Roger K. Burton and all at the Horse Hospital, James Hollands and Dr Paddy, Billy Chainsaw, Ken and Rachel Hollings, Mike Jay and Louise Burton, Christopher Fowler, Neil and Wenche Perry, Sue Smith, Tony Stewart, Tommy Udo, Damon Wise, Paul Goodhead and the Anthony Newley Society, Greil Marcus, Elizabeth Wilson, Laura Wilson, Dave Collins, Jane Bradley, Michael Dillon and the Gerry's time-tunnel.

Thanks again and triples all round for Anna-Marie Fitzgerald, Niamh Murray, Hannah Westland, Rebecca Gray and all at Serpent's Tail/Profile; François Guerif, Benjamin Guerif, Karine Lalechere, Jeanne Guyon, Hind Boutaljante and all at Rivages.

And a Methuselah of his own for Michael Meekin, the King of Swing.

The best part of going back to the 1940s was the music, due to the genius of the Andrews Sisters, Louis Armstrong, Count Basie, Irving Berlin, Al Bowlly, Bing Crosby, the Cats and the Fiddle, Nat "King" Cole Trio, Tommy Dorsey, Duke Ellington, Ella Fitzgerald, Harry "The Hipster" Gibson, Benny Goodman, Stéphane Grappelli, Henry Hall, Billie Holiday, Leslie "Jiver" Hutchinson, Ken "Snakehips" Johnson, Louis Jordan, Peggy Lee, Glenn Miller, the Mills Brothers, Louis Prima, Django Reinhardt and Fats Waller. Special thanks also to Jerry, Jan and Jocelyn at the Pink Shop for the Black British Jive compilation and for telling me the tragic true story of Snakehips Johnson, which I couldn't help but weave a little of into this tale.

The films *It Always Rains on Sunday* (Robert Hamer, 1947), *They Made Me a Fugitive* (Alberto Cavalcanti, 1947) and *Waterloo Bridge* (Mervyn LeRoy, 1940) helped evoke a lost London. Karen Livesey's 2006 documentary *The Ladies Bridge* offered an intriguing glimpse into the history of the construction of Waterloo Bridge and the story of The Ladies Bridge.

Finally, to the memory of Charlotte Greig, Dave Jennings and Ronnie Rocka, who left too soon but will not be forgotten.